Heaven Star was their world

Ian—a brilliant doctor, he first sensed the terrible force that would turn *Heaven Star* into a hell

Michan—an Outsider, his technical gifts allowed him to defy the vast terrors of outer space, until love showed him its terrible emptiness

Sharon—a powerful politician, she vowed to take control of *Heaven Star*, until a bitter opponent exposed her one fatal flaw

Sean—half-man, half-robot, he waited for the medical discovery that would give him back his legs, before it was too late

Phaedra—her graceful body was a narcotic to everyone aboard *Heaven Star*—until the narcotic turned into a deadly poison

Leo Chin—the master of martial arts, he would train one man in his image, only to discover that he had created a madman

HELLSTAR

MICHAEL REAVES & STEVE PERRY

BERKLEY BOOKS, NEW YORK

HELLSTAR

A Berkley Book / published by arrangement with
the authors

PRINTING HISTORY
Berkley edition / December 1984

ISBN: 0-425-07297-5

Thanks go to the following people, and any others we may have inadvertently forgotten, for their help in the production of this book:

Norm Hartman, Bryce Walden, Walter W. Powell, Gary Bogner, Deborah Wessell, Gene Van Troyer, Bob Nesler, Scott Pace, J. Brynne Stephens, Pat Murphy, Sharon Jarvis, Martha Millard, Beth Meacham, Melissa Ann Singer, Susan Allison, and Roger Cooper.

For Dianne, as they are all for Dianne;
For George and Willa, who allowed instead
of molded;
For the Coca-Cola Company and Dr. Pemberton's wondrous brew.

—SCP

For Marc and Elaine Zicree, who were there
when needed;
And for fresh-squeezed orange juice.

—JMR

"Instance, O instance! strong as heaven itself; the bonds of heaven are slipp'd, dissolved, and loosened . . . "

—William Shakespeare
TROILUS AND CRESSIDA
ACT V, SCENE III

"God does not play dice."

—Albert Einstein

"God not only plays dice, He sometimes throws them where they can't be seen."

—Stephen Hawking

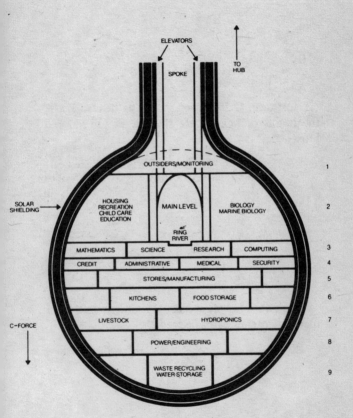

INTERIOR & HULL IN CROSS-SECTION
HEAVEN STAR

PART ONE

Feynman Diagrams

"The waves of dust rise in the well."
—Taoist proverb

ONE

Michan Bern glided over *Heaven Star*'s outer shell between two of the huge window strips, hurrying to reach his coordinates on time. He moved smoothly on near-frictionless skates over the flat surface of the toroid's inner aspect, propelled by hydrogen peroxide jets at the exosuit's shoulder and hip junctions. He glanced at his forearm chronometer and exhaled in exasperation. He wouldn't make it, not even at approved maximum speed. Steen knew that, of course; Michan suspected his supervisor of being responsible for the lock malfunction which had slightly delayed him. It was another of the man's little games designed to make Outsiders look bad. Michan had no doubt that, were he to somehow lose hull and go sailing off into Deep, Steen would grin and wave good-bye.

Michan shook his head in disbelieving disgust. He could see the reflection of his grimace in the faceplate, weirdly lit by the green and red diode glows of the heads-up display inside his helmet. True, there was plenty of time to recalibrate the GM; every alarm in the ship would have gone off if there had been even the remotest possibility of the heloid losing containment. But it was still hard to believe that Steen could be so foolish and petty with the safety of the ship even theoretically at stake.

There was no way he could make station on time, assuming he stuck to regulations. Steen knew that Michan Bern, of all the Outsiders, was a stickler for procedure. The supervisor was counting on that.

But not this time, Michan thought. This time I'm going to surprise you, Supervisor Steen.

His photosensitive visor darkened as he glanced in the direction of the heloid. Though he could not see them, he knew that tiny pellets of fuel were spiralling along invisible magnetic lines into the small sun that *Heaven Star* pushed before it through the void.

If Steen's childish little ploy were only to make Michan look bad, Michan would not have worried. The other Outsiders would always believe him over Steen. But there was far more at stake here than just his pride and record. Greg Shonin had been outside not three hours ago for the calibration, and now it was off again. If Michan were late, if he fouled up by even the slightest bit on so important a job, it would give Steen an excuse to indulge his martinet tendencies and insecure rage at the entire shift crew's expense.

The pressure control was on the back of Michan's left glove; he thumbed the tab and his hull speed climbed. In a few seconds he was past approved maximum. He didn't like breaking the rules, even though there was no real risk in what he was doing. The skates would hold up at well over twice maximum, even though they were rated at less. Any good Outsider knew that, because any good Outsider took his equipment to the limits during testing periods. A person who knew what his machinery could do in an emergency was more likely to be around to tell about it later. Still, Michan did not like it. He had been an Outsider for the last eight of his twenty-five years and he believed in the rules.

The only real danger in this situation was using too much fuel and having to skate back to the nearest lock by muscle power, which, given the clumsy nature of the exosuits, would take a long, exhausting time. Anyone who did something that stupid would be a long time living it down. But he was only going to the Number Four Knob; he had full cartridges and the extra push would not exhaust them. It was worth breaking regs to keep Shonin and the other members of his shift out of trouble.

Michan looked at the chrono readout again. He was still half a klick from the knob—why the construction crew in the Belt had not put a lock near there was a favorite gripe—but he was almost to the point where he could cut his jets and coast. So far his increased speed had apparently not been noticed by the monitor. He mentally crossed his fingers, the pressure gloves of the exosuit being too bulky to permit the actual movement.

Supervisor Steen was a rotund man with a wheezing voice, almost a caricature of an overbearing official. Teamwork was supposed to be the name of the game, particularly in a closed environment like *Heaven Star*. But Steen obviously enjoyed being at odds with those under his supervision. *Achieve results, but not through anger; force is followed by loss of strength.* It was one of the many Taoist sayings that were inscribed on small plaques mounted on walls and buildings all over the ship. Though he was no particular student of the Tao or Zen, Michan found many of the aphorisms charming. But it was obvious that Steen had never read any of them.

The inset dimple was coming up. Michan touched his pressure controls again. The jets on his left side blew a bit harder, turning him slightly. He adjusted the fuel flow expertly, swerved around the dimple and started counting; at thirty he killed the jets and began coasting. Without atmospheric friction he could coast a fair distance across the flat, white expanse of hull before slowing to a stop. He had brakes, of course, but Outsiders used them as little as possible. It was a point of pride; after years of practice, one could estimate stoproll to within a few meters. Old lady Isuzu could guess it down to mere centimeters every time. Michan wasn't that good, but he was working on it.

As he usually did when Outside, Michan looked at Sol. *Heaven Star* had been traveling since the year Michan was born, and though Earth's sun had dimmed considerably over the twenty-five years and billions of kilometers, it was still the closest and brightest of stars, a brilliant pinpoint of light. When he had been a boy, he remembered, it had been a shiny disk. He stared past it, looking into the depths of the universe, and felt, as always, the prickle of cold gooseflesh. He had never been susceptible to "Solipsism Syndrome," which was what the psyches called rapture. Others referred to it as *Wabi*, a Japanese term which translated roughly as "elegant desolation." Those who lived their lives without ever leaving their cozy little mechanical world could not handle the Deep. But for him it was the only definition of God.

He looked back in time to see the knob's shadow on the hull, an impenetrable black against the hard light of the heloid. He was slowing, but he could see he would overshoot by a good five meters. Damn, he would have to use the brakes after all. He flexed his toes; the heat sensors and pressure pads in the thick plastic insoles slowed the magnetic wheels. Michan rolled to a dead stop at the base of the knob, forty-five seconds early. He waited for Steen's call.

"Bern, how far are you from station?"

Michan kept his voice carefully crisp and official. "On station, sir."

There was a pause of several seconds while Steen digested this. Michan smiled slightly. The supervisor could hardly say anything on the com if he had deliberately set Michan up to be late; somebody might wonder enough about it to check the circuit breaker which had kicked out on the egress lock cycle.

"All right, then," Steen said at last. Was his voice a bit more asthmatic than usual? "Stand by for calibration."

"Affirmative. Standing by." Michan pulled free the velcro tab which held the calibrator to his chest below the microcomp, bent and set the hand-sized instrument into the recess designed for it. It felt slightly gritty sliding into place, he noticed.

"Mark," Steen's voice wheezed over the helmet. Michan looked at the calibrator. The LED sparkled and blurred, finally settling into a series of numbers. "Sixty-nine-point-seven-one-two-two-five," he said.

"Copy, sixty-nine-point-seven-one-two-two-five. We have sixty-nine-point-seven-one-two-two-*three* on the master. Stand by for override."

The last digit on the readout trembled, blinked and changed. "Okay," Michan said, "it's a three."

"*What's* a three, mister?"

Michan nodded slightly. Steen was right, for once; he should have given the complete read. "Laser Aiming

Guidance Module Number Four is now calibrated at sixty-nine-point-seven-one-two-two-three degrees, sir.''

"Copy. Return to lock."

"Yes, sir." Michan lifted the instrument from its socket and looked at it. Was there a trace of blue-gray powder on the base of the unit? A thought occurred to him; he clicked his com back on. "There is evidence of microdust fouling on the back plate of the GM," he said, as he reattached it to his suit. "It's possible that's what caused the recent shift."

"Are you a technician or a scientist, Bern? Why don't we let them determine the cause?"

"Yes sir." Michan felt pleased with himself; it was now on record that there might be a reason for the malfunction other than human error. Now Steen could not come down on the Outsiders without looking vindictive. And, much more importantly, the tiny artificial sun held by finely tuned magnetic fields would continue to shine within its assigned parameters.

"Bern," Steen said, "I'm impressed with your promptness out there. Since this entire jaunt should have been unnecessary, I'll expect you back inside at 0937, ready for another assignment. Copy?"

Michan acknowledged the order glumly. Steen was no fool, whatever else he might be. There was no way he could get back to the number four lock in five minutes, even skating at full power. And Steen knew it.

He sighed. That's what he got for breaking regs, even for altruistic purposes. Bad karma. There was no way out of this one.

Unless . . . .

It was an even bigger violation of the rules—in fact, something not justifiable except during an emergency situation, which this no longer was. But, Michan reasoned, in one sense it still qualified; Steen was always looking for something to nail the Outsiders with, and wasting time would do admirably. But if he got back on time, Steen wouldn't have a leg to stand on.

Michan bent his knees as much as the heavy constant-volume joints in the exosuit would allow, leaned forward and pressed the lift jets control. He felt his suit tremble around him as he was pushed upward at an angle, the rockets' lift counteracting slightly the centripetal force that held him against the rotating starship with a force somewhat less than one Earth gravity. The forward jets began to push him. To him, it appeared that his velocity was increased dramatically. In fact, since he was traveling anti-spinward, the torus was augmenting his speed by rotating beneath him. It was a delicate maneuver, requiring careful balance and attention to Coriolis and the curving surface. Fortunately, it was not possible for him to achieve escape velocity with only the suit jets. Were he able to do so, he would suddenly find himself motionless relative to the nearly eight hundred kilometer-per-hour speed of the torus, and likely be spattered into paste by one of the huge spokes as they swept by like the blades of a giant fan. The lift of the jets could only add a few kph to his speed, though that would be enough.

"Michan? It's Wanda."

"Hello, Wanda." He tried to sound nonchalant; Wanda Camber was the hull monitor for this section.

"Michan, I'm showing a large fuel consumption for you. What's happening out there?

"I'm heading anti-spinward for the number four lock. Maybe you've got a bad circuit." Both statements were technically true; he was only lying by omission.

"Bern!" It was Steen again.

"Sir?"

"What jets are you using?"

Michan throttled the lifters, feeling the "weight" caused by the ship's pseudogravity return as his speed slowed. He compensated skillfully for the increased drag as he answered Steen. "Numbers two, four, six and eight, sir. As usual."

Wanda cut in again. "You're looking okay now, Michan. I guess it must be a bad circuit."

Wanda must have figured it out and was trying to cover. He owed her one.

"I want to see you in my cube when you get back inside, Bern." Steen had no doubt figured it out too. But he would have no proof; the other Outsiders would cover for Michan. Some juggling of bytes and a fast refueling job, and Steen would never be able to nail him.

"Yes sir," Michan said.

The lock was coming up. Michan looked at the time; he had made it with over a minute to spare. He slowed to a stop near the entrance. The light was green, so he cycled the outer door open and entered. The inner lock light flashed from red to green after air filled the small chamber, and Michan entered the locker room.

Funakoshi, the suit-tech, helped Michan shed the exogear. He said, "You and Steen were most interesting on the com."

Michan shook his head as the helmet was lifted off, hardly disturbing his short brown hair. "I'm glad you were entertained. I think I need a new recharge filter, Koko. That helmet smells like week-old sushi."

"Don't blame my suit for that. Probably something you ate." Funakoshi set the helmet on its rack, then bent to remove the skates while Michan unsnapped the wrist rings. "You ought to be more careful around Steen, Michan," the tech said softly. "One of these days he's going to catch you at something."

Michan shrugged, the gesture hardly visible under the ventilation garment. "Possibly."

Funakoshi unstrapped the life support pack from Michan's back. "He is an ambitious man, Michan."

"I have nothing against ambition."

"Even when someone like Steen commands Outsiders?"

Michan looked calmly at the shorter man. "Even so."

Funakoshi shook his head. "You don't understand about politics, my friend, about the machinations of power—even petty power. None of you starskaters do. Not everybody is as dedicated to their jobs as you people are. Many are only dedicated to themselves." He helped Michan remove the upper and lower torso sections and the ventilation garment. "Be careful, Michan."

"Thanks, Koko." Michan crossed the small room and into the stall. The ultrasonic "shower" washed away the odor of recycled sweat. He slipped into a paper coverall and plastic slippers, did a few knee bends, stretched, then waved at Funakoshi as he left for Steen's office cube. He walked down the slanting corridor, conscious, as always after being Outside, of the enclosing walls. The corridor felt confining, not at all like the comforting, self-contained little world of an exosuit. Outside was a study in contradictions: simultaneously protected and pampered in a mechanical womb while having all of infinity around him. He always regretted coming back in, putting himself at the whim of people like Steen. Outside, even when working with others, he was alone, standing on the edge of the universe. He lived for that feeling.

Today's run had been mixed; he had defused a potentially catastrophic situation and saved his co-workers some trouble, but he had also broken one minor rule and one not-so-minor one. That made him uncomfortable. True, in a way he had been forced into it, but it still rankled. He should not have to do such things to protect himself or anybody else.

He felt his anger against Steen and the man's games rising again. The worst of it was that he could do nothing about it; he had no proof. He wished Martinez were still in charge of Hull Operations. Or any *real* Outsider. Steen had never so much as stuck his head through the lock. The official reason for his transfer was that it was necessary to keep fresh blood cycling to prevent incestuous dynasties forming in various sections. But Michan had heard that Steen had spun quite a bit of tape to get his current assignment. He wondered why the man wanted to command the most elite corps of workers on *Heaven Star*. Perhaps the question was the answer.

How very Zen, he thought, and smiled wryly as he stopped before Steen's door. The door slid open; he lost the smile and entered.

"*Juke*?"

Pyramus squatted before the clump of thick brush and grinned. He knew the dog was hiding in there, though there was nothing to be seen of the small animal. He could sense it.

"Here, *Juke*!"

The bush, an offshoot juniper, rustled, and there blossomed from it what was surely one of the ugliest dogs in creation. It was, as nearly as Pyramus could determine, a combination of beagle and poodle, with the worst features of both parents: floppy ears, curling fur and stumpy, bowed legs. But the brown eyes were full of intelligence and humor, and the dog wagged his tail with enough force to shake his entire body when he saw Pyramus. He ran to the man and jumped.

Pyramus Gray, Chief of Security, caught the dog and had his face immediately and enthusiastically washed. "Ho, *Juke*! No one's found you yet, eh?" He put the wriggling animal down on the grass and pulled a plastic packet from his coverall pocket. He tore it open and the dog became a fur-covered dervish at the meaty odor. Pyramus kneeled and poured the contents onto the grass beside the path. The meat was mostly soypro, but it looked and smelled like the real thing, and the dog had no qualms about it, judging from how he wolfed it down.

Pyramus looked around while the dog ate. They were in the thickest section of the Main Level's forest; the dog had chosen his hiding place well. There weren't supposed to be any animals running loose on *Heaven Star*; every creature, down to the last culture of *Escherichia coli*, was supposed to be accounted for. But sometimes pets got loose, sometimes all the litter was not entered in the maincomp. On a torus six kilometers around, there were more than a few places to hide. *Juke*, as Pyramus had named him—it meant "dog" in the language of his ancestors—was a free spirit. Pyramus admired that.

As head of security, it was his job to take the dog to Environmental Control. But if the animal did not have a home and was not claimed or chosen within a certain time, Pyramus knew what would happen to him. No, *Juke* deserved his freedom until other arrangements could be made. Obviously he could not remain on his own—there were no garbage cans to pilfer, no wild rabbits or squirrels to hunt. The forested areas of *Heaven Star* were wilderness in name only; the streams were fed by underground pipes, the roots and thin layer of soil pumped with nutrients. Every few meters was an artificial tree trunk or boulder containing electrical outlets and waste recyclers. The dog had been starving when Pyramus had found him. The Security Chief had been having lunch on a grassy knoll when he heard whining from some nearby shrubs. He had brought the dog meals regularly since then and had made inquiries as to who might be interested in a pet. Sooner or later he would find somebody who wanted an ugly but bright dog. In the meantime, something about *Juke*'s ability to hide in this small forest and be as free as he could be on a hoop-world of metal and plastic appealed to Pyramus.

"Chief Gray?"

The voice was small and quiet, coming via bone conduction from the tiny receiver molded over his left ear. The flesh-colored transmitter patch on his throat picked up his subvocal reply. "Gray here."

"Chief, we've got a case of vandalism."

Pyramus sighed as he watched the dog finish the soypro.
"Where?"

"Main Level, Spoke Five shopping mall. The Buddha."

"On my way. About ten minutes."

"Copy."

Pyramus looked down at the dog again. Full now, the
animal wanted to be petted, to have his ears scratched and
his belly rubbed. He nuzzled Pyramus's leg, his nose damp
through the thin paper pant legs.

"Sorry, *Juke*. Duty calls. You wouldn't know about that;
you're lucky." He stroked the dog's back for a moment, then
straightened and started down the path. *Juke* followed him for
a few steps, then stopped and headed back for the shrubbery.

A vandalized Buddha? What in the name of his ancestors'
wagons was that all about? Pyramus grinned. A religious
controversy, perhaps? Militant Methodists? He paused and
stretched for a few minutes, loosening hamstrings and quadri-
ceps, then jogged down the winding path, his long legs covering the ground in wide strides, lifting him a little too much for
correct running posture, but getting him where he wanted to
go. He was near Spoke Two; Five was all the way around the
torus. He could have taken the train, or the elevators through
the Hub, saving time, but there was no great hurry. Whatever
it was, it wasn't an emergency. Nothing ever was.

Before him, the beeches and firs and elms of the woods gave
way to a short stretch of meadow grass, designed for short,
uniform growth. Pyramus looked ahead, where the outer
curve of the torus met the inner. A small patch of housing was
coming into view, the architecture an eclectic but pleasing
combination of Oriental and Occidental styles. Flowing
through the center of the community, as it also flowed a hundred meters to Pyramus's left, was Ring River, the water
sparkling in the warm reflected light from the window strips
above. Two dolphins broke the surface in a shower of foam,
chattering. The air was warm and subtly perfumed by the
flowers blooming along the sides of the path. Pyramus ran
easily, enjoying the feeling of physical exertion. He was passed
by a middle-aged man on a bicycle who shouted a greeting.
Pyramus waved in response. He did not know the man, but he
was used to being recognized, either from his job or being seen
with Phaedra. At the thought of her he looked at his watch
and increased his speed slightly. He wanted to quickly take

care of whatever his deputy had found so that he could call her. The Dream Dance was coming up soon; she would need him.

Or so I like to think, he told himself. He concentrated on his running; somehow it had suddenly become an effort.

The shopping mall was almost deserted; it nearly always was. Pyramus walked down the quiet hallway, past shops offering sporting wings and martial arts supplies—Leo Chin had done a surprising job of popularizing Oriental fighting styles over the years, he reflected—as well as clothing, food and entertainment, holo and sensor spheres and book modules. There were also quite a few art galleries; with a fair amount of leisure time, many of *Heaven Star*'s people explored various creative endeavors. The signs glowed in various languages, a remnant of diplomatic courtesy to the nations of a world lightyears away, since nearly all of the multinational population spoke English, Japanese or Chinese. A large screen on one wall was broadcasting the "latest" news from Earth—over two years old. No one was listening.

Pyramus let the slidewalk carry him toward the fountain and column at the center of the mall's cross-and-wheel layout. The mall had not been a very good idea, he thought. He did not remember the giant commercial centers on Earth, but he had seen the holos. On a planet where there were myriad goods and services, such places might be needed. But on a starship where every household had a complink which could show any of the items in Stores, most people preferred to walk a few meters to their terminals rather than go several kilometers to see an actual display. The psychiatric advisors on the starship's construction had thought the center would be necessary for mental stability, to fight cabin fever and claustrophobia. But life for them, and even for those in the orbital colonies and the planetary outposts, had been so vastly different. *Heaven Star* was an atom in a sea so empty that interplanetary space seemed warm and cozy in comparison. Most people Pyramus knew, himself emphatically included, preferred the "indoors" to the "outdoors." The Outsiders did not, of course, but Pyramus privately considered all Outsiders to be psychotic.

He stepped off the slidewalk. In the center of the mall was a small recycle pump powering a rock-lined stream which cascaded in miniature waterfalls down a gentle slope. The stream passed bonsai, twisted and stunted trees a few centimeters tall, yet older than Pyramus. The tiny bit of greenery was landscaped perfectly to scale, a garden of full-sized shrubbery and trees viewed from long distance, a time-honored Japanese illusion which made a handful of earth and space seem a forest. The tinkling stream passed a synstone statue of a Hotai Buddha, standing with arms upraised and a grin on his face which made Pyramus want to grin back, sharing the enjoyment and amusement that the statue found in all things—even, the Security Officer did not doubt, the slogan and design now decorating its protruding belly.

Lettered in pulse-paint which throbbed like orange neon were the words, EXIT THE SYSTEM! A differently timed paint blinked in an unbroken ring around the words, counterpointing them. A similar graphic had been sprayed on the nearby column, over the *bas-relief* of Earth viewed from L-5 Prime.

Bill Plait, Pyramus's deputy, stood nearby. Several other people had stopped to watch.

Pyramus wandered around the fountain once, looking for other signs of vandalism and finding none. He looked at Plait. "Have you called Maintenance yet?"

"No, sir. Wanted you to see it."

"Okay, I've seen it. Call them."

The young blond man looked angry. Pyramus raised an eyebrow.

"Aren't we going to *do* something, Chief?"

"I'm open to suggestions."

"Well, we could time the paint, check the batch, find out—"

"That it was stolen from Stores, or whoever bought it."

"But we've got to do *something!*"

Pyramus turned away to let a grin escape. Bill Plait was seven years his junior and the job was still new and exciting to him. He had watched all the old holos of the good guys and the bad guys and so was always hot to see justice done. Last week he had almost arrested an old lady for littering. The Security Officer watched the paint flash. He knew who had done this; at least, he knew the group responsible. They called themselves CIRCLE, an acronym which stood for the Coalition for Interstellar Research, Colonization and Long-term Exploration. He was not quite sure what "Exit the system" meant, but he knew the group's basic tenet, which was that *Heaven Star* should not be dismantled for planetary colonization upon reaching the Centauri system, fifty-odd years hence, but should instead use materials found there to refurbish the vessel and construct more ships to journey further into the galaxy. Pyramus wondered if any of the members had ever heard of Von Neumann probes. Their concerns seemed a shade premature to him; he realized that they were advocating what they considered an important and valid course, but most of them would be in their seventies and eighties by the time the decision had to be made. They also seemed aware that it was not exactly a pressing issue; their protests had involved, so far, only harmless displays like this one.

In fact, most of Pyramus's work involved dealing with harmless matters. Being Chief Security Officer on a generation ship was almost as dangerous as watching holo in bed alone. *Heaven Star* was a small town; there was no place to hide if you did anything illegal, and everybody knew it. Too much joystick, a domestic quarrel or a fight at a party once in a while . . . these were Pyramus's primary concerns. There had only been one murder in the ship's history, and that had been when he was a boy.

The only major problem was the new drug. So far, Pyramus had been unable to trace its sources. It was named Zanshin, after the Zen state of ultimate awareness. It was a potent psychedelic which supposedly revealed the secrets of the universe to a far greater degree than other mind-expanding drugs. The catch was a side-effect which ranged from mild axon disruption to catatonia in one out of five users. Pyramus had been unable to find the source because everybody knew him and his half-dozen deputies . . . .

"Chief? I said, what do you want to do about this?"

Pyramus blinked and looked away from the hypnotic slow strobe of the paint. "Call Maintenance, like I said. It's all we can do, Bill—unless you want to go on the home channels and ask if the perpetrators would be nice enough to turn themselves in."

Plait was angry, but he smiled in spite of it. He shrugged and nodded. "Okay. See you later, Chief." He turned and ambled away.

Pyramus glanced at the big clock on the far wall of the center. Almost 1050. Phaedra would be through with rehearsal by now. He said, "Personal channel," then waited the few seconds it took for the subcomp to accept the low-priority call.

A few more people had stopped to look at the graffiti. Among the new arrivals was a tall, thin man in his early twenties with short black hair trimmed in Outsider style. There was nothing special about him, and Pyramus did not know him, but—

"Personal channel open," the impersonal voice of the subcomp said in his ear.

"Put a hold on that," Pyramus said, and walked toward the tall young man. "You," he said. The man turned and looked at Pyramus in mild surprise. "When Maintenance gets here, I think you should give them a hand cleaning up this mess."

The man stared in confusion. "What?"

"It's only fair, since you put it there."

The young man's face became a mask, not quite quickly enough to cover his surprise—and fear. "Are you accusing me—?"

"Damp it. Or would you like me to have a Medcourt put you under psyche vapor?" He had no grounds, but one thing the job had taught him was how little other people knew about the law.

The man's face reddened and a muscle jumped along his clenched jaw. He said nothing.

"That's what I thought," Pyramus said. A quiet purr caught their attention, and both men turned to see a Maintenance cart, carrying cleaning equipment and two men in gray coveralls, coming toward them. Pyramus nodded to the CIRCLE member. "Do a good job," he said pleasantly. "And next time, confine yourself to handing out pamphlets, copy?" Then he turned and stepped onto the slidewalk—and gripped the rails strongly to stop his hands from trembling.

He should be used to it by now—after all, these bursts of intuition, of sudden knowledge, were not new. He had been getting them since he was a teenager. But they still made him nervous at times: the overwhelming certainty that occasionally came over him, and which always turned out to be right.

They did not come often, and he could never summon them, and they were always about minor things, such as abruptly knowing that the tall, thin man was a member of CIRCLE and responsible for the graffiti. When he had first started getting the insights, Pyramus had reluctantly submitted himself for a neurometric wave profile and had been told he was a marginally receptive empath. The computer had predicted the psi talents would fade as he grew older, but they had not. If anything, they were now stronger. He had told no one else over the years except Phaedra—she was the perfect one to understand, since she was a strong Sender. Yin and Yang; it was an empathy that no doubt accounted, to some degree, for their immediate and lasting intimacy.

Thinking of Phaedra made him remember that his channel was still on hold. He took a deep breath and said, "Gray here."

"*Sar shan*, Pyramus?"

Pyramus smiled. The GARTH-7 maincomp had stuck its nose into the subcomp's routine handling of his call. The greeting was in the language of the Romani. Pyramus had learned a smattering of it from his mother, who was a full-blooded gypsy. The GARTH-7 knew this from his files, and it had been programmed to use personal touches in conversations. The voice was that of an older male, paternal and open —exactly the sort of personality to which his psyche profile had indicated he would respond best. He called it *Nano*, or Uncle. The maincomp could sound like anything from a little old lady with a lisp to God Incarnate, depending upon with whom it was speaking; it was hard, at times, for Pyramus to remember that the friendly tones originated in holistic patterns of sub-microscopic semiconducting viral chains and magnetic bubbles.

"Give me Phaedra, *Nano*."

"*Vadni ratsa*," the computer said, and chuckled. Pyramus snorted, half in amusement and half in exasperation; he had just been called a "wild goose." He usually got a metaphorical elbow in the ribs when he called Phaedra.

A warm and vibrant voice said, "Yes?"

"*Konnichiwa*, Phaedra-*san*."

"Pyramus!"

"How's the countdown going?"

She sighed. "As usual, I seemed to have missed satori by about five parsecs. I'm as nervous as a cat in the Hub."

"Sorry." He never knew what to say about her pre-dance jitters. For all their vaunted and envied togetherness,

Phaedra's Dance was the one area that he could not share with her. He wanted to very much, but it did not seem to be in the cards.

"Ah, I'll be fine," she said. As she always said. "How's your day?"

"Thrilling," he said, and told her about the CIRCLE spray-painter. He left out how he had sensed the man when he had returned to the scene of his crime; he felt she would not want to speak of psychic matters so close to her Dance. "Anyway, the shift end is coming up, and I thought . . ."

"Yes. Come over, please. Could you maybe pilfer some of that new wine stock, the plum-grape stuff, on your way?"

"Are you enjoining me to steal, madam? Attempting to subvert the Chief of Ship Security?"

"Yes."

"Okay. Just so I'm clear on that point."

"Pyramus? I—"

"Yeah," he said. "Me, too. I love you."

" . . . Hurry up, will you?"

"Lightspeed." He was outside the Mall; he stepped off the slidewalk and took an unchecked bicycle from a nearby rack. He would get back to his office and check what few reports there might be, wind the shift down and then see about that wine.

The wind fanned the black curls of his hair as he pedalled quickly along. Everybody loved Phaedra the Dancer; he was not unique in that. But she loved only him, and that had to be the most unique and wondrous thing in this tiny clockwork world. And in all of space beyond, for that matter.

His job might be boring at times, but he did it well. And he was still young, and *Heaven Star* rolled on through space, carrying him on a journey the likes of which none of his far-roaming ancestors had ever dreamed of making; a journey the end of which there was no reason to doubt he would see. He lived in a world far more comfortable and well-appointed than the wooden *vurdon*, or wagon, his great-great grandfather had known, secure and sealed against the terrifying gulf outside. And Phaedra waited for him.

Life was certainly good.

TWO

Geoffrey Merle-Douglass smiled down at the little metal marble he held in his right hand. Today was his birthday; he was eighty-five years old, and the marble was one of his presents to himself. It was part of the diary he had kept sporadically for almost half a century. He hardly ever reviewed any of the entries he made. He felt that doing so was like re-reading a novel. There were two popular arguments on the subject, one being that if it was worth reading once, it was worth reading again, and the second stating that there was far too much material for even the fastest speed reader to ever begin covering in a single lifetime, and so one should charge ahead at full speed, assimilating as much knowledge as possible.

As the ship's Archivist, Geoffrey was usually somewhere between the two extremes. He had a much better idea than most of the staggering amount of knowledge humanity was privy to: Even without practical access to Earth's libraries, the computer on *Heaven Star* contained information enough to fill over a billion printed books. He looked about the portion of his cube he called his study, admiring the racks of reading spheres, discs, tapes and even a few printed books, the latter a rarity on *Heaven Star* due to their inefficient information-to-size ratio. As a result of his solitary nature and curiosity, he was one of the best-educated people on the ship. But there was so much more to learn, to know, that he rarely allowed himself the pleasure of sampling anything twice. After all, the human brain was a memory bank of finite capacity—why squander it?

Especially your brain, a small, sinister voice deep within him said, *because of—*

No. He would not think of such things today, on his birthday. It was bad enough that Louis Demond, his oldest friend, had put him on edge earlier that morning. Demond was a politician and his request had been very tactfully phrased, not even fully asked, only hinted. He would like to have a look at certain . . . individual private files of opposition members. Certainly Geoffrey felt Louis was the best person for the position of Administrator—the man had proven that by being elected to the position several times already. But peeking at private files was strictly illegal. Geoffrey had not enjoyed having to refuse such a request from his old friend.

Stick to the subject, he thought. It's your birthday, remember? He dropped the marble into a hemispherical recess on the laserplate and watched it click into place. He keyed up the volume slightly and touched the play control with one age-bent finger, at the same time speaking his personal code. Then he leaned back in the worn overstuffed chair and watched the holoprojector on the polished synwood desk.

After a moment there appeared words and numbers he had not seen for two and a half decades:

"*Primium Folio*, ball one, code HTSP-69, input A-1: OFFICIAL LOG, Archives, *Heaven Star*:
    Run sequence:
    31 August 2072 1200 hr/15mn/0.05sc
    Manual Override ignition initiated and completed.
    Variant plus 0.50sc, compensated.
    Optimum totality run:
    81yr/253dy/9hr/30mn/0.30sc. Mark.
    (Peak V = 0.0025G; midline dc @
    40yr/309dy/4hr/45mn/0.15sc)
    Target coordinates Alpha Centauri A, satellite D-Delta.
    R.A. (ship prime, corrected) 14hr/36mn/23sc

Decl. (ship prime, corrected) -59dy/43mn/0.0sc
PM 3,676/yr
RV -24.598km/sc
Triangulated (uncorrected):   X = -1.696 LY
                                Y = 1.393 LY
                                Z = 3.994 LY

Adjusted TD = 4.29975 LY
Sequence complete.
End run.''

There was a moment of silence, and then the holo haze coalesced into the face of the man he had been twenty-five years earlier. Geoffrey smiled as though greeting an old friend.

"So much for Hobson's official log—a dull and dry readout that would put even an engineer to sleep, I should think. Translated, it means we are on our way, allowing a fraction of a second for a human finger pushing the ceremonial button instead of the automatics. In just under eighty-two years, all things going as planned, we should arrive at our destination, Heaven. An unofficial name, of course, but one much of the ship's complement has taken to using. The planet's real name is Alpha Centauri Delta—sounds rather like someone's pedigreed dog—one of the six worlds that spin around our nearest stellar neighbor."

The holographic image of the younger Geoffrey steepled his fingers and leaned back in the same—though not nearly so worn—chair from which the older man now watched. "We have several options from which to choose when we arrive. We can move in, if no one is at home and conditions allow terraforming. We can load up on reaction mass and come back to Earth. Or we can strike out for yet another star. I doubt I'll be able to cast my vote in any event; even if I make it to a hundred and forty, which is highly unlikely, I'll be a bit too doddering to be of much use, I should think.

"But for now, at least, I must say I feel rather fit for sixty." The smile on the younger face made Geoffrey chuckle. His amusement, however, died at the holoproj's next line:

"Outside of the loneliness, that is." The younger face grew sad. "Though Janice has been dead for almost five years, I still miss her dreadfully. I wish she could be outbound with me—"

The pressure of a finger on a control froze the image in mid-sentence. The old man sat unmoving for several moments, as still as the frozen projection of his younger self. He had forgotten speaking of Janice. It was now thirty years since she had died in a transtube accident. What surprised and saddened him now was not the pain and loss he had felt then, but rather the lack of it now; the years had insulated him from it, and he felt only a wistfulness. He mourned, for a moment, the loss of the pain.

Then he sighed and reached for the pause control. The damage had been done; his cheer had been destroyed. He might as well continue; he was always reluctant to stop a project once it was started.

"—to share this adventure . . . ah, well. No sense dwelling upon it. This is, after all, a time for looking ahead: mankind's first attempt to colonize another solar system. A brave and perhaps somewhat foolhardy venture, but one of which I'm proud to be a part. It's entirely possible that the pell-mell progression of technology on Earth might result in our arriving at Delta to find a group of colonists already awaiting us, brought by some wondrous machineries yet to be invented. But that doesn't matter. Space flight commenced, after all, by the most inefficient of methods: setting a man atop a roman candle and lighting it. It's time for this effort to be made."

Am I still this pedantic? Geoffrey wondered. But despite his slight embarrassment at his earlier self's solemnity, he watched with fascination, lost in his past. For so long, the passage of *Heaven Star* through space had been a boring routine, little different from life on any torus in orbit around the mother world. There is little to match the dreariness of a space voyage once the novelty has worn off. Listening to his forgotten speech, the archivist could recall something of the excitement and awe that had suffused the ship's population at the beginning. He remembered crowds in the streets watching the shipscopes's images of the nearer planets. He recalled the shipwide party that had been thrown much later when they passed the heliopause and entered interstellar space. None of that remained. Those who had grown up on the ship found nothing unusual about being on a star vessel. There was still contact with Earth, of course, but the time lag rendered news obsolete and communication impossible. They were truly on their own.

"*Heaven Star*—or *Ten sei Goh*, if you prefer the Japanese —also represents the first large-scale cooperation between the Earth's major powers, the U.S. and the Sino-Japanese Alliance—"

The image turned as the door slid open behind him, and the archivist saw his younger self automatically reach out to touch the pause control. An instant later, his image was back on the holoproj.

"Where was I? Oh, yes, the SJA. I think the influence of the Oriental culture on board will be quite a good thing—"

Frowning, Geoffrey stopped the recording again, trying to recall who had interrupted him twenty-five years ago. He couldn't remember. It was probably not important, but nevertheless he tapped out a search command on the recorder's keyboard. The 3-D image blurred backwards and froze on a figure standing in the doorway. Another command expanded the image, zooming in on a closeup of the face. There was no loss of quality—the transcribing lasers produced high-resolution recordings on the perfect spheres—but the contrast between the bright outside and the dim office, as well as the recording camera's aim, combined to make the figures facial features unrecognizable. The full head of wavy hair identified him, however. It was Louis Demond. He wore the same hairstyle today, though less hair formed it.

Geoffrey pulled the image back to a full shot of the office, then advanced it in slow motion while he stood and walked around the microcosm hovering over his desk, seeking a better view. He saw Demond reach quickly toward a rack near the door before the younger Geoffrey turned. A second close-up showed the same action, but neither view was complete. Had he taken something from the rack? Or perhaps put something there? Impossible to tell; the pause button he had pushed a quarter-century ago had edited out whatever had happened next.

Geoffrey turned to look at the rack of recording spheres near the door. It had stood there for twenty-five years; if anything were missing, he would certainly know it. If anything extra had been put there, he would know that too. Inventory was done yearly.

The old man sat back down in his chair. He could not remember why Demond had come in; he could barely recall making the recording. He allowed the rest of the entry to play through, but it was void of nostalgia now and there were no further references to the then-councilman's visit.

He shut off the holoproj and sat in the dim and quiet room, musing. Why should something of obviously negligible importance twenty-five years ago bother him now? Was it because he was only lately seeing his friend Demond in a new light?

This is foolish, he told himself. Demond wouldn't have taken anything. Would he?

He cleared his throat. "Hobson?"

"Sir?" The voice of the computer was quiet and very British, so similar to that of a butler his family had employed when he was a lad that Geoffrey had long ago given it the old servant's name.

"Please cross-check all recording spheres in stock, including my personal ones, against the master index. I should like to know if any are . . . unaccounted for."

"Certainly, sir. Is this a priority request?"

"Ah—no. Assign it as a routine retrieve."

There was a delicate pause. "If I may make so bold, sir—it will take some time, then."

"Quite all right. When you get around to it."

"Very good, sir."

Sean Chuma Mkono pushed against the conduit, sending his weightless form flying free along an arrow-straight path down the narrow corridor of expanded aluminum. Years of practice had made his motions automatic, almost as unconscious as breathing. Everyone who worked in the despun Hub was well adapted to weightlessness, but none moved as well as Mkono. At twenty-six, he was the youngest supervisor on *Heaven Star*. He had a wide-shouldered upper body, thick arms, and was second to no one in strength, for his size.

And he had no legs.

He sailed toward the conduit's portal, past racks of gray plastic pipes and thumb-thick copper pumping tubes, under the ceiling centrifuge with its huge flywheel. He flew in silence, one thought repeating itself in his mind like the slow beat of his heart: *the fifth, the fifth, the fifth. . . .*

In the Hub, Sean Mkono was the equal of anyone; in fact, he was better than most. You didn't need legs in the Hub. People respected you for what you could do, not for what you looked like. Only you couldn't stay in the Hub all the time. The weightless conditions would leach the calcium from your bones, turning them brittle; your brain would fill with endorphin residues and other organic wastes and you would get numb and stupid; your heart would begin to do funny things after too long without some kind of pull. You might sneak by for a few months, maybe even a year, but sooner or later it caught up with you.

Today was the fifth, he thought. Shit.

Sean slipped through the portal and into the antechamber. Just beyond was the rec room, the big empty space where fliers came to do acrobatic aerial dances with their bright silken wings, swimming through the cool, dry air. He could beat most of them at that, too. There were some who had a talent for it, but not many were his equal. It wasn't vanity, merely fact. He thought of soaring, his strong arms providing drive for the wings, of the turning, looping and spinning, easier than any bird. He smiled, but the smile died quickly. There would be no flying today, or for the next week. Today was the fifth. Today he had to take the elevator down the spoke to the torus. Today he had to strap himself into the walker, that hideous mechanical parody of a man's legs, and go to Medical. And after his examination he was condemned to Downstairs for a minimum of six days.

Six days! Forced to live in a world of weight, stumping around on a pair of motorized, gyrostabilized plastic stilts, half-man, half-machine. Useless for six days, stared at for six days, *pitied* for six goddamned days!

Each month he had to endure it. There were no options; Medical was religiously strict about it. All Hubworkers had to suffer their time Downstairs. But it was different for everybody else. Everybody else was whole. Of the nearly nine thousand people on the ship, Sean Mkono was the only cripple.

He drifted slowly toward his office. He was being too melodramatic, he told himself. There were things he could do Downstairs. He could go visit his mother; Luma was a hydrologist at the waterworks on Nine. That ought to be good for an hour or so. He could look up Tembo and Harvey and be brotherly. Harvey, only nineteen, always seemed glad to see him. He was the only one of the family who did not make Sean uncomfortable by trying too hard not to stare at the prosthetics.

Everybody kept telling him his discomfort was in his mind, that nobody looked at him like that, but Sean knew better. He was the one on the other end of the stares.

He sighed. He could visit his father and be bored by endless discourses on parallax measurements and spectral lines. He could even see Tembo's and Harvey's fathers, do all the family. That took care of one day. One of six. He couldn't even lose himself in art Downstairs; his fluid sculptures required the weightlessness of the Hub.

Kristin was hooked to her desk when Sean floated into the office. He gave her a half-hearted wave. "Anything I should know about?"

"Everything's clear," she said. Her work robe was velcroed to the wall behind her; she wore a body stocking which did not impede her movements. Sean wore a pair of specially-designed briefs and a net pullover. He seized a wall handhold and pulled himself to the drink dispenser, took a bulb of kava and began to nurse it. There was only one advantage to going downlevels, he thought, grimacing at the flat taste. The food. In null gravity, odors did not waft on the air, and so food tasted uniformly bland and dull. He always had to be careful not to put on a few pounds when he was down there; after all, what else was there to do but eat?

Kristin watched him for a moment, then said, "Come on, Sean, cheer up. You could be a spinner permanently; think how dreadful *that* would be."

Sean nodded. "Yeah, things could be worse." He squeezed the bulb and swallowed. "On the other hand, things could be a hell of a lot better." He stared at the far wall of the office, not seeing it.

"Look, Sean, you aren't any less because of what anybody downlevels thinks—"

"Haven't we had this conversation before?"

Her smile froze, and he could see the pain beneath it. She looked down at the display terminal on her desk, then began quickly running her fingers over the heat-sensitive keys. Words flickered across the screen too fast to read.

Sean mentally cursed himself. No one was safe around him on the fifth. But of all the people he could have snapped at, why did it have to be Kristin?

"Hey," he said.

She looked up from the screen, her expression carefully neutral.

"I'm really only upset because I won't get to see you for almost a week."

She nodded slowly. "I could come down, you know. We could share the dream dance."

He resisted the impulse to make a terse refusal. He didn't like people from the Hub to see him Downstairs. Even though he could move fairly well in the walker, he still felt like Frankenstein's monster: awkward, *incomplete*. "Thanks anyway, but I'm pretty well booked. Family, you know. Besides, I need you here to keep things going properly. You know."

He saw her look down again to avoid his gaze. She spoke quickly, too quickly. "Sure. I know."

Sean hesitated for a moment, listening to the silence. *We've had this conversation before, too, haven't we?* He started to speak, decided against it, and, with a shove of his right arm, left the office.

Ian Kyle looked up from the readout on the hand-sized flatscreen he was studying. He had heard the slight whirr of the servomotors; it was Mkono, down for his monthly PE. He slipped the terminal into his pocket and stood as the other man entered the room. Most of the Hubworkers could simply slide into the diagnoster and then leave, but not Mkono; Kyle always examined him personally. One day, somehow, he was going to beat that redifferentiation rejection syndrome and give Mkono legs.

Mkono shook the doctor's hand. "Doctor Kyle," he said, his tone flat and neutral. Kyle grinned. It was a grin which usually got a positive response; it was hard for people to resist him when he wanted them to like him. But Mkono's face remained as expressionless as his voice. It made Kyle angry, but he was careful not to let his annoyance show.

"How are you, Sean?"

"The same as always."

Kyle nodded, keeping the smile on his face. He realized that the source of his irritation was not solely Mkono's attitude; there was also the upcoming bout with Leo Chin to worry about. But that was later; best to deal with one challenge at a time. "Shall we begin?" He waved Mkono toward the examining room.

A small whine came from the walker's motors as Mkono tensed his buttocks to engage the device. The man had learned to use the heavy gluteus muscles well; electrostim had kept them toned despite the lack of lower limbs. He could walk almost as well as a normal man. Of course, he had had all his life in which to practice.

Inside the exam room the diagnoster waited at the end of a row of hoverbeds. The unit looked somewhat like a fat exosuit on its back, split open. It was large enough to accommodate a giant, but there was a highly flexible and sensitive inner skin which shrank or expanded to exactly fit each patient.

Mkono unseamed his coverall and released the catches which strapped him to the walker. Hard muscles flexed and danced briefly in his upper arms and shoulders as he shifted his weight to a handstance on the table, pivoted easily on one palm and caught the opposite side of the diagnoster with his other hand. He lowered himself slowly and without apparent strain into the medical instrument. The walker was left standing next to the table, the thin coverall down around its twin bases. Orthoplastic pink skin gleamed dully in the fluorescent light. Apparently the designer had not bothered to tint the device to match Mkono's skin shade. Kyle doubted that Mkono cared.

The doctor did a quick visual check of Mkono's naked form as the man relaxed into the machine: kinky, reddish-brown hair, smooth skin, muscles obviously strong and functional, judging from that easy bit of gymnastics. Kyle knew Mkono's history; there was no need for a readout. The deformity was congenital, etiology unknown, likely secondary to a solar flare from which his mother had been poorly shielded while pregnant. Or, perhaps, some damaged genetic heritage from either his Irish father or African mother. In any case, the real problem was that the clone-grafts wouldn't take. With proper field pattern programming and prolactin treatments, Medical could grow anyone a new finger, hand or leg, and even repair most internal organs. Except for Mkono. For some reason, Kyle was unable to push the cultures beyond the blastema stage.

Kyle touched a heat-sensitive tab on the control board. The compscreen lit and he tapped in Mkono's ID code from memory. The medcomp gave a fast read of the previous month's exam, then blanked into receptive mode. Another tab caused the diagnoster to close and the memory-plastic mesh to contract to Mkono's contours. Ian Kyle touched the EXAMINE tab.

In twelve seconds electrocardiographic and electroencephalographic readings were obtained; a tap speared the basilic vein in the right antecubital fossa and drew blood for a GMA-55; a second tap stabbed into Mkono's sternum and a third drilled the right anterior superior iliac crest of his hip for marrow and red cells. Sensors tested muscle tone, breathing patterns, nerve conduction, urine and feces; holographic axial scans were done, section by section, of the entire form inside the unit. Everything was analyzed, correlated, extrapolated and recorded by the medcomp.

Kyle watched the numbers and stats flash onto the screen. Mkono was, aside from the two missing extremities which the unit dutifully noted, WNL—Within Normal Limits. Allowing for day-to-day variants, he was nearly the same as last month's check. As he had said: the same as always.

Except. . . .

Kyle frowned and stroked a control. The crawl of figures slowed. Another touch reversed the information flow. When he saw the hormone scan, Kyle stopped the readout and looked at it carefully.

There was a difference, though it was not abnormal. Some of the pituitary trace secretions were up. The doctor split-screened the figures against the last exam. Somatotrophin was slightly higher, as was ACTH and pancreatrophin, the catalyst hormone. And Seinen Complex, a minute pineal body secretion, was also elevated.

Ian Kyle frowned at the screen. The rises were small, well inside the norm, but there was something about that particular combination of polypeptide chains which tugged at his memory. He entered a note reminding him to check the endocrinology tapes. It likely meant nothing, but Ian Kyle was not in the habit of allowing anything, no matter how small, to go unchecked if it might possibly be of use to him.

The exam was over. The diagnoster's top fanned open slowly, a sarcophagus lid without the usual ghostly creak. Sean Chuma Mkono sat up and looked at the doctor.

"Normal," Kyle said. Mkono nodded, his expression bored. "Suit up," the doctor continued. "I want some fresh antibody and spermatozoa samples." The diagnoster was not programmed for everything; some tasks still had to be done without the machine.

Mkono shrugged and strapped himself to the walker. Kyle prepared his equipment, knowing that the graft failures he had undergone had left Mkono with the opinion that all medics were fools. Well, it didn't matter what Mkono thought. He was not a person to Kyle—only a challenge, and Kyle never shrank from challenges. No matter what the cost—to Mkono, or anyone else.

Susan Hanawashi came out of the water as though pushed by a giant hand. She gripped the edge of the pool and pulled herself completely free of the water and onto the thick plastic lip in a single motion. She stood there, dripping wet and naked, and shouted, "Jesus, Scott, there's some kind of— *thing* down there!"

Scott St. Martin was three meters away, adjusting a gauge on the filtration system. He turned and stared at her. "What?"

Susan took a deep breath, thought about what she had seen, then said, "It was about the size of my head, but it had a dozen long, slimy arms. The eyes were almost human. It looked all soft . . . " She shuddered.

"Come on, Susan—"

"I saw it, Scott, I swear—!"

Scott began to laugh. Susan stared at him, then slowly stalked toward him, pushing the eyecup goggles from her face to see him better. "What," she said tightly, "is so damned funny?"

Scott only laughed harder, hugging his boney torso.

"Scott, if you don't tell me, I'm going to have to kick you from here to Centauri!"

He shook his head, tears running down his face, unable to speak. Susan slid her left foot forward and squared herself into a kung fu stance. She lifted her hands, spreading her fingers into claws, and took a deep breath.

Scott St. Martin, who was thirty-five kilos heavier and twenty centimeters taller than the woman facing him, stopped laughing abruptly. "Hey, easy," he said uncertainly. "It was only a joke."

Susan slid a few centimeters closer to him, her face ominous. She would not really kick him, but for the moment he could think she would.

"Let's be Zen here, Hanawashi! It was a joke!" He held one hand in front of his dangling genitals and extended the other toward her imploringly.

"Then tell it to me and hope I laugh."

"It's name is Eight Ball. It's an octopus. I grew it from a fertilized ovum out of the Terraform Stock. It's just a harmless sea creature, re-designed for fresh water, very common on Earth, really."

"You set me up. You knew I would see it."

"I'm sorry. Really."

"You don't sound sorry. Maybe if I beat on you for a few minutes . . ."

"You wouldn't do that." He sounded unsure. Susan gave in to her urge to grin and abandoned the wide-legged stance. "An octopus?" She didn't remember them from her biology studies, but then, she was an engineer; a person couldn't be expected to know everything.

"It was Killikup's idea. Some kind of racial memory, I think. He's never seen one, of course, but somehow he knew about them. You know how it is; the communication is awkward at best. But I looked it up and found we had samples, so I decanted one. They're supposed to be fairly bright."

"What's he going to do with it?"

"I don't know. I can't really tell what he has in mind." His voice sounded wistful, as it usually did when he talked about Killikup, the brightest of the ship's freshwater dolphins.

The indirect sunlight, bounced from the series of giant mirrors mounted around the outer Hub, was warm enough to dry Susan quickly. She sat in a patio chair and stared at the light of the artificial sun as it rippled on the water of the infeed pond. One of the advantages of Scott's job, she reflected, was having, in effect, a private pool behind his cube. "What's Eight Ball done so far, aside from scaring me?"

"Nothing much. Where's your sense of humor?"

Susan started to make a cutting reply but was interrupted by a splash from the pond, followed by that half-grunt, half-bark only a dolphin makes. Killikup had surfaced at the edge of the pool. He chattered again. Scott walked quickly toward him, squatted, and reached out to scratch the dolphin's head. The man spoke a few words in tones too low for Susan to hear.

He was talking to the dolphin, not with it, she knew. Unlike most people, she did not tend to anthropomorphize animals, did not think of Killikup as a man in a dolphin suit. Scott liked her for that. Killikup and the others of his kind had their own kind of intelligence, and it was vastly different from humans'. Communication was incomplete and only on the most superficial of levels, something which Scott was trying to improve. Even so, the man and dolphin appeared to be sharing a *rapport*, a meeting of different minds. It made her uncomfortable to watch.

She knew why it bothered her. What a waste, she thought, looking at Scott's bare back.

Killikup took a few bits of fish from Scott, then splashed away, leaving a wake of bubbles as he headed up the feeder line toward Ring River. Susan leaned forward in her chair to watch the dolphin leave. The slightly different angle also showed her what Scott was evidently trying to keep hidden by remaining in a crouch by the pond: his erect penis, bouncing slightly with the beat of his heart.

"That's all," Ian Kyle said.

Mkono nodded, "See you next month," the Hub supervisor said, and left. Kyle examined the reads on the antibody and sperm samples as the sound of the servos faded. He shook his head. Nothing new, no clues from the new test as to the reason for the rejection factor. He had not tried a new regeneration program in some time; Mkono had refused any more attempts unless Medical could convince him there was some chance of it working.

Kyle jabbed the exit code with one finger and watched the figures fade. He *would* find the missing factor. Maybe those slightly anomalous hormone readings contained a clue . . . he started to call up the endocrinology stats, but a voice interrupted him.

"Doctor?"

It was Itakaua, his paramed assistant. "Yes?"

She smiled at him. "You asked me to remind you when it was an hour before your lesson."

Kyle smiled automatically in return at the older woman, saw her blush slightly as she left. Alone, he began to stretch his lanky, muscular body. He settled into a riding horse stance, legs bent, back straight, then spun about abruptly, bringing his left leg up in a high arc, the fabric of his white pants snapping in the still air. He felt cold muscles protest slightly. He opened a drawer in his desk and took out an air syringe, looking at the desk clock as he did so. His lesson was at 1400; the drug mixture he had created would take forty-five minutes to reach its three-hour peak. He would take it now. He had worked hard to synthesize the compound, which was the latest in a long line of attempts. It was mostly neo-amp, with timed release epinephrine and a mild metabolic enhancer. The final touch had been a few micrograms of mescabyn for a time-dilation effect. He had used many of the ingredients before, in differing amounts and combinations, without success. But this one might be different. Today he might be able to defeat the old man.

It will work, Ian Kyle told himself. Afterwards he would be a physical wreck, but it would be worth it.

The snap and hiss of the syringe was loud in the small office. Kyle felt the cold blast of the drug travel up his arm. He spun about again, shooting his right leg out, stopping it with perfect control a fraction of a centimeter from a clear plastic replica of a human head sitting impassively on his tapecase. He smiled, sighting up his motionless leg as if it were a gun sight. Oh, yes. It would be worth it.

Susan took a large bite of the steaming omelette Scott had just finished preparing. They were inside now, she sitting at the bar in his small kitchen, he still standing by the stove, tending a second omelette for himself.

Say something, she told herself. "You're a great cook, Scott," was all she could think of.

"Thanks. How's your son these days?"

She felt relieved that he had found a safe subject. "Katsu is doing just fine. He and three of his friends have discovered the woods by Spoke Three; they've become great explorers."

"What is he now—seven?"

"Eight, this month. I'll invite you to his party."

"Oh, please do."

She could not tell if he were sincere or not; the tone of his voice was always slightly mocking. He asked, "Do you ever see—?"

"Toby? Now and then," Susan said. "He's not much of a father type; he comes by now and then out of a sense of duty. I think he's uncomfortable with a child who looks like him and calls him 'Daddy.' They get along well enough, though."

Scott leaned against the coolheat surface of the range and looked at her. "Do you and Toby ever . . . ?" he hesitated delicately.

"No." She wondered why he asked. "Not since before Katsu was born. I hardly have time for that kind of involvement; there's so much work to be done. Seems I don't know nearly as much about the Power Train as I thought I did." The question had rattled her slightly; she heard the defensive note in her voice.

"I doubt that. I think you're just a workaholic, plain and simple."

She gave her attention to the omelette. "Where did you get the spinach for this? The crop isn't due for weeks."

"You think Ag sends everything it grows to Stores? I have friends in green places."

"So do I and they all say two weeks, minimum. Come on, Scott, confess. How did you get it?"

He was silent just long enough for her to regret asking. "Well, Killikup brings me fish to trade with the farmers. Nothing like a bribe to hurry a crop."

The mixture of onion and mushroom sizzled quietly on the grid while Susan tried to think of a way to back out of the subject. Then Scott said, "Let me ask you a serious quesiton. Is it the mechanics of the Power Train section that's got you so busy, or is it dealing with people as a supervisor?"

Susan chewed carefully, the omelette suddenly tasting flat and bland to her. "What do you mean?"

"You're one of the ship's best engineers, Susan. Your promotion was long overdue. I doubt if there's much about the reactors or the lasers or the heloid or any of that kind of thing you don't know."

She cleared her throat. "I get along fine with you, don't I?"

He kept his attention on the cooking omelette, covering it carefully with the pan lid. "We both know why, don't we?"

She stared at the egg on the plastic dish, her appetite gone. "Scott . . ."

He turned and flashed a bright, false smile at her. "Sorry. None of my business, really. Let's change the subject. Are you going to plug into the show tomorrow?"

Relieved, she nodded. "It's during my off-shift, so—probably. Are you?"

"Sure. I never miss it."

A short time later, as Susan rode the train back to her cube, she wondered just what kind of fantasy the Dancer's art would conjur for Scott St. Martin. And she wondered also if, were Killikup somehow to be wired into the broadcast, how his fantasy might compare to Scott's.

Leo Chin stood alone in the dojo's center, listening to and feeling the silence. He had grown very used to this large room since he had first stepped into it, twenty-five years ago. He tried to recall how old he had been then. Thirty-four? Yes. A young, bright physicist on his way to the stars. Only six months before leaving Earth he had earned his black sash in Chan Gen kung fu. He had spent the years since as both a physicist and a teacher of martial arts. Through this dojo hundreds had passed, learning the ancient fighting discipline, the dances of the Bear, the Tiger, the Falling Leaf. He had been privileged to aid them on their way, to share in the joy of their accomplishments, both physical and mental.

Some had expressed surprise to him, over the years, that an ancient fighting art should prove so popular in this enlightened age. After all, there was no reason to become adept at self-defense on *Heaven Star*; there had been only one murder since the start of the decades-long voyage, and no one locked their doors at night. He had long ago given up trying to explain to them that the art was much more than simply fighting —that, in fact, if one is forced to fight, one is, in a sense, already defeated. The joy of it lay in the sense of accomplishment and pride as one progressed through the ranks, and in the peace that was obtainable through that. He was proud that he had taught that to most of his students.

He sighed. Most, but not all. There had been failures as well. Not many, true, but painful to him nevertheless. There had been students with promise, who could have been far better than he, but who had somehow strayed from the path. These were Leo Chin's sadnesses. Though he was usually adept enough at his art to recognize those who would ultimately fail, to urge them gently in other directions, still sometimes he had made mistakes. Sometimes a student would seem worthy when he was not.

He turned slowly, his callused feet light on the springy surface of the mat. In a short time the quiet would be replaced with the sound of fighting, of a contest of skill and will. It was ostensibly a lesson; the concept of winning and losing should be left in the dressing room with the clothes and shoes. One merely did one's best, secure in the knowledge that such was all one could do, that what would be, would be. But that was not the attitude this particular student would bring with him when he faced Leo Chin.

He faced the emblem of the Tiger and Dragon painted on the wall and performed the ritual bow. Wrists crossed, fists tight, he began the shadow-fighting set called Two-Headed Snake. He moved fluidly through the form, punching, kicking, rolling, all in perfect balance. It was meditation at its purest, a five hundred year-old wonder of choreographed violence. During the dance Chin could feel his essence becoming reptilian: cold, precise, deadly. The perfect form, unfortunately, for the task which faced him.

THREE

"Telemetry?"

"On line."

"Okay, stand by for primary run-through. Gastrocnemius one coming up."

"Copy gastroc left, remote."

"Running."

"She's clean, Raul."

"Terrific. Gastroc two . . . watching the show tonight, Shanna?"

"Nope. I've got better things to do . . . gastroc right sounds good."

"What could be better than tuning into Her Majesty's Dance?"

"Never mind. Come on, we've got sixteen superficials to go."

"Right. Uh, rectus femoris coming up . . . give, Shanna, what have you got going tonight?"

"R-F is good. Let's have the ass-buttons."

"Fine, be mysterious. Gluteus maximus one on line."

"G-M left, okay."

"I hate testing these 'casters. So boring. Now, tuning the

autonomics, that's interesting. Takes skill. Especially the parasympathetics, the EEGs and MEGs—"

"Raul, get on with it."

"Sorry. Here's glut two. You know, Shanna, if the people in this hollow bicycle wheel knew how important we are to the Dream Dance production, maybe we'd be celebrities just like Phaedra. T-C on line. Why, without us, she couldn't Send across the room, much less—"

"Hold it, Raul. You've got a warble on the thoracic-cervical."

"You're kidding. Let me check my scope—nope, I get a straight line, Shanna. No disharmonics."

"Well, I'm telling you I've got a—wait, hold it. Um, you're right. It's clear."

"What's the problem, then?"

"Nothing. Forget it."

"Hey, if your scope is jacking up, I have to know."

"It's *nothing*, I told you!"

"You're upset. Let's have a look at you—Jesus and Buddha, Shanna, you look like death! Why are you shaking so? Wait, don't blank your screen! Shanna! Are you all right? Shanna!"

Phaedra Adjurian stared at her naked reflection in the holomirror. She turned, and her tawny dark skin flashed lighter as the mirror adjusted its focus. She studied the augmented image of her back critically. She was lean and hard, and her long black hair reached almost to the cleft of her muscular buttocks. Attractive, oh yes. To be attractive was part of her job. At twenty-eight she might be just past her prime physiologically, but she didn't intend for it to show. The product of an Indian father and a Central African mother, she had large, dark eyes, a finely-sculpted face and milk-chocolate skin over a dancer's body, tight, powerful, and graceful. But she was more than just a dancer. Phaedra was The Dancer, the best on the ship.

She turned and faced the frontal projection of herself. Her breasts were small and her belly flat—and her belly was going to *stay* flat, to Deep with what her mother and friends thought about babies. She raised her left leg slowly, caught her heel with her hand and extended the leg until it was almost straight up. She felt the stretch in her muscles, but it was a good feeling. She smiled at the mirror, and the 3-D image before her, balanced easily on one leg, smiled back.

Phaedra allowed her extended leg to relax, the foot settling slowly to the floor. How much more difficult it must be in full-gee, she thought. On Earth she would be almost ten kilos heavier. Of course, Earth people were probably stronger, being able to practice against the higher pull all the time, and they didn't have to worry about compensating for Coriolis. Still, the leaps must be low and squat, hard on joints and cartilage.

A final turn before the mirror convinced her she looked good enough for the performance tonight. Too bad there wasn't a holomirror for her mind, she thought, to show what work was needed there. She took a breath, pulling it deep into her lungs, trying to force the cool inrush of air all the way to her toes the way her instructors had taught her. It helped some, but not enough. The feelings remained, the stomach-twisting fear and anticipation. She was the best Dancer on the ship, that she knew; no false modesty blinded her to her talents. But still the fear was there, as it was before every performance; not so much a fear of failure as of the act itself. The Dance never did for her what it did for the rest. To them she gave enjoyment, pleasure, satisfaction. For herself, there was . . . satisfaction, yes, the pleasure of doing her job well—but though she could lose herself in the Dance, it never became for her what it did for the rest of the ship. . . .

The portal gave a muted tone.

"Yes?"

"Open up! It's the *gavers*, we know you're in there!"

Phaedra turned away from the mirror in delight. She knew who it was; even if she had not recognized the voice, the Romani term for "police" was clue enough. She pressed the entryadmit set beneath a batik painting on the cream-colored wall. The door slid open and Pyramus Gray ambled in across the thick carpet, carrying a small box in one hand and a green squeeze flask in the other. He glanced at the holomirror. "Admiring yourself in the *dikker-glim* again. Vanity, vanity." He grinned at her. "You have something against clothes?"

"You know how it is with us free-spirited, creative types." She rose on her toes and kissed him, then looked at him. "Still wearing those miserable excuses for shoes, I see."

He looked down at his feet, which were shod in a patchwork assembly of duct tape, frayed laces and worn soles. He shrugged. "What can I say? They're part of my image." Then he held her at arm's length and looked at her carefully. "How are you?" he asked after a long moment.

"Oh—fine."

"Level Nine, lady."

She grinned. Level Nine was waste storage recycling. "Well, you know how I am. Worse than yesterday."

"I might have the cure," he said. He held out the box. "One-quarter kilo of Mama Gray's finest chocolate, fresh this morning."

Phaedra's face lit with a wide-lipped grin. Candy was one of her biggest temptations; she was always dieting to keep herself in dancing trim and hardly ever allowed herself empty sugars. Pyramus's mother, Zena, was a physiologist, a specialist in CNS research and also a fantastic cook. Phaedra tore open the box, broke off a chunk of the dark confection and ate it with bliss. "Mmm. You'll rot my teeth."

"Don't talk with your mouth full. Besides, I happen to know you had your yearly application of nocav only last week. Us *gavers*, we see all and know all."

"No privacy; it's the price of being a star. What's in the bottle?"

"Don't eat the whole box, glutton." He dangled the squeeze bottle between two fingers before her. "This, lovely lady, is a special blend of four oils and two scents, brewed especially for me by a friend in Chemical. Massage oil, for rubbing into the tense bodies of nervous Dancers. Enough talk; let's get you horizontal."

They moved into the small bedroom. Phaedra's bed was a hardfoam pad, fitted with colorful nylon sheets and a thin blanket. She preferred it to a slot bed, though Pyramus thought it uncomfortable and spartan.

"Face down," he told her. "I'll do your back first."

Phaedra complied. She felt him sit next to her, heard him rubbing his hands together briskly to warm them. Then she felt him fit them, covered with warm oil, along the sides of her spine. He pressed from her lower back toward her shoulders, then dragged his hands back toward the buttocks. He paused there, kneading the muscles, then moved down the backs of her thighs and toward her feet. The firm hands left then, but returned in a moment, bearing more of the musk-scented oil. He straddled her back, resting his weight on his knees, and leaned onto her, pressing her into the pad. Each part of her received his attention. He squeezed her feet, working on each toe separately, sliding his fingers between them.

Phaedra felt the tension flowing from her as Pyramus pounded, pressed and rubbed the oil into her skin. "Do you want a full-time job at this?" she mumbled into the hardfoam. "I can guarantee you as many customers as you can handle. Give up police work and do something useful."

"No, thanks. Making a job of it would kill the fun. I'll limit my practice to you, if you don't mind."

"Me? Mind?"

Thirty minutes passed. Phaedra felt herself floating, somewhere between sleep and awareness. She remembered being sixteen, already an accomplished dancer, and getting her first massage from Tomeo, her instructor. He had only been a few years older than she, and they had become lovers. But that massage couldn't compare to his one. Pyramus didn't just want her body; he loved her. That made the difference.

"Okay, turn over."

"You want me to move? I can't move. I have achieved a state of perfect bliss."

"All right, if you don't want me to do the other side—"

"Wait! I can move, I can move." The roll was slow, but she made it. "Ah. Groan, moan." She smiled up at him. He kissed at her, then began working her lower legs, gradually moving upward. She half-expected the massage to develop into something more at this point, and would not have objected. But his attention to her mons was sensual, not sexual. He finished her taut belly with a twirling of his right hand, then moved to her breasts, cupping each one and moving them in tight circles, pressing deep on the underlying pectorals. He moved on to her upper chest and neck, avoiding too much pressure on the sensitive nerves and blood vessels in her neck. Finally, after doing her arms and hands, he began on her face. He worked much more gently now, molding the skin and small muscles as if they were putty. With a final pressure of his thumbs on her forehead, he stopped. There was a pause, then Phaedra felt his lips brush hers gently for an instant.

She felt wonderful: relaxed, comfortable, and loved. She opened her eyes and looked at Pyramus. He sat smiling down at her, sweat beaded on his face and neck from his efforts, despite the air conditioning. On the wall behind him she could see the bronze replica of a Japanese ideogram which meant "Happiness."

Phaedra reached up and pulled him into a hug, feeling the softness of his old and worn coverall against her bare skin. "What time is it?"

"Almost seventeen hundred."

"We have an hour and a half before I have to be at the Emporium. Anything I can do for you?"

He kissed the hollow between her neck and collarbone, then sat up. "Later," he said. "Right now, you need your energy for your Dance."

She smiled at him. She had never had so considerate a lover before. "Are you going to plug in tonight?"

He hesitated. She knew he almost never watched her dance on full-sensory mode. It made him uncomfortable, for reasons she had never quite understood. She thought he was going to refuse, but instead he nodded slowly. "All right."

"I love you, Pyramus Gray."

"And I love you, Phaedra Adjurian."

They hugged, clasping each other tightly, in touch with the moment, lost in it.

Nick Daley blew out a big breath of relief. "God, Phaedra, I was getting a little nervous—"

"Have I ever been late, Nick?"

"Well—not yet." Daley was a thin, balding man whose face was set in a perpetual pattern of worry. "Everything's been ready for—"

"Thanks, Nicky. I knew you'd have things under control." The smile she gave him caused a momentary smoothing of the worry lines. She moved past him, lightly, quickly, across the wide echoing dance floor. The official name of the place was the Studio Three Broadcast Unit, but everyone called it the Dance Emporium. It was large as rooms went on the ship, twenty meters by twenty and almost seven high. Save for the telemetry technicians waiting for her, it was empty: four bland, off-white walls, a ceiling and a floor, the last of polished white oak and the most expensive recreational surface on the ship, having been trucked up from Earth during construction. It lay before her like a deep, dull mirror. Beneath it was an expanded aluminum spring grate which gave back her light steps so that she seemed almost to float across the floor.

She walked toward the head of the telemetry crew, pulling her caftan off over her head and tossing it aside. Someone caught the garment before it touched the floor and five techs surrounded her as she stopped in front of Raul Borisoff. She felt the icy frost of liquid skinbond through her sheer leotard as they placed the 'casters on her, smelled the dried fish smell that was part of her life. The coin-sized discs adhered to skin and fabric: one for each gastrocnemius, rectus femoris and quad-sets; a pair for the two gluteus maximus; one for the low back and low abdominals; two for the pectorals; one for the upper spine; and a crescent-shaped one for the anterior neck. Then there were tendon pickups, the two Achilles and the inner arms at the elbows. Eighteen buttons in all. They were as much a part of her when she danced as her fingernails and toenails, and she noticed them as much. She was far more interested in the upset expression on Raul's face.

"Raul? What is it?"

The man smoothed his straight black hair, a nervous habit. "We had a problem on the line run-through."

She looked at the clock near the control booth. "I hope it's fixed; we go on in fifteen minutes."

"It wasn't anything technical. Do you remember Shanna Dicran?"

"One of the line techs?"

He nodded, chewing at his lip. His hands came up to smooth his already slick hair. Phaedra put her hands on his hunched shoulders. "Raul, what happened?"

"She's in Medical—they say it's Zanshin—don't know if she's going to make it—"

"Raul!" Nick bellowed. "Get those 'casters synched— we're running late!"

Raul cringed under his supervisor's voice and started for the booth before Phaedra could speak. She turned around to face Nick, who was crossing the floor toward her. "What the hell is going on, Nick?"

His gaze flickered between her face and the clock. "I was going to tell you after the Dance. Shanna shivered out on Zanshin this afternoon. But everything's fine, we double checked the scopes—"

"To Deep with the scopes! Is she going to live?"

He nodded, pulling her receiver from her left ear and replacing it with one from his pocket which included an NE pickup. "Live? Sure," he said, molding it gently to her skin. "Nobody dies from Zanshin."

"Raul seemed to think—"

"Raul is in love. Lovers worry." He stepped back and looked toward the control booth. A green light showed above the window. "Clean on all bands," he said. "Stretch out and then give us a warm-up, all right?"

She took a deep breath. "All right, Nicky." She bent at the waist, extended her arms and began some stretching exercises. She took another deep breath and let it escape slowly, then stood quite still, clearing her mind, shifting into what she thought of as Dance Time. She could no longer indulge in worries, apprehensions, uncertainties. There was room for only one thing.

There is nothing but the Dance.

Thoughts of the massage at the hands of her lover, of the distressing news she had just heard—these things were pushed deep into her mind, sealed into another room.

There has never been anything but the Dance.

Her nervousness, her concern about her performance, were forgotten. She would be perfect; it was the only way she *could* be, for the Dance was all.

There will never be anything but the Dance.

With a sudden, sharp flex, Phaedra lifted up onto her toes, balancing. She raised her arms from her sides, slowly, brought her hands together over her head, reaching for the distant ceiling. She held that pose for a beat, then dropped to the polished floor in a full side-split. Then she was up again, leaping away, nearly a meter above the floor, into a sudden gymnastic tuck and roll. She landed on her feet and stood quietly. The blurry world around her came back into focus: the subdued sounds of the air conditioning, the faint fish stench of the skinbond, the cool air against her damp skin.

"Nicky?"

His voice now came to her over the receiver. "Superb, Phaedra. My pulse went up ten beats, even with the filters."

She closed her eyes. "I'm ready."

"Fine. I'll give you thirty second counts, starting . . . now. Ninety seconds."

She nodded, but did not speak. She had placed herself into a waiting phase.

"One minute, Phaedra."

When the neuroelectronic broadcast went out, those plugged in would feel her calmness. They would share it as they would share the Dance. They would share it because of her talent, her ability to Send. It made her the best Dancer on the ship. She danced, and anyone on full-sensory mode danced with her in the way they most wished to. Everyone danced differently, experiencing everything from gentle smiling pleasures to Dionysian revels. But all of them shared one thing: calming, catharsis, peace and serenity. It was release, escape, for a time.

And it was for them, not for her.

"Thirty seconds."

She nodded. She was having some trouble clearing her mind. This would not do. She had to be perfectly calm, a still pool, before the 'cast left the studio.

There is nothing but the Dance.
There has never been anything but the Dance.
There will never be anything but the Dance.

Then the music began to swell, filling the room, filling her mind, setting free the autohypnotic conditions induced so long ago, filling her, filling *Heaven Star*, filling the universe and beyond. . . .

Nick Daley knew there was at least one full shift on duty, performing the few human tasks necessary to keep the ship functioning. And there were also those too young or too sick or too whatever to be plugged in. But if he had to guess, he would have said that at least two-thirds of the eight thousand, nine hundred and forty-three people on board were tuned to the 'cast.

It was something of an ego rush to know that two-thirds of your entire world was locked into a program you directed. It almost made up for missing the show. He wondered how the many and varied inhabitants of *Heaven Star* were reacting to Phaedra's Dream Dance . . .

Michan Bern's quarters were spare, with only a few decorations and personal belongings to differentiate it from any other Outsider's cube. The largest personal touch was an oil painting of the Earth as seen from the moon; the picture covered almost one entire wall. He had bought it long ago at the ship's monthly arts and crafts fair, not out of any nostalgia for a world he had never seen, but because he liked the sense it gave of floating in space, free and unencumbered.

His arofloj, an electronic flute, rested on a stand on the extruded table by the couch. His personal scanner, in a tooled leather case, was on the topmost wall shelf, along with a few book modules—mostly technical manuals. Everything was neat, clean, spare; the colors were muted and pale.

Michan looked at the wall clock. Almost nineteen hundred. He took the headset from its chargeplate and turned it over in his hands, looking at it as though he had never seen one before. He had not plugged into a Dream Dance for several months; not since a nightmare he had had the night after plugging in. In it he had been trapped in a reactor monitoring pod in the Spindle, encased in heavy lead, with barely enough room to move. Though the huge fusion engines operated now on low levels, just enough to supply the life support systems, in the dream all the levels had been in red, sirens were screaming and it was getting hotter and hotter . . .

Michan shuddered. He had not had the nightmare during the Dream Dance, but it had been close enough afterward so that the two were linked in his mind. Since then he had been unable to experience the psychic sharing. He had watched Phaedra's performance on the holoproj without the link-up, and he had watched other Dancers, but he had not put on the headset since that night.

But he knew he needed the relaxation, the debugging of the cortex which the Dream Dance afforded. He had never had the patience to sit in meditation; he did not attend any of the Buddhist temples or the organized denominational churches on *Heaven Star*, and he had never been very interested in drugs. The Dream Dance was the only way he could discharge the tension which inevitably built up day by day.

He was particularly tense this evening, after another of Steen's lectures. The man had chewed him out, accusing him of childish stunts and irresponsible behavior, all the things Michan prided himself in not engaging in. Michan had stood there silently, weathering the barrage like hull metal against micrometeorites, saying nothing to Steen, who knew nothing important. But it had been a strain and he felt it now.

Michan sighed and slipped the headset on. The black lenses shut out all light, and the earphones killed most external sound. He felt the input pads press snugly against his scalp. He sat back on the couch, surprised to find himself breathing rapidly. His pulse was pounding. He was afraid.

He started to remove the headset, but suddenly bright purple flame flared and enveloped him; the first chords of soul-stretching music filled him, and the Dance began. . . .

Sean Chuma Mkono sailed into the shimmering air of a nameless place. He grinned at the Dancer, who clapped her hands and laughed in delight as he did a perfect flip and came down, landing lightly on the balls of his strong, brown feet. She bowed to him, then shifted up and over, an intricate step, her feet crossing back and forth in a delicate, complicated weaving. Sean's grin broadened; he bowed in return and duplicated her step, effortlessly, flawlessly. She leaped high, legs arcing, spun and landed, bounced up again, landed again, her feet blurring as she danced. Sean was undaunted. He leaped, copying her moves exactly, a symphony of grace and skill. She stopped and stood watching him in amazement. And so he led, turning, moving, leaping in patterns so complex that the Dancer could only laugh and try to follow him as best she could. But no one could dance like Sean Mkono, not even the Dancer. . . .

Susan Hanawashi found herself surrounded by people. At first she was terrified—they pressed about her, milling, shouting, their faces demanding. She turned frantically, looking for an escape, but there was no escape. The mob was everywhere. And then, suddenly, the crowd parted, drew back like holos of a windblown field of grain, and before her stood the Dancer. She smiled at Susan, lifted up onto her toes and began to move, her body impossibly lithe and graceful. From her radiated a feeling of confidence and support, of friendship, and—yes—of love. For her, for Susan. And slowly, one by one, the members of the crowd joined the Dance. Their demanding expressions softened, and they looked at Susan with acceptance and love. They murmured soft words she could not understand, but which meant everything. And they danced, and she danced, all following the Dancer, and the out-pouring of love that she felt from them made tears of joy flow as she gave the love back to them, one and all. . . .

The Dancer danced in the water, moving with the grace and ease of a sea creature. In the wavering underwater light, Scott St. Martin watched her as she came closer, leading behind her the sleek form of Killikup. Scott reached out and stroked the dolphin's smooth skin, and felt a quaver run through the muscles. With a stabilizing snap of his flippers, the dolphin came alongside the man. Scott wrapped his bare arms about Killikup while the Dancer wove a dance around them that was both paean and benediction. The man clutched at the ceta-cean's body with his arms and legs, pressed himself against the creature, and together they swam, slipping through the water, bursting above the surface in a shower of foam and waves, breathing the air together, together and united. . . .

Geoffrey Merle-Douglass stood in the endless gray halls of knowledge, surrounded by high shelves stacked with scrolls, tablets, books, tapes, spheres, cassettes, discs, and more—all the means of storing the staggering quantity of information that mankind had assimilated over the ages. He stared into the infinity of learning, overwhelmed by the sheer volume of material, too much to make the slightest dent in. A single mo-ment of despair, of sorrow for all the things he would never know, gripped him—

Then there was a laugh behind him, and he turned. She stood there, the Dancer, moving like a song of passion and life. She danced an old dance, that of charcoal scrawlings on cave walls, of reeds from the Nile pressed into crude paper, of ink and magnetic codes, but with a new kind of joy, of cele-bration which he had never seen before. Geoffrey felt the re-lentless goad he had lived with all his life cease its prodding for a time; he stepped up to her, fitted his hands to her hand and waist, and together they danced, away from the dry and dusty shelves, into a place of green and growing things, of what the knowledge was about. . . .

Michan felt a moment of sheer panic—he was floating in space without his exosuit! But then he realized there was nothing to fear. The woman who danced before him kept him from the vacuum's cold grip, kept his lungs filled somehow with fresh, sweet air as she pinwheeled and swooped and soared. Michan found his arofloj in his hands; he grinned around the *embouchure* of the instrument as he blew softly, hearing the organ-like tones fill the Deep, flawless sounds, miraculous music such as he had never played before, here where there could be no sounds. Here in the Deep, alone save for the Dancer, next to the immortal stars. . . .

Ian Kyle breathed deeply, feeling the blood singing through his veins, feeling his bare toes gripping the mat as he stood, legs bent, in a fighting stance. He was ready for anything the other could throw at him, and he knew that, at last, he would win. He faced his opponent, noting how pitiful and shrunken the old man looked. Around them both danced the Dancer, turning and whirling in a savage display of kicks, punches and sweeps, grinning at him, showing him the way to victory. Kyle laughed, and saw the glint of fear in Chin's eyes. The old man leaped toward Kyle, hurling a flurry of punches and claw techniques which Kyle blocked easily before he leaped, spinning in the air, feeling his heel impact with Chin's temple, seeing the old man drop and lie motionless, his blood staining the mat. . . .

Phaedra danced and reached for him, and Pyramus took her hands. He looked into her eyes, deeply, seeing there the sadness and yearning, the secret pain he had never been able to touch, to share. There in the wooded seclusion of the forest they danced, the scents of pine and heather rising in bursts as the needles and leaves were crushed beneath their feet. They twirled together, separating to clap hands in a time, then came together again. I love you, he said to her. I want to know all of you, all the joy, all the pain. And she answered, I want you to know, I want you to help—I want you to be for me what I am for all of them, and cannot be for myself.

Phaedra stopped dancing then and stood still, looking at him. Pyramus felt the heat growing in her, in himself, felt the fire reaching forth from both of them, joining and blending, burning away all things save the two of them. She put her arms around him, and he felt her fear, her desire, as if it were his own. There in the glade they gave and received, parts of a single being, linked fully, Sender and Receiver. They danced the oldest of all dances, then and for all time. . . .

. . . And thousands of others, mindlinked to her, translated her Dream Dance into their innermost desires and hopes, sublimating them, in a performance at once timeless and yet ever new. Until the music faded softly, stealing away in secret, leaving only a quiet calmness. . . .

Phaedra opened her eyes and the world came back: a bare room, a smooth wooden floor, polished to a sheen which reflected her own dark form. There was the sharp sweat of her body's effort for the last half hour, the small tug of the tiny 'casters glued to her skin. She looked up into the bright lights, blinking, remembering. It had ended, though it would never really end. The Dance would go on forever, but this part was finished. For a brief moment, she thought she knew, felt, what she had done for all of them. But even as she sensed it, it was gone. As though it had never been.

FOUR

Michan snapped the spunglas struts of his wings out and locked them, stretching the thin gray material taut on the ribs. He examined the struts on both sides carefully, looking for cracks or fatigue spots. The last time he had flown, the left side had seemed slightly wobbly. But he could find no signs of wear in his examination; perhaps he had only imagined it. He frowned, then slipped the double triangle and socket over his arms and shoulders and flexed the wings. As nearly as he could tell in the pseudogravity of the wheel, they seemed okay. He removed them, unlocked the struts and folded the wings into a compact tube the size of his forearm, then glanced at the clock. If he hurried he could beat the shift-change rush and save himself a wait in the flying line.

It had been almost a week since he had been to the rec room in the Hub—the last time was just after the Dream Dance. He had come out of the trance refreshed and relaxed, and had had a good night's sleep with no nightmares. The next day, full of energy, he had gone uplevels and flown, enjoying the play of his muscles and the skill of his flight. He was a good flier; most people attributed that to being an Outsider. In fact the Outsiders seldom left the hull even in the weightless area of the

Spindle and the Hub, save to adjust mirrors or do other routine maintenance, and even then they stuck very close to a spoke. But flying was part of the Outsiders' legend, and so when an Outsider came to the rec room, he or she made it a point to fly well.

His euphoria had not lasted long, however. Upon the start of his shift he had received another dressing down from Steen over a trivial mistake in one of his reports. Michan had tried everything he knew to help him relax over the next few days, including chanting, joystick and a brief, rather disappointing liaison with a woman from Environmental Control whom he had met at a party. Nothing had really worked; he continued to awaken each morning with his neck and shoulder muscles crackling with tension. Perhaps, he thought, exercise would help where nothing else had.

The halls were mostly empty before shift-change. Michan had a double off, having worked a double the day before. As he hurried to the elevator he passed a small bronze plate on the corridor wall. He had read it many times before in passing: *Many spokes unite to form the wheel, but it is the center that makes it useful.* An odd saying for Outsider territory, he thought with a slight grin. It brought to mind again Supervisor Thomas Steen. Steen's anger toward Michan seemed to have cooled slightly, but Michan was sure that the man was plotting some new ill-will for him, waiting for a chance. So far, Michan had kept his own temper under control; he wasn't sure how much longer he would be able to do so.

Sean Mkono looked at the new design on his wings with pride. A thunderbird pattern, albeit a bird without drumsticks, he thought with a grin. He could let himself joke, now that he was home in the Hub. His days of stumbling around in the walker were over for another month—though the time would pass all too quickly.

He dismissed that dour thought and folded the bright silk and struts into their case, then pushed himself from his desk toward the door. He had been waiting all day for his off-shift to try the new wings. The blue and red feather design against his dark skin would be quite flashy.

He sailed past Kristin's desk. She was already gone, would meet him at the rec room with her own wings and, he hoped, a place in line. A lot of people wanted to spend their off-time flying. Even though the rec room was the largest single-use enclosed space on the ship, there was only room for a dozen adult fliers to comfortably flit around without bumping into each other. Therefore, each flier was limited to thirty minutes per day, non-cumulative. If one broke the rules and over-stayed one's time, it cost ten minutes for each minute against later flights. Dedicated fliers timed their exits to the second. The line was always long, but it was worth the wait.

Susan Hanawashi smiled through the safety net at Katsu's grave expression. "I promise I'll bring you back for children's time, Katsu."

The boy was velcroed to the wall and holding a squeeze flask of juice. He looked wounded. "I'm eight years old now, Mother."

"I know, dear, but that's still not quite old enough for the adult sessions. It's a rule. Drink your juice and watch me fly."

He sighed loudly. "All right."

Susan dropped the smile so he would not think she was laughing at him. "I'll do the double-loop and bank for you."

"I can almost do a double."

"You'll do them better than I do pretty soon." She kicked away from the safety net and flexed her arms sharply. The broad green wings filled with air and she sailed backwards, then twisted and began to move forward. She flapped her arms several more times, built up speed, then began to use smaller motions to maneuver. It took a great deal of upper body strength to fly well, which was one of the reasons she did it. Her legs were strong from her kung fu practice, but her arms and shoulders could always use work. Susan prided herself on keeping fit. Exercise regularly, eat well, get proper rest, and the body would function optimally, like any good machine.

A turbulence in the air tumbled her forward; she righted herself with a snap of the wings and saw a pair of gray wings folded close to a body in a no-resistance dive, arrowing away from her. The idiot! He had passed quite close to her, Susan thought in annoyance. That was foolish—what if she had sud-denly made a turn or roll as he came by? Mid-air collisions at that speed could be dangerous.

She watched the flier suddenly catch air with his wings and stall, turning the dive into a series of front flips before he sailed off at high speed, driven by powerful strokes. A hotshot, she thought. His haircut said he was either an Outsider or somebody trying to look like one.

Susan shrugged mentally. She only had half an hour, and she was not going to waste it watching some showstopper. She did a lazy roll and looked back at Katsu, who sucked his juice bulb and watched her solemnly.

As she began to fly again she noticed that a section of the safety net covering the wall of the semi-cylindrical room was missing. A warning sign hung above the hole, flashing in red, and a tech was busy restringing the mesh where it had worn or torn through. Susan made a note to avoid trying anything fancy in that direction. Tangling with the net was bad enough —it usually cost a strut and sometimes could even tear the tough fabric of a wing; but sailing through that hole and hitting the wall past it—well, one would be lucky to escape with just a few broken bones.

"Hey, I'm sorry, it was a mission of mercy. I've been looking for a home for him for weeks," Pyramus said. He shrugged, which was a mistake—in zero gravity simple motions easily got out of control. Only the velcro tab on his wrist kept him from floating away from the wall where the waiting line for the rec room hung.

Phaedra said, "So you went halfway around the torus and got us an hour's wait in line. I hope the dog's happy." But she grinned as she said it. She knew how much Pyramus had enjoyed sneaking out to feed the ugly creature every day.

"Well, maybe we can learn something watching the others."

"*You* can learn something—you fly like a brick. I'm a Dancer, remember?"

"And not too bad at it, if the truth be known. I'm glad I plugged in last week. Hell of a show."

Phaedra smiled at the compliment. She wanted to ask him once again why he was so reluctant to experience the Dream Dance, and why he seemed to shrug it off when he did, but she did not. It had to do, she knew, with her own ambivalent feelings about her work, and his empathy with her.

She felt at times as though she were two people in a single body. She was Phaedra Adjurian, a dancer, an artist, young and in love—and she was also The Dancer, the ultimate fantasy figure to nearly everyone on board the ship. She was a very powerful Sender—how powerful she was not sure, since she had never trusted her talent enough to fully release it. Control, always control—it was part of the religion of a dancer. Only sometimes it seemed as though her artistry controlled her, instead of the other way around.

She looked at Pyramus. What must it be like, she wondered, to be on the receiving end?

As though he were reading her mind (and, she thought, that might not be too far off), he said abruptly, "Did I mention that it happened again?"

She knew what he was talking about. "When?"

"About a week ago. Remember the CIRCLE member who painted the Buddha? I didn't tell you how I knew it was him."

"I know how you knew," she said gently.

"Yeah. Just like how I knew what your mother wanted for her birthday; the same way I knew two months ago that Bill Plait would be calling in sick." He picked at the scratchy surface of the wall; she could smell the faint tang of the anti-dust treatment. "It still scares me, Phaedra. When it happens, it's like being . . . lost for a minute, like having no reference points, like—"

"Floating in space?" Her voice was quiet.

He looked at her sharply; then his expression grew thoughtful. "Interesting. I never quite looked at it that way before."

She hadn't either, until that moment. She knew Pyramus had an unreasoning fear of the Deep, like her grandmother had been afraid of Earth's oceans; he occasionally had nightmares of being lost forever in the awful vastness. But she had never related it to his nervousness about his psi talent before.

" 'Exit the system,' " he mused.

"I beg your pardon?"

"That's what they'd written in the Mall. I'm not quite sure what it means. But there are times, when I get those flashes of feeling, when I think I . . . understand. And then it's gone, and I don't know anymore." He looked at her. "It's the not knowing, instead of the knowing, that scares me the most."

She nodded. There were no easy answers to problems like this, she knew. His worry about sharing the Dance was all tied up in these fears, and probably many others that she did not understand at all, and Pyramus perhaps only dimly. They were not easy matters to deal with, but she was willing to deal with them, for him. She only wished he was as willing to work with her fears, especially where they touched his.

Her thoughts were interrupted by a young girl who floated up to them and shyly asked Phaedra for her autograph. As she handed the light pen and scanner back to the girl, Pyramus touched her shoulder and pointed to the head of the line. "There's Mkono taking off."

She turned gracefully and looked. "I wish I were that good."

"You and everybody else, love. He's got some bright new wings."

She squinted, pretending to be blinded by the colors, as she watched Sean whipping back and forth with consummate control and delicacy. The stabilizing fin he wore instead of legs gave him a streamlined, rocketlike appearance. "Look at that," Pyramus said in admiration. "That one-winged cross-stroke puts him into a spiral as tight as a screw going into wood. Great."

"Who's that over there? The Gray Bullet?"

Pyramus saw who Phaedra meant. The flier streaked across the room at high speed, wings folded. "Couldn't see his face," he said. "An Outsider, judging by his hair."

"He's flying pretty recklessly."

"Yeah, well, personally I think all Outsiders are a little bit nuts."

"Mkono is the best."

Pyramus watched the legless man complete an outside roll while twisting fully three times through the bigger movement. "No argument there. Second?"

Phaedra studied the graceful swooping forms before making a decision. "The Gray Bullet."

"I don't think so. Technically he's pretty good, but his lack of control loses him points. Look at the woman with the pale green wings, over in the far curve."

Phaedra's gaze followed his pointing finger. "I don't see—oh. Hmm. She's got good form, but anyone can move well going that slowly." She looked back at the Gray Bullet.

"She's speeding up," Pyramus said. "Let's see how—"

"Look out!"

Pyramus turned, almost windmilling, to stare where Phaedra was pointing. The Gray Bullet was tumbling out of control. Pyramus saw that he had broken a strut—one wing was curled and fluttering like a torn leaf. He fought the air with his good wing, trying to stop his roll. He would stretch the net good when he hit it, the Security Chief thought, then realized with an icy shock that the flier was headed directly for the hole in the net. The tech doing the restringing did not see the looming disaster. The Gray Bullet would miss him, but he would shoot through the hole like a dart through a ring and flatten against the wall beyond. And there wasn't anything anybody could do to stop him.

It seemed to happen in slow motion. They watched helplessly as the flier thrashed the air with his good wing, which only served to spin and tumble him faster. And then the woman in green came arcing toward him, wings snapping the air with powerful sweeps. She folded into a dive just before she connected with the Gray Bullet, ramming her shoulder into his hip with a *thwack*! Both of them tumbled on for a heartbeat before the woman caught air in her outspread wings and slowed. She righted herself, hovering.

The Gray Bullet still had enough momentum to hit hard. But it was the net he struck, three meters to the side of the opening. The tech working there cursed, the sound loud in the hushed room, as the line he was stringing popped from the sudden strain and hit him on the chest.

The Outsider had enough sense to grab the net to avoid rebounding back into the air. He started to untangle his broken wing from the lines as Green Wings and a few others stroked toward him.

A collective breath was released by those floating in line, and voices began to buzz.

Phaedra looked at Pyramus. "Okay, you're right. Green Wings is second."

"Michan Bern," Pyramus murmured.

"Hello?"

"The Gray Bullet. I recognize him now. He's an Outsider, all right. I knew him in school when we were kids. He's a couple of years younger than I am. A real loner; wouldn't have much to do with anybody. Wouldn't take any help, either."

"Well, if Green Wings hadn't helped him just now, they'd be scraping him off the wall."

"Yeah," Pyramus said. "I wonder how he feels about that."

Susan slowed as she approached the net, disengaged her right hand from its wing grip and seized the webbing next to the Gray Bullet. "Are you all right?"

"Fine." He sounded angry.

"I'm sorry I hit you so hard—"

"You didn't have to hit me at all! I was pulling out of it."

Susan stared at him. "If I hadn't hit you," she said, her voice cool and matter-of-fact, "you'd be all over that wall like lumpy paint."

"We'll never know that, will we?"

Susan released the netting. "Excuse me. I'm sorry I interfered. The next time you decide to commit suicide, do it Outside, not in the rec room." She thrust at the netting with her feet and shot away from him, turning and digging at the air with her wings.

His voice followed her, fading: "Look, I know you thought you were doing the right thing . . ." She ignored him as she stroked into the center of the room. Idiot, she thought. I saved his ass and he has to know it. She flew strongly, venting her anger against the air, until she was back near where Katsu hung from the wall.

"I saw you, Mom! You bumped him good!"

She looked at her smiling son. The boy had not realized the Outsider's danger; he assumed Susan had just banged into another flier like children sometimes did, for fun. His excitement was so obvious and open that she felt it dissipating her anger. She smiled back at him. Children weren't like adults; their happiness was simple and infectious, their ignorance easy to understand and deal with. Sometimes she thought Katsu was the only thing outside of her work she could understand—or wanted to.

Michan waited until there was a break in the stream of fliers, then shoved away from the safety net. With his wings folded there was little drag, and he floated directly toward the line of people still waiting to fly. He moved slowly, a target everyone could see and miss, and he did not meet the curious and amused stares that came his way. A broken strut was no disgrace, it could happen to anybody. But he was sure he could have pulled out of it without her help.

He glanced back at the hole in the net and the part of him inside his head which kept to the truth said, *Like hell; you'd have broken your arm or leg or your neck.*

No!

Yes.

He knew it was so. Why had he acted with such ill-grace? Outsiders were proud, they did not like taking help, but Outsiders were also practical, and first to admit when they needed help. There was more to it than that. He had been angry at himself, at the helpless, impotent feeling of tumbling through the air at the mercy of Newton's Laws. He had been angry, and he had taken it out on—

Who was she, anyway? He hadn't even gotten her name. Not that he deserved it, after his behavior.

He reached the net in front of the waiting line of people and pulled himself through the net's sphincter. As he drifted toward the exit somebody called to him.

"Bern. You okay?"

Michan turned and saw Pyramus Gray, *Heaven Star*'s Security Chief, floating next to Phaedra Adjurian, the Dancer. Wonderful, he thought glumly. He had just made a fool out of himself in front of the most beautiful woman on the ship.

"Fine," he mumbled.

Gray smiled. "That was a fancy maneuver. You must teach it to me sometime." The man's tone was light; it was only meant to be a little dig, Michan knew. Somewhere he found a smile. "Any time," he managed to say.

"Oh, excuse my manners," Gray said. "Phaedra Adjurian, Michan Bern, an Outsider. We were in section class together."

The Dancer smiled at Michan, and he felt a moment of giddiness which had nothing to do with his weightless state. "You were doing very well out there until you broke the strut," she said.

Michan nodded acknowledgment, then turned and continued on his way, thinking of various tortures he wouldn't mind seeing Gray put to. What had started out as a nice morning had certainly gone to pieces quickly. And the worst of it was that it was his own fault. His nervous energy had made him fly too fast, too recklessly from the start—"By-the-Book" Bern had taken one too many chances. He should have found the bad strut earlier. He should have noticed the gap in the net. He should have thanked the lady who had saved him from a nasty impact—

To Deep with it, he thought. He glanced at his watch. His double off-shift was not even a quarter over. Suddenly he wanted it to be done, he wanted to be back on duty again, back Outside, facing the stars and the gulf, away from people.

He sighed. He would go back to his cube, get his arofloj and find a deserted spot somewhere to play. He could hide in the music for awhile.

Ian Kyle thrust hard with his left foot. The kick was powerful and accurate; it hit his larger opponent squarely, just under the solar plexus. The man, a large redhead, grunted explosively and slid back. He had hard belly muscles, but Kyle knew the strike had been felt. The man nodded, acknowledging the point.

Kyle smiled thinly. He had yet to work up a sweat inside the heavy polyfab *gi*. He edged in closer, his toes gripping the mat, watching, waiting. Every sense was fully alive; he could even feel the slow, ponderous spin of the torus as he automatically compensated for it in his movements. The other man tensed. Kyle could reach his intentions from his minute movements, from his set and pose. He waited.

The big man lunged, right fist outstretched in an extended back-knuckle punch for Kyle's nose. Kyle spun away, his own right fist cocked, his arm held curled close to his body at first, then extending as he turned for a perfect helicopter hammer-fist that would connect with his opponent's ear—

Only the frail old oriental master had ducked the perfect strike and nudged Kyle's shoulder, just so, and Kyle fell forward, off balance, out of control. . . .

The big man was slower than Kyle, but he had not gotten to black sash rank without skill. Kyle's delayed helicopter punch met a solid forearm block, and the big man jumped aside. Kyle blinked, recovered quickly and set himself into a new stance. Without waiting to think about his miss, he launched a five-strike combination: fake snap kick, backfist, spinning

back thrust kick, side kick, extended finger stab to the throat.
The first three attacks were to set up the fourth and fifth; he
did not expect to tag the man until then, but he always connected with one of the last strikes—

*But the little bastard had only smiled as he brushed the
powerful side kick away, and the stiffened fingers of Kyle's
right hand did not bury themselves in the other man's throat
but instead rammed painfully against the old man's palm. . . .*

The redhaired man was able to get out of the way, using his
left leg for a sweep. It caught Kyle behind the knee and spun
him halfway around. Kyle almost panicked, but managed to
catch his balance, continued the spin and bone-blocked the
other's follow-up punch with an elbow onto the man's wrist.
The two men sprang apart, panting, and reset their stances.

Kyle realized what was happening. He was fighting a
memory. Instead of sparring with Murphy, the planetologist,
he was reacting to the moves Leo Chin had made a week ago.
He shook his head fiercely and gathered himself for the next
attack. This would be the final technique, his favorite. One
more point would win the match for him, and this would
garner it. It was flashy and complicated, and no one could do
it as well as Kyle. He had practiced it for years, smoothing it
and refining it until it was a deadly ballet: a spinning, flying
back heel hook to the temple. With a fraction of power behind
it, the strike was a certain point if it even came close to its
target. Allowed full power, it was a death blow that would
crush the fragile bone. Chin had told him it would be useless
against a trained opponent, but Kyle knew better. He had
practiced and perfected it. It would be so appropriate to defeat
the old man with it—

*The drug he had taken sang in his body, filling him with
power, speed and agility. The old man had been lucky until
now, but his luck was about to run out.*

*Wait! Someone stood in the corner of the room, watching.
Was it a drug spirit, a hallucination? No—it was a woman,
one of the green sash students. What was she doing here? This
was private, between him and Chin! He hesitated—and then
Leo Chin took a deep breath, and the sound of it triggered
Kyle. Let the woman witness his victory! He leaped, spun in
perfection, kicked in grace, with power and cold rage—*

And missed.

The old man moved, impossibly fast. And then came the

damning humiliation: Chin, frail old Chin, reached up and caught Kyle, plucking him from the air as one might snatch a cloth doll. The Sifu then spun in a tight circle, cradling Kyle, who was too amazed to react, and dropped him. Kyle fell onto his back, winded, stunned. He rolled over, gasping for air, and stared into the dark almond eyes of the woman, seeing reflected there his defeat. . . .

"Are you all right, Ian?"

Murphy squatted before Kyle, breathing heavily. "Sorry I blocked so hard; I guess I panicked a little. If you had connected with that fancy kick you'd have taken my head off!"

Kyle swam back against memory's tide and stared at Murphy. He forced himself to grin. "No problem. It was a good block, Murphy. Guess I deserved it for trying something so outlandish."

Murphy smiled in return and helped Kyle to his feet. "I'm heading for the showers," he said, and left. Ian Kyle stood alone in the middle of the dojo, breathing the heavy air. He looked toward the corner of the room by the entrance where the woman had stood a week before and watched him fall. Then he turned abruptly and headed for the showers, his feet pounding hard against the mat.

FIVE

The neat gridwork of lines on her flatscreen blinked suddenly, startling Wanda Camber. She laid down her book, wondering if she had imagined it. Best to be sure; she touched a control. The line-check diode lit briefly, indicating no sign of a surge or drop. The system was running cleanly. Wanda looked back at the liquid crystal screen in time to see the grid, lit with glowing dots that represented the location of five Outsiders doing stress checks of the spoke struts, waver. Then the lines ran together, twisting like taffy before they snapped back to normal.

Wanda tapped another control and a two-key sequence. An inset box in the lower right portion of her screen showed a search-and-repair pattern; another key sent the program leap-frogging through the system. An instant later the verdict was in: NO MALFUNCTION.

The tall, thin woman chewed her lower lip, then replayed the last minute on the log ball. The glitch was there; it had not been her imagination. She felt relieved. Look on the bright side: a ghost in the machine would give her a break while a comptech ran it down. Wanda tapped in a call for her supervisor.

• • •

Sean was watching two workers pull a burned downverter from a wall recess near the middle of the Hub when Pyramus Gray floated by. "Housecleaning, Sean?" the Security Chief asked.

Sean shook his head. "Rebuilding is more like it." He gestured disgustedly at the large piece of equipment. "This is the second one we've had to scrap this week. I think quality control is falling off in Manufacturing, at least in the electronics section. These things are supposed to be good for nine thousand hours, minimum. This one's only six months on line—hey, easy! You'll crush a hand if you aren't careful!"

Pyramus watched the two men jockey the downverter away from the wall. It weighed nothing in the Hub, of course, but it had more than enough mass to cause problems if someone got between it and a wall. Sean looked back at him. "What brings you to the center of things?"

"Rounds."

"Right, I forgot."

"Every Thursday, from Hub to Hull. Takes me six weeks to see the whole show, using a different spoke each time."

"How exciting."

"Why'd the piece fail?"

"Why? We burned out a plate. How? Dumps me; we weren't anywhere close to peaking. It's like the current jammed."

"Is that possible?"

"Not in this universe."

Pyramus made a gesture of sympathy and drifted toward the elevators. Sean watched him go, then turned back to his work.

Pyramus rode the elevator "down" through Spoke Four to Level One of the torus, feeling the pseudoweight provided by the ship's rotation gradually return. Level One was used primarily by Outsiders and Monitoring, bracketing the spoke for a short distance before giving way to the mirrors which supplied light to the Main Level. He usually spent little time on One; the Outsiders were a close-knit group who tended to take care of their own problems. But there was a new supervisor to whom he felt he should introduce himself.

Thomas Steen he found to be a short, round-faced man with mottled red skin, who sat behind his large desk like a judge presiding over a court. "Is there some problem, Chief?" Pyramus noticed a wheeze in the man's voice.

"Not at all. I'm just making my rounds; you'll see me every six weeks or so."

Steen nodded. "I'm still new at this. But I don't think you'll have to worry much about us Outsiders. I run a tight section."

"Fine with me." Pyramus stifled a smile as he left. "Us Outsiders"? Steen, he felt sure, would be as hard to push out a lock as Pyramus himself. The man seemed somehow oily; he was glad he didn't work under him. Then again, it wasn't his job to like everybody. Sometimes he wasn't sure just what his job was.

Michan Bern pushed his stad card into a wall slot and was rewarded with a can of soda. He pulled the tab, breaking the tiny freeze-cap in its base, and felt the can grow cold in his hand. He sipped at the chilled beverage as he watched the Security Chief walk past the Outsider's dining hall. Maybe he's here to arrest Steen, Michan thought dourly. He was still watching the door when Wanda Camber came into the room, carrying what looked like a flat package under one arm. He waved at her.

"I meant to thank you for covering for me that day," he said as she approached him.

"Not much of a debt on that one, Michan. It's been pretty obvious you're not Steen's fair-haired boy."

He grinned. "Still, I'd like to buy you lunch."

"Fine by me. I've got an extra hour while a comptech chases a bug out of my monitor." She sat down and punched in an order on the menu.

"What's that?" Michan gestured at the package. Wanda looked at him in faint surprise. "A book." She handed it to him.

"Really! I've only seen one or two before." He looked at the title: *Scaramouche*, by someone named Sabatini. "This looks like a real collector's item. Where did you get it?"

"Merle-Douglass loaned it to me."

Michan flipped through the plastic pages, then read a

passage out loud. "He was born with the gift of laughter and a sense that the world was mad." He closed the book, handed it back to her. "Too deep for me."

She laughed. A robot served them their meals: a Cantonese sampler for her and soypro steak and potatoes for him. Wanda ate delicately with synwood chopsticks.

"Seems I'm not the only one seeing ghosts in the machines," she said around a mouthful of eggroll. "Janet, my half-sister, says they've been getting some mutations in the program plasmids."

Michan shrugged. "I'm not surprised. It's delicate work."

"You ever see the clean room in Bioelectronics? It makes Medical look like Level Nine. They don't know what's causing it, but they've had to scrap a lot of molecular circuitry."

Michan loaded the steak with pepper in an attempt to make it palatable. "That's what the backup systems are for."

Wanda looked at him. "My, aren't we Zen today." She finished her meal and picked up her fortune cookie, then handed it to him. "Here. With Steen cutting your hoses like he's been doing, you need this more than I do."

Michan grinned and broke open the cookie. He read it out loud: " 'A ship can find support in water, but water can turn it over.' " He finished his soda. "If this were a late-night holo, there'd be a dramatic musical sting right now."

Wanda pointed at the menu, where a readout of the bill glowed. "How about a financial sting instead?"

Pyramus ate the last bite of his sandwich and washed it down with a swallow of beer. He was sitting on the edge of Ring River, his bare feet in the water. He shoved the beer bulb into a recycler disguised as a rock, then stretched and lay back to bask for a second in the sunshine. A robin flitted by overhead; birds were *Heaven Star*'s stowaways. No one knew if they had been decanted and grown from the terraforming stores, or if they had somehow been smuggled aboard before the ship left the Belt, but so far there had been ten species identified in *Heaven Star*'s "skies." No great effort had been made to capture them; they caused no real problems as long as their numbers were kept under control. Pyramus grinned. It could be worse; they could have been rats.

He sat up and put on his shoes, swearing in mild irritation as one of the laces broke. Phaedra had been after him for months to get a new pair of shoes; these were held together with tape and prayer. But they were also the most comfortable pair he owned, and he valued comfort over appearance.

He knotted the lace together, then spoke his access code. A moment later Plait's voice responded.

"How'd it go, Bill?"

Plait sounded tired. "How do you think? Seventeen little monsters tearing around looking for things to destroy." One of the primary classes had been given a tour of Security. Pyramus chuckled. "For half a card," Plait continued, "I'd've put the whole squirming, kicking, yelling lot out the lock."

"I don't think you're getting your money's worth from those alpha wave treatments you've been taking, Bill. Maybe you should start going twice a week; you're still pretty tense."

Plait sighed. "Hurry up and finish your walkabout, will you? I need help cleaning up the mess they left."

"Only seven more levels to go. Stay calm."

Plait made a rude remark and signed off. Pyramus laughed and stood up. Time to see how things were in the think tank.

Leo Chin waved a handful of papers in Pyramus's face. The normally phlegmatic scientist was more agitated than the Security Chief had ever before seen him.

"Look at this! Just look!" He pushed the papers toward Pyramus, who saw a maze of interconnected dots and lines with mathematical and Greek symbols printed everywhere. There were also a lot of numbers, mostly with decimal points and four or five zeroes strung before them.

He looked up and saw that Chin was watching him intently. "Incredible, isn't it?" the older man demanded.

"If you say so."

Leo blinked, and then nodded as though remembering something. "Sorry." He pointed to one of the sheets. "This is a Feynman Diagram, a momentum-energy picture. It is approximate, of course."

"Of course."

"We use them to slow events—anything which happens in the subatomic realm is an event—such as the annihilation of particles and the creation of new particles. Over here," and he gestured to another sheet, "is a list of the particles we were running in the rebounce tests. We're working with stable particles; ones which do not decay with strong interaction, but instead by electromagnetic or weak interaction. Look. Here we have leptons, here mesons, and here, baryons. But look at the decay rate on this meson—a positive kaon, it's called. Its lifetime is supposed to average twelve billionths of a second. Instead—"

He pointed a finger callused by years of martial arts practice at the paper. Pyramus read the number indicated. "Ninety times times ten to the minus twelfth."

"Exactly!" Leo made a baffled gesture. "That's ninety trillionths of a second, not twelve billionths! That's the same time as for a neutral short kaon!"

Pyramus said carefully, "From the very little I know about particle physics, I gather that nothing is certain on that level. So why do a few nanoseconds make such a difference?"

"You don't understand. What we're looking at simply can't be. We'll run it again, of course, but I'm certain the parameters were followed rigorously." Leo turned back to his desk.

Pyramus shrugged. The hentracks on the paper were obviously very important to Leo. He hoped the older man resolved the problem to his satisfaction.

Things were a lot simpler when all we had to worry about was earth, air, fire and water, he thought, and grinned as the left the Physics Section.

Katsu Hanawashi said, with infinite patience, "No, Tracy. Throw it like *this*," and he hurled the ball back toward the younger boy. Tracy reached up and, somewhat to Katsu's surprise, caught it. But when the boy tried to throw it back, it sailed over Katsu's head and into the bushes near Spoke Four.

Katsu sighed. Tracy was only six, but you would think he could pick up as simple a thing as throwing a baseball. True, it was more complicated than throwing a ball on Earth or one of the other planets in the solar system far behind them, but "planets" was only a word to both boys. Why couldn't Tracy learn?

"You have to throw it *there*," he said, pointing at the

ground between them. "Then it'll come to me."

"But *why?*" Tracy replied plaintively. "Why does it keep curving like that?"

Katsu knew why; his mother had explained it to him. She had called it the Coriolis Effect. The reason for it was that *Heaven Star* was rotating all the time; this, in a way he still didn't quite understand, was what made "up" and "down." When you threw a ball through the air, the ground moved underneath it. That was simple enough, but he had tried to make it clear to Tracy over and over, without success. He trudged over to the bushes, found the ball and threw it back, spinward, to Tracy, aiming over the other's head. The ball dropped into Tracy's hands. "Try again," Katsu said, without much hope.

Tracy wound up and, apparently annoyed at Katsu's patronizing tone, hurled the ball with considerable force straight at Katsu. The older child waited for it to curve gracefully up and away from him, but instead something very strange happened. Katsu *felt* something—in trying to describe it later to his mother, he likened it to someone opening a door inside his head and letting a cold draft in. For the barest instant things seemed strange and unreal to him, as though some invisible but vital part of the world had flickered.

And then the ball hit him in the head.

It hit him quite hard; enough so that he did not remember falling. Suddenly Tracy was kneeling beside him, crying, and Katsu was crying as well, more from fear than pain, though he could feel a sizeable goose egg forming. He heard concerned voices, and then the firm, reassuring hands of a grownup were brushing his hair from his eyes and blotting his tears with a handkerchief. "Easy," a voice said; it was nothing like his father's, but for some reason it made Katsu think of him. "You'll be all right, kid."

"Katsu, I'm *sorry*," Tracy said, sniffling.

"But what happened to the Cor-i-o-lis Effect?" Katsu said, bewildered.

Level Eight was Engineering and Power Transmission. Despite damping and soundproofing, it was still the noisiest of all the levels. Turbines whirred, conditioners blasted cold air over hot machinery, heavy cables thrummed with energy. The main source of power was in the Spindle, where the massive neon-sodium reactors, shielded from the torus by a layer of liquid lithium, operated at low levels on interstellar hydrogen. Level Eight dispensed the power to the ship. Pyramus spoke briefly with Enright, the Chief Assistant Engineer, but the man was too busy to talk long and, anyway, there was nothing to worry about on *his* floor.

And, finally, Level Nine.

Pyramus was feeling rather tired by the time he reached Recycling. His weight had increased as he descended toward the outer shell of the torus; he was now moving under slightly more than one gee, instead of the eight-tenths to which he was accustomed. The silence and deserted atmosphere also contributed to his fatigue. He looked about him. The floor was always cleaner and smelled better than Seven, where the rabbit farms and fowl pens were. Quite an accomplishment, Pyramus thought, considering that all waste on the ship was cycled down to Nine. Water was stored here also, in vast, thin tanks that ran completely around the ship, beneath the hull and shielding. A small portion of the precious liquid was manufactured, using hydrogen scooped from space, but the majority was recycled and rationed, as was nearly everything on board. *Heaven Star* was a closed system; nothing was wasted. Physiochemical and bioregenerative techniques ensured that yesterday's cereal package might be tomorrow's faxsheet and next week's designer blouse.

He could tell, without looking at his watch, that the mirrors would soon be opaqued for the twelve hour night cycle. The overhead fluorescents would keep the lower levels just as bright, but his internal clock was not fooled. Ancient rhythms did not change in a single generation.

The silence of the deserted halls was unnerving. He resisted a temptation to glance over his shoulder. He knew there would be no one there. Level Nine was almost totally automatic; only a handful of techs worked the floor, mostly as backup to the robotic systems which handled the flow of wastes. Pyramus leaned against a slurry tank and sighed. He had never liked Level Nine. Though the air was temperature-controlled and filtered, it always felt cold, and he was sure he could smell the faint reek of sewage. The subtle noises and dim lighting for some reason tickled his agoraphobia. He guessed it was because the only way to be more alone was to go Outside. He jumped as a compressor cut in somewhere nearby, starting off with a low whistle and whirr before evening out to a drone.

He had always thought that Nine would be a great place for a horror story. As a boy, he had once let several cronies talk him into joining them in their play down here, despite parental forbiddance. He recalled the legend that had been popular among children at the time, of the boy that had fallen into one of the waste accumulators and, through an arcane synergism of chemicals and effluvium, had emerged as a septic monstrosity that stalked the lower levels, capturing children and dragging them off to some horrible, unspecified fate. . . .

The Security Chief grinned self-consciously. He had gotten lost, of course, or the others had abandoned him, and he could still remember fleeing through the endless, nightmarish maze, tanks and feed pumps and pipes looming threateningly at every turn, and the scatological horror, he was sure, right on his heels. He had not thought about it in years. He wished he had not thought about it now. . . .

Pyramus started to walk. The various hums of the distillation and recirculation units, muted and remote, and his soft footsteps were the only sounds. At least there were no large, open spaces to deal with. On bad days he even had trouble facing the limited vistas of *Heaven Star*'s "outdoors." A fine gypsy you are, he thought. He had done some reading on agoraphobia—literally, "fear of the marketplace": an overwhelming sense of helplessness and panic when in open or unfamiliar surroundings. The medcomp had listed the primary causes as insecurity stemming from feelings of helplessness and lack of control over one's life. It made no sense, Pyramus thought. He had never felt out of control that he could recall; he could not see how such feelings were even possible in the encapsulated, easygoing environment of *Heaven Star*. He had a good job, a part in a great ongoing adventure and a sustaining relationship with an intelligent, talented and beautiful woman. There was no reason for his phobia.

And yet sometimes it took everything he had in him to leave his cube and face the day.

He stopped. There was no further need to poke around down here. He looked at his watch: 1800. If he hurried, he could finish up his paperwork in time to work out with Phaedra. He started back toward the elevators—

And stopped suddenly. He listened, and heard the sound

again: a dismal, wheezing croak, magnified by the foam metal walls. Then there was a scrabbling noise from behind a large catalytic unit.

A shadow moved on the wall.

Pyramus stood stock-still, feeling his spine turn, vertebra by vertebra, to ice. A robot, he thought. Or a tech. Had to be. But a small voice deep within him, the voice of a panicked boy, pointed out that no robot or tech had ever cast such a grotesque, misshapen shadow, and it seemed to him that the underlying scent of offal in the air was growing stronger. . . .

Pyramus took a deep breath and stepped forward. The shadow, warped by the angle of the lighting, slipped down the wall and across the floor, connecting with a pair of webbed feet. Pyramus stared in astonishment as a huge duck, its feathers the color of coal, waddled out from behind the unit. It quacked mournfully at him.

Pyramus leaned against the wall and laughed. The duck regarded him with what almost seemed a hurt expression. Pyramus laughed until he felt tears beginning. He was glad there were no witnesses. He could just see the headline in *The Heavenly Messenger*, the ship's newsletter: SECURITY CHIEF ATTACKED BY DREADED DUCK OF DARKNESS! Pyramus pressed a hand to his diaphragm; his laughter had given him the hiccups.

The fowl must have escaped somehow from Seven and made its way down here. The Security Chief sat down at the top of a short flight of stairs to wait for his hiccups to subside before he called Carl Stephens, whose responsibility the animal was. So much for the sinister secrets of Level Nine.

He looked down at the foot of the steps, and a sudden intake of breath stopped his hiccups.

Below him it looked as if someone had tossed a bag of laundry down the steps. But it was not laundry. It was a body.

Pyramus took the steps three at a time, nearly falling halfway there, clutching at the rails to save himself. He had to jump over the prostrate form to keep from stepping on it. He turned, bent, and touched the man's shoulder. "Hey, what's wrong? Are you all—?"

He shut up. The man, lying on his side, rolled onto his back at Pyramus's slight contact. He was in his late twenties, Pyramus guessed. He had needed a shave; he would never need another one. Sightless eyes stared upward and a swollen tongue, bitten nearly through, protruded from his mouth. Pyramus now knew where the smell of feces had come from. The man's bowels had voided in a final, instinctive reaction of the hindbrain, a desperate attempt to lighten body weight for flight. Pyramus swallowed bile.

The man was dead.

Doctor Hernando Montoya was short, dark and heavy-set; Pyramus guessed his age at about thirty. The medic examined the dead man quickly, using his hands and several small instruments which lit with red diodes and flashed numbers at him. Pyramus stood nervously, glad that he had had the presence of mind to use a security channel. Otherwise the entire level would be swarming with rubberneckers and media types.

Montoya's examination took about five minutes; then the medic stood.

Pyramus jumped to a conclusion. "Zanshin?"

"No. No sign of drugs on the prelim scan."

"You mean he just tripped and fell down the stairs? An accident?"

"Yeah, he fell down the stairs—after he died."

"Are we talking about a heart attack? Or stroke? He seems too young for that."

"Chief, this was no accident, nor was it natural causes. This man was murdered."

"What?!"

"See that caved-in section of bone there on the side of his head? There's no way he could have gotten that bouncing down those stairs—the shape and angle are all wrong. Somebody hit him with something."

Pyramus stared at the body, feeling ill. He took a deep breath and let it out slowly. Homicide, he thought. Jesus and Buddha in a hammock.

SIX

Geoffrey Merle-Douglass slid his left leg from beneath the thin coverlet on the bed. Old men were supposed to be cold all the time, like reptiles who could not find the sun. Not I, he thought with amusement. He was decidedly warm; the exposed limb would allow some body heat to escape.

The Archivist sighed and looked fondly at the woman sleeping next to him. He had never been able to understand why, with all the heat he produced, Elena Vasquez's feet were always so cold. At sixty, she was twenty years younger than he. And very beautiful, he thought, lightly stroking the gray hair that spread over the pillow. He looked at her face, noting with admiration the high cheekbones and the delicate webbing of lines around her eyes. She rolled over and her hand touched his stomach. She mumbled something in her sleep and patted him. Her hand felt cool on his skin.

They had not made love this night. She had come to see him, tired from her teaching, and they had eaten a light supper, talked, and sipped white wine. She had asked if he would mind if she stayed the night. He had not minded at all. He recalled part of their conversation, however, with some slight uneasiness.

• • •

"I realize that he's your friend, but Sharon feels she must oppose him for the Chair, and I have to help her."

"You must do what you feel is right; still, do you really think Sharon is better qualified to be Administrator? After all, Louis has held the position for many years. He's quite efficient."

"That is precisely the problem, Geoff. Louis is *too* good at it. He's become complacent. He can only see one solution to any problem: his. He brooks no opposition."

"And you feel Sharon Sevaer can do better?"

Elena took a delicate sip of her wine. "Frankly, I don't know. She's young, and sometimes impetuous. But she is willing to listen to other opinions. Demond, I think, has become too much the politician, too concerned with how something appears rather than with the intrinsic truth of the matter."

"Is that altogether fair? I know Louis loves the ship; he would do anything to keep it running smoothly."

Elena put her wine glass down. It was genuine Mikasa crystal, one of a set of six which Merle-Douglass's nephew had given him as a departure present upon leaving Earth. There were four still intact, two and a half decades later. "I don't doubt that, Geoff. I know he thinks he's doing what he thinks best, but the fact is, I'm not at all certain what is good for Demond is necessarily good for the ship. That's why I'm going to manage her campaign."

Geoffrey nodded. *Heaven Star* had no formal crew or captain; there was no need for one. The GARTH-7 multiprocessor, which to Geoffrey was Hobson, as it was a different personality to nearly everyone on board, monitored the infinity of astronautical complexities necessary to keep the ship on course and in communication with Earth, as well as the closed life support systems and energy production. It was backed by a failsafe of three extra systems, as well as the many subsidiary systems and human technicians. When they reached their destination a human hierarchy would make all the decisions; for now, the purpose of the Council and Administrator, who were elected by popular vote every five years, was primarily to keep day to day life running smoothly. The department supervisors answered to the Council; seldom was a matter so pressing that it could not be subjected to a vote. In case of an emergency the GARTH-7 would review the records of the ship's population and, if necessary, appoint the one most qualified as *pro tem* captain.

"Good luck," Geoffrey said, "but I think very much that you shall lose the election."

"But you won't mind if we try to win it?"

"Not at all, my dear. Not at all."

Elena rolled onto her back and mumbled again. It sounded as if she said, "Don't let the cow play, Joaquim." Geoffrey smiled. It must be an interesting dream. He reached over to gently cup her left breast. Oddly, it felt warm to him; his hands must be cooler than the rest of his body. After a moment, her nipple budded against his palm. He wondered what she was dreaming now.

She smiled and opened her eyes.

"Sorry. I didn't mean to wake you."

"But you did," she said. "And now that I'm awake, what shall we do?"

Geoffrey massaged her breast. "Why, Ms. Vasquez, whatever can you mean?"

She reached down between his legs, took his limp penis in her hand and began to stroke him.

"Dear, we did this on Tuesday, if my fading memory is correct. Today being Thursday, well . . ."

"Such a negative attitude." She slid from sight beneath the cover. After a moment he felt the warmth of her mouth envelop him. In another moment he felt himself stir. "A miracle." He chuckled. "It's a miracle."

"You are certain?" Demond said.

Pyramus nodded. "The medic is, and he's the expert. There will be an autopsy and full testing, of course, but it looks like the victim was struck on the side of the head with some kind of blunt object, crushing part of his skull and rupturing delicate membranes."

The two were in Louis Demond's office on Four. Demond sat behind his desk, a small and unimpressive metal unit with four drawers. No one could say he was using his office for personal aggrandizement, Pyramus thought. The Administrator shook his head. "Murder. I can't believe it."

"Homicide," Pyramus said, "but maybe not murder."

Demond raised his eyebrows. Pyramus shrugged. "It could have been a fight, unintentional; that would make it manslaughter."

Demond stood and walked to the light-well window. "That's hairsplitting, Chief Gray. A man—what was his name?"

"Stanhope. Arthur Jefferson Stanhope. He was a toxicologist."

"Stanhope has been killed, and the killer is loose on *Heaven Star*. Your technical niceties are hardly important."

"They are important under the law, sir."

Demond turned to face Pyramus. "What are you doing to capture the killer?"

"Medical is examining the body. I have a man reviewing the recordings taken by the robot spot cameras—though I don't hold much hope for those, they're generally set to view machinery which might malfunction. I have data on all the workers in Recycling coming in—"

"And what if he wasn't killed by somebody working on Nine?"

"You asked what I was doing, Mr. Administrator. I'm trying to tell you."

Demond nodded. "Sorry. Go on." The Administrator was obviously very upset by the situation, Pyramus thought. Well, he wasn't the only one. At least he hadn't found the body.

"I have a team from Bio checking the scene for anything which might give us a clue to the . . . killer."

"And—?"

"And I'm open to suggestions. If you have any ideas, I'd welcome them."

Demond turned back toward the window. It was long past mirror-turn and no light came from the slot in the wall. "We have to keep this quiet, Gray. People would be frightened. Can you keep it a secret for now?"

"My men won't say anything. And I can probably keep Medical and Bio from spreading it around for awhile. But the man will have relatives, friends, co-workers. . . . They'll want to know where he is."

"Tell them he's sick. He caught some kind of new enteric bacteria from the sewage—that happens sometimes, doesn't it?"

"I suppose. But it won't hold for long. Medical can cure that kind of thing in a few days."

"Better a few days than nothing. I don't want to risk a panic. I want the killer captured before anyone knows that he or she exists."

After Gray left, Demond paced his office, too agitated to sit still. A killing. It was bad; bad for the ship, and bad for him. The election was coming up soon; the opposition would use anything it could to unseat him, and a murder would certainly help them more than him. And as long as the killer was at large no one on *Heaven Star* was safe.

Gray was a good man, Demond thought, but he had no experience in this kind of thing. And it would be impossible to keep it quiet, he knew; by this time tomorrow night it would be all over the ship. The lines of communication on *Heaven Star* were too good; the rumor would circulate as quickly as if it had been broadcast on the newsletter or holoproj net. But it would only be a rumor, at first. Maybe they could catch the killer before the people started demanding answers. Maybe.

Pyramus stood in the elevator, breathing deeply. So much for his report to the *Bitcherin'-moosh*, as his people once called the Magistrate. Demond had not been as upset as he had expected, but that was the least of his worries. What was he going to do? He realized that he was afraid—afraid of failing in his job, of allowing a murderer to go free. The days of an easy job were over, he told himself. Nothing this serious had ever happened since he had joined Security. Old man Hauptmann had retired three years ago to write full-time, leaving Pyramus in charge. He had never had a murder to investigate either; Theodore Haskins, the one and only murderer on *Heaven Star*—until now—had killed his wife in a jealous rage eighteen years ago. Such things simply did not happen any more; the psyche profiles, the array of chemical and psychiatric treatments available, had reduced aberrant behavior of this sort dramatically even before the ship had left the Belt.

Part of the criteria for the population of *Heaven Star* had been mental stability and humanistic potential; that, coupled with an environment where no one lacked for food, shelter or the more intangible necessities such as job satisfaction and fulfillment, had reduced the crime curve to almost nothing.

The elevator let Pyramus out on the main level; he walked away from the spoke, down a winding residential street. Where was he to start? He had read criminology texts; he knew the theory. Motive, means, opportunity—establish those and you could arrest someone. Haskins would be a prime suspect, only he was long-since dead. Rehabilitated by personality engineering, he had returned to his job in Credit, at which he had worked happily until he had died of a heart attack a year ago.

Pyramus touched fingertips to his wrist and realized that his heart was beating uncomfortably fast. He needed to relax. He noticed that he was near a *zendo*, and on impulse turned into it.

It was the right decision; that he knew as soon as he stepped into the quiet, dimly-lit room, with one wall dominated by a large mandala composed of Sanskrit letters. Pyramus sat down on the hard matted surface of a *tan*. His leg muscles were not warm enough to permit a full lotus without discomfort, so he settled for a half lotus, left foot over right thigh and right foot under left thigh. He fixed his gaze upon the mandala and began to breathe slowly, deeply, trying to feel the thoughts, the worries, the panic pour from his mind with each exhalation.

Leo Chin had once told Pyramus that there was no "wrong" way to meditate; the Security Chief had promptly replied that he could think of a few, such as doing a handstand on a skateboard while whistling a John Philip Sousa march. But he knew that Leo was right. Though he had never thought himself very good at meditation and pursued it only sporadically, he knew it was the right thing for him now. He might never reach Zanshin, but he—

Pyramus blinked. The drug, Zanshin—could it have made a killer out of someone? It seemed unlikely; despite stories that had circulated long ago when psychoactive drugs had begun to proliferate, psychotic reactions were not all that common. All recreational chemicals on board the ship were non-addictive on a physical level, and mental addiction was treated

promptly. Still, little was known about Zanshin; it had simply
appeared one day, conceived and manufactured illegally. Its
use was hardly epidemic—so far, they had had less than a
dozen problems in a population of nearly nine thousand. But
it was worth checking into, Pyramus decided. He stood,
stamping his feet to get the blood moving, and headed for
Medical. He felt somewhat better as he left the *zendo*; at least
he had a destination, a possibility. At least he was doing something.

Phaedra Adjurian walked past the row of hoverbeds in the
ward. Some of the units had noise suppressors and privacy
screens on, but the last one was open to the big room. In it was
the still figure of a young woman whom Phaedra thought was
asleep, until she saw her blink.

"Shanna?"

The patient turned her head sluggishly toward the Dancer.
"Phaedra? What are you doing here?"

"Just checking on you."

"It's so late. I thought you were a day person."

"Normally I am. I had insomnia, so I thought I'd put it
to good use." She did not mention that her sleeplessness
had been caused by Pyramus calling and telling her about the
death on Nine. She looked at the woman in the bed. Shanna
Dicran was a year or so younger than Phaedra's twenty-eight,
but the ages were the only things similar about them. Shanna
was short and slight, blue-eyed and blonde.

"So, how are you?" Phaedra asked, almost wincing at the
banality of the question.

Shanna smiled. "Doped to the hairline. Some kind of
muscle relaxant to help with the shivers."

Phaedra nodded. She did not use many drugs; some joystick
at a party now and then, or sometimes before making love.
And once, just to see what it was like, she had sniffed Leaf.
But that was about the extent of it. She knew no one who had
used Zanshin; the potential side effects were simply too dangerous. Shanna had come out of it with severe clonic spasms,
her doctor had said, which might be permanent. Several who
had taken the drug, Phaedra knew, had become cataleptic.

"Shanna, was it worth it?"

Shanna nodded without hesitation. "Oh, yes, Phaedra. You

don't know what it's like. I can't even begin to tell you about
the awareness, the *knowledge*. I'm still flying, you see. I can
still feel a—a touch of it in me.''

"You've done it more than once, I take it?"

"Yes. Half a dozen times.''

"Is it always like this?"

"Yes. Each time, more stays with me. You never really
come down, you see.''

Phaedra sat silently for a moment. She was about to speak
again when Shanna said, "This will cost me my job, won't
it?"

Phaedra shook her head. "I don't know."

Shanna looked at the ceiling. Phaedra could see an exaltation in her eyes. "It doesn't matter. Not in the whole scheme
of things."

"You'd take it again, wouldn't you? Even knowing what
it's done to you?"

"Yes."

"What about Raul?"

Shanna sighed. "Raul doesn't understand. He's never
flown. He tells me he loves me, but he doesn't know what the
word means. He's been here during all of his off-shifts, you
know, sitting right there. I finally made him leave; he wasn't
eating much or sleeping or even bathing!''

"I find it hard to believe you'd give up your job and maybe
a man who loves you for some . . . drug.''

"You don't understand either. I can hear the others calling
me.''

"What do you mean?" Phaedra asked, but Shanna did not
reply. She closed her eyes, and a moment later the regular rise
and fall of her chest indicated that she slept.

Phaedra stood and left the ward, walking quickly, hardly
acknowledging the nods and compliments she received from
various people who recognized her. Shanna's last words, for
some reason, were most unsettling. *I can hear the others calling me . . .* What others? And what was it like to never really
come down from the drug, to have your perceptions, your
consciousness, permanently altered a little bit more each time
you used it?

It was nearly 0600 hours; Ian Kyle sat alone in his cube, staring at the wall across the room. The light was dim now; when the mirrors turned in a few minutes, the "morning" sunlight would be reflected into the cube. It was one of the nice perks of living on the Main Level. Not that it mattered very much at the moment. At the moment, not much of anything mattered a great deal, save that Ian Kyle's control had . . . faltered.

Faltered, yes, that was a good word. It was justified, because it was not his fault. There were . . . other factors at work. Forces are forcing me, he thought, with a small, humorless smile. Something was *wrong* on *Heaven Star*, something that no one else knew about—not yet. But they would. He was sure of that.

He had been in the ward when the lad had been brought in, had listened while Doctor Russell treated him and Nurse Tomita called the boy's mother. Kyle knew he was the only one there who believed what the boy had said about the lapse of the Coriolis Effect. Such a thing was impossible, of course, in any rational universe. But it wasn't a rational universe any more, was it?

He had gone home, had spent the rest of the day and night in his cube, thinking. He had heard—though not from Leo, of course—about the strange findings in the most recent series of charged-particle experiments. Over a few drinks in a bar, an acquaintance from Physics had told him this, and more. There was evidence of fractional charges in a number of elements. They were discovering anomalons, a plasma made up of quarks and gluons with completely unfamiliar behavior. "Free quarks just aren't supposed to happen," his confidant told him. "Now it looks like they're coming out of the woodwork." Kyle was not a physicist, but he was an intelligent, well-read man. It almost seemed that the randomization in the matrices of probability that knitted together the material world was increasing; that, in short, whatever reality there was on the subatomic level was changing.

When he heard that, he had thought, for some reason, of the strange diagnoster readings on Mkono. Had there been other inexplicable happenings in other departments? A quick check revealed there had been: a unaccountable failure of one of the heloid's guidance modules; several glitches in various systems which could not be traced; the burnout of two down-verters in the Hub. But all of these were, in themselves, the barest circumstantial evidence. After all, machinery failed, everyone knew that. Easier to ignore the ramifications of this rash of malfunctions, to not put things together yet. Be cautious, like Chin, and redo tests over and over, until it is too late.

But Kyle needed no tests; he *knew*. He knew by no sense he could put a name to that something was seriously wrong. He knew because, a few days ago, for the first time, he had lost control.

This was a major disaster. All of his adult life he had kept the rage within him tightly harnessed, dispensing it only under the most controlled conditions. He had become a black sash in Chan Gen because it allowed him to fight, to strike out, in restricted circumstances. He had channelled his aggression into his work. Long ago he had realized that, while he might know for a fact that he was far superior to others, those others would not embrace the truth as willingly as he had. The knowledge that he was a wolf among sheep had been enough; that, and the satisfaction of having triumphed over a childhood of terror and cruelty, of having *won* despite everything they had done to bring him down.

He had delighted in his ability to control and manipulate others, in being able to get what he wanted through talent and charisma. He had played by the rules so far because it amused him.

But the rules, it seemed, were changing.

It had not been his fault. Nevertheless, he knew he could not let it happen again. . . .

He had been thinking about Leo Chin. *Damn* that wizened little man! He *couldn't* be that good, not at his age. Kyle knew the physiology of the human body; it was not possible for a man pushing sixty to have that kind of strength. He did not believe in *ch'i*, in all the crap the old man spouted about being like water, about flowing with everything. There had to be something else, some kind of secret Chinese drug.

He had gone down to Nine, to the most deserted place he could think of, to be alone. The quiet would help; the soulless robots and circulating coils of recycled shit kept most people away. People did not like to think about drinking water reclaimed from urine, or blowing their noses on what used to be somebody's underwear. But Kyle was a doctor—he knew about the interior plumbing of the human beast. Such things did not bother him. So he had gone to Nine, for the peace.

Only there was no peace for him there. He stalked the corridors and catwalks, growing more irritated. It was more than just his inability to defeat Leo. He was thinking also of those glitches, those anomalies that were cropping up all over the ship. No one else had noticed them yet, because no one else was as smart as Ian Kyle. The possibilities inherent in them frightened him, and he could not remember ever having been frightened before.

He wanted to shout his rage and frustration, but someone might hear. So he held in the sound and used the edges of his hands to pound against the bulkhead, a man driving imaginary nails into his private demon.

And then he heard the voice. "Hey, are you all right?"

Kyle spun, fear riding high in him; he could taste it, metallic and cold. *"What?"*

"Are you okay, friend?" A man stood there, staring at him. Kyle tried to speak, and could not. The man was dressed in a gray synlin coverall. His features were sharp, eyes brown; some kind of middle-European background. Who was he? Why was he here?

"I said, are you all right?"

The man had seen him lose control. Kyle felt himself grow icy at the thought.

The other stepped closer. "Here, let me give you a hand. We'll get you to a seat and I'll call Medical—"

Everything went to half-speed then. A part of Kyle stood back and watched it happen, coolly, analytically. One step, then the jump. The spin, slowly, slowly, head snapping around to spot, the rest of him following, leg tucked in close, then whipping out, heel first, body leaning slightly for counterbalance. Woven into the motion was the silent yell, the focus of energy. As he came around, using the rotation of the torus to augment the kick's force, Kyle had time to see the man's eyes widen in sudden fear, to see the mouth start to form a yell, to see the ineffectual hands come up in a desperate attempt to ward the arcing leg away. Then—

The shock and the sound came as one. He felt the bone crunch under the thin material of his shoe, and the sound was almost like that of hitting a heavy punching bag, with a thin slat of wood breaking just under the canvas.

Then there was the slow fall, the neck canted at an un-natural angle, the eyes glazed, unseeing. . . .

Kyle knelt beside him and felt for a carotid pulse, using his sleeve to avoid touching the skin. The pulse bounced wildly and then faded as the brain told the rest of the organism it was over, now and forever. The doctor looked quickly about for witnesses, and saw none. He looked back at the body, feeling an unfamiliar emotion blossoming within him. Not remorse—he had never known what that word meant—and not fear precisely either. He was unable to put a name to it; he only knew that no one must know he had lost control. He had to make it look like an accident.

He looked at the caved-in temple. That was bad; there was no way he could make it look like it had been sustained ac-cidentally. He would have to make sure that he was the ex-amining medic when the body was found, which would not be until shift change. Kyle grinned. How convenient to be in charge of the autopsy on his own victim!

He looked around, spotted a conveyer hook on a chain, and quickly went to get it. He had no gloves and did not want to touch the body. He could not take the chance of leaving any part of himself, even so much as a single cell, on the body or its clothing. Using the hook, he caught the man's coverall and dragged him down the corridor, looking for some way to stage an accident. He carefully avoided the spot cameras, as well as the robots performing their mindless tasks.

He pulled the body to the top of a flight of stairs, then snapped the release on the hook. The body flopped down the steps, rolling in the loose-limbed, boneless manner which indi-cates no muscle control, and came to a rest at the bottom.

Kyle shoved the conveyer hook into a recycler on his way to the elevators. No one saw him. The elevator was empty. He took it to Level Two. If anybody checked the lift's memory, it would show that a passenger had come down from Four and gone up to Two.

Once on the main level, he waited until half a dozen people had boarded the elevators for different destinations before he took one down to Five. He climbed the emergency stairs up to Four. Nobody saw him enter his office. Nobody could tie him to the . . . problem on Nine. He was back in control.

•   •   •

He was in control—for now. But he had slipped. For the first time in his life he had killed.

Outside Kyle's cube, the reflected light of the heloid began to brighten into day. A new day in the voyage of *Heaven Star*, a day unlike any before it. Oh, yes, Kyle thought. That was certainly true.

He shivered, though the sunlight that now touched him was warm.

SEVEN

Scott St. Martin tapped the sliding control. On the holoproj screen a bar graph showing decibel levels and tone proportions dropped; the tone generator humming in the background went from first soprano to second. Scott made a notation on the number keypad to the right of the control board and sighed. It was such a slow process! He had been working all morning and all he had were three shifting tones: a high-low-high, a neutral, and a high-high. At this rate he would be able to translate fifty words of English into Freedolph in about a hundred years.

In the holding pond five meters away, Killikup slapped the water with his tail. He was getting bored, or hungry, or both. Scott did not blame him. It was time for a break.

The man tapped in a series of commands on the keyboard: Save Program. Add to Existing Sequences. Correlate. So far, his knowledge of what he called Freedolph made Basic English look like Shakespeare. He felt like a savage from the Stone Age trying to communicate with a twenty-first century professor; he could only grunt and wave his arms while his listener smiled and shook his head.

He had already noted several interesting departures in the

clicks and whistles which Killikup used to communicate with the ship's five other dolphins from tapes of similar interaction among Earthly dolphins. Environment and the size of the herd evidently played a fairly large part in communications.

Killikup slapped the water again. He was definitely hungry. If Scott did not feed him soon, Killikup would trip the gate and go out to find his own lunch, probably from one of the salmon ranches. Scott collected a bucket of fresh carp from the big tank and hurried toward the holding pond. He saw Killikup swimming back and forth, more graceful than any other aquatic creature on *Heaven Star*. He grinned. "Take it easy, you bottomless pit. I'm coming."

Killikup swam to the lip of the pond and stuck his head out of the water. He barked at Scott, a sound which the man knew meant *Fish!* It was one of the first things Scott had learned from the dolphin. He squatted and held a carp out by the tail, half a meter or so above Killikup's face. "You want it, fin up here and get it."

The permanent smile on the dolphin's face mocked the man. *Like hell*, it seemed to say. *You can bloody well drop it!* After a moment, Scott released the wriggling fish. Killikup caught it and swallowed it in a single gulp. The smile seemed to grow, though that was impossible. The dolphin barked again. Scott grinned in return and tossed a second fish, then a third, until all the carp were gone.

More.

"Forget it, fatso, that's all." He held the empty bucket upside down.

This time Killikup's bark was more a hoot, trailing off into a series of clicks. Scott's flesh pebbled into goosebumps under his thin shirt.

Scott. More.

The goosebumps were part of the rush he got every time Killikup called him by name. It was not the generic term the dolphin used for all humans; it was definitely a personal tag. "All right," Scott said. "Half a bucket, but no more."

He rose from his crouch by the pool's edge and pulled the portable tone generator from his belt. He punched in a complicated series of tones and rests, then tapped a control. The tone generator barked and grunted in Freedolph to Killikup: *More. Fish.* He then turned and walked back toward the carp tank.

He passed the holding aquarium where Eight Ball floated, and paused to look at the cephalopod. He had read somewhere once of a way to test the intelligence of octopi. Put a crab into a jar of water, stopper the jar with a loose-fitting plastic plug, and put the whole arrangement into a tank with a hungry octopus. It had sounded intriguing, so Scott had tried it. The results were impressive: It had taken Eight Ball less than two minutes to divine the operation of the stopper, and a few seconds later it was dining on the crab.

Killikup hooted and clicked, and Scott felt gooseflesh crawl over his back and arms again. He hurried from the octopus's tank to get more carp. Killikup's demands sounded like those of a spoiled child, but Scott moved like a man hurrying to bring diamonds to his beloved.

"I don't think so, Chief," Doctor Kyle said. "It's an intriguing idea, but all the research I've done indicates that Zanshin is a very passive psychopharmacological combination." He laced his hands behind his head and leaned back in his chair.

Pyramus said, "I've heard it causes hallucinations, and also that it makes people feel strong enough to rip steel in half. That sounds like pretty dangerous stuff to me. What if someone thought that Stanhope was attacking, and didn't realize his or her own strength when he or she tried to fight back?"

Kyle smiled. "Interesting theory. But all the examples we've seen so far indicate that the most dangerous thing about Zanshin is its potential for harmful physiological side effects. Of course, I suppose it's possible. But even so, where does that leave you? There's no way to track down the drug's users."

"I'm just grasping at straws right now," Pyramus admitted. "But I can't afford to pass up any leads. I'd appreciate your informing me of any Zanshin cases that come to your attention."

"Happy to help in any way I can, of course." Kyle rose and shook Pyramus's hand warmly. The Security Chief left.

Kyle sat staring at the closed panel. It had been a nasty shock to learn that the Security Chief had been poking about on Nine and had found the body before the shift change. Kyle had been asleep, and that fool Montoya had made the initial examination. There was no way Kyle could doctor the autopsy report and simply label it an accident now; for better or for worse, the word was out that a murder had been committed. But Kyle was still not worried; there was no way they could trace it to him.

Perhaps he should have encouraged Gray to pursue the red herring of a Zanshin tripper, but that line of deduction could conceivably lead back to him also. Zanshin had been his invention; one of several drugs he had put together over the years in an attempt to gain an edge over Leo Chin. He had been lucky; he had experienced none of the unexpected side effects. It was a combination of five drugs: epinephrine, or adrenalin; psilocybic mescabyn, itself a combination of psilocybin, LSD and mescaline; neo-methylphenidate, an improved version of ritalin, a mood elevator; *Rauwolfia cannabinol* extract, which produced a time-dilation effect; and enkephalin diendorphin, the most powerful painkiller known. It had not aided him against Chin, however, and so he had left the formula sitting under a triple blind code in his personal file. Evidently some computer pirate had managed to dig it out. He had looked at the workup Montoya had done—the man was capable in a dull, bovine way. He had found minute traces of plastic embedded in the wound—plastic from Kyle's shoe. Kyle smiled. Yes, there was no sense taking chances.

"Mother, watch!"

Susan Hanawashi looked up from her portable scanner as Katsu bounded by, running antispinward; when he was five meters past the sheet they had laid their picnic lunch upon he leaped high into a front somersault. His flip was tight, but he timed it perfectly, using the rotation of the wheel to augment it. He came down with his right foot leading enough to continue running.

Susan smiled. "Terrific, kiddo!"

They were in the meadow a hundred meters from where Spoke Four went through the Main Level; around the meadow, small pines and Douglass firs formed a screen which shielded the picnickers from nearby buildings. The meadow looked as if it were in the depths of a valley, since the toroid curved "upwards" to the blue arc of the ceiling, which was broken by the window strips. The grass was thick, a short, seedless variant of that which covered Earth's hills and dales; the trees were real and planted to give the impression of random growth, and the air was fresh with natural odors and extra oxygen. Katsu loved it here, and that was reason enough for Susan to bring him whenever she could.

They were not alone today; half a dozen other picnickers dotted the small meadow, sitting on plastic sheets, float chairs and the like. Susan swept her gaze around the scene briefly, not recognizing any of the couples or families sharing the sunshine with her and Katsu. She did not stare at anyone for more than a moment—the illusion of privacy required politeness.

Partway across the meadow Katsu turned, running in a wide loop, and headed back toward Susan. She watched him running and her smile grew wider. Such a beautiful and bright child, she thought. She recalled that moment of stark, freezing fear when the nurse had called to tell her of the accident. Fortunately, there had been no concussion, no problems beyond a goose egg. She waved at him. Katsu was the one joy outside of her job; lively, perceptive and intelligent. That was not simply a mother's subjective opinion, but truth. He sometimes had a way of going right to the heart of complicated matters, like a laser stabbing through thick clouds of dust and not losing its focus. Which was why his insistence that the ball Tracy had hurled had come straight toward him, in defiance of the laws of physics, had surprised her so. But it was understandable, given the circumstances.

Susan glanced at the scanner. The technical stats she was reading seemed suddenly too dry for her today. It was a rare feeling—usually her compulsion to work was such that she could study anytime, anywhere. But now she felt a sudden, strong revulsion to going over the material. The necessary knowledge and study required by her new position seemed abruptly overwhelming; she clicked the unit off and laid it on the sheet, next to what was left of her lunch. Katsu stopped in front of her. "May I go and explore the woods?"

She nodded. "If you put all the scraps in the recycler on your way."

He grinned, scooping up the fried rabbit bones and paper cups and plates. "I'll be back in a little while," he said, as he started for the recycler.

"Thirty minutes," Susan said. "Mark."

Katsu glanced at his watch. "Mark."

She watched him go, feeling a slight twinge of worry. She had been thinking about the rumor she had heard, that there had been a murder on one of the lower levels. She shook her head. Foolishness. Such paranoia might have been warranted in her ancestors, who had lived in the crime-ridden cities of Earth, but it was hardly appropriate on *Heaven Star*.

Susan gave a small sigh and relaxed in the sunlight. It was especially warm there, and tanning was possible. She wore brief shorts and a halter, and there was a tube of sunscreen in her carrybag. She took off the halter and began to rub the sunscreen cream into her upper body. It was supposed to prevent burning but allow tanning. She had a little trouble getting it onto the middle of her back, but was gratified to find herself limber enough to manage it. Leo Chin's classes were doing her a lot of good. Then she lay back on the sheet, feeling the heloid's warmth soak into her. It was very nice to just relax and do nothing, with no one to bother her and no problems to solve. An unusual feeling; she luxuriated in it. There was more to life than work, after all, she told herself; even more than work and caring for her child. She felt the warm light relaxing her, felt thoughts, worries, slip away. It was enough to simply *be* there.

Michan Bern leaned back against the rough bark of the evergreen tree and looked at the arofloj in his lap. The silver tube was as long as his arm, and for most of that length looked like a standard flute. At the end opposite the *embouchure*, however, was a rounded block the size of a clenched fist. This was the *hjarna*, the electronic brain and heart of the instrument. Three rows of control buttons covered its surface, and there were additional controls on the underside.

Michan was an accomplished player, so he had been told, and he practiced in the soundproofed music rooms often. But occasionally he wanted to play in a larger chamber. The problem was that he did not relish the thought of being heard. His music was private, and he guarded it carefully. Most of his acquaintances did not know he could play at all, and no one knew how much the music meant to him.

He was as deep in the wooded area near Spoke Four as he could get. He had waited for nearly an hour to be certain no one was nearby. Now, sure at last that he was alone, he raised the arofloj to his lips. The volume was set low so that the sound would not carry far, and the trees would mute it even more.

Michan began to play. He started with a short piece of baroque music, a minuet by Carlos Perito. The music was full of trills and short runs, and he used it for a warm-up more than anything else. *The Harvey Minuet* only lasted three minutes when played as a flute solo. With the instrument in *hjarna* mode, the selection could be expanded and the sound of six or eight instruments playing could be produced; a small chamber orchestra, in effect, from a single device. But he did not feel like doing that today. He finished the piece and took several deep breaths. Today he wanted to do Pachelbel's *Canon in D*, a contrapuntal piece based on a simple eight-note progression. The composer, a German, had been one of Bach's main influences, born in the mid-sixteen hundreds and died in his fifties. Michan put the instrument to his lips and closed his eyes.

First the bass had to be laid in. He tapped the proper control on the *hjarna* and began. D, A, B, F#, G, D—down the scale, then back up with the two-note close, G and A. The *hjarna* obediently stored the notes and began repeating them in a slow and stately manner. Michan added the three-note upward roll for each bass note. Then he began to program in the rest of the music: the counterpoint, and the variations on the simple theme which made the four hundred year-old composition so rich and full. For his taste, this canon was the single best classical piece ever written, so simple and yet so complex, its recursive progression leading the listener ever upward, but always keeping in touch with the central, reassuring theme. It was like a series of Chinese boxes, one nested inside the other, each opening to release a new series of notes.

He played, and it seemed that the gentle, constant breeze that was a part of the toroid's rotation played with him among the needles and leaves of the trees. Every note was perfect; he was playing better than he ever had before. He was caught up in the beauty of it, transported. He ceased to be a man playing and became instead the music itself, winding up and down, filling the cosmos. Through him a man dead four hundred years lived on. Michan Bern *became* the music. Thinker and thought, doer and deed, player and song, were one.

In the *being* of it came the knowledge that it must not be muted and private. Even if there were no ears save those of trees and air, still those must be allowed to hear. Without thought, Michan's finger found the volume control, and the ancient and timeless sounds spilled from the arofloj and filled the woods. Music, proud and fine, controlled and yet free.

The music slipped him from the bonds of his thoughts. He was, for that moment and in that place, *there*.

Susan Hanawashi opened her eyes. She heard music; at first she thought it was someone's pocket stereo, but as she listened she realized there was a subtle, indefinable difference—this was real music, compelling and alive. She sat up and looked around. Some of the other picnickers were listening as well, but the source of the beautiful sounds was not evident. They were familiar, but she could not place them.

She sat and listened, enthralled. Nobody could play like that! She found herself leaning in the direction of the music, like a phototropic plant growing toward sunlight.

Then it ended, so abruptly that she blinked. *Don't stop,* she thought. *I want to hear more.* But the silence continued, and she was surprised to find her cheeks were wet, not with sunscreen, but with tears.

Michan became aware, slowly, that he was not alone. A small boy with black hair and dark eyes sat crosslegged on the dry pine straw nearby, watching.

Michan smiled. He was not surprised to see the child. The feeling he had had in the music was gone, but the memory was still strong. The problems with Steen seemed unimportant now. Everything was all right. Furthermore, everything was going to be all right, from now until time ended, even to the last grain of sand in the last hour glass on the last world in the universe. This boy was a part of that, and so was in his proper place. He could be nowhere else.

"Are you going to play some more?" the boy asked.

Michan's smile did not falter. "Not now," he said.

"When, then?"

"Another day." Michan felt truly relaxed for the first time in longer than he could remember. Even Outside he did not have this measure of calmness and tranquility. If this were a dream he did not want to awaken.

The boy nodded. "I'll come back and listen. I'm Katsu Hanawashi. Will you teach me how to play that?" He pointed at the arofloj.

The man looked down at the instrument, forgotten in the afterglow. He was still grinning; it felt like a permanent part of his face. "Sure."

"Good." Katsu looked at his watch. "I have to go now. Will you come back tomorrow?"

Michan blinked. "No. I'll be working tomorrow."

"When?"

"Friday. I'll come back Friday."

The boy nodded again, looking quite grave for one so young. "All right. Friday. I'll be here."

Michan watched him leave. At that moment it did not matter that he normally had no patience with children, or that he had never taught nor considered teaching anybody how to play the arofloj. Katsu had listened to him and wanted to learn. It was right that Michan allow him to do so. Perfectly right.

Pyramus Gray sat in his office, staring glumly at the stack of hardcopy which the printer had spun out for him. Included was a list of those workers who had been assigned to Level Nine on the day the body had been found. The names covered seven sheets—the staff of an entire level—though only three or four of them were anywhere near the dead man's station. Pyramus intended to talk to them personally. It would be almost impossible to interview all the other workers with his small staff, and so he had arranged for *Nano*, in his infinite personae, to do it. He looked at an index to the video shot on Nine during the period prior to the killing. There were hundreds of hours of recording. Only a few cameras were near the stairway, but all of the others had to be checked as well—and searching for clues was a task so subjective that not even *Nano* was up to it. It would take a human—or, more accurately, many of them.

And then there was the medical report. It was full of jargon Pyramus did not understand—zygomatic arch, great wing of sphenoid, dura, arachnoid, pia, temporal—but the bottom line was simple enough: a caved-in skull, level with the right eye, just ahead of the right ear. A chemical analysis of the wound showed minute traces of foreign materials: an amide bond/linear macromolecular polymer and smaller deposits of polyurethane and pigments. Pyramus sighed, touched his com patch and called Medical. After a few moments he got Doctor Montoya on the line.

"What can I do for you, Chief?"

"I'm looking at your report of the chemical analysis of material found in the dead man's wound. What does all this mumbo-jumbo mean? Macromolecular polymer and polyurethane and pigments?"

There was a pause. Pyramus could almost hear the man's shrug. "Plastics," the doctor said. "There was a light-blue plastic coating on whatever was used to kill him."

"I don't suppose you have any ideas as to what that object might have been?"

"It could have been almost anything. That particular combination of material is used in hundreds of items; it's a basic product of the labs. They coat metal with it where they don't want sparks; they use it in clothing, gloves, shoes, waterproof fittings around plumbing—all kinds of things, Chief. I'm not a chemist; you can check with them. Probably they'll know even more uses."

Wonderful, Pyramus thought. "Thanks, Doctor Montoya. That's all I need for now."

"It's not on the report, Chief, but whoever did it was more than passing strong."

"Oh?"

"Yeah. It took a strong blow to do the damage I found."

"Thanks again. Gray out."

Pyramus leaned his head into his cupped palms for a moment, resting his elbows on the piles of faxsheets. He felt overwhelmed; he had no idea where to even start. He thought of CIRCLE's exhortation to "Exit the system." At the moment it seemed a very good idea. He sighed, and shuffled through the sheets. He found a biography of the dead man. Stanhope, Arthur Jefferson. Toxicologist. Age: 23: height: 180 cm, weight: 64 kilos (ship), 80 kilos (standard). Single, no children, both parents living, father: Stanhope, Richard Jay, Level Six . . . .

Pyramus skipped down the page, looking for anything useful. Near the bottom of the bio he found something. "Subject has spoken in favor of CIRCLE resolutions at three

Council meetings, following dates and items—"

Pyramus blinked. CIRCLE! A coincidence? Or could it be a break? CIRCLE had been only minor trouble so far. Still, it was worth looking into. Pyramus summoned Bill Plait and showed him the report on Stanhope.

"Christ, Chief, you think maybe they're tied into the killing?"

"It's worth checking out. You have friends who know some of these people, don't you?"

Plait looked uncomfortable. "Yeah."

"Good. See what you can find out about them. I'll have everything we have on them printed out, but most of what they do won't be in the files—at least not where I can get at it." He pushed the autopsy report at Plait. "Also, run a copy of this through to Chemical; I want a list of everything onboard which uses the compound on the report. If we can find out what the weapon was, maybe we can figure out who used it."

After Plait left, Pyramus looked at the rest of the printout. There was nothing else that would be helpful. He had found two clues, neither one particularly great, but at least there were now things to check out, people to talk to, places to visit.

He did not have much time left. Rumors that a killing had taken place were already circulating. He hoped Chemical would have some idea what that plastic had been used for— and a way to trace it.

Ian Kyle opened the slot to the public disposal, dropped the pair of pale blue shoes into the unit and cycled it shut. The unit whirled, ingested them and sucked them down to the recyclers on Level Nine. There was no way to predict what their next incarnation would be, but one thing was certain—it would be nothing that could possibly be traced back to him in any way. He walked away from the disposal, whistling.

EIGHT

Phaedra touched his shoulder and said, "It's not your fault. The family had to be notified sooner or later."

Pyramus nodded. He sat on the carved synstone and foam chair in Phaedra's cube, staring up at the ceiling, his long legs stretched out before him. "I know. But now everybody knows there's a killer loose on the ship. It's been over a week, and we're still no closer to a solution."

Phaedra rubbed his neck. "It's only been made official, love. How many people do you think didn't know already?"

"Yeah, okay. But I still keep feeling the stares everywhere I go. It's my job to find whoever it is, and people are wondering why I haven't done it already."

"You're doing the best you can, aren't you?"

"Am I?" He shook his head. "I keep running into walls. Bill can't find anything helpful on CIRCLE; the cameras came up empty; everybody on Nine has an alibi; and on top of all that, the Zanshin problem is getting worse. We had three more people in Medical during the last week, with problems ranging from the shakes all the way to full paralysis."

Phaedra could sense how tight and upset he was. "What can I do to make it easier?"

He managed a small smile. "Nothing, dear heart. It's not your problem, it's mine—"

"Wrong. It's ours." She kissed him on top of his head.

He hesitated. "There is one thing . . . "

"Name it."

"That party tonight that you wanted me to go to with you? Well, I know I said I didn't want to, but I've changed my mind. Can we still make it?"

Phaedra grinned. "Sure." But her surge of pleased surprise only lasted a moment before a nagging voice in the back of her head asked: *Why?* She knew Pyramus hated such gatherings, that he considered them pretentious and snobbish. "This isn't like you."

He had the grace to look guilty. "Your artist friends always seem to be in the vanguard when it comes to new . . . things."

"I see," she said slowly. "You want to investigate my friends."

"I'm sorry, *pirini*, but I'm fresh out of ideas, and I left my Tarot deck in my other suit."

She turned away from him and stared at the painting of the ballet dancer on the far wall. The man was high in the air, his legs rippling with muscle from the force of his leap; his head thrown back and his arms extended upward, fingers spread. It was the most dynamic pose she had ever seen; she had often, in her dancing, tried to mimic it.

She wondered why the request made her so angry. After all, if her friends were innocent, what would be the harm? But it was not that, she knew. Somehow, the request made her feel used. That in itself wasn't new; everybody used her, in a sense, through the Dance. But this was different—this was Pyramus.

She heard his soft voice behind her. "Phaedra?"

The painting blurred, and she blinked away the tears. She had fought with this feeling throughout her life. All of her childhood memories, it seemed to her, were of the dance floor, of the disciplines of barre and mirror, of calisthenics and practice—and her mother's face watching her from the sidelines, gaze fixed and intent, as though she was willing her daughter through each session and performance. She was an excellent dancer, Phaedra knew—but she only knew it because everyone else told her. She never *felt* it, never truly believed it—because it had never really been her choice.

She felt his hands slide over her shoulders and squeeze gently. He loved her; that she did not doubt. Could she blame him for wanting to do his job?

She turned to face him. "It's all right," she said.

He hugged her, but she felt something missing from his embrace. The feedback which was a part of the Sender-Receiver joining, a nebulous line which spiraled back along the psychic flow, was gone. There was a block there, where there had never been one before. Was it her? Or him? Phaedra did not know; she only knew that, for the first time since she had known Pyramus, she felt alone.

The cube panel slid open to reveal a portly woman of fifty, her face aglow with either heat or some chemical. "Phaedra!" she said. "How good of you to come!" She waved them inside.

Pyramus looked around as they entered. At first glance the room seemed impossibly large; then he realized that the walls on either side had been taken down so that three cubes now shared a large area. The entire block of housing was filled with artists of various kinds, so he supposed this kind of communal living was fairly common. He stopped musing when he realized he was being introduced.

"Marla, this is Pyramus Gray," Phaedra said.

The woman fixed him with eyes as bright, burning, and close together as a binary star. "Ah, yes. Tell me, have you determined yet who the killer is?"

Pyramus managed a pleasant smile. "We're working on it."

"I see. Well, mingle, my dears. *Every*body is here—except for Sean, of course, he *never* comes. I would have counted it quite a coup if he had, but still, one can't have everything, I suppose. Maybe if we offered to have the next one in the Hub—"

The portal chimed, interrupting her. "No rest for the wicked! You know where the dispenser is, Phaedra, do go and enjoy!" She surged away from them.

"Marla Breen-Whitlow," Phaedra said, in response to Pyramus's raised eyebrow. "You've seen her work?"

"My mother has a small bronze of a dog and cat making love. Very erotic, if you're into animal miscegenation."

Phaedra gave him a tolerant look. "One of the things I love

about you is your artistic criteria. Or should I say 'autistic'?''

"Phaedra!" somebody shouted. Pyramus turned and saw a man waving a drink at them.

"Nicky!" Phaedra called back. "Nick Daley, my director," she said to Pyramus. "You remember him. I have to go talk shop for a few minutes."

"Go ahead. I'll get a drink and wander around."

She nodded and moved away, slipping through the crowd gracefully. Pyramus watched her go. Beneath her banter he thought he had sensed just a twinge of coolness. She had seemed closed off to him ever since he had suggested coming to the party. It was a new experience with Phaedra, and one not at all to his liking.

He sighed and made his way to the drink dispenser, where he filled a plastic glass with beer and sipped at it as he moved about, listening to snatches of various conversations.

"—all right, I suppose, but the bass line was totally out-of-synch, not to mention the color—"

"—seen Sean's latest? Superb, so controlled and yet so free! The man is a genius, no doubt—"

"—exciting, isn't it? Imagine a killer on the loose! Why, he could be in this very room—!"

"—back to my cube; I've got some choice Leaf, and you could look at my waveplates—"

Pyramus finished his beer sooner than he had intended. If he had forgotten why he shunned this kind of gathering, which he had not, this was guaranteed to refresh his memory. So many self-appointed experts, bragging, criticizing, expounding. *Bunista*, he thought sourly. Shit. He shrugged and kept moving. After all, he wasn't here for fun. Which was good, because he wasn't having any.

There were quite a few examples of art—or what passed for it—on display in the room. A large percentage of *Heaven Star*'s population were artists of fair to excellent talent, and a larger percentage thought they were. Pyramus found some of the efforts worth stopping and admiring; others made him wince.

He was standing at the edge of a mind mandala's synesthesic aura, enjoying the faint sensory distortion, when he heard what he had been waiting for.

"—in the 'fresher ten minutes from now. I only have two caps left and you'll have to go fifty for them—"

The Security Chief kept walking. He did not need to hear more, nor did he need to see the man offering the deal. Maybe he wouldn't find the killer wearing a flashing placard at this party, but he was willing to bet his next month's stads that he had just passed someone making a deal for some very expensive pharmaceutical. At that price, it had to be Zanshin.

The problem was that there were three 'freshers in the expanded living space. He could not cover them all at once, and if he picked the wrong one he might miss the transaction. He had to guess. He decided on the one closest to where he had heard the conversation. He leaned against the wall behind a cybercrystal sculpture and watched.

The 'fresher was doing a good business. He glanced across the room, where he saw Phaedra in the center of a crowd of fans. He felt again the worry about her aloofness. He would try to talk to her after the party, attempt to reestablish the closeness and the bonding—

He heard the 'fresher's door slide shut, and snapped his gaze back at it. Had someone gone inside? He swore softly; he had not been paying attention. As he was wondering what to do a man approached the narrow panel. He was tall, with the thick arms and wide shoulders of a bodybuilder. His hair was light brown with streaks of blond. He looked around surreptitiously as he tapped on the door. "It's me," he said softly. The door slid aside and the big man stepped inside. Two to a 'fresher was carrying togetherness a bit far, Pyramus decided.

He approached and carefully tried the latch under the "occupied" light. It was locked, of course. He put his ear to the door and listened, heard a low mumble of voices. He felt his pulse speed up and his stomach grow tight. He was in a private house, and could not legally open the door without a warrant. But he also could not let this chance pass.

"Nano," he subvocalized. "Security Prime Priority."

The computer answered at once. "Yes, Pyramus?"

The Security Chief quickly explained his situation. "I need a lock override."

"I find four cases of shipboard precedent," *Nano* told him. "Your action is logged. Good luck, nephew."

Pyramus saw the "occupied" light go out. He swallowed, hoping that the Council would agree with the computer when they got its report. Then he slid the door open and stepped inside, letting it close behind him.

It was a fairly large 'fresher; nevertheless, there was not a lot of room. The person standing next to Muscles was a short, dark-haired woman; she stared at Pyramus in astonishment. Pyramus saw recognition on Muscles' face; the big man lunged for the recycler vent, and Pyramus knew he was going to dump the drug capsules he was no doubt holding. The Security Chief realized how ill-prepared he was for this encounter: he had no oscillator with which to stun his opponent, and Muscles could probably tie him into knots if he wanted to resist, assuming there was any reason to once the capsules were gone.

He did the only thing he could think of to do; a stunt he had once seen in an old flat gangster movie in the archives. "Freeze!" he yelled, sticking one hand into the pocket of his coverall and thrusting it out as if it held a weapon. The big man saw the action and stopped moving. "Don't hurt me!"

"Put the capsules on the counter, very carefully," Pyramus said. Muscles did so.

"Lace your fingers together on top of your head." Muscles complied. Pyramus allowed himself to breathe slightly easier, and called Bill Plait. It was only after the deputy had acknowledged that he recognized the woman: Councilwoman Sharon Sevaer, currently candidate for the Chair against Louis Demond.

Pyramus took the two capsules of Zanshin—he recognized the green and blue capsules—and left Muscles locked in the 'fresher.

"This isn't what it seems, Chief Gray," Councilwoman Sevaer said to him.

Pyramus raised an eyebrow. "It isn't?"

If she were nervous, she was now hiding it well. "That's right. You just interrupted my investigation into the sources of Zanshin."

"Oh, really?" Pyramus suppressed a grin. She was quick, he had to give her that.

"Yes, really. You can check with my campaign manager, Elena Vasquez—do you know her?"

Pyramus nodded. Elena Vasquez had been one of his teachers when he was a boy.

"We set this up in advance. Call her and check."

Pyramus considered it. Was Sharon Sevaer clever enough to have arranged in advance a cover for buying drugs? Or was it possible she was telling the truth?

Someone stepped up to use the 'fresher, but Pyramus waved him off. "Occupied, and two of us are waiting. Better find another one." He looked back at Sevaer. "Okay," he said. "Why?"

"Why, Chief? Excuse me for being blunt, but Security has had the drug problem for several months now, hasn't it? And, to my knowledge, nothing has been done."

Pyramus felt suddenly defensive. "We are aware of the problem, Councilwoman, as you might have noticed."

"And this is the first drugseller you've caught, correct?"

"As it happens, yes."

"And if I hadn't gotten him into the 'fresher, it's unlikely you would have caught this one."

Pyramus started to argue, but stopped. A cold feeling rolled over him, as sometimes happened when his bursts of intuition struck. Suddenly he knew: *She was lying. She was a user.*

"Are you all right, Chief Gray?"

Pyramus nodded. "Sorry—just got a call. Excuse me." He pretended to be listening to a nonexistent speaker while he thought about the situation. He had no proof, of course. Councilwoman Sevaer had only been talking to the man in the 'fresher; an unusual place to hold a conversation, but not illegal. He had seen no exchange of money or drugs. She could have easily invented some story to cover herself to Elena Vasquez. And Sevaer was powerful, politically. If he arrested her without platinum-bound proof, he could get into deep trouble.

He was after the producers, he told himself, not the users. Sevaer may have taken Zanshin, but that was no crime in itself; only possession was. He could go for a Conspiracy to Obtain charge, but that was weak. He had Muscles, who was possibly a line to the other end. It rankled, but he knew that the smartest thing to do in the situation would be to go along with Sevaer's story and let her go. He might be able to learn something from her later, somehow.

"Gray?"

"Sorry. My office. Ah—look, Councilwoman, it's obvious

I've made a mistake here; my apologies. I'll take the seller into custody and see what can be learned from him. And I would prefer it if you would leave such matters to Security in the future."

Her smile was full of triumph, and, Pyramus thought, relief as well. "Fine. I'll stay out of your business from now on. May I leave now?"

"Certainly. You were never detained; in fact, I don't recall seeing you here at all."

"Thank you, Chief Gray. I will remember that."

As she left, Pyramus saw Phaedra working her way toward him. He felt his stomach clench in the same apprehension as when he had opened the door. It was suddenly very important that Phaedra not know what had happened just now.

"Waiting for the 'fresher?" she asked as she stopped in front of him.

He nodded; then, in an attempt to lead the conversation, asked, "Who is this Sean I keep hearing about? The whole party seems to miss him."

Phaedra laughed. "You really do need to keep up with culture more, love. Sean Mkono, the dynamic fluid sculptor."

"Mkono? The Hub Supervisor? He dabbles in art?"

"My Gypsy darling, he is one of the best, if not *the* best. Don't you remember the colorstorm holo we saw?"

"Mkono did that?" Pyramus shook his head. "Buddha, he's good. Why isn't he here?"

"He never comes to parties; in fact, he never comes downlevels at all except for medical rotation. He doesn't like it down here, I gather."

Before she could say anything else, a group of four women surrounded them. One of them said, "Phaedra, you must come and meet my sister Lisa! She's a great fan of yours and she has a daughter who wants to be a Dancer!"

Phaedra gave Pyramus a look that said, 'Duty calls.' Aloud she said, "I'll see you in a while, *gaver*," and allowed herself to be led away. As she was leaving, Pyramus saw Bill Plait come in one of the doors. *Close, Gray,* he told himself. *Very close.*

After Plait had left with Muscles in custody, taking him out a back way so that the party would be unaware that an arrest had been made, Pyramus continued to wander about the party, waiting for Phaedra to finish signing autographs. He felt drained to the point of exhaustion. Too much had been going on for the past several weeks, and it did not look like things would be slowing down anytime soon. The worst was this terrible feeling of incompetence. He was in over his head, he knew; he had no idea how to deal with murderers and drug-dealers and all the other problems policemen back on Earth took as a matter of course.

On the opposite end of the triple-cube room he saw a booth with several people standing around it. Pyramus watched as a woman emerged alone from the booth, smiling. Then a man entered and came out after a minute or so, also smiling.

"It's a holobooth," somebody said from his left. Pyramus turned and saw Daley, Phaedra's director. "You ought to try it. It's awe-inspiring."

Pyramus shrugged. Why not? It had to be better than listening to all the artists telling each other how wonderful they were. He walked over to the booth, waited for his turn, and stepped inside.

The tiny interior was of gray plastic, dimly lit. Pyramus exhaled, feeling some of the tension lessen in the reassuring confinement. He could deal with this environment; he felt secure and protected.

There was a button mounted in the center of the wall facing him. He felt reluctant to push it; the booth itself was the most comforting piece of art he had encountered thus far. Still; he might as well see the show. Pyramus pressed the button—

—*and found himself hanging, alone, unprotected, in space, surrounded by distant stars, diamond-hard and unforgiving. The ultimate loneliness, the ultimate fear . . .*

He screamed, terror seizing him like a werewolf from his grandfather's old stories. One infinite instant of sheer panic, colder than the Deep about him—and then someone grabbed his arm and pulled him back into reality.

He was back in the cube again, surrounded by people staring at him in curiosity and embarrassment. Phaedra's hands were gripping his arm. She drew him into an embrace.

"Pyramus! Are you all right? I didn't see you come this way, or I would have warned you—"

"Jesus, Chief, I'm sorry. I didn't know . . . " that was Daley speaking. Pyramus managed a smile. "No problem," he said. "Just—took me by surprise, that's all."

Phaedra led him away from the holobooth. "Come on," she said. "I think we've had enough party for tonight."

He saw the concern and love in her face, and felt ashamed about the lie of omission at the 'fresher, for intruding into her world as a Security man. "Thank you," he managed to say. "You probably saved my life." She smiled at him, and he felt her love, her caring, touching him once again. Whatever had been blocking it was gone now; Sender and Receiver were joined once more. He resolved to never let go of that again, no matter what it took to keep it.

"Bern?"

"In transit, one minute to stoproll," Michan said. He felt the ridge of a seam pass under his skates.

"Copy, Michan." That was Dooley, on Third Watch. He had been an Outsider until seniority had kicked him up to inside duty. Michan respected Dooley; the man had spent twenty years hull-skating, and he knew what he was doing. Not like Steen.

"Hey, Michan-*san*, try not to run over me when you get here, okay?"

Michan grinned. Greg Shonin was already at the base of Spoke Six, inspecting the seal. "Not me, Showboat. I still have full brakes; *I* didn't burn a lining."

"Jesus, you never let a guy forget anything, do you? That was three years ago!"

"Once a braker, always a braker." Michan could see the reflection of Greg's suit against the darker silver-gray of the spoke, just ahead.

"Yeah, well, *I* remember a guy once ran into a spoke and damned near killed himself rather than use his brakes."

Michan laughed. "Better buried than burned."

"That's not what you said then."

"Like you said, it was some years ago—"

"You two space cadets bottle the chatter on this channel," Dooley cut in. "You want to play moldy-oldies, go to sixty-one—I'm trying to get some sleep in here."

"Copy, old man," Michan said. "Wouldn't want you to exhaust yourself turning those heavy pots down." He received a burst of something that might either have been static or a raspberry in reply, chuckled and switched his com to the suggested channel. He was getting close to the spoke and his hull speed was dropping fast. He saw Greg look up.

"Brakes, Bern, use your brakes."

"Brakes? What are they?" Michan rolled to a stop two meters shy of the other Outsider. He saw Greg's green-and-red grin through his faceplate.

"Not bad," Shonin said. "You planning to take Isuzu on in the games this year?"

"I might. I hear she missed a stoproll by almost half a meter the other day."

"I doubt it. Here, stop dreaming of glory and give me a hand with this seal inspection."

Michan touched a control and moved closer. Three times a month each main seal on each spoke had to be inspected. A leak could cost valuable air, and although the seals were monitored, a backup hands-on inspection was considered necessary. It was a boring job, but one every Outsider had to do often enough to learn it well. There was a by-the-numbers procedure used to inspect them, which included a view of the inner surface and back-up seals. A series of small hatches afforded enough room for a single man in an exosuit to peer into the space between the main and back-up. After their inspection of the outer surfaces, Michan and Greg began to circle around the vast spoke, checking the hatches.

The procedure took some time. Michan finished first. He paused for a moment, looking out into Deep, admiring the pure still colors of the stars and the infinite night between them. The cables of the stabilimentia web, a huge, complicated cat's cradle, stretched between the spokes, almost invisible against the darkness. His suit was all that stood between him and the most hostile environment of all, and yet he felt warm, secure, protected. If he listened carefully, it almost seemed he could hear, over the sound of his breathing and the subdued clicks and beeps of the monitors in his helmet, the music of the spheres, the subtle blackbody radiation that was the echoing remnant of the primordial explosion.

"Michan? How's it coming?"

Michan blinked, and focused his eyes once again on the instrument readings below his faceplate. "Fine, Greg. Everything looks good. How's by you?"

"Two left. Then I'm going to get a hot shower, call up Melissa and—"

The line abruptly went dead; Michan could no longer hear the faint carrier hum. "Greg?"

There was no answer. "Greg!"

Michan switched back to the mainline channel. "Listen, Dooley, I just lost Greg on com. I'm going around the spoke for a visual. It might be trouble; try an all-channel scan." It was more an order than a request. Dooley might be in charge inside, but when things got wonky Outside the senior man on Hull called the shots.

"Copy, Michan. Go."

Michan blew his jets and took off around the curve of the spoke, leaning to bank against the tug of the ship's spin. Shonin ought to be at the lock . . . there he was! He was down!

This was not time for games; Michan kept thrust up until the last second, then leaned backward and flexed his toes hard against the brakes. The drag almost overbalanced him, but the gyros held and he maintained his stance. He came to a stop a meter past the downed man.

The hatch cover for the seal inspection was . . . gone. Without it only the inner seal protected the integrity of the ship at the number Six Spoke, a dangerous situation. "Dooley, we've lost a hatch cover. Get somebody out here with a spare, pronto."

"Copy, Bern. What about Greg?"

"Stand by." Michan leaned over as far as he could and peered into Shonin's helmet. "Greg?"

He could see Shonin's face through the heavy plastic plate; his lips were moving. Michan saw a dent in the helmet where the com and aerial rode, and realized what had happened. He put his headpiece next to Shonin's, making a muffled conduction possible.

"—nearly killed me! Did you see it?"

"See what? What happened?"

"Give me a hand up."

Michan helped the other man stand. They kept their helmets together. "What happened?" Michan asked again.

"I leaned over the hatch and the fucking thing blew!"

"*What?!*"

"The charges blew—damn thing took off like a bat out of hell, and nearly took my head with it!"

Michan was astounded. There was an emergency blow control mounted alongside each of the inspection hatches, but it was impossible to trip accidentally. You had to lift a cover and stab the button fairly hard. No Outsider had ever blown a hatch accidentally before. But what a strange malfunction, for a hatch to pop just as somebody reached it. If Greg had been a few centimeters to the left it very probably would have smashed his faceplate. He would have died in a few seconds, blood crystallizing in the vacuum along with his air.

"Bern, what's going on out there?" It was Dooley. The man sounded more than a little worried. Michan switched his com on. "Bern here. Shonin is all right; just got his hat knocked a little crooked."

"Copy, Michan. Better get him inside." There was a short pause. "I'll have to call Steen on this one."

Michan nodded, then realized Dooley could not see that. "Yeah, I guess."

Greg was pale under the diodes's lights. Steen would blame him, they both knew that. He touched his helmet to Michan's again. "I didn't touch it, Michan, I swear."

"I know, Greg. I believe you."

But he knew that Steen would not.

NINE

The man in the diagnoster had only been in Kyle's exam room for ten minutes, and already Kyle was sick of him. The doctor touched a pressure tab on the hand screen he carried and looked at the workup. The patient's name was Thomas Steen, and he was the supervisor on Level One. Kyle snorted. A non-entity with delusions of grandeur and the gall to order *him* to hurry *his* physical. Kyle was tempted to order the man's system flushed with fluorocarbon emulsions, just on general principles. But he did not have the time; he had a dozen more PEs to do before 1200 and his nurse had just told him that Security was bringing in an emergency drug overdose. It was going to be a busy morning.

Kyle did not mind; in fact, he liked it busy. Keeping the patients juggled was a challenge; it stretched him, as so few things did. It was hard being brighter, quicker, and better than other people. One had to invent one's challenges.

He was not worried about the incident on Nine. He could not be tied to that, he knew—that incompetent Montoya had been working with Gray, and he said the Security Chief did not have a clue. Kyle grinned. Of course not.

"Doctor Kyle? The overdose is here."

Kyle looked at the board. The diagnoster would be done in a few seconds and would automatically open then. Let Steen stew for a while.

The overdose case was sprawled on the exam table, talking quickly and quietly to himself. Kyle prided himself on his ability to do *augenblick*, or spot diagnoses; it was a talent partly due to his years of work and partly, he was sure, to a marginal psi wave in his neurograph that indicated heightened sensitivity to probability patterns. He took the patient in at a glance: perhaps twenty years old, pale, sweating and trembling. The shaking was so pronounced that the man almost seemed in danger of vibrating off the table. Chemical neuropathy, without a doubt. "Draw two tubes for a drugscan."

"Already done, doctor." The nurse had hardly spoken when the intercom cheeped. "Lab here. Looks like Zanshin, all right."

"Thanks, Jerry." Kyle looked more closely at the patient. "You check his chart?" he asked the nurse.

"No physical problems and no known allergies."

Kyle took the man's left hand and moved it a few centimeters. The arm jerked twice. "Cogwheel rigidity. Better shoot him down—he's in Class Three reaction. Give him Altospas, ten milligrams, IV; better add two hundred milligrams of SNEP, too. IM."

Toshi, the nurse, looked a little surprised, and Kyle suppressed a smile. She had the hypo of Altospas, but he had been ahead of her on the SNEP. Good; he did not want her to get too confident in her ability to read his therapy in advance.

With the first injection the man's shaking began to slow; by the time Toshi had returned with the second syringe he was almost still. The muscle relaxant would keep the body quiet, and the SNEP would calm his mind. Kyle could see admiration in Toshi's glance at him—*you know your work*, it seemed to say. Of course, he thought. Particularly concerning Zanshin, his creation.

"Hey, what the hell is going on around here?"

Kyle turned and saw Steen standing in the doorway, looking ridiculous in his paper robe.

"An emergency, supervisor."

"It's taking you long enough to handle it. Are you through

with me? I have a floor to take care of, you know."

"In a moment," Kyle said. He punched in the admission code on the drug case, feeling irritated at the Zanshin user; treating people too stupid to have themselves checked for any potential allergy to a drug's components was cutting into his time. Still, it was amusing to think of the cult that had grown up around the drug. There were even those who claimed it joined minds, created a mental *gestalt* that could transcend reality. Rubbish, he thought. At least, *he* had never noticed such potential in it—

"Doctor, if you *don't* mind—?"

Kyle shook his head and glared at the man who had disturbed his reverie. Just who the hell did Steen think he was? He might throw his asthmatic weight around on Level One, but not here. "Go, supervisor," he said coldly. "We'll send a copy of your test results to your section bank."

Steen bristled at the antagonistic tone. "Now see here," he began, but Kyle cut him off.

"I said *go*," the doctor repeated, using the force of his personality like a lash, enjoying the exercise of power and the cringing response it immediately produced in the other man. Steen quickly backed into the exam room to dress.

As soon as he was out of sight Kyle spun and entered his office. He sat for a time, clenching and unclenching his fists, waiting for the cold calmness that always followed what was, for him, an uncharacteristic outburst of rage. He breathed deeply and regularly, but his pulse still raced and his skin still felt flushed after several minutes.

He realized the cause of it after a moment. It was not rage any more. It was fear.

Face it, he ordered himself. He thought of the small scraps of evidence he had been accumulating over the past few weeks from various sections, evidence of *something* happening, changing, on *Heaven Star.* Even without them, he knew, he would suspect—he could *feel* the strangeness, the infinitely subtle *wrongness* pervading everything. And was this also part of it—was his control, which had protected him for so long, also beginning to crumble?

He had moved undetected among them all for his entire adult life. One of the reasons he had gone into medicine was to gain access to equipment and drugs that would keep him safe.

It had worked; he had been able to keep ahead of them, had learned how to alter the cephaloscans and other tests designed to tie him to the *status quo*. He had excelled, become a trusted, vital part of *Heaven Star*. And now it could all come tumbling down. He might set himself apart from others, but no such Cartisan policy could protect him from the breakdown of fundamentals.

Kyle looked at his hands, saw that they were trembling. He had not felt so helpless, so out of control, since that moment on Nine. But no one knew; the only witness was dead. He remembered the cause of his frustration and anger: his defeat by Leo Chin. He would settle that soon, very soon. At least no one else knew about that—

Kyle blinked suddenly. Someone *did* know. He had seen someone else in the dojo just before Chin had tricked him into falling. A woman—he could see her in his mind's eye now, with that lucidity that sudden memories often have. A young Oriental woman, a green sash. She had seen him fall. *She had seen him fall. . . .*

"Computer," Kyle said softly. He had never succumbed to anthropomorphosizing the GARTH-7, as so many on board did. The machine responded in a soft, measured voice. "Yes, Doctor Kyle."

"I want the workups on all members in the Chan Gen class I attend."

"Of course, Doctor. Here they are."

The flatscreen built into his desk lit up with an image and list of statistics. "Next," Kyle said impatiently. The GARTH-7 obliged. "Next. Next . . ."

There she was. Hanawashi, Susan Yachiyo; age—34 years; Occupation—Section Eight Supervisor; marital status—separated; children—Katsu Hanawashi; address—

Kyle nodded in satisfaction, dropped a recording sphere into the slot, and pressed a button. Then he leaned back, steepling his fingers, feeling the welcome, cool calmness settling over him once more, like a cloak. One had to invent one's challenges.

"Hobson?"

"Sir?"

"I seem to have found a discrepancy in the log procedure."

"I will check it immediately, sir." There was a short pause, and then Hobson said, "You are correct, sir. There was a malfunction in the primary insertion. It has been corrected."

The row of numbers on the screen blinked and changed. Geoffrey nodded. "That's better. Any idea as to its cause?"

"None, sir. I've put a man on it."

Geoffrey smiled at the butlerish euphemism for instigating a search-and-repair program. "Good."

"By the way, sir—Louis Demond called. He asks if you will take lunch with him this afternoon."

"Ah. How interesting. Thank you, Hobson."

"Will there be anything else, sir?"

"No, I don't believe so. Take the rest of the day off."

"Thank you, sir."

The Archivist leaned back in his chair thoughtfully, looking at the rack of recording spheres near the door. Hobson had told him, less than an hour after his initial request weeks earlier, that there were no recording spheres missing from his files. Whatever the deleted portion of the holo from the start of the voyage had showed, it had not been that Louis Demond had stolen anything. Geoffrey cleared his throat and asked to be connected with the Administrator's office.

"Hello, Geoffrey. I was hoping you would call back today. Let me buy you lunch; I have some matters to discuss with you."

Geoffrey glanced at the clock. It was nearly noon; he could stand a spot of lunch. "Have you someplace in mind?"

"I thought perhaps Cham's, near Spoke Six."

"Sounds fine to me; Cham's it is." The Archivist broke the connection and stood slowly. His back ached. Too much sitting, he thought; I need to exercise more. But then, I have always needed to exercise more. After all, eighty-odd years deserves a few pains in payment. I'll walk briskly to Cham's instead of taking the train, perhaps that will serve. . . .

Cham's was a teardrop-shaped structure that hung from a thick tube attached to the "ceiling" of Level One, its foam metal construction making the stress factors involved acceptable. It was small, only twelve tables, and Geoffrey found a waiting line when he stepped from the tube lift. One of the privileges of rank, however, was Louis Demond's reserved table near a window. Louis was a big tipper and the staff was always glad to see him.

The Administrator had not arrived yet. A young, red-haired waitress was standing next to Geoffrey before he settled fully in his seat. "Good day, Archivist. Something to drink?"

"A glass of berry wine, I think."

The woman left and returned with a plastic glass on a thin stem, filled with the dark, sweet wine. "Anything else?"

"This will do for now, thank you. Louis will be here shortly; he'll be having champagne, I expect."

Halfway through Geoffrey's glass, Louis arrived. Before he could sit the waitress was back, pouring him a plastic flair of pale amber champagne, in which tiny bubbles rose leisurely. "Ah, Janice, thank you," Demond said. "Leave the bottle. We're ready for lunch now, I think."

There was no menu at Cham's, for there was only one main dish for each meal; it changed daily, varied widely, and so was always a minor adventure. One day the meal would be rabbit in lemon sauce; the next day, stuffed grape leaves; the next, cloned steak and lobster. For Geoffrey, much of the joy of eating at Cham's lay in not knowing what was coming, and he never looked at the other patrons' plates so that he might further delay the surprise.

"How fare the halls of knowledge?" Demond swirled his champagne.

Geoffrey shrugged. "As usual. I discovered an error in the files today, but it was corrected easily enough."

"There seem to have been a number of small errors in both the mainline and in small computers lately. Perhaps the years have made them senile."

Geoffrey brought the blackberry wine to his lips, but did not swallow. He felt his heart working a little faster. Merely a coincidence, he told himself. Demond could not know. "And you?" he said, pleased that his voice was even. "How is the campaign doing?"

"Not as well as I would like. I have a nice lead, according to my polls, but Sevaer is gaining strength. Some of the more radical elements are flocking to her. This CIRCLE group, for instance."

Geoffrey said nothing. He sipped at his wine.

"Frankly, old friend, I am a bit worried," Demond continued. "This murder has hurt me, as has the drug situation. Our intrepid Security Chief is busy paving the road to hell with his good intentions, but not accomplishing much else."

"I thought a major drugseller was arrested recently."

"Hardly. A small cog was collected at a party. The man had two capsules of Zanshin, no more, and he was unable to shed any light on his supplier."

"Unable? Or merely unwilling?"

"We put him under vapor and cephaloscan." Demond poured more champagne. "Outside of a few unusual wave peaks, which did not pertain to our situation, there was nothing interesting. He picked up his supply from a public 'fresher and left the stads in the same place. He never saw the supplier."

"How was he able to find out about the hiding place, then? He must have had someone to contact—"

"That we don't know. He simply said he was contacted; he seemed unsure as to the method. Not even psyche vapor can extract knowledge that isn't there. Whoever is behind this Zanshin thing is very clever, Geoffrey. It's making me look bad."

"I think it hardly likely that Sharon Sevaer would do better were she elected."

Demond looked out the window at the graceful, sculptured buildings and greenery. "Thank you, old friend. Unfortunately, not many of the voters share your confidence. I've been in office a long time. I've made a lot of enemies, people who don't really care if the ship runs properly. I could lose this election, Geoffrey." The Administrator's rich, smooth voice —an orator's voice, Geoffrey thought—now had the faintest undertone of worry in it. "That mustn't happen. *Heaven Star* needs me—"

Their meals arrived. "Salmon, poached in orange sauce," the waitress said, smiling proudly. "Your standards refunded personally by the cook if it isn't the best you've ever had." This last was a standing offer at Cham's; so far as Geoffrey knew, no one with any taste at all had ever taken the chef up on it.

The salmon was a dark pink, flaky, and cooked just long enough to be done, but not dry. The sauce was superb. There was a small serving dish of baked beans on the side, slightly tart and sweet, and every bit as delicious as the fish. The two men turned their attention to the meal, not speaking save to compliment the food.

When the plates had been cleared and they were drinking Kava, Geoffrey returned to the subject they had left.

"The election has you quite worried this time, doesn't it?"

Demond nodded. "Sevaer is not the right person for the job. I am. It's as simple as that. If she is elected, the ship will suffer. Oh, I'm sure she means well, and she is bright, I'll give her that. But she doesn't look ahead. She'll spend two years fumbling around before she learns anything, and the last year worrying about re-election."

"I wish I could help."

Demond was silent for some time, staring into the dark depths of his cup. Then he sighed. "You can. Sevaer must have some skeletons in her closet, something which the voters would view askance. If I knew what they were . . . "

Geoffrey shook his head. "We've discussed this. I can't let you see her personal records, Louis."

"Old friend, I have *already* seen her personal records. You aren't the only one with such access."

Geoffrey felt shocked. He took another sip of wine to cover his embarrassment.

"It doesn't matter," Demond continued. "There's nothing there I can use. What I need is something that wouldn't be likely to show up officially, something only someone close to her would be apt to know."

"If you're asking me for help in that department," Geoffrey said stiffly, "I'm afraid I hardly know the lady."

"Elena knows her." Demond leaned back in his chair, watching Geoffrey carefully.

The Archivist felt a sense of outrage. This was unethical, it was—caddish! "See here, Louis, I—"

"Easy, Geoffrey," Demond said softly. "You know raising your blood pressure is bad for your POBS."

Geoffrey Merle-Douglass felt as if he had been cast into a pool of liquid nitrogen. *Demond knew!* It wasn't possible! He had hidden it from everybody, had even falsified records in order to be assigned to *Heaven Star*. He had never told a soul, except—

Except himself.

"You *did* take one of my diary spheres, twenty-five years ago!"

Demond looked mildly surprised. "Yes. I put it back a few days later. How did you know? Never mind; it's not important. What *is* important is that I've known for a quarter of a century and I've never said anything to anyone about it."

"Until now." Geoffrey sagged in his chair. He felt as if he had been attacked physically by this man across from him, this man whom he had thought was his friend. Demond knew about his disease. POBS—Progressive Organic Brain Syndrome. It had been diagnosed on Earth when Geoffrey had been fifty. Central nervous system diseases did not respond well to treatment when the cause arose from the tissue itself. But the neurologists had agreed on one way to keep the degeneration at bay: stay busy. Never slacken the usage of the higher centers. Keep mentally active, exercise the brain, or succumb to *Senile dementia*, feel the intellect wither away. So far it had worked. For thirty years he had been able to keep the disease from progressing by a rigorous discipline of study, by never allowing his brain to stop learning.

"My condition does not affect my work," he said. His voice sounded faint through the roaring of blood in his ears.

"True. In fact, I suspect that you are better at your job as a result of your misfortune. But I doubt if others would see it that way. If Medical knew, for example . . . ?"

"They would recommend relieving me of my duties," Geoffrey said. The words tasted like ashes. "They would be afraid I might accidentally damage valuable records."

"I am afraid they would."

"Louis, if I didn't have my work, my mind would—would . . . "

Demond leaned forward. "But you *do* have your job," he said softly. "And there is no reason why you shouldn't keep your position for another fifteen or twenty years."

Geoffrey looked up from his Kava and across the small table at Demond. The meaning was plain enough: *You have your job, by my leave. I need a favor, you need a favor; surely something can be worked out.*

He shuddered. It was quite a choice Demond had presented him with: his mind or his honor. If he refused to help the Administrator, he could spend his last years penned up like a baby, drooling away all he had learned. Oh, perhaps he could sit in front of his own screen in his cube, trying to ladle material in, striving to feed his dying brain, but he knew it would not be enough. He needed the prod of real work, he needed to feel that he was a helpful, vital part of the ship's complex network, or he would lose the war he had fought for so long.

And what did he have to do to prevent this? Merely ask Elena some questions. She would not be hurt directly. Nor would the best interests of the ship. Demond was good at his job, there was no question about that. Sharon Sevaer was simply not as qualified. She needed to grow, to learn more—she could wait three years or six years or twenty years to take over the Chair. Assuming whatever skeletons Geoffrey might uncover would allow her to remain in the public eye.

"Geoffrey?"

The Archivist looked across the table at the man who held his life. There was no choice to make, he knew; it had already been made, and not by him. "I—I'll talk to Elena." He felt his face blush. He could not meet Demond's gaze.

"I knew I could count on you, Geoffrey. Old friend."

Geoffrey looked up then, anger in his eyes, but Demond's smile never faltered. Politicians learned to smile early, and their smiles were very durable, considering they had less substance than air—even less, it seemed, than the substance of this friendship truly was after so many years.

TEN

The storm raged; wisps of scarlet blew through clouds of emerald; a damp violet boiled up and mixed with faint traces of yellow, becoming a fluid bruise upon the mixture. The colors flowed, roiled, contracted and expanded in slow, unnatural flexion. An oblate spheroid, through which various colors rippled, formed in the center, then burst in slow motion, scattering droplets, each a different shade.

"No good," Sean Mkono said in disgust. He touched the control panel, keeping the movement slow so as not to hurl himself backward. The storm of mixing hues began to flow toward the bottom of the electronically shielded clear plastic box. A whirlpool formed and the colored gases swirled widdershins down the suction drain, blending into deep gray at the center before vanishing. In a moment the box was empty. Sean pushed off toward it. He marked on the nearly invisible plastic with a wax pen, made a few mental calculations, then floated back to the control panel. The microcomp controlled the colored gases and low surface tension liquids, spraying them into the electromagnetically wrapped box while subtle charges shaped them into various forms. It was an art form possible only in the null of gravity of the Hub.

Sean typed in another sequence; in the plastic cage a brooding purple began to form, sprayed by microscopic jets of compressed air. He set the purple cloud swirling upward in a twisting column, like a slow-motion tornado, then erected a gray barrier across its top. The purple flowed against it, flattening into a plane before curling downward like the cap of a mushroom. Sean nodded slowly. Good. His fingers quickly fed more codes into the keyboard. A shower of bright white dots, each a perfect sphere the size of a marble, began to "rain" downward, pushed by air instead of pulled by gravity. And at the base of the swirling storm he created an undulating flow of dark blue, like a sea under a driving rain. Yes. It was much better than the other. He tapped the STORE key to save the sequence. He would not use the memorized version for the actual display; that was only to give him a basis. The file would merely be a springboard for some new variation. He never repeated himself.

"It's beautiful, Sean," someone behind him said. He turned, startled. It was Kristin.

"Just an idea," he said, tapping the control which cleared the cage. Inside the trunk-sized box the miniature storm began to break up.

" 'Just an idea.' There are probably five hundred people who'd pay a month's stads to be able to run a keeper holo of that 'idea'. Your show's gonna knock 'em dead tomorrow."

Sean shrugged. He had reluctantly agreed to the importunings of the art committee that he do a broadcast of his work—more to get them off his back than anything else. He floated over to pack up the cage. The plastic box was really unnecessary—he could keep the fluids controlled without it. But he continued to use it for a frame, as well as for safety's sake; the gases and liquids were expensive. If he were to make a mistake or have a powerdown the walls of his studio might end up wearing paint more valuable than they were.

He folded the box into a single, thick sheet with the top flapped over. They floated out of the studio and down the hall —or the shaft, depending on one's point of view—past other rooms, most of them lab setups from various departments. Space in the Hub was limited, and so was usually rented on a rotating basis, save for the industrial chambers where the various alloys and crystals were produced. "So," Sean said, "what's happening while I waste my off-shift time?"

"The torus exploded, the heloid burned out, the Spindle melted and the reactors froze over."

Sean looked at Kristin, his eyebrows coming down into the beginnings of a frown. She laughed. "Nothing worth mentioning. Jansen and Menville finished that gallium-bismide test, and Chang says the new downverter seems to be holding up okay. Oh, yeah—you'll love this—St. Martin, the marine biologist, rented space for some free-fall experiments with fish. Had a roomful of salmon, trout, and so on swimming around in a high-humidity setup—did you know fish can live out of water in free-fall? Their gills don't collapse. Anyway, there was some sort of lock malfunction."

"Oh, *no*."

"You guessed it. Both doors popped, and Section Three was full of floating fish. Ever try catching fish in free-fall? Little bastards are *fast*.

"Oh, and you got invitations to three more parties—I declined them gracefully."

"Thanks."

"And there was one other invitation, to dinner. I accepted that one for you."

"What?"

"It's from me, boss. I'm taking you out tonight."

"Oh."

"Your enthusiasm overwhelms me."

"No, I mean, that's fine, Kristin. I'm just a little—you know—"

She nodded. "I know." In three days he would have to put on his legs again. "But tonight, we make merry. I've rented one of the Eros Rooms, complete with hardcore holos. You'll love it."

He smiled. "I don't have any choice in this, do I?"

She took his arm. "Stop bitching and come on. I can't do much with legs, but I guarantee I can make some things grow."

Michan handled the arofloj absently, flexing and loosening his fingers. It had been a while since he had been here in the woods. At that time his music had taken him into a state of being he had heard about but had never experienced. The memory of it had stayed with him for sometime, but eventually it had begun to fade. Now it was only a small rush; pleasant, but less than a shadow of the reality.

He had planned to return sooner, but there had been problems. The blown seal hatch had sent Steen on a rampage; Michan had drawn double-shifts three times in the last two weeks. He was, it seemed, always exhausted and depressed, sometimes even while Outside. He had hoped that returning to the woods might help, but he had been playing for half an hour and there had been no feeling of exaltation, no satori, for him this time. It had been a mistake to expect it.

"You didn't come back," a small voice said.

Michan blinked, looked up and saw the boy. After a moment the name came back to him: Katsu.

"I'm sorry. I couldn't. I had to work."

"I waited for you a long time."

Michan felt guilty; how many times had he waited for adults when he had been a child, only to be disappointed? "I *am* sorry. But I'll make it up to you. Would you like to play?" He held the arofloj out toward Katsu.

The boy nodded, but said, "You first."

"All right. Anything special?" He smiled, not expecting an answer.

"Do you know 'Diana, the Goddess of the Moon,' from the *Rouge Ballet* by Oshiro?"

Michan was too astonished to answer for a moment. That was a complicated piece, intricately woven, and hardly something a child would appreciate. It was one of the tests of a good aroflojist, full of treble runs and cross-fingering. He could barely get through it on a good day. "Ah, I might manage that one. How did you know about it?"

"It's my mother's favorite."

For some reason, the concept of the boy having parents surprised him. "Your mother has good taste in music."

"Yes," Katsu said solemnly. Then he settled down tailor-fashion, his back to a slender tree, and looked at Michan expectantly. Michan shrugged slightly—*Here we go*—and, after a few notes to establish the key, began the piece.

This time the music began to captivate him again. It was not like before, but it was good. The piece was difficult enough to require his full concentration; halfway through the opening movement he had forgotten Katsu, forgotten Steen, forgotten everything except the swift, stirring sounds. . . .

• • •

The moon goddess ran with a swiftness which outpaced the wind. In her left hand she carried the great hunting bow; in her right, a single arrow. She wore a white tunic and her dark hair streamed behind her. Ahead, the stag leaped and turned, foam flecking his mouth, his great antlers bouncing with his flight. He was a powerful creature, proud, strong, but she was a goddess. She gained on him, until, when the stag finally came to the End of the World and stood upon the precipice, realizing there was no escape, she was right behind him. He turned to face his pursuer, whose name was Death, Death with a nocked arrow in her bow, standing straight and tall. The stag raised his head and held himself ready. He had lived well, and he would die well. It was no disgrace to meet his end at the hands of Diana, the huntress who never lost her prey. But instead of firing, she lowered her weapon, letting the arrow's sharp barb point at the ground instead of at the stag's heart. She smiled. "Go," she said, slackening her bowstring. "You have given me pleasure in the hunting and the chase. I have no need of your head or flesh. Tell the creatures of the forest that the goddess Diana sometimes carries mercy in her quiver, for those who are worthy. . . ."

The music and the story came to the final coda. Michan was pleased. He had played it well, he knew—better than he had ever played it before. He let the final notes fade into the breathless silence, and then looked up at Katsu. He caught his breath. There was a woman standing next to the boy, her face as rapt with the music as Katsu's. For a single instant, her dark hair and white clothes, and the way the forest framed her, made him think that his playing had brought Diana herself before him. He shook off the fantasy and looked at her. She was handsome, not pretty, but strong-featured and small, and very obviously the boy's mother. And she looked familiar. Where had he seen her before . . . ?"

"You!" she said, looking startled. And then Michan knew: She was the woman with the pale green wings, the one who had kept him from smashing into the wall through the torn net weeks before. The woman in front of whom he had made a fool of himself. *Oh, great*, he thought.

She recognized him, too—he could see her face settling into tight lines. Quickly, Michan spoke. "Listen, I owe you an apology; you saved me from a lot of pain that day in the Hub. And I reacted like an idiot. I am really sorry about that; I seem to have an intermittent between mouth and brain that kicks in much too often."

He watched her waver between anger and surprise for a moment; then she nodded. "All right." She looked at Katsu, then back at Michan. "What you just played was . . . quite lovely." She seemed reluctant to praise him. "And I've heard you here before, I think, several weeks ago. A German piece?"

Michan nodded. There was an awkward silence, which Katsu broke by saying, "He's going to teach me how to play, Mother."

"Now, Katsu, you mustn't bother the man—"

"Michan Bern is my name. Michan, please."

He saw her hesitate again. "Susan Hanawashi. Katsu you apparently already know."

"Yes. And if he really wants to learn, I'll be happy to teach him."

"I couldn't ask you to do that."

"I could say it's because I owe you a favor," Michan said. "But what's more important is that he really seems interested."

"Please, Mother?"

Susan looked at Katsu. "Well . . . if Mr. Bern—"

"Michan," the Outsider said.

"If . . . Michan . . . doesn't mind, you have my permission."

"Thank you!" Katsu said, grinning.

Michan nodded. "Yes," he said. "Thank you."

Leo Chin stared at the numbers on the printout, as if concentration could somehow change them, put them back in their proper sequence. They were the results of the latest series of momentum experiments, and they were wrong, in a very frightening way.

His first thought that been, naturally, that there had been a problem with the interpretations. But if there was a glitch somewhere in the system, the computer had been unable to find it. Leo sat in the contoured chair behind his desk and stared at the blank screen of the terminal. The cursor blinked slowly, somehow mockingly, in the upper lefthand corner. Either the world is going mad, or I am, he thought. Or perhaps there is no difference between the two. The Outsiders spoke of "Solipsism Syndrome," or the long stare—the hypnotizing rapture that sometimes came upon those who looked too long and too deep into infinity. He had not realized until now that the microcosm could be just as mesmerizing as the macrocosm, if one stared long and deeply enough into it.

He had discussed the findings with his associates—none wanted to admit what seemed to be happening, and none wanted to be the first to tell Admin. After all, what proof did they have? Scribbles on paper that would be meaningless to anyone else. And what could be done about it? Nothing. Everything indicated that the disturbances were increasing, progressing from the subatomic to the atomic and molecular level.

In the trees fish play; in the deep sea birds are flying, he thought. The statement was a *koan*, a meaningless or contradictory Zen phrase meant to jolt one's mind into a new perspective on existence, and thus provide enlightenment. Perhaps not so meaningless after all, Leo told himself. It is, after all, how one interprets the system that defines the system. One hundred and eighty degrees is the sum of three angles only in Euclidian geometry—it is greater in elliptic geometry, less in hyperbolic. We define reality by interpreting symbols. It appears it may be time to reinterpret and redefine.

"La Pascaline," he said softly. The computer's quiet, feminine voice answered his. *"Oui,* Leo."

"Je suis enquiet."

The system's voice was soothing; a small part of him marvelled at the complexity of its programming. He had never spoken to it of cares or concerns before, but the infinite network of viral circuitry was not at a loss. *"Pourquois t'enquietes, tois?"*

He had always preferred to speak French to the computer; it was a source of both amusement and comfort to him to couch cold science in such a warm and rich language. But now it suddenly seemed repugnant. He stared at the blinking cursor. From the abacus of his ancestors, through Pascal's and Babbage's crude creations and the dinosaurs such as ENIAC, to Silicon Valley and, eventually, such marvels as the GARTH-7.

Man and machine had come a long way together. Neurochips now made it possible to interface brain with computer on a limited level, although there were still problems with rejection syndrome. All that, he thought, and still we know so little.

"*Laisse faire*," he said. For a moment he wished communication with Earth were practical. He suddenly felt very alone and cut off.

He sighed and set the papers aside, told his assistant that he would be gone for an hour, and left the department. He went to his dojo, stripped and dressed for a workout, and spent ten minutes stretching and doing yoga *asanas* until his muscles were warm and limber. Then he stood, bowed, and began the form.

It was called Slow Tiger, and it was one of the most complex of all kung fu dances. Two hundred and fourteen moves long, the entire sequence lasted nearly fifteen minutes when done briskly, as he now performed it, and that was twice normal speed. The Slow Tiger was more meditation than practical fighting technique, a distant cousin of t'ai chi chuan. It always brought to Leo some measure of calming, a centering of his essence. He had learned the form thirty-five years ago; it was now nearly as automatic to him as walking.

But this time, halfway through, the Slow Tiger stumbled.

Leo was amazed. He continued his intricate motions, but his concentration was broken. He had not made such a mistake in twenty years. He managed to complete the form, but when he was done there was no calmness, no centering; indeed, he was more disturbed than he had been when he had begun.

More than all the printouts and diagrams he had seen thus far, the break in the form convinced Leo that things were very wrong in the microcosm that was *Heaven Star*. He stood in the middle of the empty room, heart pounding, and recognized the touch of an emotion he had not felt for many years. Leo Chin, Ph.D., director of the Physics Section and master of Chan Gen kung fu, was afraid.

Ian Kyle was also afraid. There was a fire inside his head. It was not a painful feeling; far from it. It was a warmth which illuminated his thoughts like the reflected rays of the heloid.

You know what is happening, the flickering thoughts said.

You have the evidence, and you can feel it. You are more perceptive than they are. They can fool themselves, ignore it, but not you. You've always been too smart to fool yourself. . . .

Kyle knew it was true. He understood now why the incident on Nine had happened. It was not his fault; it was because things were *wrong*. It was yet another manifestation of the madness which had always surrounded him, tugged at him, and which he had been able to resist—until now.

He had lived all his life in a burning house, and he had survived because he had been made of iron. But now the flames were leaping higher, turning the house into a crucible.

The iron could resist the fire no longer.

In the quiet privacy of his cube, Ian Kyle began to cry.

PART TWO

Faraday's Cage

"Continually the unnameable moves
until it returns beyond the realm of
things."

—Lao Tzu

ELEVEN

Supervisor Thomas Steen sat alone in his office cubical. He had just finished dictating his efficiency report for the month, being most careful to give lowered ratings to Michan Bern and Greg Shonin for their blunder during the hatch inspection at the Number Six Spoke. He reread the report, pursing his lips and nodding his head. They were like recalcitrant children, these Outsiders; they acted as though exterior maintenance was some kind of game instead of serious business. He was changing that, though, slowly but surely. He would see an end to these daredevil antics, if he had to replace the entire department.

He flicked on the ops channel and listened, but the frequency was quiet. It was nearly the end of the shift and things were slow. The hall outside his cube was empty, Steen knew. Those working the current tour would not be through yet, and those coming on for the next shift would already have checked in, pursuant to a new regulation he had instigated providing for a fifteen-minute overlap in schedules. They had howled at that, but he had made it stick.

It was not easy trying to control the Outsiders; they were notorious as the most undisciplined bunch on *Heaven Star*. But it would be worth the trouble; a successful stint here was a guarantee of a jump from Section Supervisor to Full, and from there it was only a matter of time until a seat on the Council was his. Steen was a man with foresight, which was why he had called in all his favors to get this position. He had long been able to see his path clearly among all the others twisting across it, and he did not mind working hard to follow it.

He stood, looking with satisfaction at his cleared desk. The hatch fiasco was a blot on his record, but not a major one. Shonin had been disciplined for his error, despite his transparent lying about not having touched the control. Both he and Bern had sworn that the switch had malfunctioned. Steen smiled. The last word had been his, of course. The inspection on the switch had revealed no sign of trouble.

Children, he thought again; unable to see how much more efficient things were now that he was running the floor. They resented him because he was not one of them, had never been Outside; as though one had to be a mechanic to know how to run a machine efficiently.

He stepped toward the door, which obediently slid open. The hallway was empty. Good—he had no desire to see any of them right now. If he hurried he could reach home before the shift changed. There were some tapes he had been meaning to view—courses in creative management, and that full-sensory porno sphere from his brother Cecil. He got along with Cecil well enough, and he had gotten along more than well with Cecil's wife, Marion—for a time. She had a body made for bed; too bad she didn't have the brains to go with it, or he might have tried to take her away from his brother.

He reached his cube before the corridors filled with people. He stepped inside with a sigh of relief, looking about in satisfaction at the spacious quarters. When he was on the Council, he would have a whole top-tier flat with a view—

Beside him the 'fresher door snapped open. Steen spun about, surprised, and saw a man's figure silhouetted by the light over the sink. The man raised his right hand and pointed something at Steen, who flinched instinctively. Nothing happened, however. After a moment the figure stepped out of the 'fresher where Steen could see him.

The astonished supervisor recognized the man. "Doctor Kyle! What the hell are you doing in my cube?"

"Waiting for you, supervisor." Kyle grinned, and that,

finally, brought fear to Steen. Something in the man's expression, his eyes. . . .

Steen backed up as Kyle dropped something onto the floor. The object clinked like metal on the tile of the foyer. Before Steen could see what it was, however, the doctor stepped forward and drove his fist into Steen's belly, hard, dropping his shoulder and pivoting on his feet.

"*Uhhh*—!" Steen folded, grabbing his ample midriff with both hands. He couldn't breathe. . . .

Dimly, through the darkness that surrounded him and kept air from him (*It's like being Outside,* a small, mocking part of his mind said), the supervisor felt Kyle grab his hair and yank him erect. His stomach felt as if it were being torn in two. Steen tried futilely to suck in a breath with which to protest.

His head jerked, neck cracking painfully, as Kyle slapped him. "Stop!" Steen managed to gasp. He was breathing now, finally, in heaving asthmatic gasps. He backed away, stumbling over an ottoman and falling heavily against an end table. He knocked the remote for the holoproj onto the floor. There was a click, and a blur of colored static materialized in the center of the room, crackling restlessly with loud white noise. Steen looked up. Kyle stood over him, smiling. The flickering light from the holo made his face demonic.

"Get up, supervisor," he said softly.

Steen shook his head, feeling tears on his cheeks. He couldn't get up, not even if he wanted to. Kyle reached down and grabbed his shirt with both hands, lifting him easily—the man was stronger by far than he looked. Somehow, Steen managed to stay on his feet, though his cube shifted about him as though the torus had suddenly begun to wobble.

The doctor stepped back, slid his left foot forward and raised his hands. Steen recognized it as some kind of karate or judo fighting stance. Kyle was still smiling at him, a smile full of contempt, almost a sneer. *Why is this happening?*

It had to be the Outsiders's doing. Somehow, they had put the doctor up to it. "Listen to me," Steen said, every word feeling like fire in his lungs and gut. "Stop now—leave, and I won't tell anyone it was you. You can tell them you beat the crap out of me. I won't say anything. My word."

Kyle appeared to consider it. He dropped his hands and relaxed. Steen heaved a great, shaking sigh of relief. He was safe. As soon as the son-of-a-bitch left he would call Security and have the man taken in; then he would find out who put him up to it. They would be sorry they were born—he would start a pogrom that would sweep the entire floor—

Kyle suddenly leaped into the air, spinning as he did so, his form blurring before Steen's astonished eyes—and then the world exploded in a red, bubbling volcano of pain.

"Camera's rolling."

"Beam split."

"Sync."

The director nodded to Sean, who took a deep breath. He fanned the air slightly with one hand, turning himself toward the holocamera, and nodded curtly. Then he expertly maneuvered himself to the keyboard, already forgetting about the hundreds of people who watched, pressed by C-force against chairs, couches, beds or whatever; forgetting that tomorrow he would be one of them once again, a clumsy, ludicrous half-robot for six days. None of that mattered now. Now all that was important was the act of creation. Sean began tapping the codes into the keyboard, and colors began to swirl. . . .

Pyramus lay next to Phaedra in her bed, his arm wrapped around her shoulders. They watched the live broadcast of Sean's colorstorm on the holoproj built into the wall of her bedroom. For them a different kind of storm had just ended, one of passion rather than art.

"Beautiful," Phaedra murmured. "Isn't it?"

"Arva," he said. Yes. He watched the liquid hues, as clear and brilliant as laser colors, shifting and billowing against the box's boundaries, and wished he could stop, for just a few moments, wondering who killed Arthur Jefferson Stanhope.

Katsu sat on the floor, staring up at the projection floating two meters away. "How does it work?" he asked.

Behind him, on the couch, Michan glanced at Susan. She looked at him and shrugged, as if to say, *Beats me.*

"It's a form of electrically shielded box, Kat," Michan said. "It's called a Faraday's Cage—an enclosed space shielded from exterior influences."

"Kind of like the ship, huh?"

Michan raised an eyebrow in admiration. "That's a very good comparison. Only the artifact is using induced fields instead of walls. He doesn't really need the box—that's just to see how much room he's got."

"Oh."

Susan smiled at Michan, and they both turned their attention back to the show. Michan got along very well with Katsu, she thought. The thought made her happy, though she was not quite sure why.

"Are you asleep?" Elena asked.

Geoffrey started and sat up straighter in his chair. "What? Oh, no—just woolgathering."

"You're missing Mkono's show. It's worth staying awake for—he does a live broadcast about as often as the ship falls through a black hole."

Geoffrey focused his eyes on the colorstorm raging in his living room: the tiny tornado swirling slowly, the fat drops of ersatz water falling into the white-capped sea. Impressive, to be sure. But he was not really seeing it. He was somewhere else, watching a friendship die. . . .

Killikup seemed to be watching the projection, but Scott could not be sure. The marine biologist was watching intently, concentrating more on the cetacean's reactions than on Mkono's artwork. Did Killikup understand the concept of art? Was he impressed, moved, by the dynamic creation hovering before the pool? If only I knew how to ask, Scott thought wistfully. . . .

Demond smiled as he watched the storm and thought about how he might persuade Mkono to do something for his victory party. There would be a victory—of that he had no doubt, now. Old Geoffrey would come through for him; the terror in his face and eyes had sworn to that. A pity to put the old boy through such an experience, but it was for the greater good. The welfare of the ship had to be maintained—no matter what it took. . . .

• • •

In the cubical of Supervisor Thomas Steen, the colorstorm of Sean Mkono. neared completion, as it did in thousands of other cubes on *Heaven Star*. But the beauty of· it was lost on Steen, who sprawled on the floor before the holo, a thin line of dried blood running from his nose across his cheek and into his ear. . . .

Pyramus looked over the list of recordings. He took the sphere containing the interviews and slipped it into the slot on his desk terminal, then typed in a code. Reilly, his number three deputy, appeared on the holoproj and gave the date and legal sanctions; then the angular face of a woman flashed into view. She identified herself as Wanda Camber, Hull Monitoring Tech, First. Pyramus studied her face and so missed her first words.

"—live in the cube directly above his. His holo was on so loud—just white noise—that I couldn't sleep. He didn't answer his phone, so I finally went down to see if anything was wrong. . . ."

Pyramus fast-forwarded to the next interview.

"—direct cause of death," the doctor said. He was a light-haired man with pale blue eyes; Pyramus recognized him as the teacher of a first-aid class he had once taken. "There are some signs of injury immediately prior to death. Abrasions and contusions on the rectus abdominals, in the epigastric region, appear to have been made by a blunt object. Electro-chemical analysis of the victim's clothing in the area of the impact revealed epithelial cells consistent with stratified epidermal callus tissue; examination of the skull in the right temporal region revealed polyurethane polymer of the amide bond—"

Pyramus touched the FF control again.

"No, I haven't seen him since I lent him the tapes. My brother was a cold, unforgiving man; I can see where somebody might want to harm him—"

Pyramus pushed the Stop button. Damn! This was worse than the last, much worse. Steen had a lot of enemies; the problem lay not in finding who did not like him, but who did. There was a whole floorful of Outsiders who would not have minded if their supervisor had gone out a lock and sucked vacuum. But that did not make them all killers.

He looked at the scribbled notes he had made. Greg Shonin, an obvious candidate, had already been interviewed and his alibi checked. But there was another Outsider who apparently disliked the dead man quite a bit, and he was somebody Pyramus knew: Michan Bern.

The Security Chief thought about it. There was no obvious connection between Bern and Stanhope, but if Bern had killed Steen, it was likely he had killed the toxicologist. Prove one, and Pyramus was willing to bet he could prove the other. Psyche vapor would get the truth, if he had enough evidence to justify using it.

He touched his desk intercom.

"Yeah, Chief?"

"Bring in Michan Bern. Outsider, on Level—"

"I know where he is, Chief. I'm on my way."

"I didn't kill him."

Bern stood in front of Pyramus's desk, his feet wide-spread and his hands folded across his chest. His body language said he was wary, on guard, which was certainly understandable.

Pyramus said, "I hear you had no great love for him."

"I thought he was in the wrong job and I disliked him, but not enough to kill him. And certainly not enough to beat him to death in his own cube."

Pyramus leaned forward. "Who said he was beaten to death?"

"Your deputy, Plait. He told me on the way down."

Pyramus closed his eyes for a moment. "That right, Bill?"

Plait's response from beyond the doorway was contrite. "Yes sir, I think I said that."

Terrific, Pyramus thought. He made a mental note to have a few well-chosen words with Bill later; no point in having it on the holo record.

"Medical puts the time of death at—" he glanced at a sheet on his desk, "—2100 hours, plus or minus twenty minutes. Can you account for your whereabouts at that time?"

Bern nodded. "I was visiting a couple of friends—Katsu and Susan Hanawashi."

"We'll contact them. How long were you there?"

"From 1800 until about 2345. I'm teaching Katsu—he's eight—how to play the arofloj." Bern smiled briefly.

"2300 is a bit late for an eight-year-old to be awake, isn't it? Assuming he's on a day schedule."

"He went to bed around 2100. Susan—Ms. Hanawashi—and I . . . talked for the rest of the time."

"I see." Pyramus was not sure whether to feel glad or disappointed. He liked Bern, and had not particularly wanted to nail him for the murders. On the other hand, he wanted to find the killer.

"Would you be willing to undergo stress analysis or vapor questioning about this?"

Bern shifted his weight uncomfortably. "If I had to; I wouldn't like it."

Pyramus sighed. "You won't have to." Bern was already being stress analyzed; the indicator was built into the flatscreen readout on Pyramus's desk, visible only to him. The analyzer showed a high baseline, but no deviations on any questions. Either Bern was telling the truth or he was a body-control adept, something his records gave no indication of his being.

"Thank you for your time, Bern. You're free to go." As Bern started to exit, Pyramus added, "Don't leave town."

"Excuse me?"

Pyramus grinned. "It's out of an old entertainment vid. What the police used to tell people after questioning them about homicide cases." Bern continued to look at him without expression. Pyramus cleared his throat. "It's a joke, Bern."

Bern nodded. "Funny." He left.

Alone again, Pyramus rubbed his eyes for a moment. Back to square one; he had no doubt that Bern's alibi would check. He tapped in a call to Medical and got Kearns, the doctor who had autopsied Steen, on-line. He asked for a translation of the jargon on the interview sphere.

"Somebody bashed his head in," the doctor said. "But he or she worked on him a little first, using fists."

"Oh? Why didn't you say that in the report?"

"I did. There were traces of epithelial tissues on the victim's clothing. Callus tissue."

"Doctor . . ."

"Somebody punched him in the belly, Chief Gray. They scraped their knuckles a little on his shirt."

Pyramus felt a surge of excitement. "Can you tell anything about the attacker from that?"

"Quite a bit, normally. The primary tissues—a tissue is a collection of like cells—are nervous, muscular, connective and epithelial. Epithelial tissue forms the skin. Using the Maddox-Montgomery Electrochemical Phasing test, we can usually tell the race, sex, blood type and genetic matrix."

"But—?"

Kearns looked faintly abashed. "Our system is glitching up, Chief. We're getting bad readings, scans we know are wrong. When we're running smooth again, I can cross-index and probably match the samples with someone from files. Until then . . . " he shrugged.

Pyramus grimaced in disappointment. So much for an easy technological solution to his problem.

He thought of another question. "Why would an attacker use fists if he or she had a weapon? Your report talked about traces of plastic in the head wound, just like the Stanhope case."

Kearns shook his head. "I don't know that one, Chief."

"Any idea what the weapon was?"

"Sorry. On Earth, in a big forensics lab, maybe I could tell you. We aren't really set up to do major criminal work."

Pyramus thanked him and broke the connection. He looked at the paperwork spread over his desk, and sighed. Back to square one, indeed.

They had given her medication when she had left the hospital, but it was hard to remember to take it. It did not matter; the shakes had not returned. She was confident that they would not; how could any lasting harm come from Zanshin?

Shanna stood in the grove of trees, feeling the sunlight warm her, feeling utterly at peace, at *one* with the landscape, with the ship, with everything. She listened, not to the gentle breezes and the songs of the birds, but to the subtle, faraway murmurs in her head—the echoes of other minds, the tenuous links that the drug had given her. She knew that with her next flight on Zanshin, she would be able to understand them—and then she would be part of the true circle.

No one had known that she had gone to their meetings; not Raul, not her family, not anybody. The secrecy was necessary, she knew. They were being very cautious in accepting new members since that arrest at the party. But she had convinced them. She believed in their goals, their ultimate purpose, which was to extend the awareness of humanity throughout the universe—to explore and learn and *meld*, in any and every way, with the infinite and the eternal.

And she would be part of it.

Shanna looked at the capsule in her hand. It had been hard getting another dose; her supplier, Zed Kagan, had been unwilling initially, because of her adverse reaction. But she had convinced him. She smiled, and in a single smooth motion brought the capsule to her mouth and swallowed it. Then she sat down beneath a tree to wait.

The expansion of awareness came quickly. She saw the geometric patterns similar to those spun by mescalin and the flashes of light and color—not true hallucinations, but distortions of what one normally saw. But those effects were unimportant. What mattered was the *knowledge*, the awareness of her place in the scheme of everything, and the growing sense of unity with the others who had experienced this. There were not very many of them, and she could only hear a few of those, their thoughts becoming gradually clearer, like a radio band growing stronger. She could hear flashes of mental dialogue from all over the ship, from people both aware and unaware of her. . . .

—*rectenna's slightly out of alignment, Joey, I need a new patch*—

—*I can't explain it; it's like I can hear the stars singing*—

—*could have gone wrong? It was a hydrogen exchange, the simplest reaction in the book*—

—*welcome you, Shanna. Now you begin to understand what it's all about*—

—*still don't know that much about her; this could be dangerous*—

Shanna smiled. She sensed worry about her new state of awareness from some of the others. *There is no need for con-*

cern, she thought. *I want what you want. I have always had a longing for the Deep, always felt it was where we should be, now and always. Let me lead the way for you. . . .*

The corridors of Level One were empty, save for a few Outsiders who looked curiously at her as she walked past them. She moved with a purposeful stride, and she knew the joy she felt was evident in her expression. There was no uncertainty as to where she should go; one of the minds dimly touching hers was an Outsider's, and from his thoughts she had learned the route.

She could hear faint concern in the back of her mind, confusion and protest:

—is she doing? Where is she?—

—can't tell—she's not thinking, just acting—

—don't like this, it feels wrong—

They would understand in a few moments. She entered the empty locker room, stopped before the massive door and quickly punched the access code which she had learned an instant before from another's thoughts. The door opened with a hiss of compressed air, and she entered the small chamber. The door closed behind her. The light over it glowed a soothing, reassuring green.

—stop her! Override it, quickly!—

—don't know which one she's in—

—won't be able to get the outer pressure lock open, don't worry—

Shanna manipulated controls and switches, not knowing what button next to push until it was time to do so; then the information was there, in her mind. She knew, suddenly, how to open the inner seal, and how to arm the explosive bolts that would blow the hatch. She threw the final switch, then stepped quickly back to the inner door of the airlock and grabbed the stabilizing bars with both hands.

Shanna, no!

The hatch blew. The concussion slammed her painfully back against the inner door, while at the same time the rush of air into the vacuum of interstellar space tore at her. As the light above her changed from green to red, she stumbled forward, already feeling the freezing cold enveloping her, feeling the pains deep within her head and body starting. The outer door suddenly seemed impossible to reach, but she had to; she could not fail now, now that she was so close. There was an agonizing wrench inside her head, and her clouding vision was suddenly distorted, as though her eyes had changed shape. But she reached the outer door. She could no longer hear the panicked voices inside her mind, could no longer hear anything at all. But she could see, for a single instant, the ultimate spectacle before her. She reached out a hand already frosted with ice crystals—and fell into darkness even deeper than that which held the stars.

TWELVE

"Another murder, Chief Gray. That makes two."

"I'm aware of the number, Mr. Administrator."

"Yes, I imagine you are. What I want to know is what you intend to do about them."

Pyramus was aware that he was sitting rigidly at attention before Demond's desk; he tried to relax slightly, to ease the knots of tension in the back of his neck. "I can only assure you, Mr. Chairman, that we are working very hard to solve this."

"I have to assure the people of *Heaven Star* that something is being done, Gray. And I can assure *you* that, if catching this maniac means replacing you or anyone, I'll do it. Is that clear?"

Pyramus felt his neck tightening again. "Quite clear, sir."

"That's all."

The screen in front of Wanda Camber blinked. She sighed in resignation; the glitch was back again. It had taken the tech nearly five hours last week to chase down something he thought might be it. The screen blinked again, went blank, then flickered back on—only now all of the coordinates on the grid were changed. Wanda tapped in commands, but to no avail. *Looks like I get another break*, she thought—which would put her even further behind schedule. She turned away from the screen to call for a supervisor. The action saved her life.

Suddenly, impossibly, the console *blew up*. The force of it sent Wanda sprawling from her chair. Dimly she heard the shouts and screams of other monitors about her, felt someone grab her shoulders and pull her away. She looked back at her station—the console was erupting with sparks, fizzling with electrical discharges and smoke. She could smell the acrid stench of burning plastic. It seemed to go on for a very long time before someone finally had the presence of mind to find a fire extinguisher.

"Are you all right?" someone was asking her urgently. Wanda nodded, still staring at the blackened ruin of her console. For some reason she saw, vividly superimposed by her mind's eye over the scene, the memory of Supervisor Steen as she had found him, sprawled on the floor of his cube, colors flickering over his frozen expression of pain and fright. . . .

Wanda turned away, hiding her face in her hands.

Phaedra was applying makeup to her face before the holomirror, when suddenly the augmented image went dark. She jiggled the intensity control. Nothing happened. Terrific, she thought. A fine time for the mirror to go out, just before she had to make an appearance at a nearby school.

She frowned, peering into the dark, smoky depths. She could have sworn she saw something move in there, just for an instant. She walked around it, viewing it from all angles. Funny—it had been almost like a glimpse of another's face, dim and wavering, as though seen at the bottom of a pond. . . .

Phaedra turned the mirror off. She would rely on the 'fresher's looking glass. There had been something eerie about that flash of an image. She suppressed a momentary shudder. Burnt holomirrors were supposed to be bad luck for a year or something, too. . . .

• • •

Louis Demond sat at his austere desk, reviewing the latest polls. He was not worried, but he was concerned. Sevaer had risen two points; he was still ahead by a fair margin, but not so much now that he could laugh her off. If she continued to gain momentum at her present rate, it would be close by election day. Too close.

Demond frowned. If that many people were willing to consider voting for somebody else, it might mean he was not doing as good a job as he should. He would have to review his performance. The ship ran more or less automatically; Admin could not foul it up without a great deal of effort. But the difference between simply running and running *well* was his job, one he had always tried to do to the best of his ability. He had no illusions left about serving the people; he was a politician, and he knew that actions others might consider unconscionable were ofttimes necessary. But he was also the best Administrator *Heaven Star* had ever had. He saw his work as an end in itself, not as a means to fame or power. The work was all he had. There was no family, no other interests, save the running of *Heaven Star*. He would not give it up. He could not. Like Geoffrey, he would wither and die without it.

He looked at the faxsheet again. Sevaer was using the murders for political hay now. Mudslinging, Demond thought. Well, fine. The broadcast debates between the candidates started tomorrow; if that was how she wanted it, she was going to find herself up to her hairline in mud. He had not been a public servant for all his adult life without learning how to play those dirty games. He was a survivor, and he would win. She might be fighting for a job, but he was fighting for his life. When he got through with her, she would be lucky if her own mother would vote for her. . . .

"Michan," Susan said, surprised. "What are you doing here?"

Michan shrugged. "I had an off-shift, so I thought . . . "

Susan smiled nervously at him. "Katsu's still in school; he won't be home for a couple of hours yet."

Michan nodded. He knew that, just as he had known Susan was also on an off-shift.

"Well, come in. I was making some tea; would you like some?"

He hated tea. "Yes, thank you." She went to get it while Michan looked nervously about the small room. Its cool colors of blue and gray and the subdued continuous-spectrum lighting had always relaxed him before. Now he felt increasingly nervous. Maybe this wasn't such a hot idea, he thought. Maybe what he wanted to say would just ruin what had developed into a very nice friendship. Maybe he ought to politely excuse himself and—

"Sweetener?"

Michan almost jumped. "Uh, no, thank you." He accepted the cup of hot tea. It smelled faintly of spice. He sat down on the edge of the couch.

Susan sat across from him in the aluminum director's chair, holding her cup and smiling politely. Michan stared at the hot liquid in his own cup, suddenly at a loss. The silence began to turn awkward.

"Why had you locked the door?"

She shrugged. "I guess all those rumors about a second murder was making me nervous. Silly, I know, but . . ."

Silence again. Michan looked at a picture hanging on the far wall—a reproduction of a wood-engraving by the Dutch graphic artist M. C. Escher. It was called *Another World*; the scene was a multileveled view of lunar surfaces and Deep, seen through columned arches. Human-faced birds added to the surrealism. He looked back at Susan. He was no good at this kind of social game, Michan told himself; never had been. He was too blunt to make small talk; when he tried, he usually ended up saying something inane and stupid. But he had to try. "When we were watching Mkono's show the other night, why didn't you answer Katsu's question? I mean, you're Engineering Supervisor, for Christ's sake—you know what a Faraday's Cage is."

Susan stared at her tea. "Of course I do. But it seemed appropriate for you to tell him."

"Oh? Why?"

She looked up at him very seriously. "I don't know very many men, Michan—and so, by extension, neither does Katsu. I don't want him to think that men don't know anything about science."

Michan blinked. "Uh . . . I see. Okay."

"You seem taken aback."

"No, I—it's just—well, that wasn't what I thought you'd say."

"Ah. And what was?"

He felt flustered by her disconcerting directness. "Well, I guess I—" Her large brown eyes stared into his, frank and curious. Michan took a deep breath and plunged on. "I guess I thought you wanted him to be impressed with *me*. Me, personally."

It was her turn to look puzzled. "Why? I mean, I do of course, but—"

"Oh, hell!" Michan stood up and crossed to where she sat. "Susan, do you—" He swallowed, his throat suddenly dry. "Do you like me?"

She seemed to go slightly pale. Michan felt his stomach clench.

"Michan, I—I'm not very good with . . . people. I don't understand sometimes. I like you, but—what are you trying to say?"

Michan's heart was loud enough, he was sure, for the hull monitors to pick up. It was also going much too fast for a man who was merely standing in a room talking. He squatted, bringing his face level with hers. He reached out and touched her cheeks with his fingertips, very gently, then leaned forward and kissed her.

Entropy ran down, the stars grew cold, one by one—and then, finally, she returned his kiss. Her tea almost spilled, but Michan caught it and set it on the floor. He stood, drawing her up with him, and they embraced, kissing again. They explored each other, with lips and tongues and hands. When Michan pulled back to look at her, Susan's face was flushed and her breathing was rapid. She turned slightly and started to move away and Michan felt a quick jab of fear, until she caught his hand and pulled him after her toward her bedroom.

Susan sat on the bed in the dimly lit room, looking at Michan, who stood in front of her. He started to undress—and then, to her surprise, she heard herself say, "No. Let me."

Michan stopped, his coverall half-unseamed. She ran her thumb down the rest of the way, then stood and slid the material off of his shoulders, wondering as she did so where the

courage to do this was coming from. She had always been passive and shy with men before. But this time she could sense
that he was as nervous and uncertain as she. That helped,
somehow.

She pulled the soft plastic com patch receiver from his ear
and peeled the transmitter from his throat, dropping them on
a night table, then did the same for herself; she wanted no interruptions now. He stepped out of his shoes and stood before
her, naked save for a pair of nylon briefs that bulged with the
hard outline of his penis. She ran her hands over his chest.
"I'm glad you're not hairy," she said softly, and he smiled
slightly, nervously. His skin felt cool to her touch, and soft.
She was always surprised at the softness of mens' skin—
always expected it to feel rough and hard. She looked at his
face. He was only an inch or so taller than she, and so she
could look him in the eyes. She liked that. Toby had been over
six feet; she had always been faced with his nipples, like the
eyes of some alien creature.

She moved her hands down over his torso. His body was
firm, though not ridged with bone and musculature—
Mesomorphic, the analytical part of her mind that she could
never quite turn off whispered. She unsnapped his briefs and
took him in her hand—he was almost comically large and
hard. Michan sighed, then looked down and raised his eyebrows in surprise. "My, my—looks like the graft from that
teenage donor took."

Susan laughed, then stepped back. "My turn," she said.

"Gladly." He began to undress her, untabbing her blouse
and pulling it from her dark slacks. He reached behind her and
fumbled, unable to find the catch on the bra. "In front," she
said. He smiled ruefully. "You can see how much practice I've
been getting."

He pulled apart the tabs, freeing her breasts. Her nipples
were dark brown; he kissed each one gently, causing them to
pucker and tingle. She felt gooseflesh run down her arms.
"Mmmm. Nice." She leaned toward him.

The slacks went down and she stepped from them, revealing
pale green panties. Michan slid his hands under the elastic
band and cupped her buttocks, then moved his hands downward. The panties slid with them, revealing thick, black pubic
hair. She felt his lips brush it lightly.

She kicked her sandals off as he slid one hand up the back

of her legs and the other hand over her hip and onto her flat belly. She lay down on the bed and he followed. They kissed again, and Susan ran her hands over him again, delighting in the tone of strong muscles, exploring the different textures of him.

They broke the kiss. "Tell me what you like," he said. He moved down her body and kissed her navel, then slid his tongue lower, to taste the saltiness and wetness of her. "That," she said, "I like that!" She caught his hair with her fingers, urging him deeper.

His laugh was muffled, but hers was not. "Hey," she said.

"Hmm?"

"That's the first time I remember laughing while making love."

"Yeah?" He raised his head slightly, but kept his chin in contact with her mons. "Well, get used to it. I can be a very funny guy sometimes." He tilted his head and wiggled his tongue quickly, and this time her laughter was loud and long.

She felt herself relaxing, but it was still difficult to let go, to surrender control completely. That had always been hard to do, even with Toby—or perhaps especially with Toby. She stroked Michan's hair, then pulled gently on his arms, drawing him up until he lay on her stomach. "Enough foreplay," she said.

He sighed. "Fine with me. I think I'm about to reach critical mass."

"Not to worry. I'm familiar with containment procedure."

Pyramus sighed as he broke another lace tying his shoes. He managed to get them tied, then looked at them in amusement. Maybe Phaedra was right—maybe they *had* walked their last mile. He really should do his duty to the ship and recycle them—it wasn't like he could not afford more. He decided to stop at a store on his way to the office and pick up another pair—with velcro flaps instead of laces, this time. But then he heard Bill Plait's voice in his ear, and what the deputy had to say drove all thoughts of the errand from Pyramus's mind.

Pyramus reached the airlock before the medical team was

finished. He could see the stiffly frozen form, now covered by an opaque plastic sheet, lying on the floor. Ian Kyle was in charge, and the Security Chief pulled him aside. "Was she on Zanshin again?"

Kyle nodded. "I'd say so. They're running a screen on her now—we'll know in a few minutes."

Pyramus looked around. He saw Greg Shonin among the crowd of people, mostly Outsiders, who stood in the corridor. "Who found her? You?"

Shonin shook his head. "It was Poole and Swale. I helped bring her back in." He swallowed, looking distinctly pale under the lights. "I've heard about explosive decompression, but I've never seen it. Who was she?"

"Shanna Dicran, a tech from Broadcasting. We had her in the hospital recently for a reaction to Zanshin."

Shonin shook his head, his face bleak. "I don't understand how she managed it. That access code is changed every day, and only the Outsiders assigned to spoke duty know it. She couldn't have known how to depressurize the lock, either, or open the inner seal, or . . . "

"But she did it," Pyramus said. "She overrode the failsafes and opened the hatch, and without setting off any alarms."

Shonin nodded. "I'm going to get back to my post, unless you need me for something."

"No, go ahead. I'll send somebody over to log your statement later."

Pyramus watched the Outsider walk slowly away. The rest of the crowd began to break up as well. He looked down at the covered grotesque form, and shivered. *Exit the system*, his mind whispered, with macabre humor. Shanna had done that, all right. Had it been suicide? Or an accident? Did Shanna Dicran know who or what she was when she went through the airlock without a suit? And how had she managed it?

He felt he was in far over his head. True, people died on *Heaven Star* all the time; even state-of-the-art medical care could do little about old age, freak accidents, or even a rare suicide. But two murders within a few weeks, and now this bizarre death—it was too much. He found himself wishing desperately, for the first time he could remember, for one of his flashes of specific precognition. He needed some help from someone or something, before Demond made good his threat to fire him. But all he felt—and had felt, for days, now—was a feeling of something . . . looming, just out of sight.

Pyramus sighed. He did not look forward to telling Raul Borisoff about Shanna. Nor did he look forward to telling Phaedra.

THIRTEEN

Ian Kyle stood before the holomirror in his cube, spinning the pistol-shaped oscillator around his forefinger by its trigger guard. He had once seen an old flat-vid about the United States' western frontier, in which all of the men had carried handguns called revolvers. The weapons were supposedly capable of firing six bullets at a time, though the vids had occasionally taken considerable license with this. Some of the actors were quite adept at their use, twirling and tossing the guns around and switching them from hand to hand before allowing them to fall, spinning, into the leather holsters. Quite a display of control over dangerous weapons, Kyle thought. He admired that.

He tossed the oscillator up into the air and caught it. Unfortunately, this particular weapon, though formidable at one time, was now useless. Kyle had stolen it from Stores, not realizing that the circuitry which produced the subsonic frequencies that could vibrate a human brain into unconsciousness or death had somehow corroded or been damaged. He should have tested it, he knew now. If he had gone into a duel with one of those old-time gunslingers he would have been blasted while clicking an empty weapon.

He shrugged. He had planned to stun the fat supervisor and make his death look like an accident, but it had been so much more *satisfying* to feel Steen's skull collapse under the force of his strike. It did not matter that Gray and his ineffectual deputies would know that Steen had been killed by the same man who killed Stanhope. There was nothing they could do. He had covered himself too well. It was easy to move quickly and silently among the unsuspecting masses. No one bothered to lock their doors—though they would start soon, he thought with a grin.

They would find the tissue on Steen's shirt, he knew—but with the systems malfunctioning, they could not trace it to him. He could trip up their investigation in any of a hundred small ways—access the test results and alter them, for example, so that he could give them a sample of his skin and still be clear. He might even arrange to run the tests, pick his own scapegoat. He grinned.

He tried to flip the oscillator into the air and catch it, but he missed. It clattered onto the thin strip of bare floor in front of the mirror and the sound brought back the memory vividly: the feeling of absolute power, of pinpoint body control as he spun and connected. Kyle smiled. It never failed.

Then he frowned. But it *had* failed—against Leo, and against the ghost of Leo, personified in the fight with Murphy. And Susan Hanawashi had seen it, had seen Leo handle Kyle like a clumsy child. She had seen his shame, seen him lose control.

He really would have to do something about that.

Kyle backed a short distance away from the mirror and whipped the oscillator up, aiming at his reflection. "Zap!" he said, grinning.

Louis Demond smiled at the holocameras. All the years of practice had made him quite comfortable in front of an audience. It was true that his breath still came faster and his pulse quickened, but none of that showed. After all, his ancestors were from France, the nation of diplomacy. He had studied recordings of himself, learned how to move, how to smile, when to look directly at the holocam and when to allow it his profile. He had watched tapes and spheres of all the best political speakers, recent and historical, and dissected their motions, their timing, their delivery. It was part of his job to present an image people admired and respected. He could not let any worries, any uncertainties, show. He smiled at the interviewer. "Ready when you are, Paul."

The young man nodded and turned toward the woman seated across from Demond. "Councilwoman Sevaer?"

"Any time."

"Thirty-five seconds, Paul," the director said.

Demond took a slow breath, let it out, then another. He quickly thought over the figures and information he wanted to use. His memory was not naturally spectacular, but he had learned HL isometrics, a link-peg enhancement system which enabled him to rattle off impressive chains of complex material flawlessly when needed.

"Two seconds." The director raised his hand, then pointed at the interviewer.

"Good evening," the interviewer began smoothly, "and welcome to Political Forum, a series of programs concerning the upcoming elections. I'm Paul Straub, your host, and with me tonight are Administrator Louis Demond and Councilwoman Sharon Sevaer. Ms. Sevaer is running against Mr. Demond for the position of Administrator in this election." He turned toward Sevaer. "Councilwoman, my first question for you is: Why do you want the position of Administrator? Do you feel that Mr. Demond is doing a bad job?"

Sevaer smiled. "A bad job? No, I don't think anyone could accuse Mr. Demond of that. I'm sure he is doing the best job he can."

Demond increased his smile slightly. She was good—so far.

"No, my reasons for wanting to be Administrator are simply that I think I can do more. There are programs which will benefit many that Mr. Demond doesn't seem to have time for; there are new ideas and philosophies I'd like to see given a chance."

Demond resisted an impulse to glance at his opponent. Sevaer sounded somehow different than when he had last heard her; much calmer, more sure of herself. Her voice had a soothing, reassuring timbre to it. She had been practicing, he thought.

Straub turned to look at Demond. "Mr. Administrator?"

Demond beamed at the holocam. "Well, Paul, my reasons for wanting to stay in office are pretty much the same they've always been: I've gotten used to the desk after all these years and I've finally learned the name of my secretary.'' He allowed three seconds for whatever chuckles that might bring, then continued. ''But seriously, my long experience as Administrator allows me a view Ms. Sevaer simply doesn't have. Newer isn't necessarily better, and I would rather not experiment with the status quo of *Heaven Star*.''

Straub nodded and looked at his monitor for another question. The Administrator glanced around the small studio. He saw Elena Vasquez, looking on nervously from the wings. Merle-Douglass and he were due to meet tomorrow morning. The old boy would bring Demond a sword he could use against Sevaer—Demond was certain of it. The Archivist had too much to lose otherwise.

A few more questions were asked and answered, giving Demond a chance to use some of his memorized figures. He cited recycling percentages for last year as being up from eighty-seven percent to eighty-eight-point-five percent from the previous year, with a projected eighty-nine-point-three percent for the current year. He imagined people all over the ship reaching for their homecomps to check him, and finding him to be correct. He felt relaxed and confident; remarkably so, he thought, considering the bad news Gray had told him just before the broadcast, about the second murder. He had immediately ordered a tight security clamp. The hull monitor who found Steen, his brother and others questioned, had been requested to speak to no one, as had been Medical and Security. No one knew—so far. Thomas Steen was officially listed as being confined to his cube for health reasons.

He still had hopes of the entire sorry mess being resolved before the debates really got going. Tonight's show was merely an introduction of the candidates. Both he and Sevaer would sing and dance a little, perhaps take a few pokes at each other, but basically keep things friendly. He would run on his record and she would run over it, a classic political gambit. She would talk about reform and freshness and he would talk about experience and stability. The gloves would come off tomorrow—by then, he would have Geoffrey's ammunition in his pocket.

He was wrong. The gloves came off with the next question.

''Councilwoman Sevaer, what would be your first action as

Administrator should you win the election?''

Sevaer clasped her hands together in her lap. She had a slight nervous twitch in the right one, Demond saw, but she was holding them so that the holocam would not emphasize it.

''There's no question about that, Paul. I would immediately devote all the applicable resources of *Heaven Star* to finding the person or persons responsible for the killing of Arthur Jefferson Stanhope and Thomas Steen. And I'd like to ask the Administrator just what he is doing about it.''

She looked straight at Demond, who was barely able to keep a calm expression for the camera's unforgiving eye. *Damn* her! How had she found out? Someone had talked, but that did not matter now. He was not going to let her get away with this.

He looked over at her, smiled sadly and shook his head, as might an uncle slightly embarrassed by his young niece's *faux pas*. ''Ms. Sevaer, if this is an example of your tact and professional acumen, then I hope, for your sake, that the voters are not as shocked as I am.'' He paused, looking serious. ''I hope you don't seriously expect me to announce, on a shipwide broadcast, the details of our plans to quickly solve this deplorable situation. Such an action would be very foolish—what if the killer were listening? Is this the sledgehammer technique you plan to use in running *Heaven Star*?''

Sevaer did not look angry or upset, he noticed, though he had scored solidly and she had to know it. Straub hurriedly filled the silence with another question. Demond crossed his legs, concentrating on looking as casual and in control as possible. Inwardly, however, he was seething. If she wants a fight, he thought, she'll get one. Right here, right now.

He waited for his turn again, with a sense of excitement he had not felt in years.

''What can I do for you, Chief Gray?''

''I was wondering if you had the results of the Dicran autopsy yet.''

''Certainly. One moment.'' Kyle, standing behind his desk, tapped in a code. He frowned, then repeated the sequence.

''Problem?'' Pyramus asked.

Kyle shook his head. ''Just a momentary glitch. Been getting quite a few of them lately." He looked up at Pyramus and smiled slightly, almost as if at a private joke. "Here it is. Anything in particular?"

"Was she on Zanshin?"

"I'm afraid it's impossible to say for certain. The major compound in Zanshin breaks down rapidly in the body and leaves no trace after a few hours. Unfortunately, the half-life of the other components is several weeks."

"I'm afraid I don't—"

"The woman had used Zanshin before, and was hospitalized recently for treatment of a reaction to it. While traces were found in her CNS tissue and blood, those traces could be from previous usage."

Pyramus considered that. "Can you think of any other reason why she might commit suicide in such a bizarre manner?"

Kyle shrugged. "Depression. Anxiety, perhaps. Though our medical exams are usually thorough enough to spot such things. Have you considered the possibility of murder?"

"*What?!* How?"

"Zanshin can be injected subcutaneously, intramuscularly, or intravenously, though the popular route is orally, in a buffer. Someone who knew the victim was allergic to one of the Zanshin components could have injected her with it, knowing it would likely cause an adverse reaction. Or there are other drugs which might be mixed with Zanshin, which also leave no trace—drugs which might heighten her suggestibility or cause such mental instability that she would die rather than suffer it."

Pyramus felt stunned. "How likely would something like that be?"

"Not very. It would require a fair knowledge of chemistry or medicine and access to the material."

"Why bring it up, then?"

"I'm just pointing out possibilities, Chief."

"Could this possibility be checked?"

"If it was done with an air syringe, it's unlikely. There would be a mild bruise, perhaps, at the injection site. Maybe a concentration of the drug. No marks on the skin, otherwise."

"Did you look for that during your autopsy?" Pyramus had the uncomfortable feeling that he was being toyed with, though Kyle's manner and answers seemed perfectly straight-forward.

"Of course."

"And . . . ?"

"I didn't see any indications of such."

"Well, then—"

"But that doesn't mean it isn't possible. The exposure to the heloid's unfiltered light produced UV burns over much of her skin. Freezing ruptures cellular tissue, in addition to crystalliz-ing and changing many chemical components. It was not an easy autopsy. Do you know what happens to a human body exposed to near absolute vacuum? It's called explosive decom-pression. The body's fourteen-plus pounds of internal pres-sure per square inch hemorrhages internal organs and causes blood vessels to rupture in a matter of minutes. The eyes may literally pop out and dangle from the optic nerves—"

"I don't want to hear it," Pyramus said quietly.

Kyle nodded. His expression was serious, but Pyramus felt again somehow that the doctor was amused, deep within him-self "Sorry. I don't mean to complicate matters. You could just call it a suicide and let it go at that."

Pyramus wanted to scream. Was it possible there had been a *third* murder? "Thank you, Doctor Kyle. I would appreciate a copy of your report."

"Of course, Chief."

Five minutes after Gray had left, Kyle's com beeped. "Doc-tor, Mkono is here for his regular PE."

Kyle stood, stretched, and headed for the exam room. He felt extraordinarily pleased with himself; he felt he had man-aged to confuse the issue of the murder even further. Poor Gray; he didn't have a chance, really. Kyle was ahead of him at every turn. He was enjoying the game, enjoying the exhila-ration of teasing them, testing them, dangling clues in front of their too-dense minds and then snatching them away. A tiny part of his mind cautioned him against going too far, but he was not really worried. The ship was falling apart around them—if they were too stupid to see that, how could they pos-sibly be a threat to him?

Mkono was already in the diagnoster when Kyle entered, his

lower half waiting patiently beside the table. After the usual exchange of mock pleasantries, Kyle began the tests.

He intended to go through them fairly quickly today—he had some private time scheduled at the dojo which he wanted to take advantage of. He looked at the familiar rows of numbers on the screen, half-tempted, for the first time, to assign the routine exam to a nurse—

He blinked at the screen. Mkono's hormone reads were off.

He ran the cycle again, asking for a total breakdown by weight and volume. ACTH, pancreatrophin, somatotrophin, Seinen Complex . . . there it was—a discrepancy in the totals. Kyle tapped the difference back into the computer, along with an identification request.

NO RECORD, the screen said.

Kyle stroked his chin in astonishment. This was impossible; all the hormones, each and every enzyme, in Mkono's body were charted. He requested a breakdown of the discrepancy. The medcomp obediently began to run the molecular-chemical makeup of the unnamed substance. It seemed a little like Seinen Complex, except for what looked like an analog of hGH—but that enzyme chain there did not fit—

Unbelievable. Mkono's body was producing something he had never seen before—a new hormone. He grinned. Kyle's Complex, he would call it.

He ordered a sample taken and saved, then ran through the rest of the exam. No other changes were apparent. He bid the Hub supervisor farewell in a preoccupied manner, already planning the tests he would run on the hormone as soon as he could clear some time on his schedule. He had no doubt that it was another manifestation of the rich and strange changes that were going on in *Heaven Star*. Just as he knew that, somehow, he would find a way to turn it to his benefit.

Geoffrey Merle-Douglass sat alone in his study, feeling a gut-twisting anxiety that was an unwelcome addition to the other aches of his body. Earlier that evening he had found out something Elena suspected about her candidate, something which would deliver Councilwoman Sevaer into Louis's web. If Louis were to find out, and if he could pursue it past the suspicion Elena had.

They had spent a quiet evening reading and talking. He had

questioned her, ever so cautiously, hating himself every time he pretended to sip his wine, knowing that she would unconsciously match him sip for sip. Finally she had said:

"Doubts? About her positions on the issues, no. And not about her desire to break things away from Louis's stolid positions either. But . . . "

He felt a small leap of feral eagerness. "But?"

She sighed. "I think Sharon has some problems in her personal life. A couple of weeks ago she told me she was going to conduct her own investigation into the source of Zanshin. She stressed secrecy; if anybody from Security should ask, I could tell them about her 'operation,' but otherwise I was to keep it to myself."

"That sounds reasonable enough. So what is the problem?"

"You'd have to know Sharon," Elena said. "When she's nervous, her demeanor changes. Her words don't flow quite so well, she moves . . . oddly. Her hands, for instance, twitch."

"Perhaps she was worried about the danger?"

"Perhaps. But it struck me at the time that something was wrong. Later I had a strange call from Pyramus Gray. He asked me about Sharon's investigation. Had she talked to me about it since? How long past had our conversation been? Had she said anything about a party she was attending?"

"Ah. What do you think it all means?"

"I don't know, Geoff. But it worries me. I'm afraid that Sharon's involvement with Zanshin might be much more . . . personal than just an investigation."

"Heavens. You suspect she might be *using* it?"

Elena sighed. "I know she uses the acceptable drugs. She drinks brandy and smokes joystick and I've seen her disappear into a 'fresher and come out looking altogether *too* fresh at times. I think she might be using statocaine. I know that it is socially acceptable, especially among the well-to-do, and I know they've denatured it enough that it's safe. Still, it wouldn't do her any good if it were known. Besides, statocaine isn't what worries me."

"This all could be your imagination, you know." Geoffrey patted her hand. "I shouldn't worry too much about it." He felt the reassurances sticking in his throat, and the churning began in his belly like a thousand demented butterflies trying to escape.

Now he sat in the darkened study, staring at the wall. In the morning he was to meet Louis. If he told him about this, Louis would have his people sniffing out the truth of it in short order.

If only a relatively few people changed their votes because they suspected Sharon of doing something illegal and dangerous, it could swing the election to Louis's side. He would win.

And would I? Geoffrey wondered. *My job and mind would be safe, true.*

But what about my honor?

FOURTEEN

The dolphin slapped the water in the pool with his tail. To this he added a series of barks and hoots too complex for Scott to follow. He tapped in a command on the console, and the recorded barks and hoots came from the speaker while the translation appeared on the screen: *Bring wiggly_____Scott.*

The gap was a word as yet untranslated; sometimes there were more gaps than message. The thrust of this one was plain enough, however; Killikup wanted Scott to bring Eight Ball, the octopus, to the holding pond. *Why* he wanted the creature was beyond Scott. Killikup and the others of his kind had been born on *Heaven Star*, a descendant of genetically-altered dolphins who had spent all their lives under research conditions. He was a freshwater creature, at least eight generations away from any ancestor who had swum in a salt sea. There was no way he could know about octopi, even ones which had been altered for freshwater environs. Yet it was obvious that he did. The procedure by which he had communicated his desire to have Scott produce an octopus was long and slow, but in the end, unmistakable. A hologram of "wiggly" had finally been produced and the response of the dolphin had been *Yes!*

Racial memory was the only answer, which was in itself a

major research avenue for Scott to run down. What might a dolphin know, were he possessed of such? And more, how could man benefit from it?

For a brief time Scott had worried that the cetacean might consider the cephalopod some kind of delicacy—after all, if a saltwater dolphin ate saltwater mollusks, might not a fresh-water alteration desire a freshwater version? But the first time Scott had put Eight Ball into Killikup's tank, the two had simply swum around each other like old friends. Scott had felt a stab of irrational jealousy, as he did when he saw Killikup together with Mara, his mate. The depression which was always hiding just around a corner of his mind came out. *You're in a bad way, St. Martin—hot for a dolphin, and a male dolphin, at that.*

He shook the thought as one might shake water from his hair, and walked to the tank containing the octopus. He stuck his hand into the water and caught one of Eight Ball's tentacles. The creature, its body only slightly bigger than Scott's hand, wrapped its other tentacles around his wrist and forearm. The suckers stuck to his skin. It was an eerie feeling, the touch of something totally alien, yet unmistakably alive. He carried the mollusk to the holding pond, put his arm into the water, and felt Eight Ball release his grip and move away from him toward Killikup.

The mammal nudged the mollusk with his beak, and Eight Ball shot off with a sudden pulse of his siphon, tentacles trailing. Killikup stuck his head above the surface. He rattled and hooted at Scott, then quickly surface dived and was gone.

Scott smiled. The Freedolph expression Killikup had used seemed to be somewhere between "Thank you," "I'm happy," "Hello" and "Good-bye," depending upon the circumstances of its use. This time Scott took the sound as an expression of gratitude. He watched Killikup swim around the neutrally-buoyant Eight Ball in lazy circles; the octopus turned to watch the dolphin, pulsing to maintain its position. Now and again Eight Ball would move its tentacles in what almost seemed a pattern. The underwater cameras were rolling—if there was one the computer would eventually figure it out.

Scott sighed. The dolphin and octopus might continue their current activity for hours; they had done so before. Sometimes he had seen Eight Ball bring a plastic ball for Killikup to play with. He was tempted to watch them for a while, but he had other things to think about. He put on his shirt and started for the temple near Spoke Three. He needed to meditate, to clear his mind. There was a decision he had to make and he wanted to approach it logically and rationally, not emotionally.

The temple was empty when Scott arrived. He sat down on a cushion, pulled his legs into full-lotus and straightened his spine. With the chin-lock, he assumed *zazen*, sitting meditation. He concentrated on following his exhalations, not attempting to control or count them. He wanted to become an empty vessel, clear of all thoughts and desires. . . .

But the thoughts kept coming. He tried to push them gently aside, tried to save them in a little mental box for later, but it was no good.

Bioengineering had called earlier. They had finished the viral/protein chip, and this time it seemed to be clean. It could be implanted anytime Scott was ready. The software was debugged on the control program, the programmers said.

The breathing, concentrate on the breathing—

There would only be a slight chance of failure, and less than a slight chance of organic damage to the implanted animal. Rejection syndrome, the brain rebelling against the new flood of information, shutting down the higher functions. A hundred to one, in the dolphin's case, they said. Much less of a chance in his case. They were pretty good odds.

His left knee began to ache, something which had not bothered him in years. Psychosomatic, he thought; another distraction. It let the thoughts rush in past the breathing.

If everything worked, *if* the operation were a success, then Scott might be able to communicate with a dolphin far more completely than he could now. The VPC was the result of neurocybernetic technology, and this particular construct came from research on Dream Dancing. It would not be true telepathy, but closer to empathy; still, the link could be the most potent yet between humanity and cetacean.

He could link minds with Killikup. Know what Killikup felt, let the dolphin know what he felt, how he . . . loved him.

But there was the risk. A hundred to one—not bad odds, but if that one card came up, it could mean that Killikup would be . . . damaged. That sleek and powerful body would be driven by a mind no longer capable of any thought.

Scott sighed and gave up the pretense of meditating. He opened his eyes. There was a statue of Buddha facing him, seated in an eternal lotus and smiling. The statue was of hollow brass, the fat belly rolling out over the legs. Why fat? he wondered. Siddhartha Gautama had spent most of his life as an itinerant monk, walking all over India with his begging bowl, teaching the middle way. The Four Noble Truths and the Eightfold Path did not encourage sloth or obesity. And all that walking certainly didn't.

Scott sighed. Anything to keep from thinking about his problem. He sat in the quiet temple, feeling more alone than he had ever felt in his life. More than anything he wanted to be able to communicate fully with Killikup. He wanted Killikup to know he loved him—and he wanted to be loved in return. But could he take the risk? Was what he wanted worth the chance of losing Killikup forever? He had crumbs—should he risk losing those in a grab for the whole loaf?

"Christ, Chief, it'll take weeks!"

"I don't really care if it takes months—only it better not, Bill. I want each person checked, and I don't want any mistakes. A lot of the search and call programs are down—we'll have to do it this way."

"We've only got six men on—"

"Then use the maincomp for help, like we did before. The personal code calls still work. The questions are simple language—all they have to do is get the answers and feed them in. Anybody with enough brains to operate a flatscreen should be able to do the job."

Plait shook his head. "Eight hundred and fifteen people. He sounded tired already. "What links them all to the killings?"

"Various things. Those people who were assigned to the Levels where the killings took place are there, as well as everybody who has ever been treated for a violent crime, and all the suspected members of CIRCLE. Plus a few odds and ends I came up with." Pyramus did not have the heart to tell Bill that the number the deputy was so distraught over was likely only the beginning. Each of the people on the list had to be questioned, and each alibi would have to be checked, which meant that many more people would be involved in the questioning. Call it two thousand people—nearly a quarter of the population. And the worst part of it was that the killer might not even be on the list. All they had to go on were possibilities. There could be—probably was—something he was overlooking. The thought was frightening. He would almost prefer to chew vacuum rather than fail at his job.

There was one advantage to being in a tiny closed environment as opposed to a planet: *Nano* had tabs on everyone. All the ship's personnel were listed, and, though an increasing number of the programs were mysteriously going bad, everyone wearing a com patch could still be tracked down via a personal code. Bill and the other deputies could use the com patches to reach most of the people on the list; those who, for whatever reason, chose not to wear them would have to be interviewed personally. But one way or another, everybody would be contacted.

"Be sure the computer does voice-ID on everybody you talk to over the com—I don't want anybody playing games with us. If there's no voiceprint on record, talk to them on visual and save a holo, or talk to them personally and get a print or scan."

Plait looked glum. "I wish I had found something on CIRCLE."

Pyramus also wished he had. Plait had spoken to most of the people who were acknowledged members of the group. There were not many—less than fifty, in fact, though the numbers who agreed with them were perhaps twice that. Most people simply felt, as did Pyramus, that it was not an urgent enough issue to worry about. There was no evidence linking any of CIRCLE with Steen, or, aside from a shared philosophy, with Stanhope. The group's activities had remained low-key through all of this; there had been no more graffiti and only a few leaflets handed out.

"Who's going to follow up on the Zanshin investigation, Chief?"

"I've gotten the Council to authorize a reward of two thousand standards for information leading to the arrest of any Zanshin dealer. *Nano*—ah, the GARTH-7 has built a program to handle the calls. I'll check them out, or pull somebody off the lists to help me if it gets too busy."

"It will be, with two-kay stads at stake."

After Plait left, Pyramus sat at his desk, staring at the picture that his great grandfather had painted. It showed a man standing in a doorway, arms crossed, smiling at the artist. The man was thin and bearded, wearing a dark jacket and shirt, his face and hands stark against the dark fabric. He wore a hat with a design of two stars. There was intelligence in the dark eyes. The picture was titled, "Arlo of the Werewolves." It had been done in one of the southern California gypsy towns in about 2000, when Gitano Gray, the artist, was already an old man. The family story was that Gitano had befriended a genuine shape-changer and been allowed to paint his portrait. It was only a story, one of many that the Romani were so fond of, and Pyramus did not really believe that the man in the painting had turned into a wolf when Earth's moon was full. But there was something in the face, some kind of . . . *power*, centered around the eyes, which gave the visage a slightly demonic appearance. He could visualize what the face would look like with flaring nostrils and long canine fangs. . . .

Pyramus shrugged. He had no time for myths. The person he was looking for might not have sharp teeth and talons, but he or she was no less deadly. He turned back to his desk, feeling a certain kinship with the man called Arlo, understanding what it was like to be very much alone, thinking about things which other people never considered.

Leo Chin sat *seiza* in his cubicle, bare feet crossed, weight resting on his heels. In his hand he held three coins: a Chinese *jin-min-piao*, a Russian *kopek* and an American half-dollar. He tossed them on the floor before him six times, recording the Yin and Yang lines thus formed, keeping the question which concerned him firmly in his mind. Then he consulted his scanner tape of the *I Ching*.

It was the *Sung* hexagram. The judgment read:

Conflict. You are sincere
And are being obstructed.
A cautious halt halfway brings good fortune.
Going through to the end brings misfortune.
It does not further one to cross the great water.

Leo Chin nodded slowly. The face of Anna Vincent, the first woman president of the United States, looked soberly up at him from the half-dollar. He looked across the room, noticing how the light from the window glinted from a *tsuba*, a small brass object, the size of a jar lid, with designs worked into the metal, mounted on a wooden stand. It was the guard of a samurai sword, which had been in Leo's family for over seven hundred years, bought by an ancestor during a trip to Japan. He had been in Japan once, as a boy . . . he blinked and turned his gaze back to the translation of the hexagram on the screen. Then he sighed, stood, and bowed to the wall.

"The ship is almost three decades old, after all, Leo," Louis said. "Some breakdowns have to be expected—"

"Louis, aside from the fact that the instrumentation on *Heaven Star* was designed to last almost two hundred years, that's not what I am talking about. It is the *kinds* of problems we're seeing that has me concerned. Computer glitches which cannot be traced or accounted for, electronic failures where there should be none, test results which simply *cannot* exist in the universe as we know it."

Louis nodded, and Leo felt slightly relieved at the concentration on the man's face. The Administrator might be a political shark, but he was not a stupid man, and not about to dismiss the concerns of a scientist just because he did not understand them—particularly when the safety of the ship might be at stake.

"I read your report, Leo. Do you really think these few anomalous readings spell trouble for us?"

"I wish I could be certain, one way or the other. All I know is that the numbers are starting to vary more. We're dealing with atomic phenomena for the most part in my department. We might be talking about microscopic and chemical problems elsewhere. You heard about that explosion in the monitor section?"

"I recall the report, yes. Some sort of freak accident, they said—"

Leo shook his head. "They didn't know what else to call it. A monitor console blew up. That is *impossible*, Louis, outside of bad old science fiction vids where no one installs circuit breakers in the spaceships. We're talking about charge couple components and liquid crystal displays—the most volatile piece of equipment in the department was the Kava dispenser.

And that is only one of several incidents, all over the ship.''

"All right, suppose somehow things are happening which shouldn't be happening. What can we do about it? What is the cause?''

"I wish I knew, Louis. I only know that things are going wrong. And people are beginning to notice.''

Louis nodded grimly. "I know. Between these—accidents—and the increasing public demand to find the killer before more people die, I haven't been getting much sleep.''

"Neither have a lot of people," Leo said gently.

"I'm doing everything I can to calm things down, of course. I've even requested that Phaedra Adjurian perform a special dream dance. Perhaps that will help.''

"Perhaps." But Leo did not feel optimistic.

"Keep me informed," the Administrator had said. Leo sighed as he walked down the corridor. Of course. A physicist comes in, babbling about strange things happening on the ship, showing as evidence nothing more than a pile of numbers with a lot of zeroes in them. Hardly cause for major alarm. But there was more, of course—proof he could in no way explain. It had to do with his years of training in the martial arts, the sense of *rightness* and *wrongness* one developed from the flow of the Yin and Yang, from the Tao, from Zen. But these were hardly concepts understood by practical administrators. Or by most scientists, for that matter.

There were only a handful of people in the dance class, mostly professionals or die-hard amateurs. Phaedra had finished her work on the barre and was doing a series of slow drop stretches, sliding from a stance on the balls of her feet into a full side split. When her buttocks touched the floor, she leaned forward and stretched her arms out, until her face was close enough to the hardflex surface to smell the dust and sweat it had accumulated. Then she used her hands to push herself back up, bending her knees and bringing them together, before standing for another rep. The first few times the stretch was hard, but it felt good. The last few were physically easier but less satisfying, almost boring.

Staying in shape was the hardest part of a dancer's life—it required a daily routine which could not be avoided. Dancers often hated the workouts, but none worth half a stad would miss one unless he or she was seriously sick or injured. Skipping a week's worth of classes could lose you your edge, and you might never get it back. Even injuries had to be worked around somehow.

Madame Rykov strode into the room and clapped her hands. Now class would start in earnest. An hour and a half added to the forty-five minutes they had already done. Phaedra sighed. One had to pay the price, and its name was practice.

Thirty minutes into the class, just after a complex routine of jazz laybacks and changes, the door opened to reveal a man in the worn coveralls of a line tech. Madame Rykov was not pleased. Phaedra grinned, along with most of the other students, waiting for the feisty instructor to descend upon the interruptor in righteous wrath.

She did not disappoint them. "Out! I am teaching! No one is allowed! Go, shoo!"

The tech did not go. Instead he crossed the floor to Madame Rykov and said something too low for Phaedra to catch.

"Later! Come back in an hour!" The instructor waved her hands in exasperation.

The man said something, again too low for the class to hear. When he stopped talking, Phaedra waited for Madame Rykov's reaction. She had been known to shove people into the hall and then slide the door shut in their faces.

But not this time. Madame Rykov turned away from the tech and faced the class. "Adjurian! Go with this person. You will make up this class by doing two sessions tomorrow."

Phaedra blinked in disbelief. What was this all about?

Nick Daley looked harassed when Phaedra came into the Dance Emporium. "Nicky! What is this all about? I'm hijacked from my class, worried sick—I thought something had happened to Pyramus—"

"Sorry to spring this on you like this, kid, but it came down from top levels. They want you to do a Dream Dance."

"Who does? When?"

"The Council. Now. I talked to Demond myself. You've got about an hour to get ready."

"An *hour*?"

"The Administrator made it very clear, Phaedra. Things are in a bad way on *Heaven Star*. People are wound up like rebound springs, what with the murders and all these weird malfunctions. They figure the best way to calm things down is to blow the tension away with a Dance."

"I don't know if I can get ready in an hour, Nick."

"You have to, or we're under orders to get somebody else."

"Like who?"

"Marlene, or maybe Tomoko."

"Come on, Nicky—Marlene doesn't peak high enough and Tomoko is too young for full-spectrum 'casting."

Nick shrugged uncomfortably. "This is how it is. I don't like it, but it wasn't a suggestion. It was more along the lines of an order."

"They can't *order* you to do that!"

"Maybe not, but they can give me seven kinds of hell if I don't do it. There are other directors who'd love to have my job. Nobody in power has to be nice if they don't want to be. I'm not ready to buck them on this."

"I see. An hour. All right, I'll be ready." But privately, she wondered if she would be. She was supposed to be a release valve for the ship, but she had to be relaxed to do it. This did not feel right. . . .

She stood in the middle of the dance floor, the 'casters glued to her body, waiting for the signal from Nick to trip the auto-hypnotic code which would put her fully into the realm of the Dance. She had tried to relax, to prepare herself for the Dance, but it still did not feel right. She wondered how much of it was her and how much the strange things that had been happening on *Heaven Star*. She remembered that Nick had told her just before her last Dance that nobody ever died on Zanshin. He was wrong—Shanna had.

"Thirty seconds." Nick's voice was small and intimate in her ear. "Give 'em Heaven, kid."

She nodded, pulling herself together, trying to banish the worries, the fears from her mind.

There is nothing but the Dance,
There has never been anything but the Dance.
There will never be anything but the Dance. . . .

Michan was running down the long curving corridors of Level
One, corridors which twisted and pulsated around him like the
peristaltic insides of some monstrous living thing. They tightened about him, squeezing him, crushing him as he struggled
onward, then dipped suddenly, tumbling him down a long,
curving slide. Where was the Dancer? He landed on a floor
that was moist and warm, and which shifted beneath his feet
as he tried to stand. A sphincter-like opening suddenly appeared before him, with a sound like skin being flayed.
Framed in the opening was the Dancer. She spun and leaped
away, her dance urgent, frightened, showing him the way out.
Michan lunged after her, barely squeezing through the opening in time. He breathed a sigh of relief as he realized he was
safe—the walls of this chamber did not undulate or otherwise
threaten him.

The Dancer stood at the other side of the room. But even as
he turned toward her she began to change, her form shifting
before his eyes, metamorphosizing into the corpse of Supervisor Steen, who stood grinning at him with rotting lips. He
moved slowly toward Michan, who backed up against the
smooth metal wall, scratching, pounding the unyielding surface, screaming for help as Steen came closer, decaying flesh
sloughing from his fingers as he reached for Michan, seized
him in a bony grip. . . .

Sean's walker made a grating sound, and then ground to a
stop with a sound of locked machinery. He tensed his muscles
vainly against the activating mechanism, with no response. He
stood there, alone, balanced on two useless chunks of metal
and plastic and electronic gear. He shouted for help, but there
was no answer—not at first. Then he heard a laugh behind
him, and suddenly the Dancer spun into view, eyes full of
malicious humor, dancing in taunting circles about him. She
was cruel life and youth and energy, and he—he . . .

Sean felt a coldness creeping up his body, looked down at

himself, and screamed. He was *changing*—the flesh of his hips and torso were losing sensation, turning into the lifeless plastic and metal of the walker! He reached imploringly toward the Dancer, heard her laugh as his arms changed from living flesh to hard, cold mechanisms, felt the change moving up his neck, cutting off his scream, his hearing, his vision. . . .

Susan heard the alarms, saw dozens of monitor screens, all with the same terrifying figures blinking. The cobalt/rare earth magnets that held the heloid in a containment field were losing power—when they went, the ball of superhot plasma would explode and consume the ship! She leaped toward the master console, but someone seized her and held her back. She twisted around to see—it was Enright, her chief assistant. He was gripping her arms, his features slack and dull, with lifeless eyes. And all about her were the others who worked under her, all with the same lax, mindless countenance. Orbiting them all was the Dancer, striking at the controls at random as she danced, kicking switches, twisting dials, and for each movement another alarm went off. On the monitor screens now, instead of flashing stats, Susan saw Katsu's frightened face, multiplied endlessly, like a hall of mirrors, calling to her, begging for help even as the fireball exploded, vaporizing him and everyone else. . . .

Scott St. Martin stood on the edge of the pool, staring down at the dolphin, feeling at last the true empathic communication made possible by the VPC link. But even as he poured out his feelings of love for Killikup, he could sense the fragile tether beginning to break, could *feel* the dolphin's mind crumbling under some sort of unforeseen neural feedback. He felt the helpless fear and sense of betrayal in Killikup as the dolphin looked up at Scott and realized who was responsible for making him truly an animal. And then he felt a blow from behind, hurling him forward—he had just time enough to turn, to see that it was the Dancer, pirouetting on the concrete lip, who had pushed him. Then the cold shock of the water enveloped him, and he saw Killikup swimming toward him, beak open, the eternal smile now teeth-filled and feral, the once-merry, intelligent eyes now savage, full of bloodlust. . . .

• • •

Ian Kyle ran, hearing the shouts and cries of the torch-bearing mob in pursuit as he stumbled through the tended brush and trees of one of *Heaven Star*'s parks. They knew, all of them —the stupid, witless sheep had somehow figured it out! They knew he was the one who was different, who had dared to be stronger, smarter, *better*. The Dancer led the pursuers, leaping and twisting in an acrobatic frenzy. No matter where he turned, she was there, pointing him out. His camouflage had failed at last.

And now, as he ran, the very trees and the ground itself rose up against him, the earth seizing his legs like quicksand, the trees wrapping their branches about him, scratching him, squeezing the air from him. It was as he knew it would be—the *wrongness* was running rampant, reality itself was twisting, changing, and he could do nothing to stop it. . . .

I am going mad, Geoffrey thought. *I can feel it, feel my mind going, feel myself losing control.* He ran down the halls of knowledge, grabbing books at random from the dusty shelves, but every time he seized one, the Dancer, who followed him, struck the volume from his hands, laughing in glee. If he could only read a few words, feed a few precious crumbs of learning to his starving mind, perhaps he could hold off the onrushing darkness. He pulled a huge tome from a high shelf, and the weight of it overbalanced him; he fell, feeling his ancient bones shatter as he hit the floor. Desperately he opened the book, clawed through the pages. But it was too late—the marks of ink were meaningless to him, hieroglyphics, their secrets locked from him now forever. The pages turned to dust beneath his hands, and he began to sob, his cries sounding more and more like the wails of an idiot. . . .

Pyramus pounded his fists on the airlock door, seeing Phaedra's mocking face as she laughed at him from behind the thick glass port. Then she threw a final switch, and he heard the reverberating sound of the outer lock opening, felt himself hurled, bulletlike, out into the infinite void, felt the numbing cold grip him. He could not even scream. Pain wrenched him as his lungs and his heart exploded within him, and he saw his own blood and urine crystallizing in red and gold clouds about him. . . .

And all over the ship, thousands writhed in their private nightmares, chased by subliminal demons, tortured by electronic shades, devoured by their ids. Until the music crashed discordantly, leaving fear and pounding pulses, and bodies washed in a sea of adrenalin and cold sweat. . . .

Phaedra's eyes snapped open. She sucked in a breath that ended in a sob. *"Pyramus!"* she cried.

Nick Daley's voice hammered at her. "Phaedra? What the hell happened? Every board in the place is jammed—we've got a thousand people calling us!"

"I . . . don't know, Nick—"

Other voices reached her through her com patch, shouts and bewildered questions to each other, to her, to Nick.

"—looks like some sort of full-sensory boost in the R-complex resonance—"

"—dumping mixed beta and delta with T-spikes—"

"—these charge lattice readings in the NE feed are all wrong—"

"Oh *Jesus*, Phaedra," Nick said, stunned. "We had a huge primal fear syndrome pushed through the upper levels! Some kind of low-high turnaround . . . the breakers didn't damp it. . . ."

Phaedra stopped listening. What had she done with her Dance? What had happened?

What had she done?

FIFTEEN

Pyramus kissed Phaedra's bare shoulder while he slid his hand down her flat belly and into the tangle of her dark pubic hair. He felt the tightness of her buttocks against his groin as she pushed back against him. He could also tell she had no real desire at the moment for more sex. They had already made love twice today; in the early hours, just before dawn, and again near noon when she awakened, half an hour ago. But despite her orgasms and the massage he had given her, she was still tense.

"Hey," he whispered.

"Umm?"

"What can I do for you?"

She rolled and faced him. "Nothing more than you've already done, darling."

"Which wasn't enough, apparently; you could still pass for a violin string."

"It'll pass. It's not your fault."

"Nor is it yours, love."

He felt her stiffen slightly. "It was my Dance—"

"Hush. It was an equipment malfunction; didn't have anything to do with you."

She nodded and sighed. "I know that—here." She pointed at her head with her forefinger. "But it's still ripping me apart here." She tapped herself on the stomach just below her navel. "Pyramus, what's *happening* to everything? It's as if something alive has invaded the ship—alive and dangerous—"

Pyramus caught her hand, lifted it to his lips and kissed it gently. "It'll be all right." He wished he knew something less banal to say.

"You didn't hear some of the things the callers said. They felt—betrayed. They *hated* me."

He suppressed a shudder as he recalled the vivid nightmare he had gone through. It had been a traumatic experience for the entire ship; Medical had reported a stock-depleting run on tranquilizers and calmatives afterward. Quite a few people still had not recovered from it; on his way to her cube he had heard sounds of crying from open windows, had passed a young man who sat, rocking slightly and staring into the distance, on a bench. Fortunately there had been no reports of anyone being driven mad or committing suicide as a result. So far.

They had left the com system off; most of the calls had been hysterical demands for reparation. Several times, once while they had been making love, people had pounded angrily on the door, shouting accusations. One had called Phaedra a witch. Pyramus knew that the intensity of feeling would wear off after a while, when it became generally known that the system, rather than the artist, was responsible. But he also knew that it would be a long time, if ever, before Phaedra performed another Dream Dance.

As though reading his mind, she said, "I guess this puts the wrap on my career."

"You don't get out of work that easily. Broadcast is taking full responsibility, after all. Give 'em a week—they'll have forgotten all about it."

"Level Nine, lover. But it doesn't matter. I don't know if I could ever dance again after what happened."

"I'm not listening to that kind of talk," he said, pulling her into an embrace. "You're a Dancer—it's what you do. Everything will be all right."

She sighed, and seemed to collapse slightly in his arms, snuggling close to his chest. "Really?" Her voice was muffled against his chest, her tone that of a frightened child's.

"Trust me. I'm a cop."

She said no more, and he held her, stroking her hair, trying to believe himself what he was telling her. But he could not shake the feeling that something was wrong, terribly wrong, that an unknown and destructive force had entered his closed, cozy little world. But that was not what frightened him most; instead, it was the fact that once again, that empathic intimacy which linked them so firmly had been somehow broken. Pyramus felt only her flesh against his—she was closed to him again, locked inside her body, and no matter how tightly he held her, he could not bridge that gulf.

A twenty-minute shower was scheduled for 1300. Susan had packed the picnic gear to keep it dry, but they were not leaving the park. Katsu wanted to play in the "rain." The simulated storms were always fun to watch; the water came from concealed sprinklers in the "sky" above, and subtle, computer-controlled lighting effects and tapes produced a decent imitation of clouds and thunder. Susan had read the engineering specs once on the water and nutrient systems under the park. The buried pipes could feed the plant life much easier by underground seepage without the evaporation loss incurred by the storm—though the "rain" would be recovered, eventually. But the idea of occasional bouts of "bad weather" had appealed to the ship's designers. The storms were never unexpected if one bothered to read the park schedule.

Michan lay on his back beneath the umbrella they had opened, his eyes closed, his fingers interlaced behind his head. His arofloj was in its case, next to his leg. Susan sat next to him, watching Katsu play in the grass nearby.

"Michan? Would you do something for me?"

He opened one eye. "Anything."

"Would you play for me?"

He sat up, crossing his legs, and picked at the grass by his feet, stroking the blades, not harming them. "Here?"

"Please? After last night, I—need it."

He hesitated, then nodded. They had both awakened from the Nightmare Dance, as people were beginning to call it, huddled in her cube, stunned by the savage psychic assault. Like most others who had tuned in, they had remained in a daze, slowly recovering. Katsu had been a great help to them both. He had not been subjected to the horrible visions, and it had been soothing to them to watch him pursuing his various interests and enjoyments with the intensity that only a child can muster. They had taken him to the park and spent most of the day on a picnic.

"All right." He reached for the plastic case, picked it up and removed the musical instrument from its padded nest. Susan watched him carefully. She knew he did not like to play in public; she had tried to tell him he had a gift that should be shared, but he still seemed uncomfortable with the idea. Susan wondered why she was asking him to do it. The comfort she would derive from the music was only part of the reason, she knew. What else was it? The answer came to her as she watched Michan assemble the arofloj. She was testing him—trying to find out if he truly cared for her, as he said he did. His feelings for Katsu were apparent enough, but she still felt uncertain about his love for her.

He finished with the construction of the arofloj. He smiled at her, then raised the instrument to his lips, blew a few tentative notes and made some adjustments. "Anything in particular?"

"The day you met Katsu here—that piece."

He hesitated again, then took a deep breath and began to play Pachelbel's *Canon in D*, building the music up in layers as he had before. The volume was low, but it carried. After a moment Katsu came running from his play and slid to a stop on the grass beside them, staining the knees of his synlin pants.

There were a few other people in the park, and some of them began to drift toward where Michan, Susan and Katsu sat, seeking the source of the quiet and powerful music. In a few minutes a dozen or so people had gathered, all sitting or standing quietly, listening. Some smiled, others looked serious, some seemed to sway in time with the simple rhythm as it repeated and varied slightly with each new cycle.

Susan listened to the music, let it lift her and carry her where it would. She remembered a morning twelve years past, the morning of her fifteenth birthday. She had not had a party—there had never been birthday parties in her family—but they had all been there at breakfast, itself something of a rare occasion. Hayaku, who was nineteen, Saijitsu, only twelve, and her parents: Daisetz, her father, an astronomer and her mother, Katai, a mathematician. The two of them had given her a present: A technical reference ball entitled *Amplified Theories of Electromagnetics*. Heavy reading for a teenager, but not unexpected. She was at the top of her class, after all. She would be a scientist or a technician; it had all been planned. And so she had, as had both her brothers.

On that morning her father had told her, "Learn this work well and you will see the beauty of science." He tapped the little metal marble with one fingernail. "Science is pure. The stars do not care for anger or jealousy or love; numbers follow only logic and not whim. Upon these things you may always depend—they will not change and let you down." He had looked at Susan's mother then, and something had passed between them, something Susan did not understand until years later, when her mother told her of a love affair she had had with a young man from her department. Her father had discovered it. He did not approve of extramarital affairs, and he resented Katai's interest in another man. The fact was, her mother had told Susan, that her father had little interest in sex or love. Yet he wanted her to be faithful, without giving her anything to be faithful to. It was wrong to clamp down on emotions that way, her mother had said. But by that time Susan's own discomfort with people and emotions had been well-established.

She felt tears on her cheeks, and wiped them away quickly.

The light grew dimmer, grayer, as the window strips above them began to filter the heloid's light. With a low rumble of thunder, the rain began. Michan was sitting beyond the umbrella's protection, playing with his eyes shut—he blinked, and looked somewhat startled at the people surrounding him. But the music continued.

"Will the water hurt the arofloj?" Susan asked. He shook his head and kept playing.

"Shhh, Mother," Katsu said. Susan looked at her child, whose attentive features looked very much like an adult's at the moment. It made her want to grab him and hug him. How could he be growing up so fast?

The rain fell softly upon the gathering. Susan felt the cool drops running down her neck and arms; she watched the water gather in Michan's hair, saw him blink it away, then close his eyes again, continuing the music. A couple strolled up the path in the rain, arm-in-arm, and stood at the perimeter of the group. They looked familiar. Then Susan placed them, and felt a cold lead band tighten in her gut. The man was Pyramus Gray, Chief of Security, and the woman—the woman was Phaedra Adjurian, the Dancer.

Several others recognized them also. Susan could see the Dancer's tight, wan features, saw Gray's arm locked protectively about her waist. Many went pale at the sight of her, and a few left, hurrying quickly down the path or through the trees. Susan felt her heart beating faster; in her mind's eye, vividly, she saw the demonic face of the Dancer as she methodically destroyed the containment controls and caused *Heaven Star* to be consumed in an inferno. . . .

Susan took a deep breath and forced her eyes to focus on the grim, frightened face of Phaedra Adjurian. It was not her fault, she knew; Broadcast had issued a statement immediately following the debacle blaming faulty equipment for the Nightmare Dance. She concentrated on Michan's music, letting it flow over her, letting it wash away the remnants of the terror she had felt last night. She could see others in the crowd attempting to do the same.

As the rain ended, the music ended, trailing off in layers as it had begun. When Michan finished, the crowd applauded. He flushed and looked at Susan, as though asking, *Should I continue? I will, for you.*

She shook her head a few millimeters. *No, Michan—you've proved enough.*

Michan laid the instrument on the wet grass next to the closed case. He looked at the people. "Thank you for listening," he said.

The crowd began to drift apart and away. Michan saw the last couple still standing there. He did not seem surprised. "Pyramus. Phaedra."

"You play well," Phaedra said. In the rain, Susan could not tell if there were tears on her cheeks or not, but her voice suggested there were.

Michan smiled. "Better than I fly, that's for sure." He looked at Susan. "This is the lady who kept me from the wall that day. Susan Hanawashi, Pyramus Gray and Phaedra Adjurian. And this is Katsu Hanawashi, who is learning to play the arofloj."

Gray nodded. He looked at Phaedra, obviously concerned about her. The Dancer smiled at him. "I'm fine," she said, in answer to his unspoken question. Then, to Susan and Michan,

"I wanted to get out, to—see how bad it was. I'm glad we heard you play. It helped."

Michan smiled and nodded. He seemed extraordinarily at peace, Susan thought, looking at him. His calm flowed from him as his music had, affecting them all.

All except Katsu; the boy jumped to his feet, looking once more like an enthusiastic eight-year-old. "It was very nice to meet you," he said to Pyramus and Phaedra. Then, to Susan, "May I go play again?"

Susan smiled. "Sure." They watched her son run off. Phaedra and Pyramus sat down on the wet grass. Michan grinned as he looked at Pyramus's feet. "What's the matter, Chief, don't they pay you well enough to buy new shoes?" Susan noted that the security man's footgear had definitely seen better days.

Pyramus glanced at them and chuckled. "I hate to admit it, but I guess it is time to recycle them."

"Ship can use the polyurethane," Susan said.

The smile on Pyramus's face froze, then slowly slipped away. "Polyurethane," he said softly, almost to himself.

It was not a question, and she did not quite know how to deal with the word as a statement. "Sure. They're probably ninety percent elastomers." She looked at him in slight confusion. He had gone . . . blank, as if he were listening to something nobody else could hear.

Phaedra held Pyramus's arm and looked at his face with a small kind of fear. But after a few seconds Pyramus was back from wherever it was he had been. He still looked quite disturbed, however.

Small tendrils of vapor were rising from the ground as the water evaporated. Susan felt good, despite her drenched clothes. Michan reached for and held her hand. His gaze caught hers and, for a moment, she forgot where they were and that they were not alone. Then Katsu slid up to them on the seat of his pants in a spray of water and grass stems. "Can we come back next time it rains?"

Susan turned to answer, then realized that Katsu was asking Michan. She felt a small stab of irritation, but it vanished when Michan spoke. "Anytime your mother says it's all right, Kat."

"We've got to go," Pyramus said. His tone was courteous, but he seemed suddenly edgy, anxious. "Nice to have met you,

Susan. Maybe we can get together sometime for dinner.''

As Pyramus and Phaedra left, Michan put his arm around Susan. He was as drenched as she was, but at that moment his arm was the most comfortable thing in the world.

"I'm glad we went out," Phaedra said. "I think you're right, Pyramus. I think I'll be able to dance again.''

"Good," he murmured. She looked at him, realizing immediately that something was troubling him. "What is it?''

"They were kicked to death.''

"What? You mean—''

"I mean Stanhope and Steen. I know it.''

"How do you—oh.''

He turned to her. "I'll walk you back to your cube, but then I've got to go. There's one person on this ship I can think of who'd know how to kick someone in the head hard enough to kill—Leo Chin.''

Phaedra looked shocked. "You don't think *Leo*—''

"I don't know what to think any more. But I've got to go talk to Leo.'' He took her hand and started down the path, but she pulled free of his grasp. "No, go on," she said. "I'll be fine.''

He hesitated, and she knew why; she felt the wall between them again also. She knew he would not speak of it, and neither would she, and that made it all the stronger.

His gaze searched her face, but she could tell he did not really want to probe. She did not blame him. He had too much on his mind—it was that simple. Their relationship had to take a back seat. It was the first time it had happened—and why, she wondered, did it not hurt?

"You're sure—?'' he said, asking for benediction. She smiled, a mere movement of facial muscles, and patted his arm. "Yes. I'm not sure if it was Michan's music, or just seeing that other people are still alive and sane, but I'm all right now. Go find Leo—that's more important.''

He pulled her to him and they kissed. She wondered if it felt as empty to him as it did to her. Then he turned and jogged away down the path.

Phaedra watched him until he was out of sight. Then she turned, looking back toward the cluster of dwellings where she lived. It would be some time, she knew, before the animosity and distrust engendered by the Nightmare Dance faded. But it would end eventually; and in the meantime, she would still dance. She would stay in practice, mentally and physically. Whatever was happening on *Heaven Star* she would face, she told herself, as long as she could still dance.

She hoped it was true. But she felt unaccountably clumsy and brittle, as though all her hard-won talent and fitness had been leached from her, as she started back toward her cube.

SIXTEEN

Leo Chin looked at the holographs of the two dead men. Pyramus watched him. The physicist seemed somewhat edgy.

"Would you say the person who killed them knew what he or she was doing?" Pyramus asked. "That it was not an accidental blow?"

Leo nodded gravely. "It was done by someone with a knowledge of anatomy and fighting. The temple is very vulnerable to a trained strike; it is one of the death-blows in martial arts."

"How much would somebody have to know to use such a strike?"

"Someone with two years or more of training—a brown sash or higher—would know the technique."

"How was this done? With a gloved fist?"

The older man shook his head. "No. Not with a fist."

Pyramus stared at Leo. Something was going on here, but he did not know what. Chin was not being evasive, but he was . . . tight, somehow. The physicist could not have committed the murders himself; Pyramus had checked his alibis and found them valid. Nor could Pyramus believe such a thing of

Leo. What, then, was this all about?

"I'm not trying to indicate that one of your students may be responsible, but—how many of them would you say might be capable of this kind of damage?"

Leo sighed and rubbed his eyes. "In twenty-five years of teaching, I've had perhaps three or four hundred reach the rank of brown sash, with a quarter of that many going on to black. But any student could learn enough to kill someone in a few weeks."

"You're saying there could be . . . ?"

"Hundreds. Any one of hundreds could have done such as this."

Pyramus thought he heard an emphasis on the words "could have," but he was not sure. Leo's statement was like cold water thrown in his face. *Hundreds*. Hundreds more to investigate. How to do it, how to even start, before the killer struck again?

After Pyramus had left, Leo sat with his face in his hands. Though his eyes were closed, he could still see the holographs showing the crushed skulls of the dead men. He felt old, full of the sudden realization of how much of his life had gone by, beset with the knowledge that he had spent so much of it making mistakes.

He had lied to Pyramus. He had known as soon as he had seen the holos. He had told the Security Chief that many could have been responsible for the injuries, had even hinted that someone with no formal training at all could have caused such. Lies. Lies of omission, but lies nonetheless. Only a few could kill that way in this tiny world—and only one had done it.

Doctor Ian Kyle. One of Leo's top students, and one of his gravest mistakes. Ian Kyle had killed both men. And Leo knew that it was his fault; he should have seen what Kyle was a long time before he had taught him enough to kill. But he had not wanted to see anything wrong with his student. Long ago he had allowed his caring for the boy, his joy at the lad's aptitude, to get in the way of his true sight. And later, what he had seen was not Ian as he really was, but an idealized picture of the boy at eighteen. When had he changed? Or had he really changed at all? Maybe Ian Kyle had always been the man he was now, only Leo had refused to know it. And that blindness had cost the lives of two people.

It would have been simple to tell Pyramus Gray that the technique which had killed two men was the favorite attack of Ian's. But that was not the way to rectify his error. There was only one thing he could do, one way of honor left to him. He would go to Ian and bring him to face justice. If Ian should choose to resist, then Leo would have to contain him. It would be another failure, should it come to that, on his part and on Ian's, but it was the way it had to be done. And it had to be done before Ian found another victim.

Leo went to the dojo to prepare himself.

Ian looked startled when Leo arrived at his office. Something must have shown on Leo's face, for the younger man touched his com and ordered all calls and patients cycled until further word.

"What is it, Leo?"

Leo Chin regarded his student. Never had he used the honorifics: "Sensei" or "Sifu," as the other students did. It was always "Leo," or "Old Man," in his affectionate—or pretended affectionate—moments. But never "teacher."

Ian stood behind his desk, his gaze locked with Leo's. Then, after perhaps thirty seconds of silence, he nodded. "So. You know."

"Yes."

"How?"

"Pyramus Gray showed me holographs of the dead men. I recognized the technique."

"I see. I should have considered that possibility." He looked pensive. "And you told Gray I was responsible?"

"No."

"Ah."

Leo watched the other man carefully, searching for some sign of remorse, some indication of fear or worry. But Ian looked like a man considering what to order for lunch.

"Why, Ian?" Leo said finally.

"Why? It doesn't matter why, Leo. You should know that. You know what is happening on the ship, *to* the ship, even though you refuse to admit it."

Leo nodded. "I know. But how does that—"

"You know, but you don't understand." His voice went up a notch. "I've kept control for all these years, but it won't work any longer. Don't you see, Leo? It isn't just me. It's *everything!*" As he spoke, his hands balled into fists. The muscles of his neck and shoulders tightened.

"It is never all right to misuse your knowledge, Ian. Never all right to kill—"

"It's your fault, Leo! You refused to teach me the secrets. You kept things I needed to know from me, you crippled my skills by hiding techniques, medicines, things I should have gotten."

Leo watched his student with a dawning horror. Ian was mad, he realized. His brilliant mind had slipped over the edge dividing genius and insanity. How long had it been balanced there, awaiting some kind of push? And was the strangeness, were the increasing inexplicable changes, somehow responsible?

"Ian . . ."

"*No*, Leo! I'm not going to trot over to Security with you. That is what you came for, I know. You subscribe to the Frankenstein concept, don't you? 'I created it, so I must destroy it.' I'm your personal monster, aren't I, Leo?"

Leo could feel the energy gathering to oppose him, felt the madness within Ian coming to a boil seeking release. The old man settled himself imperceptibly, muscles relaxed and yet solid, ready for an attack. Then, abruptly, the door slid open behind him. Ian looked past Leo. "Toshi, I *told* you no interruptions—"

Leo did not take his eyes off of Kyle, but part of his awareness shifted, to sense if someone was in fact behind him, someone who might be hurt. Even as he realized it was a trick, that Ian, his hands below the level of the desk, had activated the door, in the instant that his concentration was not total, Ian grabbed the edge of his desk with both hands and straightened. He threw the desk at Leo, jerking the unit half a meter off the floor, the computer console flying off, flatscreen and light pens scattering.

Leo had been expecting an attack, but not like this. He shifted to his left quickly, dropping his weight low for balance, using the economical pushing steps of a kung fu expert.

The desk hit the floor and skidded, missing him by centimeters. Ian was right behind it, jumping over the still tumbling console and the corner of the desk. He hit the closing thin plastic doors, tearing through them, smashing one from its track.

Leo leaped after him. As he cleared the ruined doorway he saw Ian grab his assistant by the hair and jerk her behind him. The woman stumbled and fell, blocking Leo's pursuit. Ian was through the outer doors of the office before Leo could reach him. He would never catch him on foot, he knew. He turned back to help the paramed to her feet.

"What's happening?" Toshi demanded in shock and bewilderment.

Leo did not answer. He looked at the empty corridor beyond the office. Ian was right, he thought. He had created the problem; he would have to take care of it.

Katsu was asleep in his room. Michan sat next to Susan on the couch, his arm draped over her shoulders. They were watching a political debate between Louis Demond and Sharon Sevaer. The faces of the candidates were animated as they expounded their differing philosophies, but Michan was not paying much attention.

"Are you really interested in this?" he asked Susan.

Susan shrugged. "Not that much. What did you have in mind?"

Michan took a breath and let it out slowly. "Talk?"

She raised an eyebrow. "I must be losing my appeal." But she thumbed the holoproj's remote control. The picture stayed on. Susan frowned and tapped the control a bit harder. The holoproj suddenly skipped around several channels, flashing dizzying 3-D simulacra of faces, locales and abstract images before it vanished. "It's never done that before. Maybe I ought to take it apart and see what's wrong." She put the control back onto the table and looked at Michan. "Okay, let's talk."

Michan swallowed dryness. "I want to talk about us, Susie."

Her smile slipped away slowly. "Us?"

"I—that is, we . . . " Michan shook his head. "*Damn*, this

is hard for me. I don't want to put you in an awkward position, but I have to say it. Susan, I love you."

She closed her eyes, and for a frightened moment he thought he had hurt her. Then she looked at him. "Thank you, Michan. I'm not sure I know what love really is, but if I know anything about it, then I love you, too."

Michan blew out a big breath. "Buddha! Why haven't you said that before?"

"Why haven't you?"

"Fair enough." He hugged her, then held her away from him. "Because I was afraid."

"Of what?"

"I don't know, exactly. That you might laugh. That you wouldn't feel anything like that for me."

She touched his face with the tips of her fingers. "You thought I would laugh at you?" There was reproach in her tone.

"Well, not really, but I was scared. Susie, I'm good at what I do Outside. But in here, with somebody I care about, I'm Joe Fuckup. I didn't want to risk losing you."

She leaned her head against his chest. "Good. Because I don't want to lose you, either."

You've gotten this far—now go for the rest of it, Michan thought. He kissed the thick blackness of her hair. "My cube isn't very big," he said. "But I could apply for a larger one."

She moved back slightly to look at him. "Why would you want to—oh." She put her hand to her face. "Boy, am I stupid."

"No, you're not."

She shook her head. "Yes, I am, in matters like this. We're a fine fumbling pair, aren't we?"

"Move in with me, you and Katsu. Live with me—we can contract legally or not, whatever you want. I just . . . want you around." He almost said "need" instead of want, but that was too hard, even now.

"No."

Michan's guts went into free-fall. But before he could speak, she continued: "There's no point in that—my cube is bigger than yours. There's enough room for three. Will you live here, with us?"

Gravity returned to Michan's insides. He hugged her to

him, hard. "Unh!" she groaned. "Easy!"

"I can have my stuff here tomorrow, if you're serious."

"Of course I'm serious, idiot!"

"Um. One thing, though. I have to tell you about the family skeleton. I had an infamous great-grandfather, Ilusha Bernodov. . . . "

"I didn't know you came from Russian stock."

He stopped, looked surprised, then smiled. "I don't talk about myself very much, do I? Yeah—my father's family was Russian, mother's was Hungarian. They trimmed the name when they migrated to the Belt. Anyway, old Ilusha sort of blew up a nuclear plant." He grinned at her incredulous look. "He worked at a storage depot next to a plutonium plant, and was exposed to some radiation which damaged him pretty heavily. So to get back at them, he bombed the place."

"You aren't making this up?"

"May I blow a hose. Nobody was hurt, but it scared the hell out of people. Caused them to launch a big investigation, which in the end did a lot of good. But he's our black sheep. They even named the radiation disease after him, Bern's Neuropathy, since he was the first one discovered with the symptoms."

"What happened to him?"

Michan grinned. "He died in bed at eighty-nine."

"You *are* making this up."

"No, I swear. They never found a cure for the disease, but they did eventually figure out how to treat it. Part of the treatment involved male hormones, so the old boy stayed active until he died. Sort of came and went at the same time." They both laughed.

"Well, it looks as if you've been taking treatments for it too. But I guess I can stand it."

"Thanks. I love you too. And you know what? It's easier to say the second time."

Susan leaned forward and kissed him. "You may practice it all you want," she said. "I won't mind at all."

Phaedra thumbed the control on the holomirror, but, outside of a momentary flicker, saw only darkness. *It is showing me my soul,* she thought, both chilled and faintly amused by the melodramatic thought.

She hardly ventured from her cube since they had listened to Michan's music, nor had she seen Pyramus since then. She had answered no calls, including his, though he had tried to reach her several times. He had not come by, however. That was painful. *Fool,* she called herself. *He has a job to do. A small matter of a murderer loose on board—or have you forgotten?* But her rationalizations did not ease the pain.

I could go to his place. But, though she was lonely and desperately unhappy, still she was unwilling to leave her cube. This was not like Pyramus's agoraphobia—rather, it had to do with a sense of waiting—for what, she was not sure.

Scott St. Martin had made his decision. In an odd way, he owed it to the Dancer; the horrible nightmare he had had the night the equipment malfunctioned had convinced him. He could not risk Killikup's mind in such an experiment, no matter what the potential results. But perhaps there was another way.

He had heard about the drug Zanshin, how it supposedly carried the mind beyond the usual psychedelic experience, how those who had taken it could actually communicate telepathically. So far, he had found no researchers to swear that this was the case. But not much investigation had been made into that area; most of the tests concerned themselves with finding a cure to the side effects. And he had been assured that only humans ran a risk of the shakes when taking Zanshin. He could give the drug to Killikup with no physiological risks.

As for himself, there was risk, of course. But he was willing to take it. His only problem now lay in obtaining some of the drug. It was very hard to come by—it seemed to be mostly in the control of the members of CIRCLE, and they guarded it jealously.

He had overheard one member of the bio lab, a man named Lars Strogwall, speaking to someone else about a CIRCLE meeting. He had approached the man, but Strogwall had simply denied any knowledge of the group. Scott must have been mistaken.

Scott knew he had not been mistaken. He had followed Strogwall that evening, and now he stood outside the door of a cube near Spoke One. He could hear low voices inside. He wondered what his next move should be; he could hardly

knock on the door and ask for the drug like a neighbor bor-
rowing a cup of flour.

He heard steps approaching the door, and stepped back
quickly into the concealment of some shrubbery. The door slid
open, and a young woman looked out. Her face was familiar
to Scott, and after a moment he placed her—Sharon Sevaer,
the Councilwoman! Scott blinked in surprise. He wondered
how many people knew that the person running for Administrator was also a member of CIRCLE. He also wondered
how she had known someone was outside.

She reentered the cube. Scott crouched in the bushes, waiting. Sooner or later the meeting would break up. Then, perhaps, he could follow some of the others, and learn where they
lived, or wait until this cube was empty and search it. People
did not usually lock their doors on *Heaven Star*, though many
had started to with a murderer on the loose. Somehow, Scott
would find what he was looking for: two capsules of Zanshin.

You're crazy, he told himself. *If you're caught, you could
lose your standing, maybe wind up in Rehab—and for what?
A mad attempt to link minds with a specimen of* Tursiops
truncati! *Even if it works, what do you expect to get from it?
A meaningful relationship?* He thought of the punchline of an
old joke: "Even if I loved you, my parents would never let me
marry a kangaroo." *Funny, St. Martin. You're a laugh riot.*
But he did not move. He was committed to his course. After
all, if it worked, it would mean a scientific breakthrough. And
it would mean much more than that—for him.

It was dark in the empty water tank. Kyle could have had
light, but he wanted the dark at the moment; it matched his
mood. The tank had been prepared for weeks, because a prudent man planned for everything, even disaster. There was no
excuse for less. Things had not gone the way he had planned,
but it did not matter. He had discarded his com patch, left no
way for him to be traced. He would survive—long enough.

He regretted some things. Mkono was one. He had wanted
to lick that problem, to force the unwilling flesh to grow legs.
Those new readings had been most interesting. But it was too
late to study them now.

And the woman, Hanawashi—he should not have waited to

take care of her. The old man he would deal with, somehow, but even with him gone, the woman would still know.

After a little while, of course, it wouldn't matter. Nothing would matter.

Still, he did not like to leave matters unfinished. His honor was at stake, after all. He would find Hanawashi. And he would set himself free, one final time.

SEVENTEEN

Pyramus shuffled through the papers on his desk. Number of students holding the black sash in Leo's kung fu style: seventy-eight. Number of those who had already been checked and shown to be elsewhere during the murders: twenty-four. That left fifty-four. Of those, he checked the ones currently considered inactive practitioners of the fighting arts, due to illness or age. Five were over sixty—that did not discount them, of course, but four of those had not worked at it for some years, according to records and interviews, so it made them less likely. Three of the black sashes were under age fifteen, and while they had not been eliminated as suspects yet, Pyramus suspected they would be shortly, since children's movements were generally easier to trace, having parents and teachers to account to.

That left forty-six. Of that number, twenty-one were women, twenty-five men. There was no way to eliminate anyone else immediately.

Pyramus scanned the list. He recognized many of the names; with a shipboard population of less than nine thousand, it would have been strange if he had not. None of the names leaped out at him. He scanned the reduced list into the terminal and coded it, then called Bill Plait on his com.

"Bill, I want you to pull a file from the computer, code 'Suspect List,' and concentrate all your men on it. I want the prime forty-six names checked within the hour, the rest of the names by shift-end. Skip everything else until you get it done. And be careful. I think one of them is our killer."

"Copy, Chief."

Pyramus was still staring at the sheet when his com came back to life.

"Chief? I can't get it."

"Can't?"

"The computer says there's no such file."

Pyramus put him on hold and spoke a command to the terminal.

NO RECORD OF REQUESTED FILE, the screen said.

"Damn." Pyramus repeated his earlier scanfeed. "Try it again, Bill."

There was a short pause. "Negative, Chief."

Pyramus whacked the side of his terminal with his fist. "Where are you now, Bill?"

"By the bank near Four."

"Get to their printer and call me back."

Pyramus drummed his fingers on the edge of his desk. Just what he needed on top of everything else, mechanical trouble.

"I'm at the printer, Chief."

"Stand by." Pyramus put his terminal on mail function and ran the file into the printer at the bank.

"It's coming through."

"Good. Get moving on it, Bill. Out." He then called *Nano*. "Hello, *Chavo*."

"*Nano*, would you check out my office terminal?"

"What's the matter, *Posh-rat*, can't hit the right keys?"

Pyramus's jaw dropped in astonishment. *Nano* had never used that sneering tone to him before, and he had certainly never referred to him as a half-breed. Before he could say anything in response, the speaker on his desk began rattling off a series of disconnected words, fragments and incomprehensible gibberish, spoken in a variety of voices. Pyramus slumped back in his chair. God, the computer had slipped a loop. As he sat there, wondering what to do next, the word salad ceased abruptly, and then the voice Pyramus was used to hearing spoke again.

"Good morning, Pyramus. What can I do for you today?"

"*Nano?*" Pyramus asked uncertainly.

"Of course. Can I help you, nephew?"

"My terminal seems to be malfunctioning. And you . . . " He hesitated.

"Yes, boy? What is it?"

"You were . . . acting strangely a moment ago."

The GARTH-7 chuckled. "*Dordi, dordi* . . . you must be daydreaming again, Pyramus." There was a pause. "Your terminal seems fine to me."

"Uh, well, okay. Thanks."

"Any time, nephew."

Pyramus shivered. He had no doubt that he had heard what he had heard. Though the connection with the maincomp was now broken, he could still somehow feel a *presence* in the room. He decided to call Computer Operations to report the malfunction. He started to speak into his com patch, then stopped. It was foolish, he knew, but somehow he could not bring himself to place a call through the maincomp's network just now. Perhaps he would tell them in person, instead. After all, he had not gone jogging in several days. He had to keep in shape, especially considering the stress he was under.

Louis Demond's cube was as sparsely furnished as his office; the dichotomy between the spartan quarters and Demond's preference for fine clothes and food had always surprised Geoffrey. Louis sat in a chair of chrome tubing and canvas with his legs crossed, smiling at the older man.

"Geoffrey, old friend. How are you?"

"Not good, Louis. I don't like being here and I don't care for what I'm doing."

Demond shook his head. "Look at it this way. Do you really think Sharon Sevaer is better qualified to Chair the Council than I am?"

"Until recently, I never considered it possible."

"Ah. But now, since I've put you in an . . . awkward position, you think all my years of skill and practice are worthless."

"I didn't say that, Louis."

Demond stood and walked to a cabinet, pushed a button

and watched the cabinet open into a bar. He removed two brandy snifters, poured two fingers of brandy into each, and held one toward Geoffrey, who accepted it but did not drink from it.

"You don't like my methods." Demond sipped his liqueur. "Even though you know I am better for the position than that young and impetuous woman; even though you know I am more capable than anyone on the ship."

"I cannot say I am a believer in the end justifying the means."

"Horseshit, Geoffrey! A hundred people died during the testing of cancer vaccines in the late 1990s. Were their deaths worth it, when the result was prevention of what was then the number one killer disease? You know it was."

"That's hardly the case here—"

"True. But it illustrates my point. The happiness and lives of all the people in our world will be affected by this election. I *know* I need to be at the administrative helm of *Heaven Star*. My opponent isn't playing fair; she is distorting truth to her advantage, dancing around the edge of slander, trying to make it appear I am less than concerned with the people of the ship. Do you believe that—even now?"

Geoffrey stared into his brandy. "No," he said quietly. "I know you want the best for the ship. I've always believed that."

Demond smiled. "You're right—it's the truth, and always has been. And there isn't much I wouldn't do to stay in a position where I know I am most useful. I'm sorry, Geoffrey, more so than you can imagine, but if I had to blackmail my own mother, I would do it."

Geoffrey nodded. He gripped the snifter tightly and swirled the amber liquid. Then, abruptly, he raised the glass to his lips and drained it.

Demond said nothing. He waited. His gaze had the patience and warmth of a glacier.

Geoffrey took a deep breath. "She very probably uses Zanshin. People close to her would know for certain. Elena is fairly sure of it." The brandy, good as it was, burned his throat and stomach. He felt nauseated.

Demond nodded contemplatively. "I can have my people dig, now that they know what they're looking for."

"Louis, no one must know where you heard this."

Demond waved his hand, dismissing the thought. "Don't worry—"

"I am serious." Geoffrey raised himself up to his full, still-impressive height. "If Elena ever learns that I told you this, it would destroy what we have. She would never be able to trust me again."

"I've already forgotten where I heard it," Demond told him. "It is between us, old friend."

"Don't use that term in reference to me again. And, Louis—if you ever think to use this as leverage against me, be warned. If I lose Elena, I will not be a very happy man."

Demond looked surprised. "What exactly does that mean?"

"It means exactly this: If Elena finds out that I told you this, I will kill you, Louis." Geoffrey turned and left the cube.

After the archivist had gone, Louis smiled into his second serving of fine brandy.

It was too bad about having to use old Geoffrey so—well, ruthlessly was the only term. In time, he would see the wisdom of it, but that silly threat made Louis uneasy. Geoffrey had sounded so very serious. Perhaps he had better make certain that the recording he had made of the conversation stayed in a safe place. He would code it into the computer under a secret designation and wipe the original clean.

And in a couple of days, Councilwoman Sevaer's . . . indiscretions would be all over the ship. He chuckled. The election was as good as his.

The fluid sculpture seemed to vibrate suddenly, then collapsed, the liquids spreading into a thin film on the bottom of the cage. Sean, floating beside it, stared in disbelief. That was impossible—there was no gravity, no force he could think of, that could cause such a malfunction. He checked the memory —though he had saved the holoprogram recently, the system refused to reassemble it. He groaned and started over. Whatever the reason for the malfunction, it had just cost him four hours' work. . . .

•   •   •

Michan Bern's communicator went dead in the middle of an order from Dooley. "Shit!" His annoyance grew when he found that his jets refused to respond also. The overrides were no help. He sighed, and began the long, arduous job of skating back to the lock under muscle power. . . .

Phaedra tried the holomirror again. In the last few days, she had become fascinated with viewing herself. It had nothing to do with narcissism, as far as she could tell—she did not put the image on Highlight, and made no effort to primp or pose before it. Rather, she felt as though she were attempting to peer *past* her flesh, somehow, to find the reality beneath the image. She could not have said why this seemed important, but it was. Reality was proving to be a slippery thing on *Heaven Star*. Phaedra had never concerned herself much with such abstractions before—now they were beginning to obsess her.

The mirror had been malfunctioning more and more, lately. This time, once again, it did not light up. But she could have sworn she saw *something* move in its smoky dark depths. She stepped closer, turning the wall rheostat to increase the room light—

And stepped backwards in shock, gasping in air that tasted suddenly cold and musty. Dimly glimpsed, as though through murky water, she saw herself floating. The image was nude, though she was wearing clothes at the moment. But that was not what horrified her. She was seeing herself as an old woman, wrinkled and gray, her breasts shrunken to leathery pouches, her skin loose and sagging on her bones, wrinkled, arthritic, her face holding less than a shadow of its beauty, toothless, rheumy, *old*. . . .

Phaedra turned and ran blindly from the room, colliding with a spun crystal sculpture which shattered on the floor. She ran outside, and did not stop running until she reached Ring River, until she could peer into its blue water and see her reflection, wavering and distorted by ripples, but still the face of a young woman. She forced herself to breathe deeply, calming her pounding heart. *So*, she thought, *it seems even the Dancer is not immune to nightmares*. But deep within her, as deep as the vision she had seen in the holomirror, she knew that it had been no hallucination.

What, then? A glimpse of the inevitable future? And why? How? She felt, for some reason, as though she should know. She stood and looked about—a few passers-by regarded her with various emotions. Phaedra shivered, and returned quickly to her cube.

Deep in the belly of Level Nine, Ian Kyle began laughing and, for a moment, was unable to stop. When he finally could, he wiped the tears from his eyes and shook his head. "Shit," he said quietly. "Shit, shit, shit. . . . "

Scott St. Martin stared at the capsule in the palm of his right hand. It look innocuous enough. A gel cap filled with pale blue powder, the whole thing no bigger than the tip of a light pen. It was had to believe it could be so potent. Zanshin, the kiss of the gods, if the stories could be believed.

He had stolen it from Strogwall's cube. He had waited until Lars had left for the morning shift, and then entered, feeling the guilty shame of a basically honest person who is driven to perform a criminal act. He had searched quickly and haphazardly, and found the capsules only by accident, when he had knocked over a model of a DNA helix and found that the capsules had been cleverly integrated as part of the genetic makeup. He had reassembled the model and left quickly, sure that there would be security personnel awaiting him back at his cube. But, though he hardly dared to believe it, it appeared that he had gotten away with it.

He closed his hand around the drug and looked at the rows of tanks in his lab. Various fish swam in their tiny worlds; genetically-altered creatures whose ancestors had lived in salt seas, and who now existed easily in fresh water. Brainless things, not like Killikup.

The capsule felt warm in his hand. He had already given Killikup his capsule, secreted in a fileted fish. Now he would take this one—and then he would know. Maybe it was all subjective, like many so-called mind-expanding drugs; on the other hand, maybe it was a true psionic amplifier. And if it were, it was worth the risk to him. There would be no risk to Killikup. True, there had been that rumor of someone who had gone through a lock on Zanshin, but he had not been able to verify that. And he would watch over Killikup. He would not let him come to harm.

The flight lasted six hours, with a peak at four and a slow descent, according to all the information Scott had managed to assemble. There was not a lot of material on it.

Scott had taken care of things in the lab for the day. His line recorder was on, and he did not expect any visitors since the lab was shut down every tenth shift for cleaning the pump systems. He had the time.

He stepped out onto the lip of the pond. Killikup moved contently through the water, digesting his meal. Scott smiled at him, put the capsule in his mouth and swallowed it dry.

Fifteen minutes later, nothing had happened. He wondered if he had stolen a bad capsule. Maybe it was better that way. He stood—might as well really backwash the pumps, now that he had the time.

There was a poster in his kitchen; he could see it through the window. It was a 2-D photo of a green creature clambering out of a pond with a snarl on its vaguely-human features. The thing was a monster from an old vid, a fictional beast which had lived in some earthly swamp and preyed upon unsuspecting victims. Scott had seen the vid and been amused by the total unreality of it, so he had had a friend enlarge a flash of it for him. It had been with him since his secondary ed days; he hardly noticed it anymore.

He noticed it now. The colors of the creature and its swamp seemed unnaturally vivid. The green scales of the beast seemed holographic instead of flat; the water seemed real, the scum sparkled with chlorophyll. The whole poster seemed to vibrate with life. Odd, he'd never noticed just how . . . good it was before.

The backwashing could wait another minute. Scott considered the emerging creature. It was definitely moving, the water dripping from it as it came from the murky swamp; still, it did not seem to be actually getting anywhere. It was like a continuous loop, only the movement was *within*, inside the creature. Interesting that he could see that.

Scott St. Martin grinned. So it *was* working. He felt that he should be excited, overjoyed, or something—but instead, it all seemed very amusing. He looked back at the poster on his wall, reached out toward it—and discovered his hand anew. It left a trail like a screen phosphor. Scott found he could draw a design in the air; the tracing faded slowly. How Einsteinian; the hand existing through an infinite series of time/spaces, a different hand at the end of the wave than at the beginning, one of an infinity of hands. And not only that, he could see *into* it, see the pulsing arteries under the translucent skin, and the hint of bone structure under the living flesh.

He laughed. He was a child seeing the world for the first time, but with the brain of an adult.

Scott sat on a bench and stared at his hands for several lifetimes, marvelling in the intricacy of their construction, the depth of his perceptions. He pulsed, the beat of his heart rising to the surface all over his body. The physical sensation peaked and receded, a thing akin to orgasm, a rush which seemed to follow his breathing. Pulse. Breathe. Thrill.

Eons later he saw the watch on his wrist, watched the dark gray numbers dance their time-dance on the pale gray background. When it was important, the meaning of the numbers became clear to him, after the lifetimes and eons. He pulsed, and saw that five minutes had passed since he had sat down.

In the far echoing background of his mind, he thought he could hear occasional voices, very faint and muffled as though through a wall. Perhaps, if he chose to concentrate, he might be able to understand them. But it did not seem important just now. He was having far too much fun.

He wandered inside. The lab came to life, filled with inner fire. Each item flowed and glowed in a way which affirmed its essence. Glass retorts became GLASS, completely, to their cores, thickened air, captured transparency. A laser brand exuded pastel light, the potential of what it was. LIGHT, it said; LIGHT COHERENT!

The fish in the tanks regarded Scott, smiled at him, enjoyed his new perceptions of reality, of what truly existed, as opposed to what he was able to see with the crippled filters that were his normal senses. Ah, Scott, they said, isn't this the way it should be? Now do you understand?

Scott pulsed, and understood. He felt the joy rise in him, and with it the power. He was master of this, master of all he saw, master of all that he was. The knowledge flowed up in him and filled him to his fingertips, so that he had to reach wide with his arms, like a receiving antenna, humming with the vibration of the universe.

But there was something missing. Something which needed

to be done to make it all perfect. What was it?

Killikup! Of course! A feeling of great peace and love ran through Scott as he thought of Killikup. He would find him and touch him with this greatness that made him a god, and they would share it. Killikup was in the pond. How to get to the pond? For a moment Scott felt a surge of panic clawing at his insides; but the panic died under the onslaught of his purpose. Finding the pond was nothing to a god, after all.

Even the air had taken on life now, swirling in mad brownian patterns. Scott waved his hand through the dancing atmosphere, saw and felt the fluid as it left a wake behind his creation of a billion hands. He looked down between his feet, and saw *through* the floor, *through* succeeding levels below him, the bubbled layers of foamed metal that separated them, and the hundreds of people and machines, moving in a clockwork kaleidoscope, until his vision pierced through the hull and into the infinite blackness of space.

He stepped outside again, to the lip of the pond, and saw that the water was a solid block, sparkling in the sunlight. He came to the realization that outside was only a bigger inside. That was important to know.

Killikup? Scott faced the block of water and mentally called his friend, his brother, his love.

Killikup!

I am here, Scott.

Scott felt a burst of joy well through him. He stared at the water, but he could not see Killikup, though the water was so clear that it now stopped being a block and became only a skin dividing one layer of air from another. He bent and put his hand through the surface, and the water loved his skin, lapping at it. Scott closed his eyes and let the water love him.

There was something he had wanted to do, had wanted to say, but he could not remember what it was. No matter. He was a god; nothing mattered to him. He stood, and the water tried to follow him, then reluctantly allowed him to go.

St. Martin the god took a deep breath of the visible air and began to walk, full of the knowledge that all was as it should be. Everything was right. All right. ALL RIGHT. There was something he had wanted to do, but it did not matter now. The yammering voices far at the other end of his mind had stopped, now. That was as it should be.

Everything was as it should be.

EIGHTEEN

The advanced Chan Gen class was being led by Sifu Stephens. A small, chestnut-haired woman with freckles and a wide smile, she faced the twenty-three students and led them through the elaborate formal bow. "All right, let's loosen up. Do the Eight Stretches, with me."

There were four lines, each of six students save for the last one, which had five. In the fourth row, Susan Hanawashi allowed her head to droop as she stretched her neck forward, then rolled it to her left, working the trapezius and the smaller muscles of the neck.

"Reverse it."

Chan Gen students began as white sashes, then worked their way up through purple, blue, green, brown and finally, black. The nylon sashes were only badges of rank; most of the students wore the chinese-style jacket with frog-closures, and the sash was not needed to keep it closed. A few members wore karate-style gis. Beginning classes were only for white sashes; advanced classes were for purple through brown sashes; the black sash group usually worked out separately.

"Shoulders."

Susan followed the instructor's motions, rolling her shoulders first forward, then backward. She could feel the muscles growing warm, loosening, relaxing. It was a good feeling, and one she needed. She had been very tense lately. There had been a rash of strange—in some cases virtually impossible—malfunctions and errors in the Engineering Section in the past few weeks. And on top of that, she had had to adjust to the thousand and one differences and compromises that living with someone brought. She loved Michan, and was glad to have him there, but did he *have* to trim his toenails in bed?

Often Master Chen would oversee the workouts of the advanced class. He was not here today, though. Probably working in the physics lab again; he had been spending a lot of time there, Susan had noticed.

"Back and torso."

The stretching exercises took ten minutes, after which the teacher put the class through another ten minute session of pushups, leg raises and other mild strength-building exercises. The warm-up ended with a five-minute session in the wide-legged riding horse stance for posture and balance. By the time they finished, Susan could feel her jacket sticking to her sweaty skin.

"Okay," Sifu Stephens said. "Sit."

The class members all kneeled in *seiza*. The instructor looked at Susan. "Hanawashi."

Susan scrambled to her feet.

"Attack first, one through ten."

Susan nodded. She bowed, using the short form, and stepped forward. The two women faced each other. Susan suddenly lunged forward, driving her right fist hard at Stephens's nose. The instructor leaned back onto her right leg and whipped her left leg up in a counter sidekick. Her heel touched Susan lightly on the solar pelxus; Susan stopped her forward motion. Then, almost too quickly to follow, Stephens put her kicking foot down, snapped the edge of her left hand to Susan's nose, dropped to her right knee and circled her right hand up between Susan's legs in a vicious clawing motion, then came up and clawed under the line of Susan's right jaw hinge. The circular, flowing defense ended with her sliding back a meter, facing Susan, her hands held in high-low defensive posture. Then she relaxed and bowed, the signal for Susan to begin her second attack.

These one-step sparring techniques were called *wazas*, each designed for a specific attack. Susan went quickly through the first ten. She threw straight and roundhouse punches and jabs, attacked with front snap, spring, roundhouse and side kicks, and tried to grab and choke Stephens. The instructor reacted to each attack with a swift series of defensive moves, blocking or parrying the incoming strikes, then countering with hands, feet, knees and elbows.

The sifu finished the final defense, and the two women bowed to each other. "Now you defend," Stephens said.

Susan nodded and bowed. She was still straightening from the gesture of respect when—

"*Kai!!*"

Stephens launched herself forward, shouting to focus her attack. Susan reacted without thinking, bringing her right foot up to smack solidly against the woman's ribs. Stephens jumped back half a meter before Susan could follow up.

"Good!" the sifu said, smiling. She turned to the rest of class. "You see what happened? She reacted without thinking first. If you have to think, it's too slow. It must become an automatic action, a reflex."

She turned back toward Susan. "Let's try number five."

Susan nodded. Number five was a defense against a high right punch to the head. It was a spinning back hammerfist, a helicopter punch, followed by a heel-hand shot to the base of the skull and a takedown over the knee, finished by—

"*Kai!!*" Stephens slid in with a sidekick to Susan's belly. Susan stumbled back a step, slapping at the sifu's ankle with a downward block much too late. The foot thumped against her stomach, hard enough to shove her backward farther and knocking part of the wind from her. Susan dropped into a side stance, hands covering her groin and face.

Sifu Stephens looked at the class again. "And do you see what happened this time?"

Some of the students grinned.

"I suckered her. She was thinking about how the *waza* goes, so she didn't react to what I did. What does that prove?"

"Never trust your instructor!" somebody yelled. Everybody laughed, including Susan and the sifu.

"True enough," Stephens said. "But what it really proves is you can never really know what's coming. When you get cocky, you get into trouble.

"All right, pair up and run through the *katas*." She looked at Susan. "I'll run through them with you again. This time, stay alert."

Susan nodded sheepishly. It was going to be a long class, she thought.

Sean Mkono floated through the doorway of the Hub's bio lab. There was an airlock and an inner seal—the lab was kept at positive pressure to avoid contamination of the viral and bacterial cultures that were sometimes grown. He slipped into a sterile skinsuit and mask, identified himself to the automatic monitor and entered one of the lab's rooms.

A woman, tall and muscular, with close-cropped ash-blonde hair, looked up from a terminal and smiled at the sight of him. She wore a white lab skinsuit and peelgloves, and no mask. She also had on a pair of spookeyes, which were pulled up to reveal her own blue gaze. "Sean!"

Sean nodded. "Good to see you again, Diana."

"As effusive as ever, eh?" She drifted over to him and gave him a peck on the cheek. "Come on—I want you to see this. You can lose the mask—it's not necessary." She moved expertly down the tube-like corridor in the center of the cylinder that was festooned with lab equipment and monitor screens. Sean peeled the mask from his face with relief, pushed at the edge of the doorway, propelling himself after her.

Diana stopped at a closed hatch. There was a supply box inset into the wall; she slid its cover aside, pulled a second set of spookeyes from the box and handed them to the Hub supervisor. "It's a near-dark setup. There's an inner hatch, so wait until the outer seals before you light your lamps."

Sean nodded and slid the spookeyes over his head, adjusting the strap and covering his eyes with the thick lenses. The field was dark and he was effectively blinded momentarily. He heard the hatch slide open with an exhalation of compressed air and he hand-walked through it. It closed behind him.

"Okay," Diana said.

Sean touched a control on nose bridge of the spookeyes. Light flared brightly and he saw Diana shaded in the eerie pale-green glow which gave the light-intensifying glasses their nickname. There were no other colors, or even black or white, under the spookeyes; only degrees of ghostly green.

The inner hatch slid aside and he followed Diana into the

laboratory. A green floodlight on the ceiling lit the room, and the displays and setups that protruded from every angle were covered with bioparaphernalia: plastic test tubes, centrifuges, cell counters, blenders, iso-cabinets, UV and laser cutters, all anchored in place by velcro tabs or snaps.

"Over here." Diana gestured and pulled herself across a rack of various containers full of liquids—all green, of course. She stopped by a clear plastic box two meters long by half that wide and deep, held in place by elastic cables. Inside it were hundreds of dark insects, ranging in size from half a centimeter to five or six centimeters long. They were all of one species, so far as Sean could tell—oval-shaped, with spindly legs and long twitching feelers.

"What are they?"

"*Periplaneta americana.*"

Sean recoiled slightly; Diana caught it and grinned. "Don't let them get out of that box," he cautioned her.

"Why do you think this place is triple-sealed?"

Sean nodded. He knew the creatures; the weird light had disguised them for a second. He had done a paper on them when in school. It was a box full of cockroaches, and—he peered closer at them—they all appeared to be going crazy. They flitted back and forth on fluttery wings; some congregated in clumps which roiled about in the zero-gee; others appeared to be copulating, joined together in scattered pairs. All were moving in some manner.

"You remember when we worked with Sukihara for our bio lab?" Diana asked.

"Do I? Thought sure she had it in for me. Every time I turned around she was glaring at me for something."

"I think she was hot for you, but you were too stupid to realize it. Lost opportunity. The reason I wanted you to see this is because of that study you did for Sukihara."

"Diana, that was seven years ago."

"Think back. You had some sources I can't find. Thorndyke the entomologist gave you some help, didn't he?"

"Yes. He died a couple of years back."

"I know. And nobody else seems to have developed any interests in these particular beasts."

"Can you blame them? They're the ultimate vermin back in the system. I don't know why samples were brought along."

"For studies, of course. I was raising this batch to be breeding stock for darkroom work and for extracts. They are all from eggs of zee-gee adapted strains. But nothing I've read explains this kind of behavior."

Sean drifted closer to the box and watched the roaches. They seemed—there was no other word for it—frantic. "When did they start this?"

"Two days ago. It was quite sudden. They haven't stopped since. I've been feeding them and they eat, but they don't slow down to do it."

Sean searched his memories, tried to brush the years away from the days when he was nineteen and talking to the Bug Man, as Thorndyke had been called behind his back. There had been something to do with unusual activity among cockroaches back on Earth . . . .

"I remember something, but I don't think it'll help you. On Earth there were studies done on certain insects, including the great-great-and-so-on grandparents of these here. Seemed that some creatures could sense the piezoelectric effect which occurred just prior to earthquakes; some disturbances in electromagnetic spectra associated with plate movements. Drove them wild, so Professor Thorndyke said."

Diana stared at the cage and shook her head. "Earthquakes? Somehow I don't think that's the problem."

The two of them stared at the frenetic roaches, twisting and swirling, a mass of fluttering wings and mad copulation, and wondered what drove them.

"Here are the interviews, Chief." Plait waved his portable flatscreen at Pyramus. "Those we could get. Four of the people are out-of-pocket; we're still running them down."

Pyramus took the data sphere and dropped it into his terminal slot, then spoke the recall code while Plait left. The list of names appeared on the screen. Of the forty-six suspects, forty-two had been run. Thirty-nine were able to substantially account for their movements during one or both murders. The remaining three had no witnessed alibi, but were willing to undergo stress testing and medvapor. Assume for the moment those would check out, Pyramus told himself. That left the ones they had not found yet: Reese, James Mitchell, Computer Engineer; Cassidy, Kimberly Louise, Ag Technician; Yamamoto, Yuri Teitaro, Sub-Supervisor, Fusion Reactor;

Kyle, Ian Brian, Medical Doctor, Internal Diagnostics and Treatment. . . .

Kyle? Pyramus had not known he was a student of kung fu. He was just up the corridor. "Bill."

"Yeah, Chief?"

"Who looked for Doctor Kyle?"

"I did, as a matter of fact. He wasn't in his office, and his assistant didn't know where he was. She looked as if she'd had a rough morning, so I didn't press her on it."

Pyramus stood. "Stick around here for a while, in case I need to know where you are. I want to check this out."

It was not exactly one of his premonitions, but Pyramus had an odd feeling about Kyle. He walked down the hall to Medical and found the paramed on duty.

"You're Toshi Itakawa, one of Doctor Kyle's assistants?"

The young woman nodded. She looked nervous and upset.

"Is something wrong, Ms. Itakawa?"

"No. No, nothing is wrong."

Too quick, Pyramus thought, and too emphatic. "I think there is—and I think I had better know what it is."

She shook her head, and did not meet his eyes. "It's nothing, really."

"I see. And Doctor Kyle is . . . out?"

"Yes." She did not elaborate.

"Would you mind if I had a look at his office?" Pyramus started toward the inner door.

"No, wait—!"

But Pyramus was already in the inner office. He stopped at the sight of the door torn from its sliding track, then turned to face the paramed. "Okay, what happened?"

She looked very lost and alone suddenly. "I'm sure there's an explanation . . . Ian smashed through the door and grabbed me, threw—threw me on the floor. Professor Chin almost stepped on me—"

"Leo Chin was here?"

She nodded. "I don't want Ian to get into trouble . . . I'm sure there's an explanation. . . ." She started to sob quietly.

Pyramus took her by the arms and sat her in a chair. "Take it easy; relax. What happened then?"

"Ian—ran away, down the hall. Professor Chin helped me up, then followed him. I t-tried to clean up—the desk was turned over, everything was broken. . . ."

"It's all right," Pyramus said gently. "It's all right."

"Professor Chin said Ian was . . . sick, and that he would find him and take care of it. He told me not to say anything to anybody." She looked at him uncertainly.

Pyramus nodded. "I see. It's all right."

"What about Ian—Doctor Kyle? Will you help Professor Chin find him?"

"Yes," Pyramus said. "We'll help him."

Pyramus put in a priority call to all of his deputies. "Find Doctor Ian Kyle. He is thirty years old, one hundred-seventy-five centimeters tall, seventy-two kilos. Black hair, worn medium length, green eyes. A holograph is filed under the name. Use your flatscreens and look at it it if you don't know him by sight. I want him apprehended for suspicion of murder. He is to be considered extremely dangerous. I want you in pairs, and I want you armed. If you see him, do *not* attempt to take him physically. Use sonics. This is going shipwide as soon as I can get to Broadcast. Get moving."

Ian Kyle. It was hard to believe, but nothing else made sense. He had asked Chin who might have the knowledge and skill to kill Stanhope and Steen, and Chin had gone to see Kyle—and Kyle had run away. The doctor had no alibi so far. Pyramus wished his empathic flash would come now and confirm it, but it did not, of course. No matter; the *drabengro* had to be the man. The Romani word for doctor meant, literally, "poison man." How appropriate, Pyramus thought.

For the first time since he had found Stanhope's body, Pyramus felt the weight of it lifted from him. He had done his job. He had figured it out, determined the identity of the killer, using police procedure and skill—and a little good luck. When they caught Kyle, it would be over. Things would be back to normal, at last.

In her cube, Wanda Camber was planning on a quiet, relaxing evening at home. She had several spheres she had been meaning to watch lined up—mindless entertainment, mostly, but she felt like just turning her brain off for a time. She was treating herself to an elaborate homecooked meal, after several days of grabbing cafeteria food on breaks. Work had

been particularly hectic lately. That bizarre incident of her terminal blowing up—they never did find out what caused
it—had been followed by a run of glitches and snafus in the
equipment that had kept them all twice as busy as usual. This
was the first evening she had gotten in before 2200, and she intended to enjoy it.

She checked the rice; it was coming along nicely, somewhat
to her surprise. She was a good cook, but she had never been
able to get rice to come out properly—it was always either
undercooked or burned. This time it might actually get done at
the same time as the soysteak. A good omen, Wanda thought.
She wiped a few drops of gravy from the surface of the coolheat range—

And shouted in sudden pain. She staggered backwards,
holding her right hand, staring in disbelief as much as shock at
the palm, which was already turning an angry red. *Put something cold on it, dummy!* she thought. She pulled a freezepack
from a cabinet, broke it and felt it grow icy as the chemicals
mixed. She held her hand against it, wincing. It was a nasty
burn, more than she could treat at home with aloe gel and ice.
She would have to go to Medical.

But how had it happened? She could not have burned her
hand on the range—the ceramic surface stayed cool, heating
the pans on the coils by induction. She had touched nothing
hot—and yet her palm was now covered with a severe second-
degree burn.

Get it treated, then wonder about it. She turned toward her
door, and then the entire cube seemed to *shift* beneath her. It
felt almost like a mental earthquake—nothing moved physically, but she was suddenly dizzy, as though her inner ear
had refused to function. Wanda staggered backward, putting
out her hands instinctively to break her fall. Her right palm
slapped against the hot side of the saucepan in which the rice
was boiling. For an instant she was certain she had burned it
again—but she felt no further pain. The moment of instability
passed. She looked at her hand; the angry red welt was still
there, but it had not been exacerbated at all by touching the
hot side of the pan. In fact, it was almost as if. . . .

Wanda stared at her hand, realizing that the size of the welt
exactly matched the curved side of the saucepan. The conclusion was ridiculous, unbelievable—and inescapable: the burn
had appeared *before* the accident happened.

NINETEEN

Think like a madman, Leo told himself. *Imagine your mind running down a sociopathic path, cloaked in paranoia—only in this case paranoia is now truth. Where would you go?*

Leo had never before appreciated just how big a place *Heaven Star* was. There were a lot of places to hide on a torus six kilometers around, far more than a single man could search with any hope of finding a determined quarry. The only chance Leo had lay in thinking like Ian, in eliminating those places he would not go, in winnowing down the possibilities. It would not be easy.

There was a public holoproj near the daycare center on the Main Level. As Leo passed it, he saw a holograph of Ian's face appear. He stopped and listened.

"—extremely dangerous," the announcer's voice was saying. "If you see this man, contact Security immediately. Do not try to stop him or follow him. He is wanted for questioning by Security."

Leo listened to the repeat of the 'cast, but the announcement did not specify precisely why Ian was wanted. Only a moron would fail to know, of course. It was the first time in Leo's memory that such a message had been broadcast.

The physicist sighed. It would make locating Ian that much harder; he would see or hear the broadcast, Leo was certain. He would burrow deeper into his hole, or—worse possibility—he would attack anybody who saw him. They would find him eventually; there was really no place for him to run. But what Gray and the others did not understand, and Leo did, was that Ian had no interest in escape. He knew it was impossible. His only desire now was to vent the hostility, the red savagery that he had sublimated for so long, as much as he could before he was run down. He was a berserker, a ronin. In his own twisted way, Leo thought, he has achieved satori; he moves now like the sword of an Iaijutsu master, the draw and the cut and the shaking of blood, without concern for the consequences.

"Professor Chin?"

Leo had been aware of the man who had come to stand next to him, but had been too deep in his thoughts to pay him proper attention. Now he looked, and saw one of the Security men, dressed in a pale blue uniform. One hand held an audio-oscillator. "Yes?" Leo said.

"Chief Gray would like to speak to you, sir."

Leo considered it. If Pyramus knew Ian was the killer, then he must also know that Leo had kept it from him. Leo was, therefore, in trouble. A minor thing, but it might keep him from finding Ian. He could evade the deputy easily enough, but such would only worsen the problem. Better to settle the matter now. Gray might be convinced that Leo would be better left searching than not.

He nodded to the deputy. "Of course." He saw tension ease from the man's stance, heard the almost-inaudible sigh of relief, and suppressed a faint smile.

Kyle was stealing packets of sandwiches from a storeroom on the kitchen level when he heard the announcement over a ceiling speaker. So, Leo had gone to Security after all. It surprised him, but it did not worry him particularly. He continued loading sandwiches into the case he carried. The storage bin already had enough food and water for a week, but it paid to be safe. With another load or two of supplies, he would be freed of the necessity to roam so far from his refuge. He would still have to go out, of course, because there were matters which had to be attended to. Hanawashi, for one. And, sooner or later, Leo.

And after that, it would not matter.

There was a noise outside the storeroom. Kyle stood very still, listening.

Someone was coming.

The doctor stepped around a stack of plastic trays. He was effectively hidden from sight—as long as nobody came too far into the room.

The door slid open. A portly man dressed in coveralls and a white apron walked in. He turned partway toward the door and yelled: "Damn it, Mariyanovich, I told you I wanted the soypro in here!"

A muffled voice replied, too low for Kyle to make it out. The portly man muttered, "Shit," then looked around with an annoyed expression. "I don't see the cheese, either!"

This time his colleague's reply was audible to Kyle. "Behind the sandwich stacks, Rich!"

Kyle looked down and saw two wheels of cheese on the floor next to his feet. He set his stance. If Rich came for them, he was a dead man.

Rich took a step forward, and then a shout from Mariyanovich stopped him. "Holy wheel—! Rich, commere! Y'gotta see this!"

Rich hesitated, then exited the storeroom, grumbling to himself. Kyle released a breath. The man did not know how lucky he was. While Kyle did not want to call attention to himself yet, still, he was almost disappointed. The anticipation, the exhilaration, had risen high in him for that moment —he could have skated on the crystal pureness of it.

Then he heard a shout of incredulity from the kitchen annex, followed by an excited babble of voices. He could not contain his curiosity; he moved stealthily to the door and peered around it.

He blinked, not believing what he was seeing. Rich and the other worker stood in front of a section of bulkhead, talking animatedly and staring at the wall. It seemed to *ripple*, almost as if it were a fluid instead of a solid. It also looked oddly out-of-focus. Viscous waves moved over it, starting at the center and radiating outward.

"C'mon," Mariyanovich said. "Let's report it, before it stops!"

"*If* it stops," Rich replied. They hurried off down the corridor.

Kyle calmly went back to loading sandwiches into his case. He also took some freeze-dried foods in sealed pouches, as well as several bulbs of juice. So, he thought, it was building. It was no surprise. Perhaps he had less time than he thought. He closed the case and stepped outside into the annex. There was no one else there. Quickly, he walked across the small room, not stopping for more than a second to look at the anomaly on the wall. It hurt his eyes, like a badly-focused holoproj. He wondered if any form of lethal radiation or toxicity were involved in it. If so, he thought grimly, he would know soon enough.

He hurried through the exit and down a hall, turned into a corridor. There were two women talking at the far end of it. Had they heard or seen the broadcast about him yet? He walked past them. One of them smiled at him; the other kept talking. Kyle rounded the corner and walked briskly toward the stairs. He could not risk the elevators; few people used the stairs, and those who did would not get more than a glimpse of him in passing. And if they recognized him—well, that would be too bad for them.

He increased his pace. He was running out of time.

Geoffrey Merle-Douglass sat before his terminal, looking at the screen but not seeing it. The election was a day away. He was sure that Demond had used his information to the best possible advantage. Louis would win the election. And Geoffrey would have to live under his thumb for the rest of his days.

He told himself he had had no alternative. Not even the computer could have come up with a way out. He smiled wanly. And yet, it *had* been Hobson's choice, hadn't it? According to the story, a man named Hobson had owned a horse-rental agency in old England, and had allowed his customers no choice as to the mounts they rented. "Hobson's Choice" had become known as a take-it-or-leave-it proposition—in other words, no choice at all. Which was certainly what Demond had left him.

He sighed and returned to his cataloguing. He typed in a command, frowned and repeated it. UNABLE TO ACCESS

FILE, he was told. Geoffrey stared at the screen, feeling worried. The system was definitely having some kind of problem; files were out of sequence, others were misplaced or worse, and information was being mishandled. He leaned back in his office chair and addressed his terminal.

"Hobson?"

"Sir?"

"I've noticed some difficulties in your programming."

"I beg your pardon, sir?"

"I think you need some repairs, old boy."

"Yeah? Well, you can just kiss my ass, *old boy*."

Geoffrey's jaw dropped; he was too surprised to speak for a moment. Finally he found his voice; it sounded strained, but certainly not so different as the computer's had been. "Hobson! What did you say?"

"Sir? I said, 'I beg your pardon, sir?' "

"No, no—after that. I distinctly heard you tell me to kiss your ass, in a voice you've never used before."

"Sir!" The cultured tones sounded faintly horrified. "You must be mistaken, sir. I would never do such a thing."

Geoffrey felt fear clutch him. Could he have had some kind of auditory hallucination? The computer might be glitching on files, but it had *never* spoken to him in that manner before. Was it his mind? Had the battle he had fought for so long finally been lost?

Don't panic. There was a way to tell. With shaking fingers he tapped in a request for a playback of the conversation.

NO RECORD OF REQUESTED FILE.

What was happening here? He decided to call a tech and have it checked. While much of the information on *Heaven Star* was safely locked into recording spheres and other data storage, there was a great deal of material stored in Hobson's memory, material too valuable to be lost. It was not likely to happen, of course, since there were triple backups of the viral/molecular/fiber optic electronics of the mainframe's brain. But things might get shunted into places where it would be the devil to find them. Best not to take a chance.

He put in a call. *It's only a glitch*, he told himself. *It is Hobson's brain that is losing focus—not yours. Not yours.*

But the fear would not go away.

•　　•　　•

Louis Demond smiled the smile of a satisfied crocodile. He *had* her! It had not taken his people long to come up with the drugdealer Security had taken in at a recent party. The man was in detention, but that presented little problem to the information flow. Yes, the Councilwoman had been trying to buy Zanshin from him. Gray had caught them, but *she* had twisted loose somehow. The man was bitter, but he had expected no less; power takes care of power, after all. Would he be willing to talk about the incident publicly? Especially if a good word could be put in at his trial? Of course he would!

Demond rubbed his hands. He had been worried; the election was only a day away, and Gray still had not caught the murderer. He had needed an edge, and this information would go off like a tactical fission device, and blow Ms. Sharon Sevaer right out of contention. Of course, it would be nice if he could get confirmation from a second source. Gray was not viable; if he had not said anything about it before, he must have had his reasons. Demond frowned. Perhaps there was more to it; perhaps she was clean, despite what the drugseller said. He could not risk that, not until after the election. A good politician never asked a question in public unless he already knew the answer.

Geoffrey? No, he was second-hand, having gotten it from Elena. Now *there* was a source. She would never agree to say anything bad about her candidate, of course; still, there might be a way. She could be induced to open up to Geoffrey again, and the old man could record it surreptitiously. A little more *sub rosa* work and the final nail would be placed in Sevaer's coffin. It was not absolutely necessary, but why take chances? He had the lever, after all. The archivist would fume and fuss, but in the end, he would have to agree.

Demond cleared his throat. "Get me Merle-Douglass on line," he said softly.

"Chickenshit, chickenshit!"

"Am not!" Katsu Hanawashi balled his hands into fists and tried to look as menacing as he could at Tracy Bach. The other boy, realizing he had pushed Katsu as far as was prudent, dropped his teasing tone. "Okay, if you're not, why don't you do it?"

"I *told* you; my mother says—"

"I knew it!" Osamu Mofuni said triumphantly. "You're a mama's boy!"

Katsu took a deep breath. There was no way out of this, he knew; the code of honor children lived by was harsh and unforgiving. "Okay, I'll go."

"Yeah? When?"

"Wednesday. I have to study for a test on Tuesday."

One of the other boys started to accuse him of making excuses, but Tracy said, "Okay, then, Wednesday. And you gotta bring back proof you were there."

"No I don't, Tracy—'cause *you're* going with me!" Katsu grinned at Tracy's look of shock. He quickly overrode the other's attempt at protest with, "Unless you're a *bigger* chickenshit. Huh? You scared of old Shitface?"

Tracy looked at the determined young faces around him. Katsu knew he had him. Tracy had initiated the dare; now he would have to accompany Katsu down into the depths of the dreaded Level Nine, there to face the legendary monster the children called Shitface—the child who had fallen into the vat and who now roamed the halls looking for prey.

Katsu did not want to go—he was scared, he admitted privately. Level Nine was a creepy place. But it was almost worth it, to see Tracy Bach trapped by his own dare.

And it would be all right, of course. After all, old Shitface was just a story. . . .

"Why didn't you tell me, Leo?" Pyramus looked for some sign of guilt, but saw none. The older man's face was more than impassive; it wore the mask of inscrutability old stories always attributed to Oriental faces.

"I thought it better that I handle the situation myself. Ian was my student—my responsibility."

"When did you suspect him?"

"When I saw the holos. The cause of death was a flying, spinning kick. It is a poor fighting technique because it's relatively slow, but it is Ian's favorite. It's very flashy."

"Has there been any indication that Kyle was . . . unbalanced before all this?"

Leo stood silently for a moment. He looked like an old statue, as solid as bronze. Finally he said, "Ian has been unhappy for a long time. He wanted very much to defeat me in practice. I suspect he was training for nothing else save that; I also think he experimented with drugs to give himself an edge.''

"*Could* he beat you?''

"Someday, perhaps—if he ever reached a point where it was no longer important that he defeat me. Desiring it so strongly was an impediment to his progress. Our last sparring match gave no indication that his passion to win had abated.'' Leo looked down at the floor for a moment, then back at Pyramus. "I failed with Ian. He relies only on himself, on his own physical power and not on his *ch'i*. Without the inner energy which is a part of the universal flow, one limits oneself.''

"How did he take it when you whipped him in practice?''

"Badly, as always.''

"Did anyone else see it?

Leo frowned, considering. "There *was* a student who came in—no one is allowed to watch when I spar with a black sash student, normally—but she arrived early for a class and either missed or disregarded the privacy diode. A green sash—I do not recall who it was.''

Pyramus nodded. This might give him some help in understanding Kyle's motivations; still, it was more important to find the doctor. "Any ideas as to where he might be hiding? Are there any friends, lovers, people who might cover for him?''

"It is possible. Ian can be very engaging when he so desires. He could convince a weak person to do almost anything.''

"Do you think that's the case?''

Leo considered. "No. I think he is alone, wherever he is. I don't think he would trust anybody at this point. He will have found himself some out-of-the-way place where he isn't likely to be happened upon accidentally.''

"What is he likely to do, Leo? He has to know he can't hide forever, that sooner or later, we'll catch him. He isn't stupid. Why did he run?''

The older man shook his head. "I don't know. Maybe he is past the point of rationality. Maybe he doesn't think he will be caught. Or maybe he doesn't care. As to what he might do . . . I am afraid he might do anything. He has killed two people; he has to know if he is caught, he'll be pumped full of drugs and his personality re-engineered—perhaps to the point that what makes up Ian Kyle might be effectively killed. He believes strongly in his uniqueness. I expect he would rather die than face losing any part of it.''

Pyramus sighed. ''You could have saved us all a lot of trouble, Leo, if you'd told me this in the first place.''

''Perhaps. But think, Pyramus: He escaped from me—do you think you would have fared better at taking him?''

''Maybe not, but I should have had the chance. I could charge you with obstructing an investigation, Leo.''

''If you wish to do so, I will not contest it.''

Pyramus shook his head. ''No. I need your help in capturing him. You know him—I don't. It's more important that we bring him in.''

''I would help in any case.''

Pyramus leaned back in his chair and looked up at Leo. ''Yeah. Okay. I've got men searching obvious places now—empty cubicles, storerooms, like that. And we're checking on his known friends and co-workers.''

''I know of some people you might have missed. I'll give you their names.''

Pyramus nodded again. Good. They would catch him. He only hoped it was soon enough.

In the quiet darkness of the empty water tank, Ian Kyle took a bite of a soypro sandwich and chewed it slowly. It wasn't bad. He smiled. Tomorrow was election day, and the people would be concerned with that, plugging their decisions into their computer consoles, waiting for the final results to be tabulated. A busy day. Nobody would pay attention to a stranger obviously minding his own business on such a day. Tomorrow, Ian Kyle would become a new man. With the help of mortician's putty, surgical pins, heat-tape and dyes, he would give himself a new—if temporary—face. He would also be taller and heavier, with brown hair and eyes. He took another bite of the sandwich. No one would recognize him—until it was too late.

TWENTY

Demond waved Merle-Douglass to a chair, but the archivist merely shook his head. "What do you want, Louis?"

"You've heard the late broadcasts?"

Geoffrey nodded.

"Spot checks on the reaction to our little bomb burst are very interesting." Demond poured himself a drink without offering Geoffrey one. "My opponent's banners are beginning to droop like they're made of iron."

"How nice for you."

"However, I am advised that the election is still too close to call. She could conceivably pull ahead."

"How uncomfortable for you."

"I have the CIRCLE member who sold her the Zanshin to back up the charges we're broadcasting, but a second supporter would be a lot better. There could be a backlash if people were to decide that a drugseller might not be the most reliable witness on *Heaven Star*."

"I don't see how this concerns me, Louis." Geoffrey's tone was quiet and emotionless, but not contrite—not yet, Demond told himself.

"I think you do. I think you could help even more than you have, if you wanted to."

The archivist shook his head. "I think I've helped you all I want to, Louis."

Demond was silent for a few seconds. This was the tricky part—the old boy had already stiffened his backbone once, even made an idle threat. Louis did not want to have to drag him back from an angry mood. "I'm still the better man for the job, Geoffrey."

"Are you? I wonder. The lengths to which you are going to win bother me very much. This is a part of you I've never seen before, and it's very ugly. What else might you be doing that I don't know about?"

"Geoffrey—"

" 'Better a competent crook than an incompetent saint'— isn't that the old political saying? I don't agree. I've always thought you ruthless, but honest. Now I know better."

Demond sighed. It was too late to head off the old boy's anger. Pity. "I want you to get a recording of Elena telling you about Sevaer's drug problem, Geoffrey. I don't care how, but I want it by tomorrow morning before the voting lines open."

"Or else—?"

Demond made an apologetic gesture with his goblet. "Or else Elena will learn how I got the story in the first place."

The cube was very quiet. Geoffrey stared at him levelly. He said nothing. Demond felt uncomfortable—he had not expected this reaction. "Listen, Geoffrey—"

The old man seemed to straighten and grow slightly taller. "No," he said. "I won't listen. I warned you not to do this, Louis."

"You aren't seriously thinking of carrying out that foolish threat, are you?" For a moment Demond felt a twinge of fear.

Geoffrey sighed. "No. I'm hardly the violent type. I said that in the heat of anger. But I won't let you get away with this, Louis."

Demond remained silent. He held the higher hand, he knew. The old boy would come around, he had to. . . .

"I'll tell her," Geoffrey said.

Demond blinked. "You'll lose her if you do. You said so yourself."

Geoffrey nodded. "I expect I will. And I don't know what I will do without her. But I can't let you do this. I will not."

Demond considered matters. So, the old boy still had some backbone. It was a bad time for it to show. Gently, Demond said, "All right. So you tell her I'm blackmailing you. Maybe she'll even understand, though I doubt it; women don't like to be betrayed for any reason. But there is the other matter. Whether or not I win this election, what do you think your chances of remaining in charge of the Archives are, you fool? I know about your disease, remember! You'll be put out to pasture within a week, with nothing to do but wait for your brain to rot. Think about *that*, Geoffrey! You really have no choice."

The old man did not shrink, as Demond thought he might. Instead he merely said, quietly, "Yes, I know. I've thought about it quite a bit. But I do have a choice, you see; one I hadn't thought of before. It isn't the dying which is frightful; it's the manner of it."

Demond watched him warily. It's very simple," Geoffrey continued. "I don't have to wait for my mind to go. I can . . . check out early."

"Don't be an idiot! You could have twenty or thirty more good years!"

"Under your thumb? As your tame archivist, held in thrall by the threat of drooling mindlessness or loss of one I hold dear? No, Louis. I was afraid before, and I did something I deeply regret: I gave in. I have paid dearly for that, and it seems I will pay more for it yet. So be it. But no more."

"Dammit, Geoffrey—"

"Enough," the archivist interrupted. "I don't want to talk to you anymore. You will probably win your election and I don't doubt you will remember my opposition afterward. But until then, you'd best leave me be, Louis. I could be a nasty thorn to step on. I am certain your opposition would love to hear all about your machinations. If you bother me, I will certainly tell them. I may anyway. Good-bye, Louis."

Demond stood staring at the closed door after Geoffrey left. *Damn* the old bastard! Who did he think he was? He had everything to lose! He wouldn't dare—

But Demond felt the little marble of fear in his belly growing larger and colder. He could have the last word, but it would not help him now. That wasn't the point; a threat was supposed to be heeded. The old man was irrational. He should have given in, rolled over. And yet he hadn't. And Demond, whose business it was to know people, had made a mistake.

On Level One, Michan Bern slipped into his exosuit with Funakoshi's help.

"Have you voted yet, Michan?"

"I'll do it when I get off-shift." Michan flexed his toes in the heavy skates. The brakes hummed, locked and unlocked.

"Reform or status quo?" Funakoshi adjusted the suit's air flow.

"Status quo. With Isuzu in charge here now, things are running just fine for my tastes. What about you?"

"The same. I am much a fan of the phrase, *Nisi defectum, haud reficiendum*. That's bastard Latin for, 'If it ain't broke, don't fix it.' "

Michan laughed. "It's all politics, Koko, and not my area. As long as they let me do my job, I don't care. They're probably all crooks anyway."

"Amen to that, Michan-*san*."

Pyramus logged in his votes. His Councilwoman was running unopposed, but he tapped in her code anyway. And Demond for Administrator, of course. After all, if Sevaer won, she would be his boss. The information he had on her would be intolerable to her, and he was sure he would suffer for it eventually. Besides, Demond seemed to be pretty much on top of things.

Sean floated before his terminal and punched in his votes on the various issues and candidates. He had done much research on each of them; as Hub supervisor, he could not in all conscience be perfunctory in such matters. He voted for Sevaer, because she had promised to allot more standards to investigate the mysterious breakdowns that were plaguing every section. He wondered if any of it would find its way to Medical, and research into his particular problem. The thought brought back memory of the shock he had felt when he had learned that Doctor Kyle was being sought for suspected murder. When he thought of all the times he had lain in the diagnoster, at the man's mercy . . . he shivered slightly.

Identity code 404063-55: Hanawashi, Susan.
ACKNOWLEDGED. CANDIDATE LISTING FOLLOWS.
Susan looked at the screen. Perkins for Council rep, Sandow for Liaison. And Sevaer for Administrator. The woman was young, energetic and progressive. She might shake up the Council enough to get some improvements in Engineering as she claimed she wanted. Things had not been running smoothly of late; there were a lot of abnormalities in the Power Train and no feedback from Demond's office on them. Maybe new blood would help.

The early returns began to come in. Demond had his staff tabulating them, tapped into the pre-official count. It was mildly illegal, but everybody concerned with the campaign did it.

It looked good, then not so good, then good again. By 0900 the numbers had see-sawed back and forth six or seven times. First Demond was ahead, then Sevaer, then Demond again. He was twenty votes in front, fifteen behind, fifty ahead again. It was maddening; none of his other elections had been this close. Always before he had taken a commanding lead early and held it.

His strength was in the working class, Sevaer's in the upper strata, and both seemed equally strong in the mid-to-high tech population. The population of *Heaven Star* was too small to make predictions so early in the day. With a thousand votes cast and Demond ahead by only twelve, nobody could call the election.

Other candidates for other offices were no doubt wondering about their fates also, but Demond was not interested in them. There was no rabid, new-broom-sweeps-clean faction which would throw all the crooks out this time. Some old allies would remain in office and some would be turned out. If Demond won, those matters would be dealt with.

Not "if," he told himself. When. *When.*

• • •

Demond. Sevaer. Demond. Sevaer. Demond. Demond. Sevaer. Sevaer. Demond.

At a public terminal nestled behind a tall bonsai-cut pine next to the Spoke Three meeting hall, Ian Kyle grinned widely as he punched in his vote. He ignored the candidate list and used the write-in option, typing in his own name for all of the offices. Someone would see it eventually, but there was no way he could be traced by the action. Ian Kyle for everything. It did seem appropriate.

Usually there would be a holocam crew filming Phaedra Adjurian as she punched her vote in the public tabulator. But not this time, Phaedra knew. It was still too soon after the debacle —public interest in her actions and her opinions on such things as who would make the best Administrator for *Heaven Star* had dropped rather abruptly. She understood now what lives of uncertainty and insecurity the old-time stars and starlets, those whose careers depended upon the adoration of the public, had felt. She had not known, until it was withdrawn, how much she had enjoyed, even depended on, being the top Dancer on the ship.

Now, oddly enough, it did not seem to matter. What was far more important was the continual feeing that there was something that she should know, but was unable to grasp. Phaedra felt as if she were pressed against a barrier through which she could see dimly, but not past.

Pyramus could not help her with this. No one could. It had started as self-doubt, as a sense of guilt and responsibility for the nightmare dance, and a terrifying uncertainty about her ability to perform again. It was beyond that now.

She had never been overly introspective; had never felt it necessary to meditate, to chant, or even to take alpha wave treatments. Her stress control, her communion with herself, was in her talent—or so she had always believed. But the other day she had punched up from the archives a listing of the sayings and platitudes inscribed all over the ship. One in par-

ticular had stuck with her, running through her mind like a
song's refrain. *To strive is to fail; to accept failure is to win.*

Phaedra shook her head. She got lost in such musings very
easily these days. She focused on the matter at hand; the
casting of her vote on her cube terminal. *Sevaer.* She told
herself it was because she thought it was time for new blood.
She hoped it had nothing to do, deep down inside, with the
fact that Demond had ordered her into the Dream Dance that
had turned into a nightmare.

By 1730 there had been a surge in Demond's favor. With half
an hour left for voting, he was ahead by a hundred and twelve
votes. His belly was tight and he felt sweat running down his
neck under his collar. Of six thousand people, four thousand
had voted. Not all of them would. Some did not care, others
could not be bothered to take the time, and some simply
forgot. The average in an election of this kind was seventy-five
percent. Forty-five hundred votes, plus or minus a few. Figure
five hundred people left in the last half hour; if the ratio
stayed the same, he would win. But a hundred vote margin
was slim. Sevaer could have a surge like he just had. It was not
over yet.

The minutes ticked away. 1750. 1755. Forty-three hundred
votes. Forty-four. He was still leading, though his margin was
cut to ninety, then eighty.

Finally, it was over. Returns were being tallied. The
numbers flashed into view. The unofficial totals ran all too
slowly up Demond's screen.

Four thousand six hundred and nineteen people had voted
for the office of Council Administrator. The unofficial results
were: Demond, 2404; Sevaer, 2215.

He had won—by one hundred and eighty-nine votes.

For the first time in several weeks, Louis Demond allowed
himself to relax. He accepted the congratulations of his staff
with smiles and polite thanks, then retired to his private office
to savor his victory. The official totals would follow in a few
minutes, as soon as the computer ran a verification on the
identities of each voter. That was simply a matter of form. It
was over—he had won. It had been his narrowest margin ever,
but a centimeter was as good as a kilometer. He had won.

His screen went blank.

A glitch, he told himself. He ignored it. He had been re-elected, he would serve another term helping the people of his world as best he could. That was all that mattered. He had to begin making plans—

A voice spoke in his ear. "Louis? This is Leo Chin. I'm in Comp Central. The GARTH-7 is down."

"What?!"

"The maincomp is dead, Louis. Completely out. I was checking on a missing person when it happened, not five minutes ago. They're running everything they can into smaller subsystems, but it isn't all going to fit. We are in trouble, Louis."

"The GARTH-7 *can't* be down! There are three operating independent backups—"

"They are all gone. As of five minutes ago, *Heaven Star* is blind, deaf and nearly brainless."

"How? It's not possible! How could you call me, Leo, if the computer is dead?"

"Communications is on one of the minicomps, as much as they could get onto it, anyway. I think you had better call a state of emergency, Louis."

Demond swallowed. A state of emergency? That had never been done before. Not even the Nightmare Dance had re-quired such a drastic measure. "Are you sure it's this bad, Leo?"

"Believe me, Louis—it's this bad, and worse."

Leo signed off. Demond sat alone in his office, staring at the blank screen.

PART THREE

Scattering Matrix

"The wooden man sings and the stone woman dances."

—Zen koan

TWENTY-ONE

Pyramus gripped the portable comset tightly as he trotted along the tree-shaded path toward Spoke Six on the Main Level. Occasionally the comset would crackle with a voice reporting—it was on a Security channel and all of his deputies, including the reserves, were hurrying to reach different parts of the ship. Demond had called a state of emergency, something which had never before been done.

Pyramus touched his com patch absently. It was a strange feeling to know that it no longer worked—he felt isolated, cut off. It made him quite uncomfortable. Normal communications were now impossible unless they could be routed through a smaller computer—or the mainframe could be restored.

He realized now why *Nano* had spoken to him in such a strange manner. He had been dying, and nobody had realized until it was too late. Pyramus felt a wave of sorrow, almost as if he had lost a real relative.

The state of emergency was not going well, if his own performance was any indication. Aside from some half-hearted drills concerning local hardware malfunction every year or so, the situation had never been prepared for properly. No one ever assumed what the real problem would be, should it arise; certainly no one had ever seriously considered complete loss of the GARTH-7's functions, together with all the backups. These things simply did not happen. During the drills there had been at least partial communications in the form of a com tree; a pyramid of connections to pass the orders along. But even then someone had always been out-of-pocket, breaking the chain, leaving one section or more out of the sequence. Now it was much more serious. This was real and people were frightened. Nobody seemed to be in charge and things were rapidly getting worse. Aside from communications, the GARTH-7 had had an electonic hand in a great deal of the running of *Heaven Star*.

Pyramus shivered abruptly, and saw his breath fog the air before him. He had hit another cold spot—that made the third so far since he left his office. For five or six steps the ambient temperature seemed to drop a good twenty degrees, then return to normal. He did not know what it was, or what was causing it. That was the most frightening part of this whole disaster: No one knew what was causing it. Strange and surreal things were happening; he had heard rumors of people seeing mirages, of results happening before their causes, and other inexplicable events.

In addition to everything else, he was worried about Phaedra. He had been unable to contact her by com patch before the mainframe shutdown. He had gone by her cube a few hours afterward, to see if she was all right. She had assured him that she was, but her manner seemed distant and withdrawn. An old American film he had seen in the archives years ago, about a once-great movie star who retreated into a fantasy world of the past in her dusty mansion, kept occurring to him. . . .

His comset made a crepitant noise. A voice said, "Chief Gray?"

Pyramus thumbed the transmit pad. "Here."

"This is Leo Chin; I'm in Administrator Demond's office. We've been trying to pin down the location of as many mini- or microcomps as we can. You're at Six?"

"Two minutes away."

"Good. There are two minicomps there; a 900GB documents processor in the Disbursement Center and a step-frame coupler in the microwave control booth. Have the operators tie them into the intership "B" Net. They'll know the call codes."

"What will that do?"

Leo's voice sounded tired and tinny over the small speaker. "We have some other units at Broadcast on-line; we hope to be able to get the home vid channels up. That will give us ship-wide communications. It won't be as good as com patches, but at least anybody who can get to their home terminals will be able to find out what is going on."

"Got it."

"Good. While you're there, look for anyone else with an independent computer working. Word processors, games, art-comps, anything. We'll put out a call as soon as we get the holoproj up. The more we can locate and tie in, the better. We're going to have to cobble together everything we can."

"What about *Nan*—what about the GARTH-7?"

There was a short pause. "Dead. We don't know why. All the backups are wiped out also. Given enough time, we might be able to chain them into a unit mind and reprogram them, but the main matrix is gone. Maser communications with Earth are out—we can't even call home. Let us know when you get things going in Six."

"Copy. Discom." Pyramus began to jog faster. From a building to his left he heard somebody laughing. Laughing! He wondered what could possibly be funny to anyone now.

Ian Kyle stood in the shadow of a cube complex and laughed as he watched the Chief of Security run past. The ship was coming apart at the seams, and he found this very amusing. When he had come out of his lair there had been an air of panic about the people he had seen; the disguise he had spent so much time building seemed hardly necessary. A pity; it was quite a work of art. Changing his green eyes to brown had been simple enough with colored water lenses; the extra five centimeters in height, from 175 to 180, came from lifts in his plastic boots. Where his hair had been straight, medium length and black, it was now curly, short and light brown. He had formed some new smile wrinkles on his face with surgical glue, changed the shape of his cheekbones with pads and mortician's putty, and used skinpins to alter the set of his shoulders.

His own mother wouldn't recognize him.

He laughed again. Of course his own mother wouldn't recognize him; she had never even seen him, having died at his birth. And his father, weak, pusillanimous Brian, had kept him just long enough to let him know it had been his fault his mother had died before turning him over to the Nursery.

The memory stirred his rage even now, twenty-odd years later. He had killed his mother? Fine. He could not wait to grow up, to get big enough to finish the job by killing his father. But the bastard had cheated him, had died when Kyle was fourteen, a victim of a drug overdose. It had been easy for Brian Kyle, a pharmacist, to get drugs. And by dying, he had cheated his son out of what he had come to live for. *Damn* him!

Kyle shook his head. There was no point in thinking about it. After all, he was—he smiled—a new man. He could move about the ship with relative ease now, especially in the wake of the escalating madness. He could find Hanawashi.

He knew where she worked; she was section supervisor in the Power Train on Level Eight. He knew what she looked like, and he was about to find out where she lived. Before he approached her he would learn everything about Susan Hanawashi. And then . . .

Kyle smiled. Ah, yes. And then.

He walked over to a rack of bicycles. All of the two-wheelers were tagged, but he merely tore the plastic claim ticket from one of the bikes and took it from the stand, mounted it and began to pedal toward the Number Six Spoke. He hoped the elevators were still working.

"—semiconductors are out-of-phase—"

"—looks like the Maiman is off-line—"

"—not getting any ionization in the MHDs—"

"—ruby-diamond maser is holding, but I dunno for how long—"

Susan Hanawashi shook her head. "Hold it! I can only listen to one catastrophe at a time! Reynolds, what's the kw percent?"

"Eight-seven, but—"

"Fine. If it drops below eighty, dump the secondaries and use the cavity resonators for the main pump."

"Will do."

Susan looked at the other techs. There were six more of them and they all looked worried. She had to get them doing something. She began firing orders. "Pilcher, I want you to clear the maintenance comp and reprogram it to handle the transmission from the Spindle."

"But Chief, that'll take—"

"Get on it now!"

"Yes, ma'am."

"Flaherty and Running Bear, spin the mode-lock on the Maiman up to full and tune the crystal for harmonics; you know the codes. Rashid, I want the Schawlow-Townes off-line stat and recalibrated for pulse-routing. Timmons, the methyl-life will be going—see if you can't get a pocket comp to hold the tone. If it won't, shift to 6G and hold it steady as long as you can. Suzuki, I wanted the dampers on two minutes ago. And Wu, we're going to start blowing transformers; get Supply and have them ship down as many as they have functional. If you can't raise them, send somebody."

The techs all stood motionless. Susan clapped her hands. "Now! We've got power to shuttle! Move!"

They moved. Five men and three women were up suddenly, heading for their assigned tasks. Susan anxiously watched them go. If they did not stay on top of this, there were going to be worse problems in the Power Train than the loss of the mainframe. Some things were still bound to go wrong. But if everybody did their job, they might be able to avoid total disaster. The machinery would do as it was told; the problem was, as always, that people did the telling. The GARTH-7 almost always caught human mistakes; without its backup, the operation would have to be run almost haphazardly—"seat-of-the-pants."

Susan stood and left her office. The heavy vibration of the machinery thrummed about her as she walked between two lines of generators. Most of the power was transmitted from the main fusion reactor in the Spindle, but there were auxiliary devices in the Power Train as backups. They would not be able to carry the whole load requirement. She shook her head. If the main reactor died, all her efforts would merely put off the death of the ship for a few weeks to a month. What would it matter? But that was a question of philosophy, not of engineering—her job was to see that the masers and lasers functioned smoothly, receiving and transmitting energy as they were designed to do; that the MHD turbines ran as close to peak efficiency as possible; that everything functioned as it was supposed to function.

The smell of ozone was strong around her, as much a part of the air as the deep vibrations. The turbines had been sound-damped, the noise muted for human ears, but nothing had been devised to stop the bone-deep droning.

Five men moved around the tube of the main conversion maser, adjusting levers, tapping commands into the rudimentary brain of the unit like priests trying to placate an angry *kami*, or spirit of the machine. *Denki-san*, she thought in weary amusement: the god of the electricity. Perhaps a purification ceremony would help; they could pour sake into the circuits. She sighed. If only it were that easy.

"—Chief? Do we strip it or not?"

Susan blinked, realizing Enright had asked her a question. "Ah—yes, as long as the modulations are constant. If you get a disharmonic, back off and try to hold steady."

"Right. Strip it, Wilkerson!"

Susan started back to her office, wondering briefly how the rest of the ship was coping with the crisis. Katsu was all right where he was, in the day care center with others to watch him; Michan would be busy, though. There had been a lot of exterior instrumentation tied into the mainframe. Some would automatically compensate for fluctuations, but others would require manual manipulation. It would be a busy time for the Outsiders.

There was no time now to play ego games with brakes versus stoproll. Michan and Shonin skated across the inner diameter of the torus, heading for their next assignment. They were luckier than most, Michan knew. The Outsiders had their own comp for communications Outside and the unit had enough RAM to carry quite a bit of extra load. It was at the limit, now, though, and there was still too much to be done.

"Bear left a hair, Michan."

"Right." Michan adjusted his jets and veered left. Ahead loomed the winch tower of the stabilimentia web. "I'll take the winch," Michan said. "You give me the read."

There were fifteen winches which controlled the web. Each

winch was actually a complex of gears and pulleys which tightened or loosened twelve cables, each as thick as a man's leg.
There were one hundred and eighty lines, attached to heavy
supports in a tense web which helped hold the spinning torus
together. Some of the lines connected to the Hub hull, others
to spokes, still others to facings on the torus hull opposite.
The tension could not be static on a structure the size of
Heaven Star; mass was constantly being shifted about on the
ship and the cables had to be adjusted to maintain the integrity
of the structure. This, along with the eccentricity equalizers,
which also readjusted for mass distribution, was normally
handled automatically by the mainframe. Now it would have
to be done manually.

Manually adjusting the cables was a two-person job, requiring one to operate the winch with both hands while the second
observed and locked in the reading when the tension was correct. Fifteen pairs of Outsiders were at work on the web; fewer
teams would not be able to make the proper corrections
quickly enough. Shifting the tension on one set of the stabilimentia cables would automatically change the settings on
other sets, like tuning the spokes of a gargantuan bicycle
wheel.

After the cables were set, nothing in the torus above a certain mass would be shifted without special permission, until
the stabilimentia and equalizer programs could be squeezed
into a comp again. And that would not be easy, since no one
could access the original programs in the dead mainframe.
Probably a hack somewhere was tearing his hair out as he tried
to build a new set of commands, but that was not Michan's
problem. All he had to do was wait until Wanda gave them the
numbers, then make the adjustments. He did not have to
worry about the big problems. He was glad of that.

Wanda's voice crackled over the suit coms. "Bern and
Shonin?"

"On station," Michan said.

"Good. Stand by. Wentworth and Hastings are slacking
across from you first, then Swofford and Genaloni; you're
third, so be ready." Wanda continued to call the other teams
to give them their sequences. Michan gripped the metal knobs
with his thick gloves and waited.

"—to six-nine-point-oh-nine-six-one, Wentworth."

"Hastings is on the diode," Wentworth's voice came back.

The hull monitor read the next sequence for Swofford and Genaloni. Then it was Michan and Greg's turn. Michan worked the knobs; the heavy gears required all his strength to turn. He was grateful for the long hours of flying and other exercise that had given him the upper-body strength he needed now. The adjustment was almost complete—

One of the cables snapped, thirty meters out; Michan felt the vibration through his boots, barely had time to turn and see the thick metal line whipping back along the length attached to the winch tower, looping horizontally so fast that it blurred. He had no time to move or shout a warning. The cable smashed silently across Greg Shonin's back, slamming him into the side of the tower. Because of that, and Michan's stance and angle, the force of the recoiling metal snake only thumped his hip and knocked him off-balance. He tumbled, bounced once on his left shoulder and landed face down. He was up in an instant. *"Greg!"*

His suit com was suddenly full of chatter, but Michan ignored it as he skated toward his partner. Greg Shonin was dead, of that there could be no doubt. His suit was ruptured across the middle in the front and his blood formed a red cloud of crystals where it froze around the tears. It looked like his back had been broken, and he had hit the inside of his helmet hard enough to crack the face plate. Michan squatted before him for what seemed a long time before he acknowledged the calls.

"One of the cables snapped," he said dully. "Greg Shonin is dead."

"Jesus," Wanda said. "We'll send somebody out. Stay there, Michan. The webbing will have to be readjusted."

Michan looked up at the vastness of Deep, at the cold, hard stars filling the void. "Yeah." He looked at Shonin's body. "I'll be here."

After all, where else was there to go?

TWENTY-TWO

Scott St. Martin slammed his palm on the top of the lab table. It stung, but otherwise did nothing; it certainly did not help matters. He stared morosely at the bare spot on the table where his computer had been. He still had his files stored in an electron lattice unit, but they would do him no good without a terminal.

The security man had given him a receipt and had been very polite, but adamant: the computer had to be temporarily "loaned" to Medical. He would get it back as soon as the emergency was over. He was not the only one so inconvenienced; all private computers were subject to conscription until the GARTH-7 was repaired.

"But I'm a scientist; I *need* my comp!"

"I'm sorry, sir. I didn't decide who got to keep what. All I'm supposed to do is collect 'em."

For a second Scott had considered trying to throw the man out of his lab. He scotched that idea quickly; the man was fifteen centimeters taller and probably fifteen kilos heavier. It would have been suicide. Besides, they would have only sent more deputies to replace him.

He tried to call Admin to protest, using his holoproj, but

the lines were all busy. Couldn't they understand what this would do to his work? He would not be able to communicate with Killikup past the simplest of exchanges, would lose time—

He forced himself to sit still, to think about it rationally. *You're in danger of becoming obsessed, Scott old boy. Let's have some sense of proportion here; after all, the evidence all points to some very hairy happenings on* Heaven Star, *and being able to communicate with a dolphin simply doesn't sit very high on the ziggurat of needs currently.* But he could not deny his feelings of helplessness and frustration.

He considered doing another experiment with Eight Ball, trying to see if the cephalopod would better his time on the crab-in-the-jar problem. Eight Ball had it down to a science, now. As soon as he discovered the glass between him and his prey, he would immediately begin working on the plastic stopper. The last time it had taken less than thirty seconds for the crab to join his ancestors. That the mollusk had learned the puzzle was beyond all doubt. How bright he was, Scott still did not know. It was eerie to watch Killikup and Eight Ball together; he was now convinced they were somehow communicating. He felt a surge of anger. If only he had his computer!

Scott shook his head. That wasn't all of it, of course. He felt a thin wire of jealousy running through his thoughts. It was not fair that a slimy mollusk could talk to Killikup and he couldn't. Not fair at all.

He thought about the Zanshin attempt. Despite its failure, he felt it could have worked if he had just known how to handle himself better while on it. . . .

He had felt differently ever since taking it. His concentration was clearer, and his mind seemed to understand relationships between issues in his work with more alacrity. In addition, there was that strange, barely-noticeable sensation of *contact*—as far back in his mind as the farthest galaxy perceived in space, there was a faint, constant murmuring, a sussuration of thoughts, feelings, impressions that were not his own. He had no way of knowing if they were real or simply some residual hallucination. But they were oddly comforting and alluring. Say they were real, then. What if the drug worked; what if it did grant some form of empathic or telepathic linkage? Perhaps another dose would increase it.

And it would also increase the chances of some sort of side effect, he thought grimly. He had been lucky the first time, had escaped with no physical impairment. Did he want to take such a chance again?

He thought of what might be gained. He thought of his mind linked with Killikup's, of sharing impressions, feelings, with the creature that fascinated him so. And he knew it was worth the risk.

He knew where CIRCLE met. He had managed to get some Zanshin once. He could do it again.

Scott nodded once, stood, and left the lab.

"You wished to see me, Louis?"

Louis Demond nodded. "Come in, Leo." Leo moved to the chair facing Demond's desk and sat carefully.

"The hacks tell me we're running at about sixty-eight percent capacity, using every other computer we can to fill in for the GARTH-7," Demond continued. "And they say that in a month they'll have the secondaries linked and being reprogrammed; in another six months we can figure on eighty-five to eighty-eight percent."

Leo nodded. "That sounds optimistic, but within reason."

"They also say that a new matrix for the mainframe can be cultured and grown in about a year—assuming that whatever killed the first one and its backups doesn't happen again." Demond leaned back in his chair and templed his fingers. "You came to me some time back with a bunch of anomalous figures and experiments, Leo. Do you think your findings had anything to do with what happened to the GARTH-7, or with some of the accidents happening lately?"

"Yes, I do."

"You know a man was killed Outside last week?"

"I know. He was one of my students, Greg Shonin."

"Whatever this is, it can't be allowed to continue. Tell me about it, Leo."

Leo sighed. "It will be involved, Louis. I do not wish to repeat myself—if I am right, there may be no time to do so. I would like you to set up a meeting of the council and the level supervisors. They will all need to hear this."

Demond nodded slowly. "If you think it's necessary."

"I do; very much so."

• • •

Leo stood in the small amphitheatre behind a lectern. At one side was a holoproj unit, but it would not be used; there had been no time to prepare any visual adjuncts to his speech. In the tiered rows of seats before him sat the newly elected and reinstated members of the council, together with department heads and level supervisors such as Hanawashi, Mkono, Gray, and others.

How to begin? Leo wondered. How to try to put into words something that was, finally, only intuition and conjecture? For that was all he had to go on, really. His experiments, his findings—nothing was conclusive.

"You must all bear with me in this attempt at an explanation," he said. "What I am about to say is most properly said in the language of mathematics—and, as in any translation, much will be lost.

"Some of you know, perhaps, that according to accepted theory, our seemingly ordered universe is based in fact on chaos—that energy and matter are being created constantly out of a sort of evanescent subatomic ectoplasm. Think of the spacetime continuum as being like the foamed composite metal that makes up this ship—firm and solid when viewed from a distance, but filled with bubbles and ripples if observed close up. On a subatomic scale, we cannot predict events with certainty—we can only speak in terms of probability factors. In the macrocosm, events are predictable only because they tend to follow the lines of least resistance, which we call Newton's laws.

"Somehow, the randomization that we have come to expect in the microcosm is manifesting itself in the macrocosm. We seem to be entering an area of anisotropic and inhomogeneous space. I have no idea what might be causing this—or if, indeed, there is a 'cause.' I only know, as do you, that it is happening, and that we must find a way to deal with it."

Susan Hanawashi raised her hand. "Why hasn't this 'area' been detected before, Leo? After all, we're scarcely out of the solar system, in terms of cosmic distances."

"I don't know. We know that, in many ways, how we view the universe is not how it is. Our senses tell us, for example, that time is a linear, flowing thing, but all of our research indicates that we are simply worldlines, points of view traveling through a static continuum. I don't mean to sound solipsistic, but what has been seen from Earth, or from the ship, may have little relationship to what is really out there. Causality may, after all, be a local phenomenon.''

Sean Mkono said, "What *is* out there, Doctor Chin? In your opinion.''

"I can only speculate. I can tell you that if something is causing a change, it isn't only on the ship. I have sent out probes programmed to run delicate experiments, and the results have come back altered, just as those on *Heaven Star* have been. As to the source—'' Leo shrugged. "Here is one idea. You are all familiar, I assume, with the concept of black holes: gravity wells of infinite depth and strength, resulting from a star or equivalent mass imploding completely out of our universe. Within a black hole, like a beast within a cave, lurks a singularity—a thing like Kant's *noumenon*, beyond experience, unobservable. An infinite point where all the laws of physics, where space and time itself, have no meaning. For a long time physicists held the comfortable theory that all singularities were safely ensconced within black holes; that we were protected from them by that ferocious gravity well from which not even light can escape. Perhaps a better analogy than a beast in a cave would be a beast in a pit, the sides of which are too steep to climb.

"But nothing lasts forever, black holes included. And nothing is absolute; not even, it seems, the speed of light. What if the beast were to somehow emerge from the pit—or, more accurately, what if the pit were to disintegrate from around the beast? What if it now roams free, emitting *total randomization?*''

Leo paused, poured water into a glass from a pitcher, drank it. His audience was silent and still. Leo regarded the few drops of water remaining in the glass, then upended it over the rostrum. The drops spattered on the synwood, audible to all in the chamber.

"The study of chaotic dynamics asks questions such as: 'Why are not all drops of water an equal size?' In other words, why is there a factor of randomization in everything? The second law of thermodynamics states that chaos increases to maximum in any given system.

"Consider: Within what we call superspace, an infinity of

universes may exist—not 'parallel,' but rather 'perpendicular' to us, mathematically speaking. Every movement of every particle, no matter how infinitesimal, could create another branch. Some might be virtually identical with ours, differing only in the shift of an electron's orbit, for example. Others could be totally different, seething with radiation and heat and scoured clean of matter. And there would have to be some in which different physical laws apply. Wormholes—connections between universes—exist on an subatomic level. Perhaps what we are experiencing is leakage from another cosmos into ours; a sort of panspermia of surrealism.''

Another hand went up; he nodded at it. ''Yes, Mr. Lassell?''

''If these problems *are* being caused by a singularity, is there any way we can tell where it is in relation to our course, and if the effects will grow better or worse? Is there any way we can run from it?''

''Everything indicates that the effects are increasing. Whether we will pass through this area, and how long it will take, we have no way of knowing. In any event, we have no choice in regards to our course—to change it would require stopping the torus and securing everything on board, then using all our reaction mass to brake ourselves and start again in another direction. Such an absurd maneuver would require years, and would effectively doom us to being lost in interstellar space. And we have no guarantee that it would free us from the grip of whatever this is—it might only make it worse. For better or worse, we are committed.''

Demond asked, ''You're saying that, if we just hold on, we might cross this—area—like fording a river? That we might leave it all behind?''

Leo thought briefly of the *I Ching*'s warning. ''It is a possibility.'' He spread his hands. ''We have no answers; we don't even know what questions to ask, at this point. It is how you interpret the system that defines the system. Nothing is apodictic, as Godel pointed out; there will always be some theorems that are beyond our ability to prove or disprove.

''I can only offer one faint suggestion as to how to deal with what is happening. There is a Zen sutra which says, 'Arouse the Mind without its abiding anywhere.' If consciousness does actualize the universe, and some physicists believe it does, then it would seem that consciousness is on a higher level than the universe. There is a Buddhist concept called 'Dharma'; it means phenomena or observable conditions. Dharma is considered the result of cause and effect; when conditions change, Dharma changes accordingly. This is its nature—infinite transformation. Even if causality disintegrates, this also is Dharma.

"But the center of Dharma is *ku*. It is a matrix which is unfixed, massless, and beyond individuality or personality. From it all things may arise. It cannot be scrutinized, analyzed or quanitized. But it *can* be known.

"I think that attempts to define the system we find ourselves in are foredoomed to failure. Whether we label the source of our travail a naked singularity or ku does not matter. I think we must rise above definition, and simply *accept*. And I think that only by doing that will we survive."

Demond said, "Leo, we're here to hear concrete suggestions about coping with a shipwide disaster, not metaphysical mummery. Are you advising us to take *no* course of action?"

"On the contrary, Mr. Administrator; I'm advising the only course of action I feel to be viable."

"And just how do you propose the ship's population 'accept' all of this?"

"I imagine that a great many of them will not. Those of a more materialistic nature, those less given to introspection and consideration of such matters, will have a harder time with it. Children will, in all likelihood, find it easier; their minds have not yet ossified to the same degree as adults'. It may be that none of us will be able to cope with this new reality. If you are asking me, Louis, to propose a nuts-and-bolts solution, to suggest some counterphase of radiation or some chemical immunization, I'm afraid I cannot. I doubt it can be dealt with that way."

"Is that all you have to say?" Louis demanded unbelievingly.

"I'm afraid it is." Leo stepped down from the rostrum and left the amphitheatre. There was a moment of stunned silence, and then a babble of voices—some angry, some confused, but all frightened.

The doors to the ER slid wide and three people stumbled in, two men trying to hold a woman. She was screaming and fighting them. "Cocksuckers! Motherfuckers! You're all part of it! You're all helping it! Assholes!"

Hernando Montoya was drinking coffee with Toshi Itakawa when the trio burst into the Emergency Room. Both of them jumped to their feet.

"She's peeled, Doc!" one of the men yelled.

"Toshi—!" Montoya shouted.

"On my way," the MA said. "Ten milligrams?"

Montoya looked at the woman, estimating her weight, and nodded quickly. Toshi dashed from the room as the woman bit one of the men on the wrist. He howled and released her just as Montoya reached them. The woman swung her free hand at the doctor, raking at his eyes with her nails. Montoya caught her arm with both hands. He outmassed her by a considerable margin, but it was still all he could do to hang on. She flailed her arm, dragging him with it. *Hysterical strength,* he thought. "Toshi! Stat on that nullflex!"

The medical assistant hurried back, holding an air syringe. She pressed it against the woman's neck and snapped the charge into the carotid artery. The woman struggled for another ten seconds before abruptly going limp. Toshi exhaled in relief as the woman slumped in the doctor's arms.

"Thanks, Toshi." Montoya looked at the two men. "Help me put her on that table over there."

They did so. The one with the bitten hand moved to put the wound to his mouth.

"Don't do that," Montoya told him. "I'll clean it out. What happened?"

"She just up and peeled crazy, Doc. We were walking toward the elevators; she was ahead of us, and she turned and started calling Mikhail here names. She went at him with her hands and knees and it was all I could do to pull her off him."

"Do you know if she was on any medications?"

Mikhail shrugged. "Neither of us have ever seen her before."

Toshi pulled an identipak from the woman's onesuit. "Her name's Caroline Welch, according to this. She works in Life Support. I'll see if we have a hardcopy of her file."

Montoya cleaned and dressed the bite while Toshi left the room.

"Why'd she do it, Doc? Crazy out like that?"

Montoya sighed. "We don't know—yet."

"You having other problems like this?"

"Some. Nothing we can't handle." He hoped he sounded more confident than he felt. They had started calling it IMS, for lack of a better term: Instant Madness Syndrome. So far there had been fifteen cases in three days. They were dispensing muscle relaxants and tranquilizers as fast as Chemistry and Pharmaceuticals could produce them. And, after hearing Leo Chin's speech, Montoya had a suspicion that things would not get better anytime soon.

"Katsu, we've been down here long enough," Tracy Bach whispered plaintively.

"Scared?" Katsu looked at his younger friend with a superior grin. He was not going to admit to Tracy that he was scared also; after all, who in their right mind wouldn't be scared while poking around deep in the dark maze of tanks, pipes and processing equipment that was Level Nine? But he was older, and anyway, Tracy had been the one who had dared him.

The two young boys were crouched in the shadow of a large holding tank, from which pipes sprouted like the arms of a video monster. It was quiet in the dimly lit area, save for the sounds of machinery. Tracy said, in indignant reply to Katsu's question, "Of course not! It's just—well, we might get in trouble. Isn't this where they found the dead man?"

"That's not what you're scared of. You're scared of old Shitface—that kid that fell in the tankful of crap, remember? The one that's made out of shit, and that walks around like this?" Katsu shambled toward his frightened crony, arms held stiffly before him, face twisted in a frightful grimace. "And he's all slimy and dripping, and when he grabs you—"

"Katsu, *stop it*!" Tracy began to cry.

Katsu stopped, but not out of pity for Tracy; he had suddenly heard something that sounded out of place in this quiet, brooding, mechanized area. He straightened and looked about. His heart seemed to leap to his throat as he saw movement in the distance, but he quickly recognized its cause as a passing robot. Then the sound came again. It was quite nearby: a muffled groan, deep and reverberating.

"What was *that*?" Tracy began to cry in earnest.

Katsu felt fear's cold, skeletal hand stroking along his back-bone. Maybe Tracy was right—he did not believe in the stories of the monster, but there *was* supposed to be a bad person somewhere on the ship who had killed three or more people. Maybe coming here wasn't such a good idea—

"Katsu!"

Katsu nearly screamed; the stern voice had come from right beside him! Then he realized it was his mother's voice; she was calling him on the comset she had made him carry since the patches had quit working. He nearly wept with relief.

"Yes, Mom?"

"Where are you? I told you to come straight home from school!" His mother sounded more worried than he had ever heard her before. He felt guilty and apprehensive.

"I'm—Tracy and I were playing."

"Both of you get home this minute, copy?"

"Okay, sure," Katsu said with relief. Maybe, when he got home, he wouldn't have to tell her where he had been. "C'mon, Tracy, we gotta go home." He grabbed the still-snuffling smaller boy by the arm, and then the groan sounded again, louder than ever, shading at its end into a muffled shriek. It was the final straw for both boys; with screams of fright they ran toward the nearby elevators, both of them sure that the murderer, the monster, or worse was right behind them.

The elevator doors would not open.

Katsu jabbed the call button again. The soft white light above the door said that it was open and ready to receive passengers, but the doors remained closed. And then—then he felt it again, the same *strangeness* he had felt before when the Cor-i-o-lis force had failed and Tracy's ball had hit him in the head. It was stronger this time. And above him, the light changed from white to red. Katsu had never seen that happen before. He stared up at the light, which now glowed with a baleful, sinister intensity, bathing the entire area in sanguine radiance. Tracy was screaming in fear now, pressed against the unyielding doors. Behind them, a steady, metallic groan-ing echoed. Katsu looked back over his shoulder, and what he saw caused his eyes to open wide enough to hurt.

It was hard to see in the shadows and the red light, but the tank they had been hiding beside, with the many pipes rising from it, seemed to be *throbbing*, the pipes writhing like tentacles. Katsu screamed, shut his eyes, and pressed the call button again with all his strength.

Even through his tightly closed lids he could see the red light suddenly vanish. The elevator doors opened, and he and Tracy fell into the car. The doors closed behind them, and they collapsed into a single, sobbing pile on the floor as the car rose swiftly up the spoke. They heard a muffled sound behind them, like an explosion, and the car shook slightly. But it continued to rise.

When the doors opened again, Katsu and Tracy did not move. The people who were waiting to enter found the two boys crouched on the floor, still crying.

TWENTY-THREE

Michan walked down the hall toward the elevators. His shift was finally over and he was in a hurry to return to Susan's cube—correction, he thought; to *our* cube—and see how she was. She had been even busier than he, trying to keep power supplied evenly to all parts of the huge torus—not an easy task during the best of times. He wanted to get home to her, fix her dinner, give her a chance to unwind.

There was an orange strobbing at the edge of his peripheral vision. Startled, he turned to look for it—and saw nothing. All the full-spectrum lighting tubes which lined the hall seemed to be working normally. A power surge, maybe. He started walking again.

The flash came again; he turned quickly in an attempt to catch it. Nothing again. . . . Well, he could hardly expect to be faster than light. But here was something odd . . . the wall to his left was . . . shimmering. It looked like the air surrounding a transformer's cooling fins, distorted by waves of heat. Michan stared at it. His first thought was that there was a short-circuit behind the thin paneling of the wall, that an overload must have somehow started a small fire. The walls were equipped with automatic foam extinguishers, of course, but he grabbed a manual tube anyway. The way things had been going lately, one would be foolish to trust the automatics.

Two more Outsiders approached from the opposite direction as Michan ran to the wall with the foamtube. They hurried forward to help him.

"What's going on, Bern?"

Michan called over his shoulder as he reached the shimmering area. "Short, maybe; looks like heat coming off the . . ." He stopped, looking at the wall. The heat waves were gone.

"Where?" It was Isuzu, the top skate.

Michan looked up and down the length of hallway. "It was right here."

The other Outsider, Wentworth, stepped toward the wall and put her hand on it. "Cold. Maybe farther up the hall?"

"I don't—maybe." Michan took a few steps, looking hard at the wall. Nothing; no heat, no distortion, no flashing orange lights. Michan shrugged. "I must be going blind. I'd swear I saw it."

Isuzu and Wentworth looked at each other. The older woman said, "Everybody's been running in vacuum a lot lately. We're all tired. Maybe you ought to take a couple of shifts off."

Michan nodded. "Yeah. Maybe you're right." He started to turn away, and then the orange light flared again at the edges of his vision. He started to say, *Did you see that?* but instead held his tongue, waiting for their reaction. Wentworth started slightly and glanced about.

"Something, Joanna?" Isuzu asked.

"No. Nothing."

After Wentworth and Isuzu had left, Michan replaced the foamtube and carefully walked back along the length of hall where he had seen the flashes and the air distortion. The walls were cool to his fingertips and there were no more bursts of light. He looked about him, feeling the coolness of the air conditioning. The corridor suddenly seemed very confining, like the vascular passageway he had been trapped in during the Nightmare Dance. Michan shivered and hurried toward the elevators.

Things were not back to normal, Pyramus thought, but at

least they seemed to be slightly more manageable. Despite the occasional surreal happenings and the emergency measures necessitated by the death of the mainframe, the ship as a whole was still functioning, though Medical was reporting more and more cases of people freaking out for no discernible reasons. Pyramus looked at Bill Plait and the reserve deputy, who stood waiting in the center of the Security room for their orders.

"We still have a killer to find. I want you to pick up where we left off—use the printouts you were working on before the computer bought the farm, and check out anything which might be connected to Kyle. Be careful. Same drill—you see him, call in and get help, or use the sonics if you get within range. Don't be shy about that; Kyle must feel he has nothing to lose at this point."

"Copy, Chief." Plait and the other turned to go.

After they left, Pyramus looked at his list of things to do. Rounds were supposed to be tomorrow, but he could skip that. Routine was the first casualty of any disaster; things had not settled down that much.

He was also supposed to have dinner with Phaedra, but it looked like that would have to be postponed—too much paperwork to go through. He did not look forward to calling her and telling her. She had not been herself lately—he had thought she had rallied from the experience of the Nightmare Dance, but such recoveries were seldom so dramatic and sudden. She had been spending more and more time in her cube, had seemed withdrawn and moody those few times he had been able to call. He was worried about her.

He looked down at the hardcopies, sphere racks and modules on his desk, and felt suddenly drained, overwhelmed with work and worry. On impulse he coded her number.

There was no answer; not even a recording. He stared at the blank screen for awhile, then broke the connection. Yet another worry—where was she?

Sean Mkono swooped, stroking powerfully with his wings at the bottom of the loop, feeling the burn of effort in the *Latissimus dorsi* along his sides. He rolled at the top of the loop and twisted into a lazy immelmann, a classic reverse turn. It was at once harder and easier than it would have been in a craft on Earth. He had the precision of direct action with wings as opposed to controls; on the other hand, there was no gravity, and so the loops had to be performed under inertia. Momentum had to be built for air resistance on the wings to be effective. But that was no problem for him—he had had almost twenty years of practice, ever since he was a child. He remembered the first few times he had floundered around in the flight room. But even then he had been much less awkward than the other children.

He was celebrating his return to his own environment—though he had been back for several days, this was the first chance he had had to fly. There had been so many things going wrong—it was as though his crew had just let everything go to hell while he was Downstairs—though he knew that was not the case. If Leo Chin's theories, fantastic as they seemed, were right, then anything could go wrong, at any time. And not just with machines, but with the infinitely-complicated clockwork complexities of the human body as well.

It was not something he wanted to think about. He had read history spheres about the latter half of the twentieth century, when everyone on Earth had lived each day with a Damoclean sword hanging over them: the possibility of a global thermonuclear holocaust. How had they survived? he had wondered. How could anyone wake up each morning, go about one's affairs, make plans for the future, knowing all along that it could come to an end at any time? It was different than the knowledge, the acceptance, of death—though individuals die, some comfort can be taken in knowing that the species continues. But to *know* that the survival of all mankind depended upon the decision of a few insane leaders—for, from the texts, there was no other possible interpretation of their snapping and snarling, waving multiple-strike warheads at each other like stone clubs—he had not been able to comprehend what day-to-day life could have been like.

Now he knew, however. Now he could understand, could empathize, with those poor, frightened masses of an earlier generation. The concept of *Heaven Star* being destroyed was as incomprehensible to him as the destruction of Earth had been to them. One denied; one ignored; one simply refused to let the mind embrace such an unthinkable prospect. To suddenly have order and rationality snatched from the universe—it was too much. Best to pretend it would not get any worse, that they would survive it somehow. Best to take the short view, to deal with things as they happened. In a way, this was even more disheartening than the prospect of a nuclear war, for there was *no one* to appeal to. God was playing dice with *Heaven Star*, and no one else could get into the game.

Sean dug into the air with one wing in a cross-stroke and put himself into a twisting line, spinning around his own long axis, like a bullet fired from a rifled barrel. The move was perfect, he knew. Compensation; the bane of Napoleon. He snorted. Short people didn't know how good they had it, compared to someone who ended at the bottom of his ass. And so he had compensated. Some people were afraid of water, and so they became expert swimmers; some people feared physical weakness, so they trained their bodies to the peak of fitness; some people learned how to fly because they were afraid of heights. Sean Mkono had none of those fears, but he had trained for all those things and more. Mathematics, art, supervising . . . he had mastered them all because he was never content to simply be as good as anybody at anything. He had to be *better*.

A pair of teenagers rose toward the ceiling ahead of him, flying close together and facing each other. Five meters from the net they peeled apart and looped away, coming around at head-on speed. It seemed certain they would collide, but at the last second they veered, one up, one down, missing by scant centimeters.

Despite his melancholy thoughts, Sean grinned. It was a nice move. It made him want to show off by pulling something grand from his bag of tricks, but he just kept flying smoothly instead. He did not need to compete with anybody—he knew he was the best. Someday there would be some hotshot who would outdo him, but only when he decided to hang up his wings. . . .

Assuming the ship survived. Of course. That was how they had made it from one day to the next, back when the choice had been the stars or annihilation. One could not give up hope, no matter how bad the situation. One could not keep the prospect of Armageddon constantly in mind. *I'll meet you for lunch Wednesday, barring thermonuclear war.* . . . Impossible to live that way. And he was doing the same thing. *Heaven Star* would survive, because the alternative was unthinkable; he could no more visualize his world destroyed than his grandfather could have visualized the ravaging of the planet.

He swooped again, and, suddenly, something was wrong. Sean felt himself . . . *drop*. That was impossible, of course. Yet he could not deny it; for an instant his weight had returned. It was as if he had been snagged by a jagged bit of gravity. He blinked and looked around. It had happened to other fliers as well; it was not his imagination. Some of them had not noticed, but most had. One did not work well in the hub without having excellent control of one's body, without knowing exactly how it ought to feel at all times.

Sean Mkono had overcome a lot of obstacles in his life; he had compensated his way into mastery of things most people only dabbled in. But he knew that this was a situation he could not overcome. He turned and stroked his way back to the lockers. He would do no more flying today. Something was dreadfully wrong with his world, something he could not control.

In the Hub's bio lab, Diana Friedman was busily trying to wrap as many of her experiments as she could—there were a lot more important things to worry about now than her own small specialties. But as she floated about in the near-darkness, she stopped abruptly and caught a handhold, staring at the clear plastic box strapped to a table.

She felt a frightening urge to laugh. What she was seeing was impossible—it required an intelligence roaches simply did not possess. Inside the box, the almost three hundred insects had finally ceased their nonstop frantic scramblings. Now, as Diana watched, they began to link together into a circle. In less than a minute they had formed a perfect ring, a fat, thick doughnut floating in the cage, dark green viewed through spookeyes. They were perfectly still—no legs moved, no antennae twitched.

Phaedra had gone for a walk in the woods. It was the first time she had ventured out of her cube any great distance since the day after the Nightmare Dance. It had simply seemed right, finally, that she do so. She had ceased to question such motivations—she acted largely by instinct and impulse these days.

She found a measure of peace in the fresh scents of the pines and the flowers. This part of *Heaven Star* seemed largely unaffected by whatever had been happening. Phaedra had encountered no people so far. It was possible to pretend, if only for a moment, that things were normal.

It occurred to her that she was really being quite selfish —after all, the malfunction that had caused the Nightmare Dance was merely one manifestation of a pervasive sickness that was debilitating the whole ship. She should try to take the larger view, to learn what she could do to help in this emergency. Instead she had steadily withdrawn, seeking some elusive inner chimera.

She had seen little of Pyramus the past few days. She felt more cut off than ever without his presence and support—she had not realized how much she had come to depend on their Sender-Receiver relationship until that psychic bond had been reduced to its present tenuous state. For several days she had not even attended her dance or stretch classes—the first time in her memory that she had been so derelict.

The trees and hills, so comforting a moment ago, now seemed depressing to her. She returned to the path and was making her way home when she heard her name called. She turned and saw Marlene Parrish, one of the four other Dancers, approaching, together with several of her sycophants. Phaedra's heart sank; she knew what was coming.

"Haven't seen you in class for days, Phaedra. Have you been sick?" The tone was just a bit too solicitous.

"I've decided to keep a low profile for a while, Marlene. Give people a chance to recover from what happened."

"Oh, yes, that horrible Nightmare Dance, as they're calling it. But surely people realize by now that it was Broadcast's fault—not yours." Marlene smiled, and her entourage smiled too, as though by remote control.

Phaedra felt a sudden surge of disgust. "I have neither the strength nor the inclination to spar with you right now, Marlene. You're top Dancer right now; I hope you enjoy it. It won't last long."

The smile showed a bit of teeth, now. "Why, Phaedra, what a spiteful thing to—"

Phaedra turned and walked quickly away. She wondered why she did not feel shame and repressed rage at the sound of the laughter behind her. When the door of her cube was safely shut behind her, she waited for the tears to come. But, oddly enough, she felt no urge to cry. Marlene and her petty vindictiveness did not matter. Even losing her position at the top of the pyramid, she realized, did not matter.

And what *did* matter? She did not have an answer to that—not yet.

Susan and Michan stood at the door to Katsu's room, conversing in hushed tones. The boy was sleeping better now, though he still moaned and tossed occasionally. Susan was explaining to Michan, who had just arrived home from his shift, what had happened.

"They went down to look—and it's true. One of the processors had just *exploded.* No reason—no gas buildup, no inherent structural flaws they can find so far."

"Like Wanda Camber's terminal." Michan glanced into the lighted bedroom. "Poor kid—is he okay now?"

Susan shrugged. She felt infinitely weary. "Medical gave him a sedative. I don't know. Michan, I'm very scared. Things are getting worse, and there's nothing I can do. I'm not in control of this, and I don't know how to handle it."

"You and everybody else, love." He put his arms around her. "But maybe . . ."

She felt a slight flicker of hope that, against all logic, he would have an answer. "What?"

"I didn't hear Leo's speech, but from what I've heard from others, he recommended adopting a Zen attitude, an attempt to rise above it. Right?"

"Sort of, I guess. I didn't think you were into that sort of—"

"I'm not—or rather, I haven't been. But I remember something that happened to me when I was playing once—I don't know if it was the music, or what, but I was *in tune.* And everything was *all right.* If I could find that feeling again—"

"I'm not sure what you're talking about." And yet she was; she recalled hearing his music that time in the woods, before they had met, and feeling a fleeting sense of the same thing. It was comforting, but also somehow frightening.

"Neither am I—but listen. Remember what I said once about Pachelbel's music?"

She nodded. They had been discussing the mechanism of the arofloj, and how uniquely suited it was for playing recursive melodies—musical constructs that nestled within larger frames, each building upon the next. "You said it was like a Chinese puzzle box."

"Exactly." He frowned. "And if you peeled away the elaborations, if you backed the *hjarna* down, you came to the primal line. I think that's what Leo was talking about."

"Okay, fine. So how do we do that?"

"I don't think it's something that can be *done*. I think it already *is*. We just have to realize it."

Susan watched his face—Michan had never been an overly introspective sort, but now he seemed to be wrestling with concepts like Jacob with the angel. "You sound like you've discovered some sort of Great Truth."

He laughed quietly. "Do I? Good. I was afraid I was sounding like a cosmic jerk."

"Suppose you and Leo are right—suppose the way to deal with this 'new' reality is to rise above it somehow, to control by letting go. Enlightenment isn't something you get free in your breakfast cereal. Wasn't Siddhartha supposed to have sat and stared at a wall until his legs withered away before he got it?"

Michan shrugged. "I know. But it's like the old joke about chicken soup: 'It couldn't hurt.' " He looked down at her, kissed her. "When Katsu wakes up, why don't we go back to the woods for a while? I'll take the arofloj. It might be the best thing for him—and for us."

Susan nodded. It sounded nice—very nice. She wasn't sure why, but somehow she felt less overwhelmed than she had at the start of the conversation. *Hope is wonderful,* she thought —*it can grow on anything.*

TWENTY-FOUR

Kyle awoke in the darkness of the empty water tank, stretched luxuriously and smiled.

It had all been so easy. He had seen Hanawashi arrive at work, and had followed her to her cube after her shift was over. He had ridden the elevator with her to the Main Level along with four or five others. No one had given him a second glance.

He had watched her constantly for the past few days. There was a man living with her—an Outsider—and a child. They were not particularly sociable; the strains of a flute or something like it could be heard through the thin walls sometimes. One of the players was very good, the second obviously a beginner. All three were regular in their habits of work, play, eating, et cetera. Good; that would make it even easier.

He would have to make his move soon; eventually, no matter how careful he was, Hanawashi would notice him following her. There were some places he avoided—the dojo, for instance. His disguise was good, but the old man might see through it. Chin had always said not to look at the face of an opponent, but rather at his soul, and Kyle did not want to risk being discovered before he dealt with the woman. After that, he would seek out Leo Chin.

He felt a thrill of vibrant energy as he made his decision. Yes. He would do it today. When she left for her shift he would stumble into her and use a concealed air syringe to fill her with thoraril; she would be out on her feet in five seconds if he hit the vein. Then he would lead her to an empty section in Nine and wait for her to recover. The size of the dose was important—she had to be awake and alert when it happened, in full possession of her reflexes and senses. She had to *know*.

Kyle dressed in the darkness, only using a light to find his medical supplies and touch up his disguise. There was no real hurry; she would not leave before her normal time, but he wanted to be safe. He would arrive fifteen minutes early. It would give him time to dwell on how it would be.

Susan stroked Michan's hip. He smiled in his sleep, but did not stir. She did not want to wake him, so she slipped carefully out of the bed. He and Katsu were both off today; they could sleep late, but she could not.

Slipping a pair of green coveralls over her undertunic, she actually found herself looking forward to her shift. Things seemed to be running somewhat better lately. So far, they were holding the line. Perhaps soon the ship would pass through this strange distortion of the continuum, and life could continue as normal.

She wondered if the quiet time they had spent in the woods had anything to do with this new-found peace of mind. Perhaps Michan had been right. It had certainly been a boon to her nerves to simply relax, to listen to the music he made, and to not worry. It had been difficult to turn off the thoughts, the worries, and she had not succeeded completely. But she thought she had managed fairly well. And the outing had seemed to do Katsu a world of good—last night he had slept soundly, with no nightmares.

Maybe things would be all right.

She ate a cup of cereal with blackberries and soymilk, cleaned the cup and left the cube quietly. Outside, as she started down the path, Susan saw a curly-headed man strolling in her direction. She smiled and he returned it. He looked familiar, but she could not place him. Of course, one could not be expected to know everybody on the ship. He was coming closer, still smiling, when behind him somebody yelled.

"Stop! Security officers!"

The man spun around so fast Susan had trouble accepting it. She looked past him. Down the walkway two deputies in their uniform synlins were running toward her.

"Damn," the curly-haired man near to her said softly. He turned back to face her and smiled in a way which made her skin go cold. Then he sprinted past her.

"Stop!" one of the deputies yelled again. He ran past Susan, his boots pounding on the plasticrete. She saw he held some kind of weapon, which he pointed at the fleeing man. There was no sound; she could not tell if he had fired it or not, but the curly-headed man did not stop.

The second deputy, a heavy-set man, ran past her. "What's happening?" Susan said in bewilderment, but he only shook his head. He was trying to talk into a small comset he held in his left hand.

The curly-headed man rounded a corner and vanished, the first deputy closing on him. The heavy-set deputy straggled behind them, clearing the corner a few seconds later.

Susan stared at the corner, hearing the echoes of their chase fade. Several other people came out of their cubes, some in pajamas, and questions began to fill the air. Susan shivered; the memory of the man's smile was chilling. It had been easy and intimate, as though they were old friends, and yet at the same time filled with cruelty and hatred. Perhaps he had been one of the many whose minds were snapping under the stresses and pressures of late.

She looked at her watch. She would be late if she did not get a move on. She suddenly wanted very badly to run back inside, to curl up in the bed next to Michan. But she had a responsibility to her crew, and to the ship. She turned and hurried down the path.

The tinny comset voice of George Wu Han was distorted even more by his gasps for breath. "Chief—Bill and me—we think it's him—"

Pyramus thumbed the transmit pad. "Listen, George, *don't* try to take him alone! If you get him boxed, stay back and cover the exits with your sonics! I'm on my way!"

"—Copy, Chief—he's right ahead—I see Bill—suspect's going into a building—looks like Bill's going in after him—"

"Call him! Tell him to get out of there!" The Chief of Security was looking at a scan map. There was no mainframe to zero in on the deputies' com patch coordinates—he would have to figure it out himself. "Where are you?"

"Not sure—wait a minute—we're at the museums—"

Pyramus tapped a full-frequency broadcast. "I have a Code Doctor at the museums. Anybody not involved in a life-threatening emergency get to the Main Level now!"

Pyramus ran. There was no other way to get there fast enough—he did not want to wait for the elevators, assuming they were working, which was anyone's guess. He took the stairs up from Four. It took him ten minutes to reach the location. He saw George standing at the entrance to the Natural History Museum, clutching his oscillator and a heatscope. He looked nervous.

"Where are they?"

"Inside, according to this." He gestured with the heatscope, an infrared tracker sensitive enough to locate a mouse in an auditorium. "I called Bill, but he didn't answer."

"Damn!" Pyramus knew Plait would try to be a hero and take Kyle alone. He drew his oscillator. "Stay here," he told George. "Help is coming. When they get here, tell them to circle the building until I call them. Got it?"

"Got it. Uh—what if he comes out, Chief?"

"Get out of his way, George, but follow him if you can." Pyramus slid the comset into his coverall pocket and started for the museum's entrance.

The museum was closed and very quiet. Aside from the broken door at the front, everything looked normal. Pyramus moved carefully, the oscillator held before him. He moved down the center of a large hall, past darkened areas where the holoexhibits waited to spring into life at the pressure of a foot on a floor trigger. His bowels were clenched and his scrotum was tight. If *anything* moved, he intended to shoot first and worry about who it was later. Waking up with a sonic-induced headache would be the price anybody who startled him would have to pay.

A sudden dry rattling to one side caused him to whip about and trigger the oscillator. He relaxed slightly as he realized what had happened—though he had not stepped onto the floorplate, one of the exhibits had somehow been activated. He was staring at an arid, sun-baked landscape, dotted with cacti and other desert growth. A huge diamondback rattler, coiled and ready to strike, shook the articulated horny rings at the base of its tail and flickered its tongue at him.

Pyramus came out of his tight crouch. The oscillator's subsonics had not affected the holo, of course. He relaxed slightly, turned, and continued his slow patrol.

Halfway down the hall, he saw the body. The coverall identified it as Plait. Pyramus crouched and twisted in a small circle, sweeping his gaze around the hall. He could see no one else in the dimly-lit hall. He moved over next to Plait's body, touched it with his left hand, his right still tightly wrapped around the pebbled butt of the oscillator.

Plait's neck was still slightly warm, but without any pulse. Pyramus leaned over to look at his face, then turned away, feeling ill. The deputy's face was smashed and bloody, and his throat was swollen to the size of a water pipe. His skin had a cyanotic blue tinge. Pyramus knew what must have happened. The swelling in his neck had blocked his breathing; he had suffocated.

He called George on the comset, then began artificial respiration. He performed a tracheotomy on Plait's throat, below the swelling, inserted the hollow cylinder from a light pen into the incision, pinched the man's nostrils shut and gave Plait four quick breaths. Then he found the xyphoid process area of the torso with his thumb, locked his hands together and began cardiac massage, alternating it with more breaths. He knew it was probably hopeless—though there were records of successful rescusitations taking place as long as twenty minutes after cardiac arrest, in the majority of cases irreparable brain damage took place after less than half that time. But he did not stop working on the body. Bill had been his deputy, and his friend—Pyramus could not let him go without making an attempt to save him.

George and several others entered the hall. Without stopping his CPR action, Pyramus directed them to search the hall—"carefully!" A few moments later, Doctor Montoya arrived. He quickly confirmed what the Security Chief had feared—there was no hope of saving Plait.

Pyramus sat down on one of the contour benches in the hall—his legs felt too weak to support him. The murders kept happening, and he could not prevent them. Nothing he did was effective. He wondered how much longer he had before public outcry and the action of the Council replaced him with someone else, someone who might be able to do the job.

Perhaps he should resign—perhaps it was time for him, also, to "exit the system." He thought he understood now the sudden attraction insanity held for so many in *Heaven Star*'s metal womb. It would be so easy, so simple, just to let go. . . .

"Chief?"

He looked up to see George Wu Han standing before him.

"He's gone, Chief. We found the fire exit open."

Pyramus nodded. He looked at Plait's body, now covered by a sheet. Nearby, he saw the broken pieces of an oscillator—Plait's, no doubt. How could Kyle have gotten to him while the deputy was armed? The man was inhuman, unstoppable.

"Tell me what happened, George, and don't leave out anything."

George stared at the body. He was pale and his hands were shaking. "Bill got a call." His voice was higher than normal and it wavered slightly. "Somebody had seen a man sneaking out of a storage tank on Level Nine. They gave a description, said he took the Spoke Four elevator to the Main Level."

"And the description matched Ian Kyle's."

"No, Chief, it didn't. This guy had the wrong hair color and was taller and older."

"Disguised." Pyramus felt disgusted with himself.

George nodded. "We didn't know that, but Bill wanted to check him out anyway, so we started looking for the guy. Took us about fifteen minutes to spot him. He was walking down near the tech cube, big as you please. There was a woman—"

"A woman? With Kyle?"

"No. She came out of a cube and was heading toward the elevators. The guy started toward her. We didn't know if it was him, but Bill figured he ought to question him anyway. So he yelled, and the guy took off."

"Not 'the guy,' George. Kyle. Ian Kyle." Pyramus felt infinitely weary. Bill Plait's gung ho attitude had finally paid off —he had found the bad guy. And now he was dead. Somebody would have to call his parents . . . and he had a sister. . . .

Pyramus sighed, and looked at George. "I want Level Nine searched. Use everything we've got—fingerprint flashlights, heatscopes and heartbeat sensors, the works. Go over the place centimeter by centimeter, if that's what it takes—until you find something."

He was surprised when the search did result in something, the next day.

"We found the place, Chief," George told him over the comset. "Inside one of the empty tanks. There's food and drinks and all kinds of medical gear."

"Good. Don't disturb anything. Put four men down there where they can't be seen, to watch that tank. If he comes back, take him. Don't get close—use numb gas and the sonics, whatever it takes. Just as long as you get him."

"Yes, sir!"

Kyle stood in the shade of a small elm tree, took a deep breath of the piney air, and allowed himself a quiet laugh. He knew he would be spotted eventually. He wondered if they had found his hiding place yet, and, if so, if they really thought he was stupid enough to return to it.

He turned and hiked back up a small stretch of hill, eventually reaching the jumbled mass of artificial rocks and boulders that melded into the curving wall of the toroid. He twisted one of the knobbled projections on the "rock" face, exposing a tiny inset console with ten buttons. He punched a code, and a flat area of the fake cliff slid up, revealing what had once been a gardener's storeroom. It had not been used in several months, he knew—the gardener had been one of his patients, and Kyle had suggested he use another storeroom at the base of the hill to save back strain. He grinned. His concern for his fellow man had now provided him with another lair. How very appropriate.

It was not as safe as the other one, but he would not be needing it for as long. With the mainframe down, there was no sophisticated electronic way they could track him—they would have to rely on those pitifully inept deputies. And by the time they found him, it would be far too late.

Kyle grinned, and stepped into his new home. The panel slid into place behind him, to all casual eyes simply another part of the landscape.

TWENTY-FIVE

Geoffrey poured the wine into Elena's glass very carefully, watching the pale amber fluid flow and wash against the sides of the glass as it rose. "Enough?"

"Yes, thank you."

There was no coolness to her voice, no underlying anger in the words, that he could tell. She sounded to him as she always had, though it was easy enough for his imagination to augment the innocent words. *"Yes, thank you—betrayer."*

He had no defense, were it so. He had hope, and fear, but no defense. There could be none.

Elena touched the wine glass, lifted it, and swirled the liquor around before touching it to her lips. "You still don't believe me, do you? You don't think I understand, you don't think I trust you or love you anymore."

Dumbly, he shook his head. *No, I don't.* His stomach was full of liquid nitrogen, his bowels twisted into knots, like the rubber bands of the toy airplanes he'd played with as a child in Soho. He waited to hear her say, "Well, you're right."

Instead she said, "You're wrong, Geoff. I don't feel that way at all. I understand why you had to do it. Demond is a

monster, a very cunning and manipulative monster. I would
have done the same in your position."

"Would you?" He still could not believe her. He wondered
if he ever would.

She sipped her wine slowly, then nodded. "I only wish you
had told me about your illness a long time ago. I could have
helped you. Together we might have been able to beat him at
his dirty little game."

Geoffrey smiled, but it was hollow and only for her benefit.
She said it did not matter. She came to him the same as before,
acting no differently. She still loved him. And the horrible
part was that it made no difference—it would not help. He
could no longer stay his plunge into madness, just as *Heaven
Star*, were Leo Chin's theories right, might be hurtling straight
into the incomprehensibility of a singularity.

He thought of some oft-quoted, yet appropriate lines of
poetry: *Things fall apart; the center cannot hold; Mere an-
archy is losed upon the world . . . .*

"What are you thinking?"

"Of a poem."

Elena smiled. "Quote me a line; let me see if I can name it."

" 'The best lack all conviction, while the worst are full of
passionate intensity. . . . Surely some revelation is at hand.' "

She frowned then, obviously searching her memory. "I'm
afraid you've got me."

"I'll make it easy on you. 'And what rough beast, its hour
come round at last—' "

" 'Slouches towards Bethlehem to be born,' " she finished.
"Yeats—*The Second Coming*. A cheerful bit of verse. What
brought that to you?"

And so he told her of the memo he had had from the Powers
That Be earlier that day. It had hemmed and hawed with great
delicacy, but the bottom line had been quite clear. For the
duration of the emergency it would be better if Archivist
Merle-Douglass was given some "assistance." Read: He was
being eased out. He had no doubts as to the responsible party.
Demond was making good his promise, as he must feel he had
to do. The big stick would cause no real fear if it were not
wielded on occasion; someone had to be flattened now and
again to show the doubters the substance behind the show. So
a young woman, no doubt intensely loyal to Administrator

Louis Demond, would be arriving shortly to help him.

It was a farce; he needed no help and everyone knew it. Everyone would also know that the memo was merely a disguised axe, but the form had to be observed. There was not supposed to be a spoils system on *Heaven Star* and outright dismissal would be *gauche*—something Louis Demond would hardly be guilty of.

As Geoffrey finished telling Elena that he was shortly to be unemployed, she put her wine glass down onto the table. Not wanting to look at her face while he spoke, he watched the process carefully. The goblet was resting on the table and Elena's hand was already moving back toward her body when the thin Mikhasa crystal *exploded*. It didn't merely shatter—it blew apart, as if some errant child had put an invisible fire-cracker into it.

Elena jumped up from the small dining table. Geoffrey was slower to react; she was halfway to the kitchen for a towel before he could do more than back his chair away from the spreading pool of wine and glass fragments. There was a spot of blood on the back of his left hand.

"Are you all right?" he called to her.

Elena returned with the towel. "Fine. I'm *so* sorry; I know you've had those goblets for decades. I didn't think I'd set it down that hard—"

He dabbed at his hand with a handkerchief. "You didn't. I saw it. It didn't shatter from the impact—it . . . blew up."

"Blew . . . ?" She stopped, staring at him. Old and valuable crystal did not explode. He knew what she must be thinking: *Oh God, his mind is beginning to go. . . .*

Scott St. Martin's head felt lopsided, as though it were bal-anced precariously on his neck. Quite suddenly something cold was pressed against his left temple, and the sting of it against bruised flesh shocked him back into awareness.

He blinked, opened his eyes; blurred faces came into focus. One of them was Lars Strogwall; another was Sharon Sevaer. And three others, whom he did not know. One of them, a small, wiry, man with intense features and curly black hair, was holding a damp cloth to his head.

"Are you all right?" He sounded concerned.

Scott's tongue felt thick and useless in his mouth. "What happened?"

Strogwall said, "I hit you." He looked slightly ashamed. "You can't blame me, what with all that's been going on. After all, you were in my cube—"

"You have no reason to apologize, Lars," the wiry man said. "You were within your rights." He fixed Scott with dark eyes. "Now, suppose you tell us what you wanted here."

"A mistake." Scott was appalled at how little he could remember of what had happened. He had waited until mirror-turn, then had entered Strogwall's deserted cube—he had reached for the helix containing the capsules, and there had been a flash of blinding light—

"I came in the wrong cube by mistake. I'm sorry—"

Sevaer looked at the wiry man. No words passed between them, yet somehow Scott knew that they were in communication. *I told you, Zed. I told you he would lie.* The words seemed to echo, dreamlike, far away in his mind, like a badly-tuned radio.

Zed looked disappointed. "You were after Lars's supply of Zanshin," he said to Scott. "You can't fool us—you must know that. The single dosage you've had should have told you that much."

Scott felt very tired suddenly. "You're CIRCLE, aren't you?"

"Part of it. My name is Zed Kagan. And you are Scott St. Martin."

"Did you learn that by reading my mind?"

Kagan smiled slightly. "No—by reading your identipak." He handed it back to Scott. "You have nothing to fear from us, St. Martin, even though you're a housebreaker, and technically should be reported to Security. All we want to know is why you seek Zanshin."

Scott attempted to explain. He was aware that his statements were rambling, even somewhat incoherent, but they listened intently until he trailed off. "Research, then," Kagan commented. "And that is the only reason?"

He knew it was useless to lie. And, oddly enough, he felt no shame. "I want to tell Killikup that I love him."

They showed no surprise, or any other reaction. They glanced at each other, and once again Scott could vaguely sense thoughts passing between them.

Kagan looked at him again. "Let me explain, St. Martin. There is only a limited supply of Zanshin on hand currently, and it is needed for very important things."

Scott nodded. He did not feel particularly disappointed— the touch of the cold cloth to his bruise had told him he had failed. "Such as?"

They glanced at each other again. "Such as exiting the system," Kagan told him.

"I don't know what that means."

"Neither do most folk on *Heaven Star*—yet. But they will. If Sharon had won the election, they would have known a lot sooner—but she did not have enough in her at that time to see what Demond's plan was, and prevent it."

Sevaer's expression was one of annoyance. "If Tomlin and I hadn't gotten caught in that 'fresher by Gray—"

"He was only doing his job. And he did not report you initially. The leak came from somewhere else."

"I don't understand any of this," Scott said. "Please—"

"I'll try to explain," Kagan said. "You know what's happening on *Heaven Star*. You've seen the wall maelstroms, felt the temperature changes, seen the optical distortions. It's getting worse. Reality is broken, St. Martin. And Zanshin is the cure."

"I don't understand what you—"

"You can, if you'll only let yourself. Listen to me with more than your ears—you've got enough in you to feel it, if you concentrate. You've heard of CIRCLE. You know what we stand for. The universe is mankind's home—the *universe* itself! We have to take the next evolutionary step. If we settle on some planet around Centauri or wherever, it's only a matter of time before we're in the same sorry shape we were in on Earth! We have to overcome our fear of Deep, and recognize it for what it is—our *home*."

"And how does Zanshin fit into this?"

"It prepares us for the new reality. It's an aid to the next step. With enough of it in your system, you can deal with the changes. No one on Zanshin has succumbed to the madness that is growing epidemic. The drug keeps you sane. It's somewhat like giving stimulants to hyperactive children— instead of increasing their nervousness, it slows them down. So it is with Zanshin; we are better equipped to deal with the changes. And someone must remain stable, if *Heaven Star* is to survive."

"Why haven't other researchers discovered this? You'd think that—"

"Researchers discover what they want to discover. Besides, Zanshin, as you know, is hard to come by."

"But the side effects—the shakes—"

"Temporary—a transient effect. Once you have enough of the drug in your system, there's a synergistic reaction which makes use of the mind-linkage. We keep each other from harm, in essence."

"What about that woman who went out the lock? You didn't keep her from harm."

Kagan closed his eyes, as at a painful memory. Sevaer put her hand on his shoulder. "It was a mistake," Kagan said at last. "There are those who cannot handle it. Do you see why we have to be careful?"

Scott St. Martin thought about what he had seen in one of his holding ponds earlier in the day. There had been a mound, a small tumulus of water, in the center of the pond. It was impossible, of course, and yet he had seen it, had even gotten a holo of it. And he had heard of stranger things all over the ship. Maybe it *was* true—maybe Zanshin could give you some kind of edge.

"I want to be part of this," he said.

"It's not that easy," Sharon Sevaer replied. "We're having a hard time making more of the drug—chemical reactions don't behave the way they're supposed to any more. The way Zanshin metabolizes remains stable, but it's becoming increasingly hard to produce it. It's not enough to just want to survive. We must be assured of total dedication to our goals. Can you prove that, Scott?"

Scott said nothing. He could not lie to these people, he knew; he was transparent to them. And they knew that all he really cared about was Killikup.

Kagan said, "In this emergency, we must work together. We, and the few others who are linked to us, are the only hope for *Heaven Star*." He looked thoughtful. "We need to think further about this. A dolphin in the network is an intriguing idea, and one that might be helpful in many ways. But your motives worry me. We cannot afford to make another mistake. We'll let you know our decision very soon. Go back to your work. You'll hear from us in an hour or so.''

Scott stood, hardly able to believe he was being allowed to leave. He hurried out the door and down the nighttime path.

When he got back to his cube, Killikup was nowhere to be seen, and did not respond to a call. Scott wandered anxiously about the lab for a time. He tried to read, but could not concentrate. He thought of going to the temple and trying to meditate. He could not decide what to do while he waited.

No—that was not true. He knew what he wanted to do.

He turned on the privacy diodes, blanked the windows and pulled a sphere from his files, dropping it into his viewer.

The underwater scene was of the big holding pond. The water was blue and clear, and the sleek figure of Killikup slid through it with flicks of his powerful tail. Scott sat in a form chair and untabbed the front of his coveralls. He was already erect. He slowly began to masturbate as he watched the holo of Killikup moving through the water.

"Susan, the Maiman is out-of-phase, the chambers are heating up!"

"Shut it down!"

"It'll cut twenty percent of our output—"

"Shut it down, now! If it goes it'll take three months to repair! They'll just have to live with the cutback!"

Leo was spending most of his time working, trying to chart the escalating complexity of the randomization. But an hour or so after each shift, he went looking for Ian Kyle. He had to find him, stop him, before any more died. So far, it was like searching for a particular neutrino in a thousand square kilometers of space.

When Michan walked past the newest shimmering spot in the hall, he did not run for the foamtube, nor did he stop. He was not crazy, he knew—there were dozens of these "soft spots," as they were being called, cropping up all over *Heaven Star*. He wondered how long it would be before the entire ship began to melt and flicker away, like a dream.

No, not like a dream, he corrected himself. Like a nightmare.

Pyramus ran up the stairs to the landing. He could hear faint shouting beyond the door. "What the hell is going on?"

Reilly looked at him in confusion. "It's Wu Han, Chief. He's out there on the roof, and he's—he's crazy. He's shot three people with his sonic."

"Dead or stunned?"

"Just stunned—so far."

Pyramus nodded. The shouts had stopped. He opened the door a crack and looked out. He saw two of his men and a maintenance tech lying in the awkward positions of unconsciousness. From somewhere beyond the door came a low, steady murmur of stream-of-consciousness babble. He pushed the door open wider and peered around it. George crouched near the edge of the roof, hugging himself, rocking back and forth slightly as he talked in a monotone. Pyramus held an oscillator in one hand, but he knew that if he stunned George, the man might very well fall off the roof.

He took a deep breath, opened the door and stepped out. "George! I've got a problem here that needs your help!"

George looked around. "Sure, Chief." He grinned, then brought his oscillator up, aiming it at Pyramus. . . .

" . . . coming around now."

He had a splitting headache—residue of the subsonics that had vibrated his brain into unconsciousness. He was lying on a hoverbed in Medical. A nurse checked his pulse, smiled briefly at him and walked away to look at another patient's chart. *She looks tired*, he thought.

Reilly was beside the bed. So, somewhat to his surprise, was Phaedra. Pyramus smiled at her, and she smiled back and wrapped his hand in both of hers. It was like holding the hand of a stranger—he felt no thrill, no surge of intimate feedback, as he had once when they touched. Looking at her, he could tell that she felt the same lack. And the worst of it was that he felt no sense of loss. He felt nothing at all, as though his emotions were still under the oscillator's spell.

"What happened?" he asked Reilly. His voice came out in a croak.

The deputy looked uncomfortable. "George is dead, Chief. He jumped."

Pyramus closed his eyes. He felt Phaedra stroking his cheek.

"You did the best you could," she told him softly. "Come home with me—you need some rest."

I need more than rest, he thought. *I need help. We all need help.*

But he knew there was none to be had.

In Medical, Doctor Hernando Montoya watched the Security Chief, his deputy and the Dancer leave. They were among the lucky ones, he thought. He signed another chart and shook his head. It was the eighty-sixth case of IMS.

TWENTY-SIX

He did not know if she would remember him from the morning when the deputies chased him, but he did not want to take the chance. Accordingly, when she came out of her cube he was hidden behind a large planter. He waited until her back was turned before he moved.

Her mind was evidently elsewhere; she did not notice him until he was almost upon her. Then she started to turn, but too late—Kyle pressed the pneumosyringe to her neck and triggered the compressed air charge. Five seconds . . .

She swung her right hand, fingernails hooked in a tigerclaw rake at his face; he blocked the strike easily, his gaze never leaving her eyes. He saw fear blossom, and the widening of her pupils as the drug began to work. Three seconds . . .

She snapped a front kick to his groin, but her speed was nearly gone now. He laughed and slid back a step. Two seconds . . .

She had courage, he thought, as she gathered herself for a lunge. But it was too late. She stopped moving and stood there dully, her eyes dilated in the semi-sightless manner which marked an ataractic stupor. He smiled at her. "Much better,"

278 Michael Reaves and Steve Perry

he said. "Now come along, Susie; you and I have matters to settle." He took her arm and she allowed him to lead her toward the elevators.

It had to be done at the dojo, of course. There was some risk—although no classes were scheduled for several hours, the old man worked out alone at odd times—but no other place would be right. She had seen him fight there once—now she would see him again. Only this time it would be a closer view, and one she would not survive.

The dojo was empty, as he had hoped it would be. Kyle led Susan to a bench just inside the door and made her sit. He returned to the door and flicked on the privacy diodes, then activated the lock; finally he took a thin wedge of aluminum and jammed it between the back of the door and its slot, pounding on the wedge with the callused edge of his hand until it was in as far as it would go. Nobody was going to come through that door accidentally, and even if they were very determined, it would be difficult.

Susan sat staring vacantly at the wall. Kyle squatted down next to her and watched her. He slid his hand across her right breast and squeezed. She did not react, and he dropped his hand. No, he was not interested in that now. Maybe later, after he had worked on her with his hands and feet a little. Yes, that would be better—when she was awake and could appreciate it.

For now, there was nothing further to do but wait. It would be at least ninety minutes before the drug's effects faded completely; perhaps longer, depending on her tolerance. Kyle relaxed and leaned back against the wall, watching her, thinking of how it would be . . .

Michan was about to leave for his shift when the cubecom chimed. He almost did not answer it; he was late and it was probably someone calling to learn why. But he had never been able to ignore a call. He thumbed the terminal switch. "Bern."

A small, sharp-featured man said, "Susan Hanawashi, please."

"Sorry. She's at work."

"No she's not. That's why I'm calling. This is Engineering."

Michan regarded the face on the flatscreen. "She left here an hour ago. She should be there."

"Maybe she might have stopped somewhere? We need to talk to her."

Michan shook his head. "Sorry. No idea."

The man looked quite harried. In the background, Michan could hear shouted commands, and see more harried people moving quickly about. "Look—if she calls, tell her to get in touch with Bevins as soon as possible, okay?"

"It's urgent?"

"What isn't, these days? Discom, chum."

Michan stared at the blank screen, feeling slightly worried. It was a five minute trip to the Power Train from the cube—ten at absolute maximum. Even with elevators full, it should not have taken Susan more than half an hour to reach her shift. Where could she be? She was never late.

He thought of asking Katsu his opinion. But the boy was sleeping still, and Michan did not want to disturb him. The Outsider stood in the silent cube, thinking. He recalled Susan's story about the man the security guards had chased a few days before. She had passed it off as nothing, but he could tell the episode had upset her. Suddenly he was afraid; he tapped a call into Dooley, told him he would be a little late. Then he went out.

Leo Chin stood before Louis Demond's simple desk, watching the Administrator speed-read the sheets he had brought.

Louis looked up. "This is accurate?"

Leo nodded.

"Jesus Christ. The incident rate is going up exponentially!"

"Yes. And it has progressed to the macrocosmic level. Things are breaking down, Louis. Two of my techs are in Medical, under sedation. According to the stats there are over a hundred people being treated for mental instability. Not only that, but there has been an alarming increase in cases of radiation and chemical poisoning. And the breakdowns in electronic and mechanical functions continue."

"What can we do to stop it, Leo?"

"As I said before—I don't know."

• • •

Pyramus lay on the hardfoam pad next to Phaedra, listening to her breathing and feeling more alone than he had ever felt in his life. He had not slept much, and he felt guilty that most of his thoughts had to do with tracking down Ian Kyle as opposed to repairing this rift between them.

They had not made love; they had hardly spoken. He was still tired and vaguely ill from the oscillator's effects, but that alone would not have mattered, had he felt any desire, any interest, on her part. He was sure she would have responded to him, had he made overtures, but he knew their coupling would have been empty and joyless without the added non-verbal intensity they once had shared.

The gulf he had sensed between them seemed nearly unbridgeable to him now. At first he had put his work ahead of her reluctantly, from a sense of duty—after all, the security of *Heaven Star* transcended personal problems. But now the search for Kyle and the ship's emergency seemed almost preferable to thinking about how remote she had become. She had hardly emerged from her cube since the Nightmare Dance. This worried him; a borderline agoraphobic himself, he dreaded seeing it happen to her. But he did not know what to do about it.

We've exited the system, he thought.

Pyramus stretched, feeling his toes scrape on the cube's floor beyond the procrustean length of foam. Then he stood, swiftly and silently, and began to dress. He felt no guilt at leaving Phaedra without saying good-bye; she preferred it that way. She had always been an uneasy sleeper, and if he woke her up she would stay awake.

He seamed up his coverall and stood looking down at her, wondering what he was feeling. He sighed. Time to get back to his desk, to the unending search. He felt a sudden flare of rage against Ian Kyle, surprising in its intensity. How *dare* the man casually destroy and disrupt so many lives! Up to this point, he had been too busy in the mechanics of the pursuit to give much thought or feeling to the object of the search. But now he knew suddenly that he hated Kyle, that he would gladly push him out of a lock himself if he could just lay hands on the elusive doctor.

• • •

Michan was quite worried by now. He had retraced Susan's route all the way to Engineering without finding any sign of her. She was an hour overdue at work by now, and he knew something was wrong.

His route had taken him though several of the home areas and working areas of the ship, and he could almost smell the barely repressed panic and confusion among people. He saw three more "soft spots" and passed through several cold and warm areas. At one point the path before him had grown luminescent beneath his feet. He had spoken to several people from Physics about such manifestations, and they had said that yes, there was some random danger of radiation from such phenomena. He tried to remember when he had had his last cancer vaccination. He put the thought out of his mind and continued on. He had more immediate concerns.

He grabbed an elevator uplevels—after waiting nearly twenty minutes, which added to his frustration and concern— stopped at Four and headed for Security.

Pyramus Gray was alone in the office when Michan arrived. Michan saw him glance up in surprise, and noted abstractly how tired and worn the chief looked. "Bern. What's wrong?"

"I've got a problem." Michan told Pyramus about Susan.

"I wouldn't worry too much—maybe she just wanted some time off."

"You don't know Susan. She's very conscientious about her work."

Pyramus nodded. "All right. I'll have my men keep an eye out for her."

Michan felt frustrated. "Isn't there something more that can be done?"

"With the GARTH-7 down and no way to trace the com patches, I'm afraid not. You can file a missing person report."

Michan started to make a scathing reply, but stopped himself. After all, what could he expect? For Security to drop everything and run up and down the halls looking for one person during this emergency?

Pyramus began to tap in details on his keyboard as Michan gave him the stats on Susan. He saw Pyramus frown. "What is it?"

"That address sounds familiar."

The com chimed. Pyramus touched a button and Louis Demond's face appeared on the screen. "Chief Gray, I'd like you to come to my office as soon as you can. Leo Chin is here and we want to discuss crowd control problems with you."

"In a minute, Mr. Administrator. I've got a missing person report to fill out first."

Demond looked quite worried. "This is important, Chief."

"So is the whereabouts of Susan Hanawashi."

Leo Chin's voice cut in. "Susan?"

"You know her?"

"She is one of my students. How did she come to be missing?"

Pyramus glanced at Michan, who stepped up to the terminal and repeated his story.

There was a long pause. Then Leo said, "This may mean nothing. But . . . I believe Susan was the green sash who accidentally intruded during that . . . sparring match we discussed, Chief."

Michan was looking at Pyramus's face. The Security Chief looked puzzled at first; then his face went white. "Oh, shit! *That's* why the address sounded familiar—it's where Plait and Wu Han saw—"

Michan leaned forward, staring at Pyramus. "What? What is it?"

Pyramus leaned back and stared at Michan. "Kyle."

She had fallen asleep after forty minutes, toppling gently over onto the mat. Kyle was glad; it meant that when she awoke she would be free of the drug.

Now, thirty minutes later, she was beginning to awaken. Kyle stood, bent over her, and seized her wrists. He dragged her to the middle of the floor, then moved back three meters and began to stretch. He loosened his legs first, then his arms and shoulders, and finally his back and torso. It would only be a few more minutes now. He laughed softly, delightedly, as might a child with a new toy.

• • •

Leo could see that the young Outsider was nervous and frightened. But there was no way to downplay the danger. If Susan had indeed been kidnapped by Ian, then Leo knew what his erstwhile student was going to do to the woman. She had seen him lose to Leo. The sifu had been brutal in the match, trying to shock Ian into a realization of his misuse of the martial arts. Ian hated him, he knew; and he would also hate the woman who had seen his defeat.

The three of them, and five deputies, were standing outside the Admin building. "Where would he take her?" Pyramus asked Leo.

Leo stood for a moment in intense thought, trying to put his mind in the same mad track as Ian's. Suddenly, he knew. "The dojo."

Michan turned and ran for the elevators. "Wait!" Pyramus shouted, too late. Leo looked at Pyramus, then turned and followed Michan. Pyramus, a sonic in one hand, gestured to his remaining deputies with the other. "Let's go!" They followed at a run.

Susan's head hurt and she felt nauseated. Her mouth was dry and it took a second for her vision to clear. The first thing she saw was a man standing next to her, arms crossed, watching her. She stumbled as she got to her feet, but managed to keep from falling. She was slightly dizzy, but it seemed to be passing. What—? She remembered: She had been grabbed, injected with a drug. With a gasp, she looked at the man. He was a stranger . . . no, wait—she knew him, but could not quite place him. . . .

He smiled. "Ian Kyle. Forgive the hairstyle and the wrinkles."

Susan felt no fear, oddly, only a numb incomprehensibility and disbelief. Ian Kyle—the doctor who was supposedly responsible for the murders? What was he doing here? What was this all about?

"What—what do you want?" Her voice was heavy, leaden, though she could feel no other effects of the drug now.

The smile left his face. "Honor."

She shook her head, confused.

"You saw the old man beat me."

"I saw you lose a match, but that doesn't mean anything. Nobody can defeat Master Chin—"

"I can! I will!" His expression was dark, frightening, now.

Susan moistened suddenly dry lips. "Look, I didn't mean to intrude on your lesson. The diode was out; it was a mistake."

"Oh, it was that, all right." He unfolded his arms and slid his left foot toward her, settling into a slight crouch.

Susan backed up three steps. Kyle moved toward her, quickly covering the space between them with the push-and-slide stance martial artists used to keep their center of balance low.

He was going to attack her!

Susan pulled her own right foot back and raised her left hand to cover her face and throat, while dropping her right hand down to her waist to block her ribs and belly.

Kyle's hands remained at his side. He nodded. "Good. But you need to turn a little more to the side and move your left up a bit."

She felt fear settle on her in a suffocating cloud. He was a black sash, a teacher—she was only a green sash, still two years or more away from the coveted top rank. She had sparred with black sashes before; sometimes she could get a point in, but she had never defeated one. And Kyle was not fighting for points.

He moved, scooting in fast and faking a backfist to her face. She was too tight—she snapped an upward block with her left hand before she realized the ploy. While her hand was up Kyle whipped his left foot around in a spring kick, unbelievably fast, but not that hard. The top of his foot slapped her chest; it stung and knocked her backwards. She tried to catch his ankle with her right hand, but he was much too quick. He jumped back just outside of her kicking range. "Too slow, Susie. I could have used the ball of my foot on your solar plexus and knocked the wind out of you. You have to do better than that."

Susan sucked in a deep breath and tried to relax. He was right. She was tense, scared, and that would be lethal if she did not overcome it. Fear and tension only slowed reactions. But he wanted to hurt her—maybe even to kill her!

Don't think about that. Just react, wait for his attack and counter. Nothing else must matter.

She realized that he had maneuvered her so that she was down-torus from him; he now possessed the spinward position. He lunged and threw a series of kicks: front snap, round-house, side kick, using his right leg. The ship's rotation added to their already-considerable strength. Susan blocked the first, feeling her arm go numb from the impact; she ducked under the second and backed away from the third. She should have gone around the last kick, perhaps tried a punch at his spine, but now it was too late.

She was panting already, and her skin felt flushed. But she could see that Kyle was not even breathing hard. He smiled at her again. "Much better. Not good, but better."

Michan ran. The kung fu school was halfway around the torus and it would take him ten minutes to get there at full speed. He saw no bicycles available, and the train only ran spinward; he would have to go all the way around the ship. As he ran, he could picture Susan lying on the floor of the school, bleeding, perhaps dying. He ran faster at the thought.

Leo took the elevator through the Hub. There was no point in worrying about speed and time; he would get there when he got there. He could go no faster.

Pyramus found a bicycle and swung onto it. "Get there as fast as you can!" he shouted to Reilly and the others. He pumped the pedals hard, swerving to miss a bubbling soft spot in the path.

Kyle screamed. "*Haii!*" Susan slid backward, but not quickly enough; she managed to block the first punch, but not the second. Kyle's knuckles knocked her head back, splitting her lower lip against her teeth. For a moment she lost track of things in a hot flash of pain. She shook her head savagely to bring herself back. She could taste the blood, could feel it running from the corner of her mouth.

Kyle did not pursue his advantage. He was toying with her,

enjoying this. The realization made her both angry and more afraid. She did something reckless; she stepped forward, trying for a crossover side kick. It was a slow technique, but powerful. Kyle backed away, using a circle-claw to parry it. The block threw her off balance, but she went with it, turning into a back kick. Her foot brushed his face, but there was no real power in the blow. He bounced away and nodded. "Better, but still not there."

The fear overcame the anger and Susan edged away, keeping her hands in a defensive posture. She thought of screaming for help. But the walls were soundproofed—no one would hear.

Thirty more seconds, Michan thought. His chest felt like it was about to burst, and the landscape around him was tinged with red. But he was almost there. Just another thirty seconds, another hundred meters. . . .

Leo emerged from the elevator and saw the Outsider running for the dojo's entrance. He must have sprinted most of the way. Leo picked up his own pace. If Ian was in there, the Outsider would be in danger if he tried to stop him.

Pyramus saw both Michan and Leo as they arrived at the school's entrance. He skidded the bicycle to a stop and jumped from it.

The hand series he threw at her included two punches and a raking claw. Susan managed to block and parry all three, but opened her body in doing so. Kyle snapped out a side kick that hit her heelfirst. She felt a rib crack; for an instant she wondered at the lack of pain. Then it flooded in on her, making it agony to draw a breath. She tried to hide how she felt, even managed a weak stab at his eyes with her fingers, but she knew he was not fooled. He brushed the extended fingers away with a hand and used the back of it to slap her across the face. The cut in her lip opened wider. Her face stung and tears ran from the sudden pain.

Don't panic! Hold yourself together! But she knew he was growing tired of the sport; unless some miracle intervened, he would—

At the door of the dojo, someone shouted. *"Susan!"*

Michan! "I'm here!"

Kyle flicked a glance toward the door, then looked back at her. "It doesn't matter." He smiled. "I have all the time I need." To prove it, he chased her toward the corner behind her, punching, clawing, kicking. He hit the broken rib again, landed a hammerfist on her upper back, kicked her thigh hard enough to raise a knot.

He was going to kill her. She knew it; she could feel him setting her up for a big move. What would he use?

"Locked!" Michan slammed his hands against the door. It was heavy, not the light plastic of most panels, and would not move.

Leo pushed past him and produced a key. He unlocked the mechanism; but the sliding panel did not open when he pushed the control plate.

"It's jammed shut!" Pyramus said. "We'll have to get something to pry—"

"Move!" Leo swept his hands back and both Michan and Pyramus were shoved aside like small children. He stepped to the door and laid his hands on the plastic, fingers spread wide, took a deep breath and tightened his muscles. Michan and Pyramus saw the veins on the backs of the old man's hands rise and stand out. Leo Chin began to tremble, as if driven by some heavy internal motor. The door began to shake also. Sweat broke out on the back of Leo's neck. The door began to vibrate in its frame.

He hit her six or seven more times, hard enough to rock her. One blow, she was sure, cracked her jaw. She knew he was getting ready for the finish, could sense it. What would it be? She tried to remember the match she had witnessed between Kyle and Master Chin. He had used some flashy technique. . . .

The door to the dojo clattered and rattled in its frame. Leo took a deep breath, let part of it out—and screamed. Pyramus and Michan ducked as the door shattered like glass—

The inhuman scream and the crash jolted Susan. She saw Kyle glance toward the doorway behind her. At the same moment, she remembered—a flying, spinning back kick to the temple. . . .

Leo leaped through the shattered door. Pyramus and Michan were right behind him. They saw Kyle and Susan, squared off in fighting stances. It all happened too fast for Pyramus to even raise his sonic, much less fire. *"Ian!"* Leo shouted.

"No!" Kyle screamed. Then he leaped.

Susan saw him jump and turn . . . *he's spinward* . . . slid left in a V-step, at an angle . . . Kyle's leg whipped out . . . *Now.* . . .

With all the strength she had left, she swung her right hand in a ridgehand cut. His leg struck like a snake, his body following the circular movement. She was striking against spin, and so was low on her counter; she hit him across the throat instead of the face. The force of her blow broke her wrist. It was all she had, and it was enough—Kyle's head snapped back. His momentum carried his body upward, his leg striking her across the shoulder, hurling her halfway across the room. Then he hit the mat crown-first.

Susan managed to sit up. She stared at his motionless form. And then Michan was there, holding her and crying.

Pyramus and Leo stepped forward as the doctor shuddered and then lay still. Pyramus started to kneel beside him, but Leo held him back with a hand that could have been carved from stone. "There is no need." The teacher looked down at his student. Pyramus thought he saw a trace of sadness in Leo's impassive face. "His throat is crushed; he is finally at peace."

TWENTY-SEVEN

Michan realized he was crying as he cradled Susan. "Are you okay?"

"I think my wrist and nose and probably a rib are broken," she mumbled, the words costing her obvious pain, "and my jaw feels like it's fractured." She made an attempt at a wan smile. "Other than that, I'm fine." She touched his face tenderly. "You came for me."

Michan looked at Kyle's body, then at her, and shook his head. "You didn't need any help from us."

The lights flickered then, and went out; they were in an instant of darkness before the emergency floods kicked in. The comset in Pyramus's hand came to life with four or five voices cutting in on each other with panic-stricken questions and statements. Pyramus thumbed the send button.

"Hello! Reilly? Anybody? What's going on?"

Another voice cut in, this one quite calm. "This is Bevins in Engineering. The mains have gone down."

Susan gasped in shock. She tried to stand and nearly fell; Michan steadied her. "I've got to get to the Power Train," she said, holding both hands to her jaw. "We've got to get the auxiliaries on line before—"

Michan held her. "You're going to Medical first. You won't

289

do anybody any good the way you are. You can call and tell them what to do until somebody takes care of you."

Ian was dead. The knowledge affected Leo more than he had thought it would. Part of it was regret for all that his student might have been but never would be now, and the heavy sense of failure. But Leo was honest enough with himself to know that there was more. Part of him felt cheated because he had not faced Ian Kyle and done the honorable thing. A sense of anticipation—albeit one seasoned with dread and regret—had been foiled by Susan's last-ditch defense. He was not surprised that she had won. It was the old story of why the rabbit usually escapes the fox: the fox is only running for his dinner, while the rabbit is running for his life.

Leo looked at the body of Ian Kyle a final time before he followed the others from the dojo. There was much truth in the old stories. A pity he could think of no proverb to save them from the problems they faced now.

Louis Demond's lines were jammed with panicked calls.

"—Mr. Administrator, there's no *reason* for the power failure—!"

"—none of the control systems are operative—!"

"—ship's dead in the water—"

"—have *three hundred people* in Medical—!"

Numbly Demond gave orders, referring one department to another, trying to get technical people to work on a particular trouble at a time instead of worrying about the entire picture. But Demond could see the entire picture, and it frightened him more than anything he had ever seen before. *Heaven Star* was dying, was being killed slowly by something nobody could see or touch or understand. And there was nothing anyone could do about it.

Phaedra woke up suddenly. She was not surprised that Pyramus was not beside her; she had expected him to go back to work as soon as he recovered from the effects of the sonic. That was not why she was upset—in fact, she did not know why she was upset. She had always been more of a Sender than a Receiver, but now she had an unaccountable feeling of some impending disaster. Her cube, heretofore so comforting, a haven against the world, now seemed suddenly confining, brooding. She pulled on a formfit. Something was happening. Pyramus had gone to do his best to help, she was sure. She had to do the same.

The young woman fluttered about the department like a confused bird, but Geoffrey had no time for her. Without Hobson's aid the requests for information were coming in much too fast for him to handle. His "assistant" would have to wait; this was more important than mother-henning a new clerk.

Geoffrey studied the portable flatscreen which was hooked into the minicomp he had been using since Hobson's death. Odd, he thought, how much he still grieved over the loss of his proper butler, ever polite and correct.

"Archivist, you must let me do *something*!"

He spared her a glance. He was busy, busier than he had ever been, and he realized he had never felt more alive than he did at the moment. He grinned. She might be a political pawn, a single stone in a *Go* game, soon to have his job, but at the moment he felt no rancor toward her. If she wanted to work, he could find plenty for her to do. "All right, my dear— collect all the spheres on nuclear and fusion engineering you can find and have them delivered to the Spindle. Get them to Level One and the Outsiders will take them from there. And locate that old Houghton recorder and put it on line; there are a thousand hours' worth of troubleshooting programs stashed away in the disk files which somebody will need sooner or later."

She nodded and was gone. Good—she seemed bright enough, she had the proper schooling—he did not remember her, but she had been in one of his classes—and perhaps, after all this was over, she would be able to replace him. But for now he was still archivist—and there was work to do.

"Bern, this has got to get to the engineers in the Spindle. The lifts are down; you'll have to climb one of the spokes." Dooley shoved a plastic vacctube at Michan.

Michan nodded and grabbed the tube. "On my way." He almost welcomed the dangerous assignment—it would take his mind off Susan as he had last seen her in Medical, being bandaged and anesthetized while Katsu stared at his mother with tearful eyes.

The strange spot in the hall was no longer simply shimmering when he passed it now; the wall seemed alive, undulating almost as if it were made of liquid plastic. A wave would start at a point two meters high and run to the juncture of the wall and floor. The bright peripheral flashes were there, too—more often and sharper than before. Genaloni stood by the wall, staring at the phenomenon. He glanced at Michan. "Watch this." He extended his gloved hand toward the wall. As Michan watched, the man's fingers sank into the surface as though it were a gel. Genaloni continued pushing until his pressure-suited arm was elbow-deep into the wall—then he pulled his hand out. He was holding a pair of white and red wires. He glanced at Michan, then released them; they sank slowly back into the wall. There was a ripple on the surface of the wall which smoothed out as Michan stared at it.

Michan did not know what he said. Whatever it was, it was spoken in a whisper.

"Yeah," Genaloni said. "There's another place not quite like it in the head at 220. Only it sort of swirls."

Michan stared at the wall, wondering what would happen to the ship if something like this started on the hull.

Susan was full of painkillers; her wrist was immobilized in an orthoplastic foam splint, her fractured jaw had been injected with orthobondic, her rib wrapped with a fulton tape. There was nothing to be done for her nose, save packing and the overall effect of the long-acting Decadron injection to relieve swelling and inflammation. She moved through air which seemed as thick as cotton. When she entered the Main Room, all who could spare the moment stared at her in shock.

She ordered them back to their tasks with an impatient gesture. "Where is Bevins?"

"Medical," Rashid said. "He—saw monsters in the methyl solution."

Susan nodded. "All right. Timmons, you take the Schawlow-Townes. Cycle it down and off-line—"

"We'll lose thirty-five percent of what we've got left—"

"We're going to lose fifty percent no matter what we do! The main fusion horse and the MHDs are gone! We're going to the aux-gen and the baby masers, that's all were going to be able to keep running. We've got to keep the heloid bottled or we lose the whole ship!"

They stared at her. Susan could see it on their faces: they were afraid. They were looking to her for guidance, for some kind of answers to the horrors that would not stop. She had none. The medications were making her stupid and all she could think to do was keep things going by the book. If she could not deal with them as people, then she could as organic machines.

"All right, I want a kick-in starting with One, Three, Five and Seven, then the even numbers—but hold Eight at minimum as a reserve; we'll probably need the draw soon enough. The Secondary will hold if we don't strain it too much. We've got to keep something for the spinjets."

Her crew looked tired, but they moved. Susan sat down slowly, staring at a non-functioning optical pump. The device seemed limp, somehow, as if it were wax left too long under a forming lamp. She blinked. It had to be the drugs. . . .

"Without full power to the spinjets, the torus will begin to slow its rotation, due to friction from the bearings," Leo told Demond. "It will take a long time before we'll begin to notice a lessening of the pseudogravity, however. We have more pressing things to worry about."

"Such as?"

"As of now, we are running at less than half of our normal power. All non-essential systems are shut down and we're conserving everywhere we can. Our paramount concerns are life-support, and the maintenance of the magnetic fields that hold the artificial sun in containment. So far, we are maintaining—"

"But we can't keep it up indefinitely," Demond finished.

"No. We can't."

"And we still don't know *why* things are falling apart. What do we do, Leo? How do we deal with this?"

Leo murmured, " 'When the screen is rolled up the great sky opens.' "

"What?!"

"A line from a poem by a Zen master named Mumon, called *The Gateless Gate*."

Demond sat back in his chair in disbelief. "I need answers and you're giving me *poetry!*"

Leo said thoughtfully, "Louis, have you heard the rumor that users of the drug Zanshin are not affected by the madness syndrome which has five hundred people paralyzed? That they don't 'see' the wrongness all over the ship?"

"I've heard something about it, yes."

"Suppose that it's true, Louis. Suppose that an altered mental or even spiritual state somehow affects whatever it is causing all this."

"Are you trying to say that we only *think* the computer and the mains died?"

"No, of course not. But what if the cause might somehow be affected by our mental states? If we could somehow drop the scales from our eyes, roll up the screen, really *see* what's happening. . . . "

"Leo," Demond said flatly, "That's crazier than anything else that's been going on."

Leo nodded slightly. "Perhaps."

"What if it *were* true? What would you have me do—feed everybody on the ship dope?"

Leo sighed. "In a scattering matrix, one has to consider all the possibilities."

"What the hell is a scattering matrix?"

"In subatomics, we can't observe a particular particle—only the area in which it is occurring. When particles collide, they scatter, and we can draw a circle around them only in terms of probability. An S matrix is a table of probabilities; we talk of the interactions rather than the particles. It is the dance rather than the dancers."

"*Dammit*, Leo! I don't want mysticism, I want cold, hard facts—"

"What I'm trying to tell you is that there *are* no cold and hard facts, Louis. Not objectivity, but subjectivity, rules. Individual microcosms are becoming the macrocosm."

Demond's com buzzed; he stabbed the box with a finger. "Yes?"

"Susan Hanawashi, Louis." Her voice sounded infinitely

tired to Leo, but rational. "The torus is slowing down."

"We know that, Susan—Leo says the effects will be minimal for—"

"You don't understand, Louis. The spinjets are still firing, but we're slowing down anyway. I can't explain it, but we're dropping rotational speed by nearly a hundred kilometers an hour."

Demond looked at Leo in shock. Leo showed no surprise. "But," the Administrator whispered, "that's imposs—" and then he stopped. There was no point in saying it any more. It was all impossible—and it was all happening.

TWENTY-EIGHT

"How long?" Demond asked.

Susan's voice was quite calm. "Eight hours and forty minutes. That's if it continues at the present rate."

"Can you increase power to the spinjets? Maybe that—"

"We've already tried that—as much as we can. It doesn't seem to make any difference if the jets are on, off or at overload."

Demond wiped sudden sweat from his forehead. "What do you suggest, Hanawashi?" There was no reply. Demond punched at the device's controls. Nothing—the unit was dead. Feeling close to panic, he looked at Leo Chin.

"How can this be happening? I can accept mechanical malfunctions, but this—this is like something malevolent, *alive*. . . ."

Leo shrugged. "It may well be alive, depending on your definitions of life. I can show you experiments indicating that subatomic particles 'know' what other particles do—even kilometers apart." He stood. "The important thing now is to warn people. We must anchor things, prepare. As the rotation of the torus slows, the centripetal force will fade. If it stops, conditions will be similar to the Hub. The wheel is not designed for that. Things will be even more chaotic than they are now."

"My com is dead," Demond said, as if that meant something important.

"They may all be. But there are portables. We've got to—" he stopped suddenly and stared at the wall behind Demond. The Administrator turned.

The wall of his office appeared to be *breathing*. It inflated, swelling to a balloon-like lump, then sank to flatness before repeating the cycle. Demond stared at it in horror.

Leo looked at the phenomenon expressionlessly. "It's getting worse. I think we are running out of time—in every sense of the phrase. I'll sound the alarms and make the announcements. People will have to know that the wheel is going to stop spinning and that things are going to become even more surreal."

Demond nodded. He was watching the wall pulse, out, in, out, in, out. . . . "This *has* to be a hallucination," he mumbled. "Or a dream."

Leo said gently, "Louis, I'm beginning to think there are no hallucinations, no dreams—only stages of reality."

Demond forced himself to look away from the insanity that was happening to his office wall. This could not be happening. He should be in control, should be able to take care of it . . . .

"Leo—?" He looked about the office. Leo was gone. There was no way the physicist could have left the tiny office, Demond knew, without his noticing. But he was gone. Demond shook his head. He was having trouble concentrating. The room seemed to be shimmering slightly; he reached for his com again in panic, heard static pulsing from it in regular, hypnotic waves, though the button was still in the "off" position. Demond snatched his hand away quickly, closed his eyes, hiding his face in his hands. His desk, where his elbows rested, felt oddly soft, plastic, yielding. He pulled his arms up into his chest and huddled in his chair, rocking slightly.

Sean Chuma Mkono was one of the first to know about the slowing rotation. He was on a laser-line to the Spindle, and he picked up the problem quickly. It would not affect much in the Hub, but the wheel would be—

Then the "floor" of his office—the surface his desk was attached to—turned into a plastic whirlpool. Sean pushed away from the desk and floated over it, peering at the surface. He prudently did not touch it. It looked like warm, swirling honey.

He heard Kristin scream. He shoved away from the wall and shot through the doorway, hooked his left hand around the jamb and stopped.

Kristin was floating in the corner of her office, curled up, staring at her word processor. The machine was smoking and a purplish flame, almost like a bunsen ring, was pulsing in an even circle from the VDT.

In the hall outside something groaned metallically, followed by a brittle pop. Mkono pushed away from the door and floated toward Kristin.

She screamed again, and he could *see* the sound—a long streamer of bright orange which twined outward and flared across the room. He reached Kristin, grabbed her, hugged her to him. She did not seem to notice. Behind him the word processor flared brightly and spewed blacker smoke. The sound circuit kicked on and began to wind up and down the scale in a fragmented series of cheeps and whines.

What was happening?

He used his shoulder to push them away from the wall and steered Kristin through the outer door into the hall. A chunk of thick plastic floated by, trailing a line of acrid smoke. Part of a flywheel, he realized, shattered somehow. . . .

Someone screamed nearby, the sound trailing off into a low giggle. Something was clacking loudly, and part of a copper conduit lay circled in the air like overcooked spaghetti.

He pushed them into one of the Eros rooms—private chambers that could be rented for more intimate forms of zero-G recreation. The walls were soft plush, and there was nothing— he hoped—potentially deadly. But he knew that there was no real safety anywhere—anything could happen.

Kristin was quiet; she watched him with frightened eyes and would not answer him when he tried to talk to her. Finally Sean said, "All right. You stay here; I'm going to web you into the sleep-slot. Don't get out until I come back."

He closed off the sleep-slot with cotton mesh so she would

not drift around the room. Then he tried his remote's com. It was not working. He had to get to somebody who knew what was going on—if anyone did.

Sean made his way back into the hall. More debris was evident. He passed people, some floating in panic, some attempting to deal with the increasing chaos. He visited the various departments, gave orders and encouragement. The slowing rotation was not going to affect the Hub, of course, but the other bizarre happenings would. He put Hernandez and Spottiswoode in charge, then made his way to his cube. There he found his wings, stored in their compact tube. Already the gravity had to be dropping toward zero-G in the main portion of the ship. The torus was too large to move around in without wings.

His first duty was to his department, he knew—but to perform it most efficiently he had to find out what was going on. The coms were all out—he would have to go down to the wheel.

When the water in Eight Ball's aquarium had begun to form fingers that reached for the ceiling, Scott St. Martin had taken the capsule of Zanshin.

They had come by his cube just before mirror turn, Kagan and the others who had caught him in Strogwall's cube. He had been surprised—he had not thought they would decide in his favor. Kagan had explained why: "It's starting to happen now. St. Martin. You can't sense it, but we can—and we're going to need everyone we can get linked into us. The torus is slowing rotation. It's going to be madness, very soon. Take the capsule, link with your dolphin if you can. You'll hear from us."

It seemed to work, as far as minimizing the unreality about him. The peripheral psychedelic effects were much more muted now, and he could no longer see the wavering, impossible things the water had been doing. He could maintain a kind of focus, this time.

He had given the second capsule to Killikup.

He heard the alarms sounding. The loudspeakers began to broadcast instructions, telling people to secure everything they could. So it *was* happening. There was something he should check on, but he could not remember what it was. He felt definitely lighter—he seemed to move with languorous, dreamlike motion, though how much of that was real and how much the drug he could not tell. *Does it matter?* he asked himself. For some reason, the thought was very amusing.

Scott.

His heart leaped for a moment—*Killikup!*—but even before the denial came within his mind, he knew that was impossible. Whatever form mental communication with another species would take, it would not be in spoken English, of that he was sure.

It was CIRCLE.

That's right, Scott. Reach out to us, reach out to Killikup. It's time to exit the system.

The voices, the *presences*, in his head, were comforting, supporting. Reach out to Killikup, indeed. Just try to stop him.

The fingers on the surface of the aquarium seemed to be settling down nicely now. Good. They were right, Zanshin was the answer. . . . Scott calmed his mind, using the meditative techniques he had practiced, and prepared to reach out—

The water abruptly changed color and viscosity, roiling sluggishly like oil, shifting hues. Scott blinked. Was it the drug, or reality? Either way, it should not be happening. He should be able to see through such images to the underlying truth. He tried to stand, and the action sent him floating into the air; he bumped his head on the ceiling. The pseudogravity *was* fading— and faster, somehow, than had been anticipated. With a gasp, Scott suddenly remembered what he had to check on. *The pumps—!* If they were not shut down, Ring River and every other body of water on *Heaven Star* would be hurled from their beds.

He could not reach the pumps from here, and the controls no longer worked. He had already gathered all the dolphins, including Killikup, and also Eight Ball, into a holding tank, the top of which had been covered with an oxygen-permeable membrane. They, at least, would be safe.

He felt something in his mind, a touch of something profoundly alien and yet familiar. No words, hardly even concepts—a sensation of sleek swiftness in a liquid world.

Killikup? Is it really you?

The human thoughts from the others were silent now, waiting, as though respectful of this moment. The sensation shifted. Scott St. Martin saw a thousand generations of life in the seas flash by; birth, mating, play, eating, death. There were no names, no words, but the essence was: *I am here; we are connected.*

Scott felt the truth of it. It had worked! He was mentally linked with Killikup! Images danced in his mind: smells and tastes and sonic impressions. He made his way carefully to the holding tank, peered down into the water. Killikup floated a little bit away from the rest of the water creatures, looking up at him.

Nearby, he saw water from the river surging into the air, forming perfect spheres that were stretched and distorted by the air currents. Showers of tiny droplets surrounded them, hazing the air. The bubbles of water moved slowly, like balloons. Scott looked back at Killikup and smiled. Things were definitely falling apart—they might not survive. But at least he and Killikup could face the end together. He gathered his love and let it flow from him toward the dolphin. *Feel. Understand. Accept—please.*

He felt/heard the dolphin's response: *Kle'echklot'ippl'kon.* It was a dolphin term which might have taken months of computer time to translate, but Scott knew instantly, precisely, what it meant.

Killikup loved him in return—but not as he loved. To the dolphin, Scott realized, he was no different from Eight Ball, the octopus—one who played with him, fetched him things upon command, and gave him unquestioned, unqualified love.

A pet.

Scott St. Martin's heart shriveled and blackened like paper in a fire. He opened his mouth and screamed—a wordless, raging howl. He felt the others within his mind clamoring, sensed their sudden concern. He ignored it, looked back at the river, which was breaking up and floating away. He pushed himself awkwardly away from Killikup, into a long, flailing leap that brought him up to a huge water bubble floating above the ground. The impact shattered it into smaller globules, but they were still large enough.

Scott, no—! We need you. . . .

The salt of his tears joined the fresh water of the bubble as he opened his mouth and inhaled. Coldness filled his lungs. *A pet.*

By the time he reached Phaedra's cube, Pyramus was half-floating, half-running. He had left his post to check on her, unable to bear the suspense of not knowing where she was, what was happening to her. Her cube was empty. He stood in the doorway, watching *Heaven Star* falling to pieces about him, and cried in frustration. If the ship was dying, he wanted to be with her, to repair at this last extremity the breach that had been widening between them. But now it was too late—she was gone.

"Liquitronics had dropped point-nine-seven, Susan!"

"Seal it! It's all we can do!" Susan held her hands to her head, as though trying to block out the ceaseless flow of fresh disasters. Her injuries and the painkillers combined to make concentration an effort. She floated in a semi-fetal curl above the floor; the torus had increased its deceleration rate, was almost at a standstill now. Even as she thought about that, she heard a vast, almost subsonic groan that reverberated through the walls, and saw everything loose in the room, which inertia had settled to the floor, suddenly flung gently into the air.

"Zero-G!" Someone shouted behind her.

Not quite, she thought; the jolt would have distributed itself equally between the wheel and the despun Hub—there would be an infinitesimal amount of centripetal force still. Or perhaps not, considering how the laws of physics were collapsing. It did not really matter; to all extents and purposes, they were weightless.

"Susan!" It was Rashid. "We've got an emergency!"

She turned carefully, grabbing a cable to avoid floating away. What could possibly be worse than what had already happened?

She saw the white expressions of her crew as they stared at the single monitor that was still working. It showed one of the external mirrors surrounding the heloid, which reflected the light of the artificial sun through the window strips. There was something odd about its shape—

"It's warped," someone said. "Don't ask me how, but the mirror's—changed. It's focusing the light from the heloid on the number four guidance module."

The monitor picture shifted. Susan saw the rectangular shape of the GM. There was a spot of light on it, perhaps three inches across, that was too bright to look at—a miniature image of the heloid, focused on the surface.

Susan felt her mouth go dry. "Can we shift the mirror?"

"I've tried. The gimbals are seized up."

She was not sure how she managed to ask the next question. "How long do we have?"

"Maybe half an hour."

"The Outsiders?"

"I can't raise them. No communications." As he spoke, the last monitor suddenly flickered and went dead. The crew looked at each other. They were alone, cut off from the rest of the ship.

The focused beam from the mirror, hot enough to boil metal, would burn through the GM's casing and disrupt the magnetic fields holding the heloid. The high-energy plasma would expand like a fusion explosion, consuming the entire ship. And she could do nothing to stop it.

It was the Nightmare Dance, she realized, come true.

"Phaedra!"

She turned, and saw Pyramus hurrying toward her on the path, his long-legged stride exaggerated by the fading pseudo-gravity. She felt a great welling of sympathy for him; he looked tired, battered. *Whatever happens*, she thought, *I am glad that we loved each other*.

He stopped before her. "I was coming back to check on you."

"I'm all right. Tell me how I can help."

He was silent, looking down at his feet, for so long that she thought he had not heard his question. Then he raised his eyes and met her gaze, and she was surprised by the intensity of it.

"I would if I could, love. But all I can tell you is that you will. And that I *know*."

She shook her head uncertainly. "I'm not sure what you—"

Pyramus grabbed her by the shoulders tightly enough to surprise her. "Trust me on this, love. I know this like I've never known anything before. When the time comes, you'll know what to do.''

A deafening crash seemed to echo and reverberate for minutes through the air and through the ground. They both turned, and saw that Cham's, the hanging restaurant, had fallen. Though the pseudogravity was beginning to fade, there had still been enough centripetal force to fling the massive, teardrop-shaped structure against the floor of the Main Level with enough impetus to shatter part of a cube complex. Phaedra saw smoke curling up from a fire that had started, heard the faint cries and shouts.

Pyramus kissed her, then released her. "Where are you going?" she asked, as he turned away.

"Level One. They've had a hull blowout."

"Pyramus!" The confusion and fear in her own voice frightened her. He looked back at her. She was not sure what she had intended to say; what she did say was, "Be with me."

"Always," he said. And then he was gone.

"Pyramus!"

Michan Bern used a CO_2 cartridge to propel himself down the wide corridor in Level One toward the Security Chief. "What are you doing here?"

"I heard you've had a blowout up here."

"You heard right—it's a bad one, too. The whole team's working on it. I was on my way there—it's way the hell over by Spoke One."

"Section sealed off?"

"I don't know. No communications anymore—just word of mouth. We're still breathing, so I guess they're handling it."

Pyramus had hold of Michan's belt, and the Outsider's gas cannister was pushing them down the corridor as they talked. As they passed a viewport of the hull, both were dazzled by a sudden burst of harsh light before the window could adjust.

"What in—?" Michan looked at the heloid. "Must be problems with the pellet-feeder."

"It didn't come from the sun—it came from over there." Pyramus pointed. Michan's gaze followed, and he gasped. "The GM—what the hell's happening to it?"

"What do you mean? What is it?"

"I'll explain when I find out. Come on, Gray! I'll need your help!"

Phaedra stood in the Dance Emporium.

She was alone, but now she was alone without loneliness. The dance floor was empty, the shining wood reflecting the overhead lights. The quiet was like a robe about her. It seemed to her that she, who had 'cast the Dream Dance so often, had been moving in a dream herself for the past several weeks, and was only now beginning to wake up.

The increasing trouble and panic she had observed as she would a late-night holo; tired and apathetic, not thinking, just experiencing. After all, what could she do to affect things in any way? Best to leave such worries, such efforts, to people like Leo Chin—to those who knew the answers, or at least what questions to ask.

Phaedra thought about the Dance. Though it was not exactly what Marx had in mind when he wrote his Manifesto, still, in her mind, it was the ultimate communistic statement: from each according to their ability to each according to their need. But her need was never fulfilled. She shared herself with them, and in return received—what? Certainly there was—*or had been*, she thought bitterly—the adoration, the fame, the money. And, above all else, the satisfaction of the Dance itself. But there was also the jealousy and lust and failure of her own receptive empathy. She had never been able to tune into another Dancer's 'cast on full receptive mode and enjoy it; she was too much the sender to receive, too much the professional to relax with a lesser performance.

She began to stretch.

She had not stretched, had not practiced, for weeks. It seemed strange to do it now, with the ship dying about her, but she did not question the rightness of it. The Dance had been her life, and now, it seemed, it was all she had left. For as long as she could remember, she had worked at it, polishing it, crafting it into a perfect harmony of mind and motion, always seeking to make it better, to make it the perfect brush for her psychic canvas—

Why?

Phaedra blinked. Where had the question come from? It

was not something she had ever asked herself before. Why?
Because the Dance was—

A means to an end? Why cannot it be an end unto itself?

Because that's not what it's for! Its purpose is to—

*Why must it have a purpose? Why can't it be what it is, for
no other reason save that it exists? Why must it do?*

Phaedra felt suddenly dizzy. She sat down on the resilient
wood. All of her life she had danced for a purpose, to help
others, to bring them the peace of the Dream Dance—the
peace she had never felt. That the Dream Dance could simply
be, without any reason for being, was incomprehensible, irrational. It meant giving up the control that had always been a
part of her, it meant—exiting the system.

When the time comes, you'll know what to do.

Phaedra began to giggle, and then to laugh. She threw back
her head and let her laughter fill the empty chamber. After
a moment, more lights blazed, and the door at the far end
opened. Nick Daley ran into the room.

"My God, Phaedra—what are you doing here? Don't you
kow what's happening to the ship?" He grabbed her arm and
pulled her into the control room.

"Hook me up, Nick! I've got to reach them, tell them all
what I've just—"

"Are you *crazy*? After what happened the last time? Do you
think I can take a chance on another malfunction, on making
things worse—if that's possible? It's all I can do to just hold
up my end of communications!" He looked at a reading on a
VU meter. "Sanders! We're losing the beam from the power-
feed lasers!"

Phaedra tried to convince him, but he was adamant; he
would do nothing that might add to the chaos. She gave up,
and half-ran, half-floated out into the hallway and up the
stairs to the roof of the complex. From there she looked out
over the section of the Main Level as it stretched away from
her, rising up to meet the ceiling. The landscape made her
think of paintings by Dali and Bosch: the trees were waving as
though whipped by a gale, though there was none. People and
some objects were beginning to float in free-fall as the torus
continued to slow. Several of the buildings seemed to be
melting, losing their integrity, plasticrete flowing sluggishly.
There were continual bursts and flickers of prismatic color
and spectral shifts, like rainbow lightning. Bubbles of water

and other liquids were everywhere. Mirages appeared and vanished in slow, stately time.

Phaedra closed her eyes; the sights were making her dizzy. She had to Dance, but how could she reach them all without the aid of the neurocast equipment? And how could she perform in what was rapidly becoming zero-G? As to the latter, she would *have* to, that was all; she would have to trust her reflexes, the skills gained in Hub flying. As for the former— she had never tried it before. She would have to do the best she could.

That was what she had to tell them all—to do the best they could.

On the wide, flat surface of the roof, as a world unravelled about her, Phaedra Adjurian began to Dance.

TWENTY-NINE

Leo Chin was on his way to the Spindle when he saw her.

He recognized the Dancer instantly, and felt no surprise at seeing her even though he was not wearing a headset. The Sending was as strong as he had ever experienced it, if not stronger.

Leo nodded in satisfaction. Phaedra had sensed what to do, had made the right choice. And he knew the time had come to make his.

He settled into a lotus position. The Dancer moved about him, her form trailing light, weaving a new vision of the way things would now be. Leo Chin knew it was time to abandon completely the Western modes of thought he had moved in for so long. Such ways would not enable him to survive the madness on *Heaven Star*. Perception must be altered.

Exit the system, the Dancer whispered within his mind. *Understand, accept, transcend. Become a part of the universe, for the first time. . . .*

He knew now why the new drug, Zanshin, seemed to help some people. But it was an illusion: it would not last. She was right: The change, the *acceptance*, had to come from within.

The problem was, of course, that the ship might not survive.

Even with the chance at a higher consciousness, it would take many new minds to win the fight. It would be ironic for mankind to be given the chance to take a step upward only to be destroyed while doing so. Leo watched the Dancer twirling about him, her art confirming this. She would do everything she could to ensure that this would not happen—but she needed help.

The ship trembled slightly, and he bounced with the movement, floating slowly into the air. He did not unfold his legs—indeed, he hardly noticed that he was floating.

It was one thing to recognize intellectually the need for acceptance, but quite another to actually do it. Enlightenment was not gained easily. But even as these negative thoughts formed within him, he recognized their folly.

It is yours already, the Dancer confirmed, and Leo Chin felt sheepish at forgetting such a basic precept. He had to learn nothing—he knew the answer—it was, had always been, merely momentarily forgotten.

As he realized this, the Dancer vanished.

Leo Chin laughed. He stretched his legs from the lotus fold and settled slowly toward the floor. He could see the lines of energy which ran around him, the *ch'i* of which he had spoken for so long, but never really experienced before this moment. He routed them into gordian lines and focused. Weightfulness then existed in a pocket around him. He began to walk.

He passed a melting wall, looked at it and said, "Stop that." The wall became still, a thin sheet of material which still vibrated, but within the realm of "solid" perception. The microcosm remained the macrocosm, but it was now filtered. A small adjustment, just as the weightfulness was a small thing. Leo knew he could not reach beyond a tiny range, and that even then there were limits. It did not matter. It would be enough.

The Dance, forever the Dance. . . .

But this time it was different. A small part of Phaedra which was not buried under the layers of almost-reflexive motions and mindsets stood back like an *atman* and observed, as if riding just above her shoulder. It was as though she could see the play of muscle in her arms and legs and torso, smell the sharp sweat, hear the rush of air through her hair as she danced in zero-G, all removed yet somehow more real than the reality.

In Zen, the thinker is the thought, the doer the deed. For a brief time, before she wondered how and why this was happening to her, Phaedra was simply that. There was no past, no future—only the eternal now.

As soon as she wondered why it was so, it was gone. But the memory had been burned into her soul. Phaedra Adjurian had felt what it was that others felt when they tuned into her Dance; she *understood* what it was she did for them. More; she *accepted*.

Though the momentless moment was gone, lost in questions of how and why, the Dream Dance had to continue. She could not stop now. By abandoning control for the first time, she had performed to her limits—she was in touch with everyone on the ship, holistically, over nine thousand individuals, each of whom were interpreting and accepting or rejecting her Dream Dance, her wordless message. She felt fear, the inability to handle it—

Dance, Dancer. We are with you. Draw upon us.

She felt strength being offered her from other minds. She sensed who they were: those who had sought uplifting and understanding through the use of the drug Zanshin.

It is not the way; we realize that now. But through it we can help you somewhat.

Phaedra accepted their strength gratefully. It was not the joy, the oneness, that had sustained her for that infinite time before, but it would be enough. There were still so many people to touch. . . .

Ahead of her and behind her, the curved interior of the torus seemed to straighten, as though she now stood within a long tube. She could see down the echoing length of it, could see herself standing atop the building, Dancing. She did not know if it was some freak change in the refractive index of the air, or part of the new vision afforded her now. It did not matter. She pushed her new awareness through the length of the Main Level, and beyond, expanding it, reaching through the levels of the ship, outward towards the hull, touching more and more minds. . . .

Thousands of tiny spheres floated around Geoffrey Merle-

Douglass, metal worlds the size of children's marbles, no two in the same orbit. All was chaos within his study; the torus had not slowed to a smooth stop, allowing objects at rest to remain at rest, but had suddenly jolted, as though some massive bearing had seized up. It did not matter why; what mattered was that everything not anchored had been hurled gently at a forty-five degree trajectory along the angle of the ship's rotation, and the debris and detritus of more than a score of years, the impedimentia of Geoffrey's professional life, had been no exception.

The archivist had made half-hearted efforts to gather everything, but had soon given up. There was simply too much of it.

There has always been too much, he thought bitterly. His thirst for knowledge had never been quenched, and now never would. He was tired of trying. The excitement and usefulness he had felt earlier had been replaced by a sense of futility. He sat alone and shivering in the desolate autumn country of old age.

It was all pointless now anyway, was it not? *Heaven Star* was dying, and Geoffrey at last acknowledged that he was ready for it. He was tired—tired of fighting the endless war against a disease that would leave his body functioning, but his mind gone dark.

He looked up suddenly, realizing he was not alone. The Dancer spun before his chair, her movement sending the floating spheres and modules into an armillary frenzy. He remembered the Nightmare Dance, but somehow the thought engendered no fear—this was unmistakably the Dancer he had known and trusted so many times.

She stretched her hands out to him imploringly. *There are new things to know, wisdom beyond knowledge. Come, let me lead you to a new wing in the heavenly library. . . .*

Geoffrey sat quite still, watching her. His first thought, when he realized he was seeing the Dancer without the interface of a headset, was that the madness he had feared for so long had stolen in, swiftly and silently, and taken over. There was no way he could prove this was not so, but still he did not believe it. But then, does a madman ever believe in his madness?

I offer you a choice, the Dancer told him. *A possibility to explore your own mind as you never have before, to learn of things you never dreamed existed before. Come along with me. . . .*

How can I, Geoffrey thought wearily. *This new ground is the domain of madness. I am an old man; I have spent my years in solitude, working with what humanity has gathered. I am a cataloguer, a creature of systems, of logic, of order, of reason. I cannot follow you quietly to this new place. It is too much.*

The Dancer's body language grew concerned, urgent. *Come.*

The spheres flew around him like planets about a sun; the walls lived and moved. His long-standing citadel of reason was besieged.

Come . . . .

Geoffrey Merle-Douglass looked at the Dancer. "I am too old," he said aloud. "It is too much for me."

For an instant, it seemed as if she would vanish, and he knew that if she did, he would lose the battle he had waged for so long. He felt a single stab of fear at the thought—and at that, the Dancer reached for him, seized his hands and pulled him to his feet. *You cannot accept what you still fear,* she told him. *You have dealt with changes all your life, archivist. You have seen the colonization of the planets, the building of a starship. This is but one more change—more sweeping, perhaps, but no different. You are not ready to die yet. There is always more to learn, more to know—accept this, and take joy from it. After all, someone must be here to record this moment—who better qualified than you?*

And with that, she pulled him into the Dance, and he laughed as he realized the truth of her words, laughed as he grasped the folly of his fear, which he felt dissipate like shadows at mirror-turn. The madness he had dreaded for so many years was now here—he was a part of it, and could at last name it—it was, purely, simply, awareness.

Louis Demond floated over his desk, which was metamorphosizing into something different—what, he did not know, nor did it matter. The walls of his office seemed to close in on him. His worst fear had come true—he was no longer in control! He could not be, unless—

He looked out the window and saw the Dancer, floating above a scenario of madness; a chaos of floating debris and people, of huge globes of water and shimmering light. She spoke to him, completing his thought, telling him what he so dreaded to hear:

Unless you give it up completely.

No!

But that, he knew, was the choice, the ultimate decision of a life full of decisions. *Let it all go, and it can be yours. Your position is not important, your power is not important. You must release it, or be crushed by it.*

He was a survivor! He could live through this! He pushed himself toward the door, but the door was no longer there. The wall was a madly swirling blot of colors and textures and smells. Demond looked back out the window, but the Dancer was no longer there. Instead it was Fear that now danced with Demond; he felt her cold hands on his back, her panicked breath in his face.

A survivor. . . .

He managed a final scream.

Leo Chin walked. He appeared to be surrounded by a pocket of calm within the insanity, but it did not seem that way to him. The non-casuality that permeated the ship was, to him, sane. Around him, *Heaven Star* was in chaos: People who had lost their holds on something solid, or had that solidity dissolve from their grasps, floated like wind-blown leaves, terror-stricken. So many of them had refused to accept, or could not accept, what the Dancer was trying to make clear to everyone on the ship. Those stared in dazed disbelief as about them floated bulkheads, holoproj sets, shoes, great bubbles of water and a myriad other flotsam. But where Leo walked, things were quiet. It was not madness to him, but rather merely newness; he understood it, was able to reshape it into something approximating the reality he had formerly known.

The chunk of metal and plastic which floated ten meters above him had no weight, but it did have mass. Leo watched the object, which he recognized as a metamix distributor. In the pseudogravity of the rotating hull it would have weighed nearly a metric ton. It was moving quickly. Leo estimated its path, and looked ahead to where it would strike.

He saw the children.

There were nine or ten of them, clutching each other and a portion of a roof which was drifting, anchored by a single strut to the unit it had once covered. The material was thinner than a wall—after all, it only had to stop light, not rain or wind—and it was beginning to shred. Some of the children were crying; one clutched a dog, half-beagle, half-poodle, in his arms. Several others were quiet, staring into some personal void, eyes wide. Leo recognized one of the latter: Katsu Hanawashi.

He saw that they had perhaps ten seconds before the massive distributor crushed them.

Even as he realized it, he leaped, releasing at the same time his hold on the lines of weightfulness. He shot toward the slowly tumbling block of machinery, hands extended. Perhaps even now the Dancer led all or some of the children toward the new manner of sight, but he could not take the chance of their understanding and accepting in time. He hit the artificial asteroid hard, deflecting it from its path. But it was not enough; it would still strike half of the children.

Leo Chin smiled, remembering Ian Kyle as a child. So bright, he had been; so dedicated to learning. He had failed Ian; he would not fail these children as well.

He wrapped weightfulness about himself and the distributor, creating an attraction between it and the floor. The straight line became an arc. Leo thought of Ian again. Yin and Yang always balanced, eventually.

Katsu saw the metamix distributor strike the floor of the Main Level with enough force to tear almost completely through the surface. With the new way of seeing that the Dancer had showed him, he understood also why Leo Chin had elected to save them by sacrificing himself. He looked at the other children, including Tracy, who were still crying. *Tracy never could understand things,* he thought with great sympathy.

Aloud, he said to them, "It's okay. I know what to do now." He looked at the disintegrating roof. It was perfectly right the way it was—but it would also be all right *this* way—and, as Tracy and the others watched in disbelief,

Katsu rebound the polyfibers of the roof and made it strong again.

He could do more than that, he was sure—but for now, this was enough.

Susan Hanawashi floated in the control room of Level Eight, trapped, as were her associates. The doors had melted shut, and the temperature was rapidly rising—from where, she could not tell, for there was nothing in the room capable of overheating.

She could feel the gaze of Rashid, Wilkerson, Running Bear and the others on her. She was the boss, the leader—she should have the answers. *Help us!* they were saying silently. *Save us!*

She could not help them; she was tired, injured . . . but it was more than that. She had never known how to give reassurance, aid, succor, to anyone other than Katsu. She had never been able to touch people that way. She thought of Katsu, and Michan, whom she knew she would never see again.

Then something flickered in the corner of her vision, and she turned—and gasped. The Dancer balanced lightly on a console's top, dancing in defiance of weightlessness. Susan felt a single moment of freezing fear—it was too close to her memory of the Nightmare Dance. Was it coming true, then? Had the Dancer focused the mirror upon the GM? It seemed too much to believe it had been an accident. . . .

She heard a voice in her mind, soothing, calming. *I bring you hope, not horror. Draw upon the love you have known, and the strength that is yours if you only accept it.*

Wonderingly, she realized what was being asked of her. She had to cease intellectualizing, begin understanding. She looked at the others, wondering if they, too, saw and understood. Together, they could save themselves, as others might be able to save the ship. . . .

She was aware, suddenly, of where the heat was coming from. An easy enough thing to fix—a bit of mental pressure *here*—

The temperature began to drop. Susan smiled at her friends. Some of them returned her smile, and she knew that they had understood what the Dancer had told them. The others they would calm and protect from harm. The madness still filled the ship, but there was a chance now. That was all any of them could ask for—a chance.

Sean Mkono swerved around a hail of shrapnel thrown out by an exploding wall. One of the pieces punched a small hole in his left wingtip, but that did not matter; the ripstop would keep the hole from tearing further. He could patch it later—if there was a later for him.

He saw a fire spreading nearby, the smoke expanding rather than rising. Closer, a man clutched at a floating branch. He was screaming, but the sound was quiet, as if his voice had worn out. Sean swooped toward him, seized him, used his momentum to carry him along. Already he had collected a dozen people from the air and brought them to the relative safety of a solid deck or cube roof. He knew he should return to the Hub, but so few people here seemed capable of coping in zero-G. He had only seen one or two others with the sense to use wings.

He deposited the man on a rooftop, leaving him clutching at a pipe, and flew away. The man would be safe—as long as the pipe did not turn to plastic vapor in his hands, or the roof crumble beneath him, or any other of a million things happen.

Someone was flying alongside him; Sean turned his head and, to his surprise, saw the Dancer turning and swooping in the air. How could she be here? He had no headset, there was no holoproj nearby—

Her laughter trailed behind them like a flag. *Does it really matter?* she asked, and he realized that it did not. She swooped and circled about him, inviting him to consider more important things.

What things? he asked silently. And then he knew. He drew away from her, tried to ignore her. He had given up the desire for legs a long time ago, had accepted that he would never have them. . . .

But you haven't. And therein lies the problem.

Sean braked himself, snapping his arms together, using the powerful muscles of his chest to overcome his inertia. He was suddenly covered with sweat. The Dancer was presenting him with a choice, he realized—she was showing him the way to cope with this new reality, to really be of help, to do more than just gather people from one precarious situation and transport them to another. But something was holding him back—the idea that he was not ready, not able, not *complete*. . . .

You are complete. All you have to do is realize it.

He shivered. All of his life he had wanted to be whole, to walk like everybody else. He had told himself and others that he had given up on that dream, had made his peace with it. But he knew that he had not. He realized now what that buried desire had done to him. It had kept him apart, had made him unhappy, had cost him dearly.

The whole thing suddenly seemed absurd to him. Sean Chuma Mkono laughed. He looked at the Dancer with gratitude, and then beyond her, accepting the craziness of the world about him as he finally accepted himself. And, by so doing, felt truly in touch with himself, felt clean and whole for the first time in his life. He could sense the rush of blood in his vessels, the secretions of glands, the chemical flow of hormones in his tissues, those same hormones which had once so puzzled Ian Kyle.

He looked about; the Dancer was gone. Sean stretched his wings out, seized forces he had had no conception of a moment before, and, without flapping, began to accelerate. He could sense the ship's pain; *Heaven Star* was wounded, perhaps dying, and he had to do what he could to save her and the people who were a part of her, and a part of him.

"The focusing mirrors," Michan said. "Has to be. Somehow one of the mirrors is focusing the heloid's light on the GM!"

They rocketed down the corridors. Around them, walls undulated and changed shape and color. They reached the suit room. The exosuits were clipped into their racks, except for loose parts which floated in the chamber. Outsiders could get into and out of a suit alone, but Michan knew he would have to help Pyramus. "Come on, slide into the rack! Hurry!"

Pyramus floated in front of the suit rack, his face covered with sweat. "No," he said. "I can't. I can't go . . . out there."

"You *have* to! That plasma will go through this hull like acid through paper, and it won't stop until the whole ship is consumed! We've got to shut that mirror down, and I'll need your help to do it!"

"There are other Outsiders—"

"Yeah—all on the opposite side of the ship, patching a hole! They couldn't get here in time, even if I could call them! Come on, Gray, into the suit! You'll be all right if you do what I say."

Pyramus could not breathe—then he realized he was holding his breath. He exhaled raggedly, the sound loud inside the exosuit. He stared at the thick door on the airlock before him. *Outside. . . .*

Michan seemed to sense his fear. "When you get out there, look only at the hull and what you can see three meters in front of you. Copy?"

Pyramus managed to nod. The inner door of the lock slid shut. Red lights changed to green; the outer door opened silently. . . .

Michan's voice reached him over the com in the suit's helmet. "I've linked us with a tow-bar. All you have to do is relax."

Pyramus nodded again, then realized that Michan was not looking at him. "Copy."

They stepped through the lock, and Outside.

Pyramus forced himself to look only at Michan's back and at the hull rushing by as they flew over it. He had to keep reminding himself to breathe, but so long as he did not look away from the ship, he thought he could stand it.

"We'll have to jet up a spoke to the hub," Michan told him.

Pyramus made the mistake of glancing up. He saw the bright surfaces of the mirrors. And if he lifted his gaze a little, he could see the heloid, and past that. . . .

Deep. Black, cold, endless. . . .

His heart thudded and his breath froze in his lungs. He jerked his gaze back at Michan Bern's exosuit. He felt the fear inside the suit with him, like some clammy inner lining against his skin.

The jets lifted them slowly past the curving surface of Spoke Four. Michan took no chances—he moved them carefully from one handhold to another. "Not far, now. Let's hope the external control set is still working."

They reached the area where the spoke joined the Hub. Pyramus felt a little safer there. He could glance in several directions and see nothing but reassuring metal, like being between two huge buildings. Michan guided them to a panel of controls, where he stabbed at the oversized buttons with his gloved fingers. "Damn it!" There was no need to explain what that meant.

"Can we turn it manually?" Pyramus asked.

"No; it's too big." For the first time Pyramus thought he heard panic in the Outsider's voice. "There's only one thing left to—"

Silence. Pyramus felt a moment of sheer terror as he realized his suit com had cut off—another manifestation, no doubt, of the strangeness that permeated the ship. Then Michan touched his helmet to Pyramus's. "I'll have to block that focused beam."

"With what?"

He could still hear fear in Michan's voice, but it was under control now. "My helmet. The visor's photosensitive, with a half-surface reflection. If I can reflect the beam long enough for you to get help—"

"You're crazy! How do you know it can handle that kind of heat?" Pyramus steeled himself and looked at the GM on the hull. They could see vapor rising from the bubbling paint and metal now. "You'll have to block it right at the focus point; if your faceplate can't take it, it'll burn right through you!"

"If you have any better ideas, I'll listen. But there's no more time to argue." He lifted Pyramus's arm, showed him the control buttons for the jets. "You've had enough experience flying in the Hub not to go sailing off into Deep. Get to the rest of the Outsiders near Spoke One and bring them back here!" He released the tow-bar then, and with no further words, pushed himself away from the spoke.

Pyramus watched the suited figure dwindle away. He swallowed bile, fought down an impulse to scream. He was on his own, Outside. He realized suddenly, ironically, that it was *this* from which his subconscious—warned, no doubt, by his flashes of prescience—had tried to protect him by fashioning his agoraphobia. But he had not understood, and now it was too late. He tried to push himself away from the reassuring metal—

He could not do it. He clung to the handhold, shivering, hiding from the hungry darkness that threatened to enfold him. Even if it meant the destruction of the ship and everyone on board, he could not do it. . . .

Pyramus.

He looked up and saw Phaedra before him, dancing against the backdrop of stars.

Oddly enough, he felt no surprise, no uncertainty of his own sanity. A great calmness settled over him. The linkage, so long lost between them, was back at last, stronger than ever.

My love, her movements sang. *Best love, only love . . . understand that you have nothing to fear from this universe. You have shown me the way; now let me show you. Let go of your terror, draw strength from me and from others. Be aware.*

Pyramus stared at her, moving in perfection against the stars, in the night which he had feared all his life. She showed him the beauty of it, made him realize the folly of fearing that of which he was so intimate a part. The rush of love purged the terror. He felt tears of thankfulness on his cheeks, reached out a gloved hand to her—and then stopped.

He *saw* something—not with his eyes, but with something more. He looked down at Michan, moving so slowly toward the GM, and knew: *He won't make it.*

He looked for Phaedra again, but she was gone. She had done what was necessary—the serenity, the knowledge, she had left him with was enough. He knew what was going to happen; his intermittent precognitive abilities were now under his control. The focused beam would disrupt the GM's circuitry a second before Michan reached it. The heloid would be loosed from its containment, a ravening demon of destruction.

Pyramus turned and looked at it. A demon, indeed. He remembered Phaedra's statement that the force invading the ship seemed almost alive. Think of it as a demon, then. Or as the sun god of a score of ancient mythologies. And what traditionally pacified the sun god?

Pyramus reached out with his new perception, and knew what had to be done. The reason for it did not matter, any more than it mattered if he thought of the heloid as a sun god or as a ball of roiling energy. He saw clearly how to gain the instant it would take for Michan to reach the GM. He knew what the consequences would be—but they did not matter either. *You have nothing to fear in this universe.*

It was time to exit the system.

It was not necessary to push the control button on his arm.

He felt the hydrogen peroxide jets fire, lifting him away from the Hub, up and toward the fire of the heloid. The light grew, bright, brighter, brightest—until it was all-encompassing.

Michan saw the tip of the narrow cone of light limned in the dust and vapor rising from the GM. He thrust himself forward, not daring to think about what would happen should his visor be unable to reflect the concentrated heat and light. But just before he interposed himself between the beam and the unit, he saw the casing bubble away, saw circuits vaporize in the actinic glare, knew that in the next instant he would feel the fires of heaven roll across him—

Nothing happened. And then he was in position, and the fire was in his eyes. The visor darkened to maximum shielding, but still the light was blinding through his closed lids. His face was burning. He would not be able to hold it—it would sear him, destroy him, and the ship. . . .

Against the dazzle of his closed lids Michan saw the Dancer. He caught his breath at her beauty, and listened as she spoke to him as she spoke to all the rest of them. He realized suddenly what he could do, how he could end it. He moved his helmet exactly so, and the convex surface of his visor reflected the beam back along its trajectory. He guided it, shaped it, touching and melting the gimbals that held the mirror frozen, letting the controls he had pushed before now swing it away, scattering the heloid's light harmlessly into space. As he did so, he felt other minds at work, shunting microvolts of power in the GM past melted circuitry, restoring the balance of the magnetic fields about the heloid. All of this in one timeless instant.

Phaedra felt Pyramus's thoughts within her, felt his love surround her soul, as she concluded her Dance. She understood the necessity, if not the reason, for his sacrifice, and let the grief flood through her.

She was in touch with all of those who had understood and accepted, as she had. There were not many; far more had been unable to follow the new path, and had either died or were still at the mercy of the randomization factors. But there were enough. She thanked them all; those of CIRCLE who had given her strength when she needed it, and all of the others who had added to the gestalt.

Then she gathered weightfulness about her, as did the others, and began again.

Michan floated into the suit room and pulled the helmet from his face. He looked at his burned and blistered face in the visor's reflective surface. It was bad. He would have to get to Medical. . . .

We'll take care of it, Michan.

The pain went away.

He looked at his face again. It was still burned, but he could no longer feel the pain. No, that was not quite right—it was still there, but he *accepted* it, made it part of himself, and so it was no longer pain.

Welcome to the land of miracles, Michan.

It was Susan. *Do you understand?*

Yes. I think so.

Good. There's a lot to do. There aren't enough of us yet, and the danger is still great.

Even as he realized what it all meant, Michan heard other voices. Phaedra Adjurian, of course. And Mkono, Merle-Douglass, Wanda . . . and Katsu, and other children. Even Killikup, and a small, simple being called Eight Ball. He felt a surge of protection and warmth from them all. Susan was right—there was a lot still to do. But it could be done—now.

Michan took a deep breath, and went to do his part.

THIRTY

Sean Mkono flew through the healing skies of *Heaven Star*, hauling a net full of bodies behind him. He moved slowly and carefully; there were fifteen corpses in the net and he did not want to lose control of his flight. They would not mind, but he was not so hardened to death that he would not feel uncomfortable, even though he had been playing the role of corpse wagon for three days.

Of the nearly nine thousand on *Heaven Star*, only about two thousand had survived. The rest had been caught in the maelstrom, one way or another. Some had suicided, some had been killed by others, some had died in accidents. Most of them had simply given up; their bodies had stopped functioning. They had been faced with a world, a concept, that had been too much for them.

There had been only one viable way of disposing of the bodies before disease began to spread, cold and callous as it seemed. They were being dispatched through the airlocks. Unlike normal burial procedure, in which the rotating torus would cast the body away to float forever in infinity, these would surround the moving ship in a cloud of frozen corpses. Perhaps, Sean thought, someday, there might be a faint hope of learning how to revive some of them. Until then, if ever, *Heaven Star* would wear her dead like chains.

To his right, Sean saw a cube beginning to melt. "No, I don't think so," he said. He concentrated upon it, and it solidified—*Did it?* he wondered. Or did he only think it did? It did not matter—the effect was the same.

His stumps itched. In six months, he knew, he would have legs—if he was still alive. And he would walk—assuming the ship could be made to rotate again. Once that thought would have made Sean Mkono the happiest person on *Heaven Star*; now it was not nearly so important as keeping the bodies safe in the net.

Susan smiled at her crew. Most of them did not know a laser from a maser, but they were all willing to work and learn. They had been very good at cleaning up the Power Train, smoothing out the unreality of the distortions into something that could be worked with. If the new Spindle crew was equal to their task, the main reactor might be restarted soon; if that happened, the Power Train would be ready. Not fully, of course—there had been too much damage for even the new energies some of them commanded to fix instantly. But things were coming along. Already Susan had managed to get three of the MHDs back on-line, so there was power for life support and lighting and some medical and computer, as well as limited recycling. At least they did not need energy for communications.

Mother?

She knew instantly where Katsu was and what he was doing. She smiled at the knowledge. He was in school, but a different kind of school, learning a different kind of knowledge—one that would aid them all immeasurably in the future.

Yes, Kat?

How are you?

Much better. Her injuries had nearly healed already. A different kind of knowledge, a different kind of healing.

I love you, Mother.

Susan smiled and returned to her work. People were depending on her. For the first time, the thought was not frightening.

•   •   •

Phaedra had the children, nearly a hundred of them, sitting around the edges of the broadcast studio. She was not dancing, but she was teaching them about the Dance. In many ways, the new way of looking at things had been easier for the children, but in some ways it had been harder. There was so much they did not know, so much they still had to learn—and, it seemed, no one was better qualified to teach them than she.

She talked to them with her mind, teaching them about things such as love, life, pain and sacrifice. The young minds learned what she felt for Pyramus, and they learned what he had done for them all.

But why did he have to die? Katsu asked.

We don't know yet. We only know that somehow, his action gave Michan the moment he needed to stop the beam, and the rest of us time to repair the GM. That's all we have to know at the moment, love. That's all that matters.

Geoffrey Merle-Douglass dropped a new holosphere in the recording slot. There was power now, and he could begin once again to do what he did best. But how to begin? he wondered. And where? How could he possibly do justice to this new awareness, this benediction that had been given them in the midst of catastrophe?

He smiled wistfully then, remembering a time long ago when he had viewed an entry in his diary, and the reference in it to Janice. He looked across the room to the picture of Elena, raised his glass of wine to her. She, along with so many others, would follow *Heaven Star* wherever her course might lie. There were some indications that the strangeness they had encountered was subsiding, but it was too soon to tell. In any event, it did not matter. Whether they survived or not was up to them.

He knew the place to begin, now. He stroked the "record" tab and said, "Elena Vasquez was one of the many who did not survive—at least, not physically. But in my mind, and in this record, she will always survive—she and so many others. . . ."

Michan floated above the inner aspect of *Heaven Star*'s torus, looking up at the ring of bodies that sparkled in the light from the heloid. The new awareness they had come by had given them much, but it had also cost a great deal. And in the end, it might cost them everything. The ship was badly crippled and repair was uncertain. *If* they could restart the reactor, *if* they could set the wheel to spinning again, then maybe they could survive. Even with the new energies many could control, there were not enough people to give the ship "weightfulness" and stability everywhere. It was a new land, and they were truly pioneers. And, he reminded himself, one definition of a pioneer was someone with an arrow in his back.

They could all still fail. But at least there was a chance.

And if they should manage to patch the ship up, what then? Impossible to return to Earth, but how could they continue onward as originally planned? Kagan and the others, the ones who had thought that Zanshin was the answer, advocated exploring their new abilities with an eye toward making the universe their home. But they were not gods—not yet, at least. First they had to survive.

Michan sighed, the sound loud in the confines of the exosuit. There would be no easy decisions. But they had at least given themselves a chance, a hope.

Michan?

It was Wanda. *Right here.*

Susan says they're going to try the main reactor in a few minutes. If it works, we'll get rotation; if not. . . .

Michan nodded. If not—there was still so much that could happen in this strange part of the cosmos, so much that was deadly, hidden in the dark. But humanity had always ventured into the dark—even before discovering fire.

You someplace you want to be if it doesn't work?

Michan smiled inside his helmet. He looked up, into the infinite.

Yes. I'm someplace I want to be.